STAR WARS®

AN IMPERIAL COMMANDO NOVEL

501ST

Also by Karen Traviss

STAR WARS®

AN IMPERIAL COMMANDO NOVEL
501ST

KAREN TRAVISS

DEL REY • NEW YORK

Star Wars: Imperial Commando: 501st is a work of fiction. Names, places, and incidents either are products of the author's imagination or are used fictitiously.

A Del Rey Mass Market Original

Copyright © 2009 by Lucasfilm Ltd. & ® or ™ where indicated. All rights reserved. Used under authorization.

Excerpt from *Star Wars: Darth Bane: Dynasty of Evil* copyright © 2009 by Lucasfilm Ltd. & ® or ™ where indicated. All Rights Reserved. Used Under Authorization.

Published in the United States by Del Rey, an imprint of Random House, a division of Random House LLC, a Penguin Random House Company, New York.

DEL REY and the HOUSE colophon are registered trademarks of Random House LLC.

This book contains an excerpt from the forthcoming book *Star Wars: Darth Bane: Dynasty of Evil* by Drew Karpyshyn. This excerpt has been set for this edition only and may not reflect the final content of the forthcoming edition.

ISBN 978-0-345-51113-3

Printed in the United States of America

www.starwars.com
www.delreybooks.com

14 13 12 11 10

*For the 501st Dune Sea Garrison
and Tom's Mando Mercs*

THE STAR WARS LEGENDS NOVELS TIMELINE

BEFORE THE REPUBLIC
37,000–25,000 YEARS BEFORE
STAR WARS: A New Hope

c. 25,793 YEARS BEFORE STAR WARS: A New Hope

Dawn of the Jedi: Into the Void

OLD REPUBLIC
5000–67 YEARS BEFORE
STAR WARS: A New Hope

Lost Tribe of the Sith: The Collected
Stories

3954 YEARS BEFORE STAR WARS: A New Hope

The Old Republic: Revan

3650 YEARS BEFORE STAR WARS: A New Hope

The Old Republic: Deceived
Red Harvest
The Old Republic: Fatal Alliance
The Old Republic: Annihilation

1032 YEARS BEFORE STAR WARS: A New Hope

Knight Errant
Darth Bane: Path of Destruction
Darth Bane: Rule of Two
Darth Bane: Dynasty of Evil

RISE OF THE EMPIRE
67–0 YEARS BEFORE
STAR WARS: A New Hope

67 YEARS BEFORE STAR WARS: A New Hope

Darth Plagueis

33 YEARS BEFORE STAR WARS: A New Hope

Cloak of Deception
Darth Maul: Shadow Hunter
Maul: Lockdown

32 YEARS BEFORE STAR WARS: A New Hope

STAR WARS: EPISODE I
THE PHANTOM MENACE

Rogue Planet
Outbound Flight
The Approaching Storm

22 YEARS BEFORE STAR WARS: A New Hope

STAR WARS: EPISODE II
ATTACK OF THE CLONES

22–19 YEARS BEFORE STAR WARS: A New Hope

STAR WARS: THE CLONE
WARS

The Clone Wars: Wild Space
The Clone Wars: No Prisoners

Clone Wars Gambit
Stealth
Siege

Republic Commando
Hard Contact
Triple Zero
True Colors
Order 66

Shatterpoint
The Cestus Deception
MedStar I: Battle Surgeons
MedStar II: Jedi Healer
Jedi Trial
Yoda: Dark Rendezvous
Labyrinth of Evil

19 YEARS BEFORE STAR WARS: A New Hope

STAR WARS: EPISODE III
REVENGE OF THE SITH

Kenobi
Dark Lord: The Rise of Darth Vader
Imperial Commando 501st

Coruscant Nights
Jedi Twilight
Street of Shadows
Patterns of Force

The Last Jedi

10 YEARS BEFORE STAR WARS: A New Hope

The Han Solo Trilogy
The Paradise Snare
The Hutt Gambit
Rebel Dawn

The Adventures of Lando Calrissian
The Force Unleashed
The Han Solo Adventures
Death Troopers
The Force Unleashed II

The STAR WARS Legends Novels Timeline

STAR WARS®

AN IMPERIAL COMMANDO NOVEL

501ST

PROLOGUE

INTELLIGENCE REPORT (Extract)
CLASSIFICATION: Restricted
TO: *Director of Imperial Intelligence*
FROM: *Section Controller J506*
SUBJECT: *Special security risks.*

I regret to report that a number of security threats to the new Empire remain unresolved.

Among them is a small but worrying number of desertions by clone troopers from the former Republic's special forces. We consider it unlikely that they are unreported casualties because of patterns of association. They are:

1. Null-batch ARCs N-5, N-6, N-7, N-10, N-11, and N-12. Highly dangerous and volatile black ops commandos whose loyalty was always suspect due to their strong association with their training sergeant, Kal Skirata.

2. Alpha-batch ARCs A-26 and A-30. (Others are unaccounted for, but they may be genuine casualties.) Equally dangerous, and—should you need to remind the Emperor—trained to be "one-man armies."

3. An unknown number of Republic commandos—at least three complete and partial squads. Experts in sabotage and assassination.

4. Mandalorian mercenaries and military advisers working for Special Operations Brigade GAR, also known to have trained the missing clones—Kal Skirata, Walon Vau, Mij Gilamar, and Wad'e Tay'haai.

5. *Among the known fugitive Jedi—in other words, those not confirmed as eliminated in Order 66, or reasonably believed to be—is General Bardan Jusik. Interrogation of several Padawan Jedi before execution suggests that Jusik renounced his Jedi status and joined the Mandalorians as a mercenary. I hardly need spell out the special risks of a Force-using Mandalorian.*

The prisoner Dr. Ovolot Qail Uthan is also at large after being taken from Republic custody. Whether this was carried out by former Separatists, or is linked to Skirata's alleged industrial espionage for an unknown commercial clonemaster, the biologist remains a threat to the Empire because of her work on FG36, a genome-targeted biological weapon specific to Fett clones. She is a Gibadan citizen, and Gibad is still refusing to observe the cease-fire.

Recommendations:

1. *That we continue to search for the missing special forces personnel.*

2. *That we carry out reprisal action against Gibad, both as Uthan's most likely source of technical support for bioweapon terrorism, and as a deterrent to other dissident governments.*

3. *That we closely examine those Imperial clone commandos who have missing squadmates—such as the former Omega Squad—and whose loyalty may be in question. If they prove reliable, we should use them to track their former comrades.*

4. *That we anticipate encountering former special forces clones in future military operations against rebels and malcontents, and ensure that Imperial stormtroopers are equipped to deal with the unique threat they pose.*

Submitted this day by: Sector Controller J506, Officer Marigand, H. F.

1

Malcontents and troublemakers will always be with us. They exist to dissent. A galactic cease-fire is exactly what most of them don't *want, because it takes away the cover for the small and implacable grievances that give their lives meaning. If they happened to win—they would be lost in aimless despair.*
—Emperor Palpatine, on being told that opposition to Imperial rule was continuing on a number of worlds, despite the end of the Clone Wars.

Commercial freighter *Cornucopia,* Mezeg Sector freight terminal; third week of the new era of the Empire

Ny Vollen had never broken her word to anyone, but now seemed like a sensible time to start.

I must be out of my mind. This is going to get me killed. And them, *too. What was I thinking?*

She didn't even dare imagine the word; her two passengers were just *them.* The brief time she'd spent with Force-sensitives had made her nervous at a gut level, and she was now irrationally afraid that her thoughts, feelings, and anxieties were somehow broadcast to anyone with the skills to detect them. It was crazy, she knew . . . but she *didn't* know.

She couldn't be sure her mind was still private territory. And that was what bothered her.

Just keep your heads down and shut up, both of you.

Is that so hard? You can do your Force stuff to make guards go away, right? Well, do it.

The Mezeg terminal smelled of lube oil, blocked drains, and those sickly sweet hot buns that were sold with near-undrinkable caf wherever freight pilots gathered. She gnawed unenthusiastically on a bun, trying not to imagine what the hard chewy bits were made of. The scent of artificial vannilan always made her feel sick. Now it added to the turmoil in her stomach, threatening to overwhelm her as she stood under *Cornucopia*'s fuselage waiting for her vessel to be inspected.

She rehearsed a convincing reaction in case her hidden passengers were discovered.

Never seen them before in my life, trooper.

These refugees get everywhere, don't they?

Thank you, trooper—now get them off my ship.

But none of those lines would have convinced her, so she doubted they would persuade any of the Imperial stormtroopers searching vessels entering and leaving Mezeg. If the stowaways were discovered, then at least they had no idea where *Cornucopia* was headed. And she hadn't yet programmed a course for Mandalore, so there was no data to extract from the new computer and lead the authorities to Kyrimorut.

At least the worst wouldn't happen.

But I know exactly where we're heading, all the names, all the places, so the worst that can happen . . . will happen to me.

She was far too old to be embarking on a life of lawlessness. If she was caught and interrogated, she had no idea how long she would hold out before she revealed what she knew of Kal Skirata's refuge for clone deserters. Her chances of escaping from the search team of four fit troopers, a civilian guard, and an akk hound looked close to zero.

Come on. Are they really going to suspect me of anything? I'm a woman. I'm old. My ship's even older than I am. As to which of us is in worse shape . . .

"Waste of kriffing time." The Rodian pilot in the line

next to her had a tiny courier shuttle that couldn't have concealed a jackrab, let alone stowaways. He kept checking a chrono hanging from a fob on his jacket. "This is *costing* me."

"Can't argue with the Empire," Ny said. "Suck it up."

The white-armored stormtroopers didn't scare her. She knew they should have. They weren't Kal Skirata's adopted sons, the special forces clones she knew, like A'den, Mereel, and Corr. They might have looked identical under those helmets, but if she thought they were friends—that was all wrong, *deadly* wrong. These men had their orders. They probably didn't include being kind to old women who thought they were all nice boys at heart. Anyone aiding fugitive Jedi was an enemy of the Empire by definition.

And why am I doing this, anyway?

The freight port security guard held his search akk on a choke chain as he went from vessel to vessel, letting the animal snuffle around cargo bays and hatches. Four stormtroopers waited to pounce if the akk reacted to a scent or a sound.

"I suppose they're bored now they haven't got a proper war to fight," the Rodian said. "Nothing better to do with their time. And how much has Palpatine spent on all that new armor? What was wrong with the old style? *More* taxpayers' credits wasted."

"They're looking for Jedi," Ny said. *And my friends, like A'den . . . and Ordo . . . and Kal.* She wondered if the Rodian actually paid any taxes at all. "We don't know how many escaped the Purge. Enough to worry Palps, obviously."

But Etain Tur-Mukan was one of the many Jedi who didn't get away, although she hadn't been executed in the Purge. She'd died *stupidly.* She got herself killed. Ny was used to the angry phase in bereavement, and the guilt that followed blaming the dead for being dead and leaving you so lonely that it wasn't worth taking the next breath, but she hadn't even known Etain before she took her body home to Mandalore.

Crazy kid. If she'd just walked by instead of getting in the way, defending that clone trooper, then she'd be alive now. And Darman would have a wife to come home to, and their baby would have a mother. What a waste. What a terrible, terrible waste. A war for absolutely nothing except a corrupt old barve's ambition. Or a whole bunch of corrupt barves, if Kal's right.

My Terin should still be alive, too. Stang, I miss you, baby.

The pain was at a manageable level these days, although she wished she hadn't found out the details of how her husband died. But if she hadn't, she would have imagined worse. Her old man was dead, gone in a matter of minutes, and that was all there was to it. He wasn't the only man in the merchant navy to die in the war; she wasn't the only war widow in the galaxy. Her grief was nothing special.

"I hope they find all of them, *fast*, and then we can get back to normal business," the Rodian muttered.

"Who?" Ny was miles away, walking with the dead and trying to resist asking them why they'd done such uselessly brave things that hadn't made the slightest difference to the course of the war. "What?"

"*Jedi.* I never trusted them anyway. My buddy—he lost his ship once, no compensation, *nothing*, when one of their fancy Masters commandeered it for some getaway. No *please, thank you*, or *here's some creds to tide you over, friend.* Just *took* it. Higher authority. Mystic and righteous work. Piracy, more like—government-backed thieves. Well, they got theirs. Good riddance."

Ny thought of Jusik and Etain, and bit back a defense. "Would you turn them in if you found any?" she asked.

"Even without a reward." The Rodian snapped his fingers. "Like *that*."

Ny wondered what he would have thought if he knew that it was another Force-user still running the show anyway. But she wasn't even sure she could blame it all on this . . . Siff? Shith? *Sith*, that was it. Whatever kind of saber-jockey Palpatine was—if he'd engineered the whole war, like Skirata said—then he hadn't needed to encourage some worlds to fight each other. Old enemies were just waiting for an excuse to start.

Ny hadn't even heard of Sith before she met the renegade clone clan. Bardan Jusik had explained the ancient feud between Sith and Jedi, as pointless as the sectarian war on Sarrassia, where two factions of a religious cult had been fighting for thousands of years over the proper ritual for handling some holy relic—a goblet, a statue, a set of bones, Ny forgot which. They just seemed to define themselves by *not* being the other faction. She didn't understand any of it.

Osik. That was the word. Mandalorians knew how to cuss, all sibilants and explosive consonants. It was all a load of *osik.*

There were plenty of other things Ny didn't know or understand that were much closer to home. She hadn't known Etain, so she couldn't fathom the depth of Skirata's guilt about the girl. She hardly knew Darman, come to that. She didn't understand why Mandalore had allowed an Imperial garrison on its home turf. And she didn't know how she fitted into the gathering of misfits that was Clan Skirata, only that she now thought of Kyrimorut as her home base and that it had happened almost overnight.

But that didn't matter now. She was doing this for two reasons, two *good* reasons, but the second one was starting to trouble her more the closer she got to Mandalore.

I gave my word. And . . . stang, why do I trust Kal Skirata so much?

"At *last*," said the Rodian. The akk handler was heading his way. The Rodian turned to her and nodded in a way that seemed to transcend species, the gesture of an exasperated pilot on a tight schedule whose timetable had been messed up by idiots. "I'm going to lose my on-time bonus thanks to this."

Ny stood with *Cornucopia*'s manifest in one hand. That was the drill; to have your admin data ready on your 'pad for inspection, stand clear of your vessel, and wait for the security guy to talk to you.

Speak when you're spoken to. Some things never change.

"Don't point that out to them, will you?" she said. "Or else they'll keep you here until Mustafar freezes over."

She realized her pulse was racing. If the akk got a whiff of her two passengers, she'd be finished. It was a huge gamble. But then her passengers had everything to lose, too, and she knew they could make themselves a lot harder to find than the average stowaway.

Ny waited. She concentrated on feeling impatient, imagining the time and creds she would have been losing if this had been a real delivery, and hoped it was enough to disguise her fear from both akks and humans.

She wouldn't have been the first freight pilot to find illegal stowaways in her vessel, or the first to deny all knowledge. And sometimes that was true; illegals knew all the tricks when it came to slipping past security checks. But what had once been routine and occasional searches by assorted authorities for a variety of reasons—like Boriin not wanting skilled metalsmiths leaving its territories, or Mil Velay not allowing anyone with a criminal record to enter its space—was now a matter of life and death.

The akk strained on its leash as it came toward her. Both of its front legs lifted clear off the ground as the handler leaned back against the animal's weight to restrain it. He slackened the leash, and the akk raced up *Cornucopia*'s open ramp and vanished inside.

Ny handed her datapad to the stormtrooper. She couldn't see his eyes behind that visor, but she was used to guessing where folks who wore helmets might actually be looking, and he seemed to be reading the 'pad.

"Name, ma'am."

"Nyreen Vollen."

"Cargo?"

"Food and basic supplies, bound for LodeCorp Mining asteroid Nine-Alpha-Four, Roche system."

"Any passengers?"

"None."

"Have you left your vessel unattended or unsecured at any time?"

"No."

"Have you checked the vessel for beings, life-forms, or objects not loaded by you?"

"Yes."

Well, that was true. She'd checked. The *beings*—she'd done the loading personally. The stormtrooper took some time going through the list on her 'pad, probably to give the akk enough time to do its search. There wasn't much that anyone could extract from her manifest. It really was just supplies—flour, grassgrain, pickles, powdered milk, sacks of denta beans, soap, dried fruit, all the staples that would come in handy for a siege. Kyrimorut was that kind of place. It gave its residents a siege mentality, if they hadn't already arrived with one. And she had.

The stormtrooper handed back her datapad. The others began walking slowly around the freighter, looking it over.

That hold stinks of tar-fuel, too. The akk can't smell anything through that . . . can it?

But akks could do a lot of things. They weren't anywhere near as smart as strills—ah, yes, Mird, she had a treat for Mird in her cargo, too—but they were employed as search animals for a reason. They were *good* at it. They smelled all, heard all, saw all.

No noise. No barking. No reaction. Please, please . . .

Ny had never known time pass so slowly in her life. How could the akk possibly miss what was hidden in the empty water tanks? It would start whining and scrabbling at the inspection plate. She must have been crazy to think she could get away with this, *her*, a lowly freight-jockey. Running errands and doing a little low-level spying for A'den had been nowhere near as outrageously dangerous as this. Even helping that ARC trooper Sull desert had been a relatively safe trip. Ny knew she was out of her depth now.

It's all my fault. Kal didn't even want this. My bright idea . . . my problem.

The Rodian's shuttle, now cleared for exit, taxied to the landing strip and lifted off. Ny watched, hoping she just looked anxious to complete her deliveries and get paid. Searches took less than ten standard minutes, from what she'd seen, and the akk had been nosing around in *Cornucopia* for about that long.

It's nearly over. Nearly out of here. Nearly . . . home.

Where was home now, anyway?

Then it started. The hacking bark of the akk hound, that distinctive *ack-ack-ack* noise that gave the animal its name, echoed from the open hatch. Ny knew she wasn't going home now, ever, and she struggled not to panic. Three stormtroopers rushed to the ramp, blaster rifles ready. The fourth held his sidearm on her.

"Wait here, ma'am," he said. He craned his neck to see what was happening. "Officer, what's going on in there?"

The akk stopped barking. Ny heard one set of scuffed footsteps accompanied by scrabbling claws, and she simply couldn't draw another breath. This was it. The animal must have sniffed out her stowaways.

"Sorry, boys." The guard's voice emerged from the hatch. "He's still a pup, despite his size. Needs a bit more discipline."

The akk came trotting down the ramp dragging a bantha's thigh bone, the huge pelvis end clamped between his jaws. It was Mird's treat; bantha meat wasn't easy to get hold of on Mandalore. Ny's knees nearly buckled. The guard tried to take the bone from his animal, but the novice akk wasn't having any of it. His lip curled and he growled deep in his throat, teeth still locked hard on the femur.

"Look, I can get another bone," Ny said, feigning exasperation rather than flinging her arms around the akk and telling it what a good boy it was for sabotaging the search. "Keep it. I need to get moving."

One of the stormtroopers tilted his head at her. "What do you need a bantha bone for, ma'am?"

Ny's answer was out of her mouth before she even thought about it. The ease and speed with which she conjured up a complete fabric of lies shocked her.

"One of the miners has a pet nek," she said. "You don't find many banthas on your average asteroid."

It really *was* getting that easy to lie. She was disappointed in herself, her old self before widowhood had made her into a more marginal creature, but she also felt a thrill of excitement—and shame—at her newly discovered capacity for defiance. *Yes, I'm wrong, I'm breaking the law, but I did it—I pulled it off.* The guard was still trying to get the akk's mind back on search duties as she closed the hatch.

Stang, she hoped those two could still breathe in that tank. She couldn't check until *Cornucopia* jumped to hyperspace and she'd set the autopilot on course. Getting out of Mezeg orbit seemed to take hours rather than minutes, and the moment the stars in the viewport stretched from points of light to frozen streaks of infinity, she checked the course and handed the controls over to *Cornucopia*'s nav computer.

The aft cargo section was silent except for the throb of the drives and the rattle of loose fittings. Ny took a deep breath and began unbolting the water tank inspection plate on the deck, wondering if she'd find bodies rather than live Jedi.

"That was too close." Ny lifted the metal panel and reached down. It was a tight fit in the space between those tanks even for a short, skinny kid like Scout, so the Kaminoan must have been very uncomfortable indeed. "How did you get away with that?"

Scout scrambled out of the hole in the deck, her ginger hair disheveled. She looked like she hadn't eaten in a week. It took a little longer to extract Kina Ha, not only because the Kaminoan was much taller, but also because she was a lot older—exactly how old, Ny wasn't sure, but the Kaminoan was a venerable lady by anyone's standards. Ny usually couldn't tell the age of a non-human, but Kina Ha would have looked obviously old to anyone, with deeply lined gray skin and drooping eyes. She moved slowly. It made Ny feel positively teenaged.

"I influenced the akk to find that bone when it got too excited," Scout said. "But we're fine. Aren't we, Kina?"

"We are *alive*," said the Kaminoan. "And that is a bonus. Thank you for risking so much for us."

Ny would have taken that thanks in her stride a matter of days ago, but now it triggered a pang of guilt. Neither of the Jedi knew where they were going, and they hadn't pressed her too hard for an answer. But she hadn't told them exactly who their hosts would be, either.

And that was going to be . . . interesting.

No matter: like Kina Ha said—they were alive, and that was a bonus.

Cornucopia was a typical old CEC *Monarch*-class cargo ship, boxy and basic, with a long bench along the bulkhead behind the pilot's and copilot's seats. Kina Ha settled on the bench like a crotchety duchess and fastened her safety restraints. Scout slid into the copilot's seat next to Ny.

Ny broke out some ration packs and passed them around. She had no idea what Kaminoans ate—fish and other seafood, she guessed—but Kina Ha wasn't going to get any yobshrimp here. Skirata had said that Kaminoans hated bright sunlight and were happiest when it was cloudy and bucketing down rain. That was going to be a challenge to achieve on Mandalore, too. But that was going to be the least of Kina Ha's problems.

"We're going to Mandalore," Ny said at last. Somehow she expected at least a gasp, or even a cry of protest. But the two Jedi were silent. "You heard me, didn't you? Mandalore? *Manda'yaim*?"

"Yes, we did hear, thank you," Kina Ha said. "Suitably remote and forbidding. I commend your ingenuity."

"You don't have a problem with Mandalorians?"

"Should we?"

"Well, a lot of them have a problem with you. Jedi, that is."

Kina Ha peered into the open pouch of the ration pack as if she was divining the future from its contents. "I have a vague recollection of Mandalorians fighting for the Sith," she said. "But I've kept myself far from the political detail of the galaxy for a long time."

Ny wasn't sure what *a long time* meant, but she imagined centuries. Kina Ha wasn't just any old Jedi. She was genetically engineered; all Kaminoans were, of course, and Skirata said that was how they survived their global flood and turned into what he described as *loathsome eugenicist scum*. But no Kaminoan had been engineered quite like Kina Ha. She was unique. Her genes had been modified for a very long life span, and that meant she would be useful to Skirata in ways she probably couldn't begin to imagine.

That genome was the only thing that was going to save her from Skirata's wrath. He was banking on finding something in her genes that would stop his clone sons from aging at twice the normal human rate.

"Is that where you're from?" Scout tidied her hair with her fingers. It didn't look much different afterward. "Mandalore?"

"No," Ny said. "I'm not Mandalorian. I just help them out when they're busy."

How do I explain Kal to them?

"I'm not being ungrateful," Scout said. Kina Ha selected something from the ration pack and chewed it thoughtfully. "I'm just scared."

Oh boy. "I'm taking you to a safe place," Ny said. "Quite a few other folks are hiding from the Emperor."

"Other Jedi?" Kina Ha asked.

Ny wasn't sure how to describe Bardan Jusik. Lapsed Jedi? *Very* lapsed Jedi? Apostate? Born-again Mando? It could wait. Scout would be able to decide for herself soon enough.

"In a way." She couldn't sit on this any longer. "Look, you're going to stay with a Mandalorian clan of clone troopers who've deserted. Some of them don't have very happy memories of Kamino, Kina Ha. It's only fair that

I warn you. And the place belongs to Kal Skirata. He's an old mercenary who trained clones in Tipoca City, and . . . well, he hates Jedi and Kaminoans for using the clones. So relations might be frosty for a while."

Ny felt a little better for getting that out in the open, but not much. Kina Ha tilted her head gracefully.

"Well, it could be worse," she said.

Scout lowered her chin. "And that place is *safe*?"

"Kal's a good man." Ny was instantly defensive again, was already far too fond of Skirata for common sense. "He's dedicated his life to rescuing clones. But Kamino left a big mark on everyone. One of the clones had a baby with a Jedi girl who got killed in the Purge. So it's one big painful mess at the moment. But you'll be safe there. Kal's given me his word."

Mess didn't quite cover it. Ny decided not to plunge the two Jedi into anxiety overload by mentioning the rest of the problems. They'd find out about Dr. Uthan soon enough, and Jusik the definitely-not-Jedi, and the bounties on everyone's head, and Jango Fett's serial-killer sister back from the dead, and the Imperial garrison, and Fenn Shysa's resistance plans . . . yes, it really did sound like less fun than falling into a sarlacc's corrosive gut when she looked at it all in the cold light of day.

But Ny still couldn't help feeling better when she thought of Kyrimorut. The place was isolated, desolate, and spartan, full of the grieving and the dispossessed, but the warmth of the tight-knit community there transformed it.

It held no memories of Terin, either. When she was there, she felt able to imagine a future. The days ahead were no longer an empty void to be endured or escaped.

"What happened to the Jedi's baby?" Scout asked.

"Kad? He's fine." Was that telling Scout too much? Ny had grown a major caution gland when she started dealing with the Grand Army, but the girl would see for herself anyway. "Growing like a weed."

"And the bone? What was the bone for? Is it some

primitive Mandalorian ritual? I heard they crown their leader with a real skull."

"I think the skull's symbolic, Scout." Was it? Ny liked Mandos, but they did have a penchant for anatomical trophies. "The bone was for Mird. If you've never seen a strill before, they're quite something. Very rare native animal."

"Never heard of them."

"Then you're in for an education."

Ny settled back in her seat and realized that she hadn't escaped from the Empire. She'd simply skipped one crisis and was hurtling at multi-light-speed toward the next.

"I recall strills, I think," Kina Ha said absently. "But that was just before the Sith went into hiding."

Ny was only half listening now, checking *Cornucopia*'s instrument panel. "Sorry, when did the Sith disappear?" She glanced over the back of the seat. Very few ordinary folk had even heard of Sith, so it was odd to hear Kina Ha drop the name. "I'm not good at history."

The Jedi frowned in concentration, furrowing her wrinkled brow all the way back to where her ears should have been if Kaminoans had them.

"Oh . . . perhaps a thousand years ago?" She swayed her impossibly long neck like a snake. "It's been so very long . . . and so many wars. I forget."

Ny wasn't sure she'd heard right. And then she realized she had, and the galaxy changed out of all recognition for her—again.

Special Operations barracks, 501st Legion headquarters, Imperial Center (formerly Coruscant)

Medical technology could do just about anything, Niner decided, except mend Darman.

He watched his brother put on his newly issued Imperial armor, dark charcoal gray and black. The color was much like their old matte-black Katarn pattern plates, but there the similarity ended; everything about the shape, from helmet to chest plate to greaves, was just that bit different. It made Darman look like a stranger. And he felt like one, too.

Darman had changed overnight. Niner couldn't really expect anything else. How would any husband react to having to stand by and watch his wife killed? But this was more than grieving. Both he and Darman had lost brothers in the war, and they'd had no choice but to get on with life and carry on fighting in the very next moment.

Grieving was dealt with slowly and privately. Eventually, you came to terms with it. But Niner had never been in love with a woman or fathered her child, and so he realized that Darman's grief was probably something new and indescribable, bound up with shattered hopes for a future that no clone had thought he'd ever have.

But we can *have those lives. The little ordinary things. Fi's got a wife. So has Atin. And Ordo. They're living as Mandalorians, free men. I know what I can be.*

Niner had never seen Kyrimorut, and now he had to forget that he even knew its name. At least he didn't know where the homestead was. Nobody could beat that information out of him. He was scared to talk about anything in their new quarters, even in the locker room, in case the Emperor had installed surveillance to check on who was loyal and who had ties to the past regime.

It might have been the same boss with a new title, but the new Empire already felt like a different world from the Republic.

Darman attached his armor plates to his undersuit, and clung to his DC-17 rifle like a comfort blanket. The 501st had let the commandos keep those for the time being. There was probably a brutally pragmatic reason for it; they were used to the Deece, and that saved training time on new weapons, but it still felt like a kindness, a concession to ease them into the new and unsettling world of the Imperial Army. Niner kept trying to work out why it felt so different. It wasn't the vast influx of new clones produced on Centax 2 by fast Spaarti processes. He'd met very few of those men. No, what bothered him most was simply the absence of things that had been the core of his life for thirteen years.

People.

He couldn't call Skirata. There was no General Jusik, either, or Fi, Corr, or Atin, or any of the people he knew he could count on if he needed them. There was just Darman.

And Darman needed him, whether he knew it or not.

Dar could have escaped with the rest of them and been with his baby son now, but he didn't; he'd stayed with Niner. Nobody in the galaxy could buy that kind of loyalty and brotherhood, and now Niner had a debt not only of honor but of *family*.

Darman flexed his fingers, making his new gauntlets creak. "You going to stand there scratching your *shebs* all day? Buckets on. Mustn't keep Lord Vader waiting."

"I know you're not okay," Niner said, "so I'm not even going to ask."

"I'm fine. Are *you* up to this?"

Niner had broken his spine on that awful night when Order 66 was called. Darman had refused to leave him, afraid he'd end up like Fi, on life support waiting to have the plug pulled because nobody had a use or a place for crippled clones. Niner didn't need reminding that it was his fault Darman was stuck here and not raising Kad.

"I'm good as new," Niner said. He did a few twists from the hips and bent over straight-legged to put his palms flat on the floor. "See? Actually, that's better than I used to be. I couldn't quite do that before."

"Come on. Let's get this over with."

"Dar, whatever Vader's got in mind for us, it'll be business as usual."

"How can it be? We haven't got a war to fight now."

"Oh, you think it's all over, do you? You been watching the holonews?" News was all that Niner had to occupy him for days after his spinal cord was repaired and he was confined to a brace. "There's still trouble. Still places where the locals are fighting. Places that won't accept the Empire."

Darman flipped his helmet over between his hands a few times. "Little border wars. They don't need special forces for that."

"Okay—what do you want to see happen? No, don't answer that."

Niner grabbed Darman's arm, steering him down the corridor to the parade ground. This wasn't Arca Barracks. He couldn't trust anyone or anything. When they got outside, he walked into the center of the parade ground, took off his helmet, and gestured to Darman to do the same.

This had to be done in silence. Normally, they could have switched to a secure comm circuit and safely discussed anything within the privacy of their helmets, but Niner had no idea if the new kit had comm overrides that he didn't know about. It was the kind of thing he could have handed to Jaing or Mereel to pull apart, but the Null ARCs were half a galaxy away. He'd improvise.

"What are you doing?" Darman asked.

Niner held up his forefinger for silence. "Testing the proximity sensors. Put your helmet down."

As far as onlookers were concerned, they were just two clones testing new and still unfamiliar armor systems. Niner laid his helmet on the ground and walked away from it, beckoning Darman to follow suit. When they were far enough from the helmets to be out of audio range—and then some, just in case—Niner stopped.

"Okay, Dar, we walk back toward those buckets in a few moments, like nothing happened. Got it?"

"You're paranoid."

"I'm *sensible*. Look, Dar, what do you want most right now?"

"Does it matter?"

"Yes. It does. Do you want to leave? Do you want to

go to . . ." Niner hardly dared say it, but at some point it had to be said. "You want to go find Kad? Look after him?"

Darman's expression was unreadable. If only *Bard'ika*—Bardan Jusik—had been here now; he could have Force-sensed Darman's real mood. But he wasn't, and Niner could only guess, because the Darman he knew didn't react the way this Darman did. Niner had spent two days reading medical texts while he was recovering. He didn't understand a lot of it, but he now knew there were states of mind called dissociative amnesia, where the mind shut out the memory of terrible events just to be able to cope with everyday life. He was sure Darman was doing that.

"I don't know that name," Darman said at last.

Niner had no idea how to handle this. All he could do was keep an eye on his brother and hope that time really did heal. "Okay," he said. "You want to stay here."

"What else would I want to do? I'm a commando."

"It's all right, Dar. You're going to be fine."

There was nothing else Niner could say. Darman hadn't mentioned Etain since the night she was killed. Niner decided it was still too risky to raise the subject. But he made up his mind that he'd get Darman out of the Imperial Army by brute force if necessary. How—that was another matter. But he was a commando. He'd think of something.

"Are we done?" Darman asked. "Because Vader's giving us our briefing in a few minutes, and I hear he's pretty tough on bad timekeeping."

There was no more Sergeant Kal, the indulgent father, and his loose regulations. There was a command structure of officers, and things were a lot tighter all around. The only part of their previous lives as Republic commandos that they'd kept—apart from the Deece—was their ID numbers, now with an *IC* prefix.

They'd think that changing our numbers was like changing our names, wouldn't they?

Niner began to wonder if he was making excuses for

the Empire, attributing gestures that it simply wasn't making. Perhaps that was his own way of staying sane.

They kept up the pretense of walking toward their helmets to see if the alarm kicked in, which at least told Niner that something in Darman still knew he had a secret to keep. For a moment he wondered if Darman's paranoia about the Empire was even worse than his own, and this was just a conscious act maintained twenty-four hours a day so that it never slipped. But it was hard to tell. Darman put on his helmet, killing any further chance of private conversation, and they strode off in silence to the briefing hall.

Niner wasn't sure what he was expecting to see when he got there. The ranks of commandos waiting for Lord Vader weren't the entire strength of the former Special Operations Brigade. Niner estimated it was less than a quarter, maybe a thousand men, so he wondered how they'd been selected. He had no way of recognizing any of them until they spoke or moved, though, because the individual paint schemes they'd been encouraged to apply to their armor, Mandalorian-style, had now been erased by a sea of uniform black. It said more clearly than anything that the galaxy had changed. Niner didn't even spot Scorch until the man slipped into a space beside him. His vivid yellow armor flashes were gone.

Funny. We're used to recognizing individuals with identical faces, but then I'm thrown for a loop when everyone's got the same armor.

"How are things, *ner vod*?" Scorch asked. "You've been keeping to yourselves lately."

Niner decided it was probably a bad idea to speak *Mando'a* in front of strangers, although he wasn't sure why. By *strangers,* he meant any of the 501st stormtroopers who hadn't started life as Republic commandos on Kamino, trained by Mando sergeants. He wasn't sure if he could think of them as brothers.

"I've not been well," Niner said, deadpan.

"Heard about the injury. Nasty." Scorch didn't say if he knew the detail of the fight at Shinarcan Bridge. But it was no secret that a woman had been killed when she stepped between a clone trooper and a Jedi's lightsaber. Just how many people knew it was Etain was another matter. "I think we've got some ARCs here, too. Imagine that, the ARC boys having to slum it with us lesser mortals . . . so how are you, Dar?"

Darman shrugged. "I hate this new armor."

"Yeah, it's a waste of creds. Nothing wrong with the old kit. Fixer hates it, too. Boss couldn't care less."

Niner had to ask. "Any news on Sev?"

He said it as neutrally as he could. Darman wasn't the only man here with painful memories. Every commando knew that Delta Squad had lost contact with Sev and left him behind when they banged out of Kashyyyk. Quite a few men thought the squad should have told General Yoda to shove his order to pull out, and gone back for their buddy. But Yoda was now gone, too, along with the rest of the Jedi. Sev was one more tragedy in a grinding, oddly pointless war, the extra agony piled on by losing comrades in the last days of the fighting.

Like Etain. She was minutes—no, seconds away from getting off Coruscant for good. It's just cruel. It shouldn't have been like that.

"No," Scorch said, his voice a little hoarse. "Sev's still MIA."

He didn't ask about Etain. But Delta Squad knew about her and Dar. Niner just hoped that the gossip hadn't reached Vader.

Vader . . . Vader was as far from General Arligan Zey as any being could be, a huge figure encased completely in black armor, helmet, and cape. His voice and rasping breath didn't even sound human, although rumor said he was. He swept into the hall and didn't even introduce himself. He didn't need to. In two or three weeks, he'd become the name whispered in messes and canteens. This was the Emperor's right hand, and he could do things that only Jedi could do, like moving things—and smashing them—without touching them.

Someone said he'd been a Jedi once. But so had

Dooku. It would be no big surprise if that was true. Niner didn't know or care about that, but he'd treat Vader with caution anyway. He stood to attention. The last thing he wanted right then was to be singled out as an individual. He wanted to vanish.

Vader stood with his thumb hooked in his belt, his rhythmic, wheezing breaths sounding like a machine. "We have tracked down many of the traitors who escaped the Purge, but our work is not finished," he boomed. "There are still Jedi evading justice, and we have deserters from our own ranks to deal with. You will live up to your name as Vader's Fist. You will hunt down the remaining fugitives."

Niner expected some reaction from Darman, at least a flinch. But he stood frozen. Nobody moved or said a word.

"Your former special forces comrades are adept at causing death and chaos," Vader continued. "So you are the ones best placed to locate and neutralize them. I expect no quarter given to them. They were your brothers once, but they are now traitors, an insult to all of you and your sacrifices. You are now the Imperial Commando Special Unit. Do *not* disappoint me."

A list of fugitives was transmitted to the clones. Niner knew that every clone in the hall was doing the same as he was at that moment. Each man was adjusting his focus to look at the head-up display in his helmet to check the images and text superimposed on the view through his visor.

He knew he'd see names he recognized. The faces didn't matter, of course. Except for the Jedi and a few others, they would all look identical; and there they were, listed as numbers.

ARC trooper Captain A-26 and ARC trooper A-30— Maze and Sull.

Maze? Old misery guts, AWOL? Him, of all people . . .

Niner was genuinely surprised by that. Maze was Zey's aide, a man who did things by the book. Niner wouldn't have bet on him making a run for it, but then there were others there on the list who seemed equally unlikely: Yayax Squad, Hyperion Squad, and individual Republic commandos he remembered. There was even a regular clone commander missing, Commander Levet, who'd served under Etain on Qiilura.

Corr and Atin were on the list, of course, but Fi wasn't. At least his faked death had convinced the Empire's new record keepers. But most civilian personnel were exactly the same beings who'd served the Republic just weeks earlier, at the same desks and with the same salaries, and nothing much had changed for the vast majority of Coruscant's population except the name of the place. It was Imperial City now, and the planet was Imperial Center. The biggest task the desk jockeys faced was revising the holocharts. Niner still found that hard to take in after so many lives had been torn apart in his own small circle.

Coruscant. Corrie. Triple Zero. Trip Zip. I'm easy. But it'll never be Imperial City as far as I'm concerned.

The deserters list was short but significant. Rolled together, they made a brutal little army to be reckoned with. Niner had seen how much damage a single ARC could do, from blowing up key targets to destabilizing whole governments. Come to that, he knew how much damage *he* could do with a few brothers and the right kit. They were dangerous. They'd been bred and trained to be that way.

Do I want to stop these men?

Do I want to kill them?

Of course I don't. They're our own.

And then there were the other names, the ones that needed pictures as well, because they were random beings with their own distinctive features—the Jedi on the run. Bardan Jusik was only one name on a list that was longer than Niner expected, all little Padawans and minor Knights but relatively few Masters.

But there was one Knight on the list nobody would have to look for. This far back in the ranks, Niner doubted that Vader could see him. He put his hand under Darman's elbow, knowing the effect that seeing Etain Tur-Mukan's name and face would have on his brother.

So they don't know she's dead. And that means they really aren't sure who's dead and who's missing.

Etain's picture wasn't a flattering one but it still broke Niner's heart. He could only imagine what it did to Darman. She was a thin, freckled girl with wavy brown hair and green eyes. If he hadn't known her, he'd have thought she was just another young woman; a librarian, a store assistant, a clerk. She didn't look like a general who'd fought a war and put everything on the line.

"It's okay, Dar," Niner whispered. If anyone picked that up, it wouldn't have meant a thing to them. But Darman didn't react. "*Udesii.* Take it easy."

"I sense that many of you are dismayed by these names." Vader had a knack for saying the most unsettling things. "You have been commendably loyal to some of these beings. But they deceived you, and they deserve no mercy, either. Your specific missions will be assigned to you soon. *Dismiss.*"

The lines of commandos filed out of the hall and broke up into groups heading back to the barracks. Niner kept checking his datapad for assignment details. It was a lot of trouble to go to just to tell them they'd be getting a list of folks to kill. But maybe it was about seeing Vader in the flesh and realizing that the guy meant business. General Zey had never had that effect on him, and as for Yoda—Niner couldn't actually remember seeing Yoda in person, but he just knew the general didn't have that gut-gripping presence that Vader had.

Scorch sidled up to Niner and matched his pace.

"I *hate* this," he said. "And we've got some new guy taking Sev's place. It's temporary, though. He'd better understand that."

Niner remembered Corr joining Omega Squad when Fi had been whisked off to Mandalore. It was obvious that Fi was never coming back, but nobody ever admitted Corr was a permanent replacement. Niner understood Scorch completely. *Permanent* meant you'd given up hope of seeing your brother again, and made you worry that you'd somehow sealed his fate by accepting he was gone.

"Well, there you go," said Darman, walking toward the canteen, eyes on his datapad. At least his appetite was unaffected. "Look at that."

"Who did we draw?" Niner asked, suddenly not wanting to look at his own 'pad.

"We're with two new guys from Galaar Squad—Ennen and Bry. And we're just Squad Four-zero now."

"I meant who are we supposed to go after."

Darman swallowed just hard enough for Niner to realize that he really was distressed by all this, even though he seemed to be numbed by events. There wasn't a lot one clone could hide from another, not when every small gesture and sound had to be examined to distinguish one brother from another.

"Some guy called Jilam Kester," Darman said. "Never heard of him."

It was still an assassination, but Niner was relieved that it wasn't *Bard'ika*. Then he wondered if they hadn't been assigned the people they knew best because someone thought they'd never pull the trigger.

Niner couldn't imagine the Empire—or anyone—being that tolerant of clones who might not carry out their orders because of sentiment. It felt like a test. He waited until they were on their own on the parade ground before taking off his helmet.

"Who's got Skirata and the Nulls? And Vau?" Niner couldn't see the names anywhere. He scrolled through the list on the 'pad, looking for the numbers: *Null ARCs, N-7, N-10, N-11, N-12, N-5, N-6*—Mereel, Jaing, Ordo, A'den, Prudii, and Kom'rk. "Palps can't possibly believe that they're all conveniently dead now. They were on the bounty hunters' wanted list before this came out."

Darman shrugged. "What if they are? We haven't heard from anyone in more than two weeks, not since . . ."

He stopped. It was the first time he'd come anywhere close to mentioning the night of Order 66 since it had happened. But he didn't go on.

Niner checked the 'pad again before he was certain that only the Alpha ARC deserters, Jedi, and Republic commandos were on that hit list. The Jedi Masters and some Knights were marked for execution, and Padawans and other fugitives were to be detained alive. Either Palpatine already had the Nulls and the Mando sergeants—Niner doubted that—or he was sending someone else after them, like Imperial Intelligence.

Good luck, spooks. You'll need it. Especially if you're unlucky enough to find them.

"Okay, grab Ennen and Bry," Darman said. "Let's get this done."

That wasn't Dar talking. That was the pretend Dar.

"You okay with this?" Niner asked.

"What, hunting Jedi?"

"Yes."

"They took everything I ever cared about," Darman said, suddenly more like his real self for a few seconds. "You bet I'm okay with it."

He didn't say anything else. And Niner didn't press him. He wasn't sure that he was ready to hear Darman spill all that buried pain.

Southern outskirts of Keldabe, capital of Mandalore

Jusik had never seen the thing before, but now that he had he still didn't believe it. And he wasn't sure he wanted to.

It was a vast skull, a mythosaur skull, with huge downturned horns that curved to the jaw, slanted eye sockets, and long teeth. It was the iconic symbol of Mandalore in every sense, both *Mand'alor*—commander of supercommandos, chieftain of chieftains—and the world itself, *Manda'yaim*. But it still looked ludicrous on that scale.

The skull and the rest of the unconvincing skeleton structure was big enough to house a battalion. Keldabe wasn't the loveliest city in the galaxy, but Jusik was still surprised that anyone had built something that ugly where folks had to look at it. It was, as Coruscant architects might have said, *unsympathetic* and *not in keeping with the vernacular.*

"Ugly as *osik*," Ordo said, getting straight to the point. "And useless."

Jusik slid out of the speeder and leaned against the door to watch a procession of stormtroopers and repulsors taking equipment into the skull itself. It was hard to imagine what was happening. He hoped they were going to demolish it for offenses against aesthetics. It was the most useful thing that the Empire could ever do for Mandalore.

"What is it?"

Ordo stood considering the abomination, arms folded. "Beats me. Maybe it's some promotional stunt for MandalMotors." He drew an imaginary skull in the air with his fingertip. "It's their logo."

"You seriously think the average *Mando'ad* would buy their products on the basis of a giant mythosaur skull? That's *aruetyc*."

"No, but it's so bizarre that I struggle for an explanation."

"Is Fenn Shysa having some coronation there as the new *Mand'alor*?"

"Definitely not his style." Ordo got back into the speeder. "In fact, I don't think new *Mand'alore* have had crowning ceremonies since . . . well, I don't know. Vulgar. Very wasteful."

"*Aruetyc*." Jusik shut the hatch and started the drives, realizing how often he used that word lately— non-Mando, traitor, enemy, or just not one of *us*. He'd embraced his new identity completely, just as he'd once been wholly Jedi, and it still surprised him when he considered it. *Converts are the worst, they say. Is that me?*

Yes, it is. "Now let's find out what the Empire's doing with it."

Jusik started up the speeder. He wasn't bothered by the presence of an Imperial garrison here—yet. Kyrimorut was so remote and hard to find in the thinly populated wilderness that made up most of Mandalore that Keldabe might as well have been on another planet. But he knew that Palpatine hadn't sited a base here for the benefit of the local economy, so everyone was waiting for the inevitable catch. As long as the Empire employed Mando mercenaries and paid rent for the land, then the jury—on the surface of it, anyway—was still out as to whether the garrison was a threat.

Privately, the decision had already been made.

Shysa was making plans for a guerrilla war against the Empire. He could already see that it would be an unwelcome lodger in years to come. Kal Skirata—*Kal'buir,* Papa Kal—didn't want anything to do with Shysa's secret army. He had enough trouble of his own. But then he'd never wanted the Empire here, either.

It had come anyway. Everyone knew where this would end, and only *when* remained in doubt.

"Ordo, you know *Kal'buir* is as dear to me as he is to you," Jusik said carefully, steering a couple of meters above the riverbank. "But do you think he's wise to let Ny bring Jedi here?"

Ordo read his datapad and didn't comment on the irony of the question. He seemed remarkably relaxed about things now. "It's not without risk."

"How do you feel about having a Kaminoan around?"

"We coped with having Ko Sai as a houseguest . . ."

"Actually, we didn't, and she didn't handle it too well, either. She killed herself. And Mereel—she just pressed all the wrong buttons in him."

Jusik realized that was the most stupid phrase he'd come out with in a long time. *Wrong buttons.* No, that didn't even come close. Mereel, like all the Nulls, was just a faulty product as far as the Kaminoan clonemasters were concerned, something to be put down like an ailing farm animal before they went back to the drawing board. Any normal kid would have been deeply traumatized by that kind of treatment. But kids who had been engineered to be perfect black ops troopers, ferociously intelligent killing machines—their reactions were likely to be a lot more extreme.

Jusik still marveled at how normal the Nulls managed to be most of time. Mereel was charming and affable, a ladies' man, always the one with the jokes. And then something would trigger the other Mereel, the tormented and haunted child buried within, and he'd change instantly for a moment before snapping back to his old self. It was as if all the Nulls knew this damaged animal within them only too well, and built new personalities on top to keep it on a leash.

"Sorry," Jusik said. "I'm not making light of what happened to you."

Ordo shrugged. "Mereel took it the worst. But we're all messed up." His frank assessment of his own mental health was almost touching. "Imprecise term, but it sums up the effect Kamino had on us."

"Have you discussed it with *Kal'buir*?"

"Yes, and I agree with him. Kina Ha's genetic material is too valuable to pass up just because we have nightmares about the *kaminiise*."

Jusik chewed over the implications of that again as he parked the speeder as close as he could to the *Oyu'baat* cantina. Kina Ha was another long shot in the bid to find a way to reverse the clones' accelerated aging, and all of those so far had unraveled into dangerous missions and betrayals. If the Kaminoans had engineered some of their own kind to live exceptionally long lives, then there was something—some set of genes, some technique—that Dr. Uthan might exploit to reset the clones' aging process to normal. Yes, Jusik could see how important it was; Skirata lived for his clone sons, and giving them a normal life span had become a sacred quest. But *this* . . . it had to be traded off against the risk of Kyrimorut's location leaking, and whatever would happen to Ny Vollen's regard for Skirata when she worked out that he would turn Kina Ha into soup if he thought it would save his boys.

That's going to hurt Ny. Maybe him, too.

"Let me ask you a question, *Bard'ika*," Ordo said. "Does it trouble you that Kina Ha is a Jedi?"

"Why should it?"

"Old memories."

"Not bothered at all."

Ordo looked dubious. "But Kaminoans aren't a compassionate species, so what kind of Jedi will she be?"

Jusik thought about it. He'd never heard of a Force-sensitive Kaminoan. And one who lived for centuries, maybe even millennia—that made her a one-off in every sense. "A lonely one, I think."

Ordo raised one eyebrow. "Inside, I'm crying. Really. So is *Kal'buir,* I'm sure." Then he dropped the subject. Jusik decided that Ordo thought it was perfectly normal to try to erase your past because he'd done it, too, or as best he could. He seemed to be worrying that the arrival of real Jedi might shake Jusik's resolve.

No. No, it won't. Now now.

Keldabe was a few hours' flight time south of Kyrimorut and the climate was much milder. The snow hadn't reached this far. Jusik ambled through the narrow streets and down alleys overhung by rickety buildings, relishing the sheer impossibility of the city. One moment he was in a street that hadn't changed in the best part of a thousand years, all time-twisted wooden frames and ancient plaster, and the next he was in the shadow of a stark industrial warehouse or a polished granite tower. Keldabe was an anarchic fortress of a city on a granite outcrop on the bend in the Kelita River, almost completely surrounded by the Kelita River, a natural moat that changed from picturesque calm to a torrent within a kilometer. Jusik loved the place. It captured everything about Mandalore for him, and he was happy that intelligence gathering would bring him down here more often.

The clones had to keep their helmets on, of course. No Mandalorian cared if his neighbor was a deserter from the Grand Army, but the Imperials were around, and the last thing anyone needed was a clone stormtrooper coming face-to-face with a man who looked exactly like himself.

The stormies, as everyone now called them, hadn't come into town yet. They probably wouldn't venture into the *Oyu'baat* anyway. It was the oldest cantina on the planet, open for business when the Mandalorians fought against the Old Republic, which was also the last time anyone seemed to have changed the menu.

The place was clean but somehow enticingly *seedy*. The smells that wafted out when Jusik opened the doors were an adventure in themselves. He felt the thrill of ages, because everything happened here; as a Force-sensitive, the echoes called to him as vividly as if he'd been present when the events took place. If Mandalore had a government of any kind, then its business was done in the *Oyu'baat*'s booths and at its long counter as chieftains of the clans debated, reached agreements, and struck deals.

So the *Oyu'baat* was the obvious place to hear gossip about the Imperial garrison. Mandos tended not to keep secrets among themselves, and it saved a lot of high-risk observation time just to sit and listen—and enjoy an ale.

Jusik took off his helmet and bought a mug of *ne'tra gal*. He didn't look much like his wanted poster behind the counter—all bounties were posted there, for the benefit of patrons who were in the hunting business—but nobody would have turned him in anyway. Jusik was a Mandalorian now, just another adult taken into the fold like so many others, whose past no longer mattered and wasn't discussed. But maybe they left him alone because anyone who knew his past also knew that he was under the protection of Kal Skirata. Jusik remained wary.

Ordo kept his helmet on and settled in a booth. Jusik

ordered a bottle of ale for Ordo to take away. The barkeep gave Jusik a sympathetic look.

"Clone on the run, eh, *ner vod*?" Locals knew why some men kept their helmets on. He held the glass mug of *ne'tra gal* at arm's length until the foam settled. "Don't worry. Imperials don't come in here. Made sure of it."

The barkeep didn't say how he'd achieved that, and Jusik didn't ask. He could hear a group of men convulsing with laughter. The word *kyrbes*—mythosaur skull, the *Mand'alor*'s traditional crown—jumped out at him.

Well, they thought the thing was funny, too. Jusik decided to gather a little intel.

"*Vode,* what's going on with that skull?" he asked. "Why are the Imperials moving in?"

One of the group, a thickset man in his fifties with deep brown armor and knuckles tattooed with *Mando'a* runes, was laughing so hard that he started coughing. He tried to answer. But every time he almost got a word out, the guffaws overtook him and he bent over with his hands braced on his knees. His friends were in the same state. One of them could only manage a wheezing *hurr-hurr-hurr* sound. The whole cantina was watching now.

"You don't know what that is?" the man said eventually. He wiped tears from his cheeks with the back of his hand. "Really?"

"Really. We don't usually go south of the river, so we've never seen it before today."

"Go on, Jarkyc, tell him." One of the group shoved the man in the back. Mando humor could range from sly to unashamedly lavatorial, so Jusik couldn't guess what was coming. He just sensed in the Force that Jarkyc found something both hilarious and confusing. "It's the best thing I've heard all year."

Jarkyc got his breath back and cleared his throat. "It was the dumbest idea." He jerked a thumb at one of his companions. "Hayar's idiot brother thought Mandalore could attract adventure tourists. He built the skull as a theme park years ago. A place where folks could be entertained with mindless *aruetyc osik*. Needless to say, it never opened."

The men started laughing again. Jusik couldn't piece it together. "So why are the Imperials interested in it?"

"We've been bad boys. We told them it was an ancient Mandalorian temple that held great magical power for us simple folk, and so . . ." He took more wheezing gulps of air. "Well, they wanted to build the garrison in there, on account of it having so much *significance* to us. So we *sold it to them*."

The whole cantina erupted in raucous laughter. *Beskar* gauntlets hammered on tables. Yes, a combination of *aruetyc* gullibility, playing dumb, and getting paid a good price for it was a fine Mando prank.

"Mythosaurs weren't that big, were they?" Jusik said.

"Maybe not, but *they* don't know that, do they?"

"*Aruetiise*," Hayar said. "They'll believe any old *osik* you tell them. They think we're superstitious savages."

"Hey, retract the *superstitious* bit!" someone shouted over the laughter. "Think we should leave some offerings at the temple, just to show how pious we are?"

Other drinkers joined in. "What, the ones with five-minute detonation timers, or the incendiary sort?"

"Proves that someone on Kamino forgot to use Jango's brain cells."

"Nah, it's not the *clones*. It was that garrison commander—some aristo from Kemla. *Kaysh mirsh solus*."

It was a lovely Mandalorian insult: *his brain cell's lonely*. Mandalorians had more words for *stupid* and *stabbing* than any other language, and Jusik couldn't help thinking the two were somehow inextricably linked.

"So what does that tell you?" Jusik asked Ordo, sliding into the booth.

"I'd take a guess that the Empire wants to inspire awe and wonder among the natives," Ordo said. "Or they think it's going to curry favor with us. Either way, it tells me that whoever's making the decisions doesn't know Mandalorians very well. And that means it's not Palpatine, because I think he *does* understand us, in an exploitative sort of way."

"Like *Kal'buir* says, it'll be about *beroyase bal beskar*—Palps wants our mercenaries and our iron ore." Jusik drained his ale in eight gulps. He'd never enjoyed ale on Coruscant, but it all felt very different here. He was filling out, putting on weight and muscle, and he felt happier being *Bard'ika* than he ever had in his life. "I wouldn't mind taking a closer look at the skull."

"It's like watching a speeder wreck, isn't it?"

"I'm having one of my *feelings* from a previous existence."

Ordo shrugged and pocketed the unopened bottle of ale. "Come on, a quick walk around town to see who's about, and then you can go admire the *kyrbes*."

A walkabout normally resulted in buying odds and ends they couldn't get in Enceri; engine parts for Parja's workshop, toiletries for Dr. Uthan, and candies for everyone. Jusik hoped Mij Gilamar included dentistry in his prodigious range of medical skills, because clones and sugary food went hand in hand. Their accelerated aging seemed to demand a lot of calories.

By the time they found a safe observation point for the grotesque mythosaur theme park, Ordo had already chomped his way happily through a half-kilo bag of candied nuts and was starting on the second.

"You'll regret that when your *beskar'gam* doesn't fit anymore," Jusik said, watching the skull from the speeder's side screen.

"I'll burn this off *easily*."

"Yeah, that's what I used to say."

Jusik was beginning to wonder if his Force senses were getting slack. He had an uneasy feeling about the garrison, which he filed under O for Obvious, but there was something else bothering him. He watched the procession of stormies, construction droids, and Imperial officers—who certainly got their new uniforms faster than Jusik ever received kit requests in the Grand Army—

and looked for anything out of the run of normal-for-despots.

"I see they've got Mando help," he said, focusing on a figure in red *beskar'gam*. It was always hard to tell a male Mando from a tall female because the armor often obliterated the curves and gave women the same gait as the men. But he was sure it was a male. "Well, as long as Shysa hasn't gone public with his resistance, what can they do?"

Ordo shoved his bag of nuts in the speeder's dashboard compartment and held his hand out for the electrobinoculars. "Let me look."

"There. The guy in red, black undersuit, talking to the Imperial."

Ordo froze. "Ah."

"Something wrong?"

"In a way."

"What?"

"Gilamar won't be happy. You don't know who that is, do you?"

"If I did, *Ord'ika*, I wouldn't have handed you the electros."

Ordo watched in silence for a little longer until the man took off his helmet for a moment to scratch his scalp.

"Yes, that's definitely him," Ordo said. "Former *Cuy'val Dar*. One of Jango Fett's less inspired choices for training sergeant—good soldier, but a complete nutter. Mij Gilamar had to be dragged off him more than once. Had a lady friend called Isabet Reau—also a sergeant, also mad as a box of Hapan chags."

"I need a name." Jusik recalled all the gossip and filed names mentally. He needed to know who could upset the good-natured Gilamar that much. "Come on, who is it?"

"The man who wants the old Mandalorian empire restored," Ordo said, seeming to have lost interest in his nuts. "To the bad old days, that is. His name's Dred Priest. And he's a dead man already."

2

*If we've defrauded the galactic banking system out of a
trillion credits, stolen the industrial secrets of the top
dozen clonemasters, assassinated government intelligence agents, and spied upon, thieved from, sabotaged,
and generally ticked off Palpatine at every level—well,
harboring escaped Jedi really isn't going to make things
any worse for us, is it?*
—Deserter, Null ARC trooper N-10—now Jaing
Skirata, Mandalorian mercenary

Kyrimorut, Mandalore

"**S**o you know what you're doing, Kal, yeah?"

Mij Gilamar rarely gave advice outside of his two
fields of professional expertise—killing or curing—but
sometimes he used a certain tone that made Skirata's
shoulders hunch.

It was a rebuke, a clip around the ear, however kindly
put, and all the more cutting for it. No, Skirata was *not*
sure what he was doing. He would have been the first to
admit it. In fact, he was going to admit it right now. He
stared up into the clear dusk in the general direction
from which the freighter *Cornucopia* was due to make a
low-level approach, and wondered if this was the moment when his talent for pulling off impulsive gambles
had finally reached its limit.

*But it's not just my neck, is it? It's my boys. And it's all
the other unlucky* shabuire *who put their faith in me.*

"Okay, I've risked everyone's life by letting the Jedi come here," he said. "The more folks I gather in, the greater the odds that we'll be found. But be honest, *Mij'ika*—if you'd had the chance of getting your hands on someone the aiwha-bait engineered to live longer, could *you* pass it up?"

Gilamar kept his eyes on the sky. "No, probably not."

"I hear the *but* coming."

"It's too late to change plans. I'd just be sniping."

Skirata heard something rustle in the undergrowth. His first thought was that it was Mird, but the strill was with Vau, light-years away in the Kashyyyk sector looking for leads on Sev. After long years of hating Mird, Skirata now missed the animal, and much as it surprised him, he missed Walon Vau, too. He thought of all the times he'd drawn his knife on both of them, and bitterly regretted years spent on infighting when there were so many real enemies around.

The rustling turned out to be Mereel and Jaing strolling through the bushes. Jaing was either keeping an eye on Mereel, knowing his temper when it came to Kaminoans, or else planning to show off his distinctive gray leather gloves to Kina Ha to remind her what could happen to Kaminoans who didn't behave.

Am I sure this isn't a setup? How could a Kaminoan Jedi with those genes land in my lap? She's probably the only one of her kind. And I'm not that lucky.

Gilamar sighed. "Maybe Ny's had the sense to blindfold them. But they're Jedi. They've got that radar ability, that *direction* thing."

"Yes, thanks, I do realize that once they get here, they know our location." Skirata took out a strip of ruik root and chewed to calm his nerves. "They can have this location dragged out of them if they're ever caught. So once they're here . . ." He hadn't thought that through yet. *What the* shab *have I done?* "But my priority is keeping the boys safe. So I won't hesitate to put a round through both saber-jockeys if I think that needs doing. Is that the question you really wanted to ask, Mij?"

Gilamar turned his head slowly to look at Skirata. "Kal, did you tell Ny why you were willing to hide the Jedi here?"

No, he hadn't. At least, he hadn't spelled it out; he'd just reminded Ny that he wasn't the good man she thought he was, but that he loved his boys. She *knew* what the stakes were, what was happening to Ordo and all the other clones. She should have put two and two together. He didn't plan to apologize for doing his duty as a father.

"I never told her I wanted Kina Ha for spare parts, no," he said.

"She's only seen the nice paternal Kal." Gilamar held out his hand for a piece of ruik. "You might want to think how to break it to her. Maybe I should do it. Doctor's bedside manner and all that *osik*."

"Tough. She's a fine woman, but this isn't about her."

Skirata liked Ny, so much that it scared him. He should have grown out of all that nonsense by now. And he owed her. But if A'den tried any harder to throw the two of them together, they'd break something.

A'den would have to wait to get his own way for a change. Skirata had a mission, and he would *not* be diverted from it. His reason for living was his adopted sons, and without them . . . sometimes he wondered how long he would have lasted if he hadn't taken a chance on Jango's summons to Kamino. He was pretty sure that within a year, he'd have been dead in a gutter with a blaster hole through his head for pursuing one bigger, faster, younger bounty too many. He might even have ended up putting the hole there himself. He hadn't enjoyed being the old Kal Skirata.

And then he met the Nulls, breathtakingly courageous little kids barely big enough to grip a hold-out blaster, and his life began again as if he'd been resurrected. He'd been given a second chance to make a better job of it.

I owe them everything.

"Okay," Gilamar said. "You trusted her with the location, and you trusted ARC troopers you didn't even know, like Spar and Sull. So maybe you can find a way to trust these Jedi."

Jaing walked up behind Skirata and draped one arm on his father's shoulder. Mereel appeared on the other side. They moved in like a close protection team.

"I'll make sure they know the house rules, *Buir,*" Mereel said. "Regardless of how much I want a nice pair of gloves like Jaing's."

"Get your own Kaminoan, *ner vod.*" Jaing gave Skirata a rough hug and back-slap. "I need a matching belt to go with these."

Gilamar just smiled. Like Skirata, he'd never been one for trophies. Come to think of it, neither had Vau. The three of them always looked pretty harmless for Mandalorians, with no scalps, hides, strings of teeth, or unidentifiable remains of their kills dangling from their shoulder plates. Maybe they needed to roughen up their image a bit and sport a few shriveled body parts that weren't their own. Skirata tried to imagine what he'd be able to stomach hanging from his shoulder plate. He couldn't think of anything. His own squeamishness surprised him sometimes.

Mereel cocked his head. "Listen . . ."

"Is everyone inside?" Skirata asked.

"I don't think a teenage girl and a senile Kaminoan are going to be a security problem, *Buir.*"

"What if it's not just them?"

Jaing chambered a round in his Verpine rifle. "Then I'll just have to empty the whole magazine, won't I?"

Skirata's hearing had been wrecked by too many years of using noisy weapons, but his eyesight was okay. He watched Ny's freighter skim just above the trees, no navigation lights visible, bringing with it a heady blend of hope for prolonging his boys' lives and the real risk of losing everything he lived for.

Every waif and stray that ended up here was potentially another mouth to betray the existence of the bastion, whether they intended to or not.

And that included Ny Vollen.

Skirata trusted her because A'den did. And she'd put herself on the line; she'd brought Etain's body home, spied for the clan, and refused all payment. All she wanted was to find out how her husband's ship had been lost, but now she had that information—she was still around, still doing favors.

"So you have a woman at your beck and call now, *Buir*," Mereel said, not quite managing to stop himself from grinning. "We're irresistible, we *Mando'ade*."

"It's not like that," Skirata said. "She's lost. She's found us. That's all."

He'd never thought of himself as a man who put the slightest faith in anyone beyond himself and his lads, but now he saw just how long the list of trusted strangers was becoming. This wasn't what he'd planned.

Cornucopia settled on its dampers, hissing vapor like a panting animal. Jaing and Mereel took up firing positions with their rifles trained on the main hatch and the emergency escape plate. *Shab*, it was just like Tipoca City again. The little Nulls reacted like that on the first night he'd met them, when an unexpected knock at the door sent them scurrying to take cover or stack either side of the doors.

I mustn't forget what Kaminoans did to my boys. No two-year-old child should know how to do that. It's wrong. It's just plain wrong.

Skirata felt better now. The clone army might not have been Kina Ha's doing, but he had no reason to apologize to her, either. The hatch opened. Light spilled on the snow and the ramp extended in jerks and scrapes. *Cornucopia* was in need of a major service.

"Hey, Shortie." Ny stepped onto the ramp and jerked her thumb over her shoulder. "They followed me home. Can I keep them?"

"That's Fi's line," Skirata said. He tried hard not to smile at her, but failed. He was instantly fourteen again, desperately worried what a girl thought of him, wishing he was taller, crushed or overjoyed depending on the look she might give him. He didn't even notice that Ny wasn't his usual type; she'd struck a spark in him, and he wished she hadn't. "He's made an uj cake for you. Parja taught him how."

"Mando men," she said. "No end to your talents, is there?" She looked over her shoulder. "Scout? Kina? Come on, I need to get this ship under cover. We're still on a war footing here."

Skirata braced himself. He didn't dare look at Jaing or Mereel.

Relax. It'll be easy. All Uthan needs is samples, right? Nobody can object to that. No decent Jedi would want to deny another living being a chance of a proper life. And if she does—too bad.

Skirata took Jusik and Etain as his benchmark of what decent Jedi should be. He was going to measure these two newcomers against that, and he felt he had the right to. But he'd been so fixated on the Kaminoan, so focused on what her genetic material might mean for the clones, that he'd almost forgotten about the kid Ny called Scout.

She came out of the hatch first, and he simply wasn't prepared for the punch in the gut that it gave him.

Scout was all freckles and skinny determination, a Padawan Jedi in a grubby beige robe, shivering in the cold, hair in need of a good brushing. When she hitched up her belt and Skirata saw the lightsaber dangling from it, she reminded him so much of Etain that he simply couldn't handle it. He put his hand to his mouth, more in shock than to stifle the sob.

Gilamar let out a long breath. He'd seen it, too.

"I'm Tallisibeth Enwandung-Esterhazy," she said, giving Skirata a formal bow of the head. "You'll probably want to call me Scout. Everyone else does. Thank you for taking us in, Master Skirata."

Skirata wasn't even aware now of Jaing and Mereel behind him. Kina Ha was temporarily forgotten. He held his hand over his mouth, blinking away tears, and struggled to compose himself.

"You must be freezing, *ad'ika*." He could hardly keep

his voice steady. *Ad'ika* just slipped out. It was what any Mando father called his kids, regardless of their age. "Get indoors and have some hot food."

Ny had told him that Scout was a lot like Etain, but she'd only said she was weak in the Force and almost didn't make the grade as a Jedi. He took it more as a bid to convince him Scout was no danger to anyone. Ny had never warned him that the girl was so much like Etain in other ways, though.

But Ny had never seen Etain alive, of course. She couldn't know.

Gilamar led Scout away, and Skirata was still so stunned and upset that Kina Ha was—mercifully—an anticlimax. The old aiwha-bait shuffled down the ramp, still with some of that grace that they all had, but she was obviously ancient. He'd never seen a Kaminoan who looked like that. Knowing how they treated him as defective because he'd limped, he wondered what they'd make of Kina Ha in Tipoca City.

She bowed her head. "Nyreen has explained your *difficulty* with my people, Sergeant." She used Ny's full name, adding to the impression of ancient formality. "Which makes your generosity that much more commendable."

Skirata was too gutted by the shock of seeing Scout to say anything but the first thing that came into his head.

"I'm not a saint, ma'am," he said. "There'll be a price."

Kina Ha nodded. "That's the way of the galaxy."

Ny guided Kina Ha to the farmhouse as if she was reluctant to leave her to Jaing or Mereel. When she looked at Skirata, she seemed shocked, but it wasn't as if she hadn't seen him cry before. Maybe she couldn't see what he saw when he looked at Scout.

Fingers gripped his right arm, careful but firm. "*Buir,* you better get indoors, too." Mereel marched him away while Jaing boarded *Cornucopia* to move the vessel into the camouflaged hangar. "Are you okay?"

"Are *you,* *Mer'ika*?"

"The old aiwha-bait's irrelevant," he said. "I'm not giving *all* of them the power to upset me. But remember something, *Buir*—the other one's not Etain. Scout's just a little Jedi who reminds us of her. Okay? Don't let her get under your skin."

Skirata felt like a fool. He was a fool because Ny Vollen left him feeling vulnerable. He was a fool because a teenager who was a little too much like Etain could reduce him to tears. He was a fool because he let all this *osik* get to him. His war wasn't over. He had to stay sharp and keep thinking like a soldier; there was a lot of unfinished business.

"I know, *Mer'ika*." He had to stop reliving the past and focus on the future. "I'm just old and tired. You'll be like that one day. But no sooner than you need to be."

Mereel chuckled and wandered off in the direction of a hangar hidden by netting and half buried in the soil. He never seemed upset by his accelerated aging. But then Skirata had never been conscious of being a short-lived creature compared with the Hutts he'd done business with, so maybe the reality hadn't sunk in for Mereel yet.

It would sink in when he started overtaking Jusik on the road to mortality, though. Skirata, painfully aware of an implacably ticking chrono, braced himself to have dinner with a ghost.

Kyrimorut, Mandalore

"Is it compulsory to like *gihaal*?" Ruu Skirata asked.

She opened the metal container, letting the pungent aroma of dried smoked fish escape into the kitchen. *Gihaal* kept for years without refrigeration, one of the staples of Mandalorian ration packs. Ny filed it under Acquired Tastes. She was grateful she'd never had to prepare it from raw fish. It must have smelled a whole lot worse while it was drying.

"I doubt it," Ny said, trying to hold her breath. "I think a lot of Mandos hate it, too."

Ruu wrinkled her nose as she inhaled. She was so much like her father. "Good. I'd hate to let the side down."

With more than twenty mouths to feed, meals at Kyrimorut had now acquired an industrial scale. The complex was more than a house. It was *yaim*—part barracks, part hotel, part married quarters, part farmhouse, the archetypal Mandalorian clan home. They were lucky that Laseema, Atin's Twi'lek wife, had worked in a restaurant and so could manage a kitchen. She knew all the complicated stuff about portion sizes and making sure everything was ready at the same time. Ny was happy to take orders from her.

"I vote we get a droid," Jilka said, dicing amber-root. "Why is Mandalore the only place where everyone does everything by hand?"

"The dignity of labor." Besany tasted the bubbling vat of stew to check if it needed more salt. "Hard work's good for the soul. Very grounding."

"My soul's fine," Jilka said stiffly. The angrier she got, the faster she diced. "My body is another matter."

Jilka looked at her hands, red and sore from kitchen chores, and Ny could almost read her thoughts: *How did this ever happen to me?* Like Besany, Jilka had worked for the Treasury as an investigator. But unlike her, she hadn't followed a clone husband to Kyrimorut. She was an innocent bystander, set up by a Gurlanin spy to draw attention away from Besany while she leaked government information to Skirata, arrested by the secret police—and sprung from prison by Ordo and Vau. Jilka's life had been wrecked before she even knew why. She hadn't actually punched out Besany yet, but the atmosphere between them was pure ice. It was only a matter of time.

"You don't have to do this." Besany held out her hand for the knife, which was probably a bad idea. Jilka ignored it. "You've got no obligation to us at all."

"If I'm stuck here, then I *pull my weight,*" Jilka said, and went on chopping.

What else could Besany say? That it was better being stuck at the *shabla shebs* end of the galaxy—Ny was picking up all the profanities—than being held by Palpatine's thugs? None of it should have happened. Jilka had just been friends with the wrong woman at the wrong time.

Well, they weren't friends now.

Corr poked his head around the kitchen door. Ny wondered if Jilka could tell all the clones apart yet.

"Can I hide in here, please, ladies?" He gave them his best cheeky-boy smile and swaggered in. "The atmosphere's a bit intense out there. Aiwha-bait alert."

"Since when does the kitchen have a FEMALES ONLY sign outside?" Jilka asked. "Make yourself useful, soldier."

Corr winked, took the knife from her hand, and began chopping with surprising speed and skill. The more surprising thing was that she let him.

"If it *did,*" he said, "you'd give me special exemption, right?"

Jilka fixed him with her tax investigator's stare. "Maybe."

He smiled and chopped faster. He was being a bit too cocky, paying more attention to Jilka than the knife, and the inevitable happened. He nicked his finger. He swore and paused for a second before carrying on.

Jilka stared. "You're not bleeding."

"Oh, these aren't real, neither of them." Corr flexed both hands. "But the sensors work. I'm in pain. You can kiss it better if you like."

"Not real?"

Nobody had told Jilka much about Corr, then. The fact that he'd lost both hands and forearms in a blast when he was a bomb disposal trooper just hadn't come up. It had now. Prosthetic limbs were commonplace, but losing both hands somehow shifted the injury from routine to distressing.

Corr's smile didn't waver. He stripped the synthflesh covering off one hand and waggled metal rods and servos for inspection.

"Bomb disposal specials," he said. "I was in EOD, but I got a wire wrong. Now, *these* babies—special bomb disposal standard. Also issued to surgeons. *Very* fine motor control. *Very* sensitive, too, when I put the synthflesh back on."

He gave her a sly smile. Jilka looked like he'd defused her as efficiently as any explosive device.

"I'm impressed," she said.

"Understandable," said Corr. "The rest of me is all my own, of course."

Jilka seemed to thaw a little. She was either embarrassed by his injury or very taken with him, and Ny bet her creds on the latter. Corr carried on chopping until Skirata called him from the passage. It sounded like Ordo and Jusik were back from Keldabe.

"Keep the blade warm, gorgeous," Corr said, pressing the knife's handle back into Juka's palm. "I'll be back."

He vanished. Jilka turned her head slowly to Besany. "So, your idea? Peace offering? A clone of my own?"

"Not at all." Besany looked put out. "He was very shy when I first met him, but Mereel decided to . . . broaden his outlook on life."

"I see it worked."

"You could do a lot worse, Jilka. Clones value the things we take for granted. They never expected to have any of them."

Ny was surprised by the rebuke, but Jilka didn't snap back. She went on chopping, eyes fixed on the table. Atin came in carrying a plastoid bowl full of gleaming freshly caught fish.

"Kaminoans eat fish, don't they?" he said, as if he was having second thoughts. "I never asked back in Tipoca. We didn't eat with them."

Laseema picked up a fish by its tail. "Did you gut them properly?"

"Of course I did. And it's going to take me ages to get the smell off my hands."

"You're a darling. Now all I need is some *gihaal* stock to poach them in."

"You know that's what Dad and the boys call the Kaminoans, don't you?" Ruu spooned the dried pieces into a jug. "*Gihaal*. Fish-meal. When they're not calling them aiwha-bait, that is."

Jilka seemed unmoved by the odor, but then her tax enforcement duties brought her into contact with a lot of Hutts. "Well, we can make some ironic broth, then. *Gihaal* for *gihaal*."

"Twenty-five *gihaal* broths, coming up. Or however many it is."

"None for Fi." Laseema tasted it, frowing. "He can't stomach it after what happened to Ko Sai."

Jilka gave Ny a look that said *tell me what happened,* but she decided that could wait a few months. The woman was unhappy enough as it was.

"Okay, so how many *have* we got tonight?" Laseema checked quantities on her datapad. "Are Cov's squad in or out at Rav Bralor's place? How about Levet? Uthan—is she staying in her room, or what? Arla won't come out, I know."

"I know we couldn't leave her in the asylum," Ruu said, "but did anyone think how the poor woman would feel about being surrounded by strange men in Mando armor?"

"But we're not the Death Watch," Besany said. She'd fallen into the role of alpha female by virtue of being Ordo's wife. "We're not the ones who killed her family."

"And she's not Mando." Ruu seemed to have embraced her father's culture despite the long separation. "She's from Concord Dawn. Not the same thing. Jango joined us, but she never got the chance. *Everyone* probably looks like Death Watch to her."

Laseema arranged the fish in a pan and set them on the stove. "Do you think she knows Jango survived?"

"I don't think she even knows what day it is. *Bard'ika*'s the only one who can talk to her. And you, Laseema."

"Maybe that's because Bardan doesn't look like her brother, and Laseema's a Twi'lek," Jilka said. "Arla's *got* to notice the family resemblance in the clones, even if she never saw Jango as an adult."

"That must be upsetting her even more." Laseema arranged tidbits on a tray with a few flowers. Arla certainly never got touches like that in the Valorum Center. "And I don't so much talk *to* her as *at* her—just odd words. Maybe she doesn't understand much Basic."

Ny had to remind herself that Arla Fett had been banged up in a secure mental unit because she murdered a few men, and a court decided she might kill more. But everyone here seemed to assume she had her reasons until proven otherwise. It was a bafflingly Mando attitude. Skirata never seemed to worry that the men of Kyrimorut were at risk.

"Gosh, it's going to be a fun evening," Jilka muttered. "My family had dinners like this on Republic Day. No serial killers, of course, although we were never entirely sure about Uncle Tobiaz."

Ny thought that summed it up pretty well. The atmosphere around that huge veshok table was *sliceable,* although not for the reasons she expected. Skirata looked lost and upset. She'd expected to find him being dragged off Kina Ha, knife in hand. But it was Ordo and Mereel—those two always paired up when they smelled trouble—who looked grim and disapproving. Kina Ha sat next to Atin. Ny decided to sit on the other side of her and offer moral support.

"I'll make the introductions." Skirata's voice was husky, as if he'd been swallowing unshed tears. "Kina Ha, Scout—this is my family, and my guests." He pointed out who was who, who was married to who, who *should* have been married if only they'd get on with it, and who the guests were. Dr. Uthan was introduced as *a friend* concerned for the clones' health. Skirata had a talent for sly euphemism.

But something had knocked the stuffing out of him, and Ny guessed that it was Scout rather than Kina Ha.

Little Kad, *Kad'ika,* sat on Jusik's lap for a change, staring at the two Jedi. He was around eighteen months old now, walking and talking, but with an unsettling tendency to just pause and study things in a way that looked too adult. He held his toy nerf in one hand, its fur charred from his mother's funeral pyre. Ny found it heartbreaking that this tiny kid had put it on there. She tried to work out if he felt cheated that Skirata had rescued it from the flames, that he'd been denied the chance to give his mother a farewell offering, but he refused to be parted from the toy now. Skirata had planned to keep it for when Kad was older and could understand its significance. That plan had lasted a few hours.

The baby already knew. Ny could see it.

Kad never asked where Etain was, or when Mama was coming home. As soon as Skirata showed him her body, he seemed to understand perfectly that she was never coming back, so now he kept asking where *Dada* was. Sometimes he said *Boo,* asking for his *buir,* the *Mando'a* word that could mean mother or father. But Ny doubted he was asking about Etain. He was just picking up the language he now heard most often. He wanted Darman.

Kad stared at Scout as if he knew her, then shook his head.

"He's very cute," Scout said. "I feel that the Force is stronger in him than in me, but that's not saying much. I have to do most things the hard way. I'm not much of a Jedi."

"Kad's mother wasn't strong in the Force, either," Skirata said, "and she was a *terrific* Jedi."

Ny caught Ordo's eye and saw that slight raise of the eyebrow. He was fiercely protective of his father, always ready to intervene. But it was Jusik who stepped in.

"Kina Ha, I've never heard of another Force-sensitive Kaminoan," he said. "May I ask a very personal question? Did they try to engineer your bloodline to maximize midi-chlorians?"

Ko Sai had been excited to get her hands on blood and tissue samples from Etain and Kad. It was an obvious question to ask when it was clear that Kamino had its own Jedi test subject all the time.

"Oh no, not at all," Kina Ha said. She sounded like a Kuati dowager duchess, imposing and matriarchal, even with that misleadingly gentle Kaminoan voice. "My Force abilities seemed most unexpected and most unwanted. I was bred for *longevity*, for deep-space missions. We never carried out those missions, of course, so there I was, something of an *embarrassment*, and the only one of my kind—I didn't fit the standard at all. So I felt it best to leave. As a species, we learned to fear too much diversity because controlling our genome was the way we survived the flooding of our world. A *one-off*, as you might call it, looks very much like a threat."

Kad's gaze was now fixed on Kina Ha. He didn't even blink. Jusik carried on.

"If Ko Sai was so interested in midi-chlorians, then, why did she seem to have no record of you?"

"Bardan." Kina Ha sounded as if she'd known him all her life. "This was all a *very* long time ago, *centuries* ago, and I suspect that my particular genetic records were erased before Kamino became such an *industrial* clonemaster. I'm not the kind of relative you'd want the neighbors to know about." She almost laughed, a strange bird-like trill. "I do enjoy human holovids, as you can tell. I've had a great deal of time on my hands to watch them."

The clones sat completely still, watching Kina Ha like snipers. Ordo wasn't even eating. They seemed mesmerized by a being who was nothing like the Kaminoans they'd grown up with.

"I have a lot of questions for you," Jusik said. "But I'm stopping you from enjoying your meal."

"It's very good fish broth," Kina Ha said. "I confess that I hadn't expected hospitality."

"We didn't expect you to laugh," Mereel muttered.

"None of us meets the other's expectations, then." She

reached past Ny and put her long three-fingered hand on Atin's arm. "I saw you, young man. Not as you are now, but I had a vision centuries ago that Kamino would unwittingly create a clone army for the dark side. They created so many clone armies, of course, a foolish and terrible thing to do anyway, so who was to say which one would be the army of my vision? So here we are, both of us unaware of the nature of those who used us."

"We know now," Fi said. "I don't suppose you can tell me the winning numbers for next week's Corellian lotto, can you?"

Fi always knew when and how to defuse a tense moment. Kina Ha looked him right in the eye with the dignity of immense age.

"Ten . . . fourteen . . . eighty-four . . . sixteen."

Fi and Corr laughed. So did Jusik. Ny tried to look at Skirata as casually as she could, checking how he was holding up, but it was Uthan who diverted her attention. The scientist seemed fascinated, watching like a stalking tusk-cat. She just couldn't take her eyes off Kina Ha.

Ny wondered if Uthan saw a fascinating old being, or a product full of genetic puzzles. It was an interesting reversal of roles for a species that saw humans as their top product line.

"Master Skirata," Kina Ha said, "you said there would be a price for your generous protection. I would like to know what it is, in case I can't afford it. Not fortunetelling, I hope? I'm very *vague*."

Skirata looked up as if he'd suddenly started paying attention. "Well, I was hoping for some fortune *changing*. Your compatriots designed my boys to live half a life. They age at double the normal human rate. I think that's unfair, all things considered."

"I agree. I take no pride in Kamino's capacity to manufacture slaves, whether they be soldiers or factory hands."

"I see you've *briefed* her, Ny . . . ," Skirata muttered.

Ny had already worked out why Skirata had agreed to

let the Jedi come here. She had no illusions. He'd made
it clear from the start; his boys' needs came first, and
he'd do whatever it took to slow their decline.

"Never said a word, Shortie." Ny steeled herself to
taste the broth. It was much better than it smelled. "The
lady thinks for herself."

"Then we live in an age of miracles." Skirata sounded
as if he'd rehearsed being nice and didn't want to let the
facade slip. "Kina Ha, Dr. Uthan is a geneticist and mi-
crobiologist, and maybe some other ologist I don't
know about, and she's trying to put my boys' body
clocks back to normal. Taking a look at some tissue
samples from you might give her a clue about how to
undo Ko Sai's maturation process."

"You don't want the secret of eternal life, then."

"No, I don't. But you're not immortal, by the looks of
it."

"Well spotted." She glanced at Jusik. "And you're
quite capable of taking what you want from me, by the
Force or by force."

"Is that a *no*?" Skirata asked.

"Merely remarking that you asked first, and I think
the request is reasonable. It *is* unfair. Beings are not
commodities to be designed and marketed."

Skirata let out a little bark of a laugh. "I bet they
loved your freethinking attitude in Tipoca. Shame you
weren't on the Jedi Council, too." He inclined his head
in a bow, and Ny decided it was genuine. "*Vor'e*. Thank
you."

Skirata went on eating, gazing down into his broth as
if he was ashamed. He'd managed not to call Kina Ha
aiwha-bait, or lecture her on the evils of commercial
cloning—so far. Ny wondered if he felt he'd betrayed his
principles by compromising with both a Jedi and a
Kaminoan.

*How would I have handled what he saw on Kamino
all those years? Look at Ordo, or Mereel. They'll never
be normal. How can I expect Kal to forgive Kaminoans*

for that? Or the Jedi, for turning a blind eye to it all? And how can I get him to give these two a chance?

There were two kinds of bigots: the kind that melted when face-to-face with the individual, and the kind that smiled politely but wouldn't let their daughter marry one of *those*. Skirata took a Mandalorian approach to it all, that individuals were only judged by what they did, not what they were, so everyone got a chance—just the one—to change his mind. Ny tried to understand how hard it was to suspend ancient hatreds when folks had a joint history like the Mandalorians and Jedi. A four-thousand-year-old enmity was more than she could begin to grasp.

But if she still had things to learn about Mandalorians, then she'd only just started on the reality of living alongside Jedi.

They really weren't like other beings at all.

Kyrimorut, Mandalore; next morning

Life wasn't going to return to normal for Ovolot Qail Uthan, and she'd accepted that the moment the cell door had swung shut in the Valorum Center.

But she'd held out for three years, and now she felt she could handle anything life threw at her. It was all a matter of looking at the situation from another angle and deciding to be content with whatever she could wring from it.

There was always something positive to seize upon. *Always.*

At least she had a pleasant room here, plain but comfortable, with a generous mattress—Mandalorians didn't shun comfort, however ascetic they appeared—and a fine view of the countryside through an arrow-slit of a window. And she could open the door and walk outside anytime she pleased.

But she wouldn't get far. There was nowhere to go that didn't involve struggling through deep snow for the best part of a hundred klicks to the nearest town, Enceri. Fi, the clone recovering from a brain injury, told her that Enceri was the pimple on the *shebs* of Mandalore and that she'd like Keldabe a lot better. She worked out what a *shebs* was fairly fast.

Now Fi brought her breakfast. She wasn't sure if he'd taken a shine to her, or was simply curious to see what a creator of genocidal weapons looked like at close quarters. She was sure they all saw her as a monster. What else could she expect when their mission had been to destroy her project, and hers had been to destroy them?

Yes, I can kill every one of these young men. I still don't know how I feel about that.

"Eggs again," Fi said, appearing at the door. "You're a woman of habit, Dr. Uthan."

"Protein," she said. "I believe in protein."

"So what do you think of our ancient aiwha-bait?"

"Is that what you call Kaminoans?"

"Fair's fair, Doc. They called us *units*."

"I think I might have *depersonalized* you somewhat, too."

"I never felt a thing. Honest."

"Did Kal send you to charm me, so that I might see the error of my ways?" Uthan uncovered the breakfast tray and admired the spread. Mandalorians *ate*. It wasn't elegant food, but it was certainly filling. "Make me ask myself how could I possibly want to wipe out such witty and charming young men?"

"Well, I am, yes, but do you still want to kill me?"

Uthan had to laugh. She was used to oblique people with hidden agendas that she had to hunt and dissect, so Fi's child-like directness was disarming. But that was probably the whole idea.

"Nothing personal," she said. "I just wanted the Republic to get off my homeworld, and quite a few other governments agreed with us."

"So you don't hold it against us for getting you shot and then locked up in a loony bin for three years."

"We're probably even, aren't we?"

He gave her a big grin. "I reckon."

Uthan settled down at her table and beckoned him in to sit down. He didn't move quite as crisply as the other clones. He was a little thinner, too.

"So," she said, "you were in a coma."

"Yeah. They switched off my life support. But I went on living anyway. I'm stubborn when it comes to not being dead."

"And?"

"Besany rescued me from the medcenter at blaster-point and the next thing I remember is *Bard'ika* healing me. They said it was really exciting. I missed it all, unfortunately."

"If this is what Jedi healing can do, I'm more than impressed." Uthan passed him one of her mealbread rolls. Clones definitely craved carbohydrate, and looking at Ko Sai's research on rapid maturation and metabolism, she could see why. "Do you all think of yourself as Mandalorian? Not just clones. All of you. Besany, Laseema, Jusik?"

"Sort of. Jilka doesn't, but then she didn't have any choice. Arla Fett—well, the poor woman's totally *dini'la*. But she's not Mando anyway."

"I never really thought about it before, you see. I only knew Ghez Hokan, and he had a very different view of the world from Skirata's."

"He did after . . ." Fi's voice trailed off, the only time that Uthan had seen that permanent good humor fade. She took a guess that he was going to make a joke and then recalled something distressing. "Our old boss, General Zey, said he used to be in the Death Watch but they threw him out. *Kal'buir* says he wasn't."

"Hokan thought the kindest thing was to kill you all rather than let you live as slaves to the Jedi."

Fi smiled. "It's good to know everyone has sensible reasons for wanting us dead, Doc. I'd hate to be killed on a pointless whim."

A voice from the doorway made Uthan jump. "That's a dirty word around here, *Death Watch*. Two, actually."

Mij Gilamar leaned against the door frame, rattling a flimsi bag that sounded as if it was full of glass. "And Hokan was never a member, just a hard-liner, so never believe intel or gossip." He held up the flimsi bag again as if he was tempting Uthan with a gift. "I took some samples from Kina Ha, Doctor, seeing as I'm the qualified scab-lifter. You're not a physician, are you?"

"Oh dear, you're going to use big confusing words," Fi said. He filched a couple of extra rolls and stuffed them in his pocket. "I'm off."

Uthan was still trying to place Gilamar in the Mandalorian scheme of things. He looked like everyone's idea of a holovid Mandalorian—broken nose, scarred armor, grim expression, buzz-cut hair—but when he spoke, he was another stereotype entirely: a highly educated man. She found the idea of a doctor working as a mercenary and still practicing medicine almost too much to take in. But then Mandalore itself was one big contradiction, with heavy industry and shipbuilding sitting cheek by jowl with farms that hadn't changed in centuries, sophisticated electronics and ancient metalworking skills side by side in the same suit of armor. She really wasn't sure what a Mando was anymore. All she knew was that they weren't quite what she expected. She hadn't met two the same yet—not even the clones.

"No, I'm not good with needles," she said. "You seem to be a polymath, Dr. Gilamar."

"Got to be." He sat down and took an assortment of vials and slides out of the bag. Some contained dark purplish blood, one seemed to be urine—clear and colorless as distilled water—and other containers held tiny globs of bloody tissue. "We're a long way from Coruscant Medical School. Every Mando needs to be able to do half a dozen jobs."

Uthan picked up one of the sample vials. "Biopsies? You know your way around Kaminoan anatomy, then."

"I spent more than eight years in Tipoca City with them. I know how those things are built. Now, how do you want to play this? I'll run the analyses for you if you like."

"Is she really a thousand years old?"

"No reason to doubt it. I've never seen a Kaminoan like her, and I've seen plenty."

"Extraordinary."

"You're looking for switching techniques rather than actual genes, right?"

"Most life in the galaxy has some genes in common, so perhaps not."

"We thought the maturation control was linked to silencing genes H-seven-eight-B and H-eighty-eight, but we didn't get anywhere with that. No artificial or nonhuman genes in the mix, either. I can assure you we menaced and leaned on some of the best scientists in the field."

Uthan smiled. She liked keeping things up her sleeve. She'd had to, just to stay alive these last few years. How could these strangers think she would trust them? Everyone used her.

"Do you know how my engineered pathogen targeted clones?" she asked.

Gilamar smiled back. "I think targeted bioweapons are a load of old *osik*, actually. Against humans, anyway."

"And why would you say that?"

"Because, unless you have some way of identifying a complete genome—not just a few genes, not even *ninety-nine percent* of the genome—there just aren't convenient Corellian genes or Mandalorian genes or whatever for a pathogen to hook up to. Not even if you call it a nanovirus, which I also think is *osik*, by the way. You'd have to find a way for the virus to identify the whole genome, or nothing."

Gilamar didn't sound as if he was gloating. He must have known the virus wasn't quite what she'd told Palpatine's minions it. He leaned forward across the table and smiled. Once, Ghez Hokan had lost his temper with her and hauled her across her desk by her collar, and for a moment she thought Gilamar would do the same. These were, after all, men who lived by violence.

But he just picked up the vial of urine and shook it carefully as if he were mixing a leisurely cocktail. "Am I right, Doctor? Either your virus has to find the intact Fett clone genome, or else it's useless. Which means it won't affect the Nulls, because their genome was altered from the basic trooper template, and it won't touch *Kad'ika*, because he's got half his mother's genes. Or maybe it goes to the other extreme, and kills most humans indiscriminately. Because the differences between human genomes across the galaxy are so *tiny* and populations *so mixed up* that your killer cocktail *can't tell the difference*. Can it?"

Uthan wondered if Gilamar had been in contact with Hokan during those few days of crisis on Qiilura. He was right. At that time, she hadn't been able to stop the virus attacking all human genomes and make it single out Fett clones. There just weren't enough genetic differences between humans to exploit—bar one. Hokan had been furious, thinking he was guarding a failed experiment.

"You're an analytical man, Gilamar."

"Call me Mij." He smiled. "You don't have to be a hotshot geneticist to work through the logic. Of course . . . if your magic potion *does* work, and really *is* that selective, then it has two possible methods—either the whole-genome approach, which sounds a bit too complex and would be totally borked by routine mutation anyway, or it would have to zero in on something that the average clone has, but the average random human hasn't . . . the gene sequence that controls their accelerated aging. Did I get the right answer, Dr. Uthan? Am I a clever boy?"

Gilamar was right. No, he didn't need to be a geneticist to work that out, but he needed to be smarter than the idiots who'd held her captive, and he was. Yes, she'd been working on a highly selective virus, all right. She wanted to identify the aging markers as badly as Skirata had, but for wholly different reasons. She couldn't unleash a virus that might wipe out the whole humanoid population of a planet. She had her ethical limits, however much of a monster others might have believed her to be.

And I'll still catch some nonclones who just happen to have that same genetic quirk—but perhaps one in ten million. Safe enough, I think. A reasonable margin of error.

She leaned back a little and finished her eggs. It took more than a table covered in Kaminoan tissue samples to dent her appetite.

The galaxy's different now. The war's over, but there's still an army full of Fett clones out there. So what happens next?

She only knew that she couldn't trust the Empire not to kill her, and that the best deal she'd been offered so far had been from a gang of Mandalorian criminals.

Or maybe not *criminals. Patriots? Amoral opportunists? Rebels? Terrorists? Depends who's doing the defining.*

"That's what I get," she said, with as much dignity as she could muster, "for thinking Mandalorians are all mindless thugs."

"Stereotypes," Gilamar said. "Don't you just *hate* it when that happens? You Gibadans are all the same."

Uthan fought back a smile. Gilamar stared at her for a long time, not remotely aggressive, but all the more worrying for that. Then he grinned.

"Why do you suppose Palpatine wanted me to keep working on the FG thirty-six virus instead of destroying it?" she asked, wishing she weren't enjoying the discussion. "It wasn't asset denial. If he wanted the CIS to be deprived of my expertise, he could have killed me anytime."

"Oh, I think you know the answer."

"It did dawn on me, eventually. Insurance."

Gilmar nodded. "Can't blame the old despot, really. If the clones decided to turn against Palps for any reason, one of the Grand Army's contingency orders was to relieve him of office the hard way. Order number five, if I recall. There was an order for every eventuality, from the old *chakaar* himself to whacking the Jedi." He stood up and stretched. "Just tell me something. What *did* you leave Palps with? A working targeted nanovirus, or the one that kills most humans it infects?"

"What would *you* leave him with?"

"One that wouldn't even kill bugs. It's a dangerous toy for a man like that."

"The strain I was working on when you removed me from the Valorum Center wasn't actually . . . finished. I had to have my own insurance, remember. He wouldn't have needed me alive once I delivered it."

"So Palpatine's got a less choosy version of your doomsday bug? The one that might affect *everyone*?"

"I believe so."

She hadn't planned it that way, not at all. She just hadn't known that she'd be plucked from Republic custody without warning. But if the fool used it, he'd wipe out most of Coruscant, his own power base.

That'll teach him . . .

"*Wayii* . . ." Gilamar blew out a long breath, eyebrows raised. Uthan rather liked him. It was a pleasant change to have intelligent and challenging conversation, especially with someone who didn't think she was clinically insane. Three years in solitary with only a substandard psychiatrist for occasional company had nearly made her genuinely crazy. "Does the *shabuir* know what he's got?"

"I don't know," she said. "His scientists are mediocre at best. But if he does, then he'd better be too smart to use it carelessly."

"What's an Empire if you lose most of your subjects? No fun lording it over a few Hutts, two banthas, and a Weequay, after all."

"Well . . . a Weequay might not be resistant to the virus, either."

Gilamar laughed. He could afford to, perhaps; Mandalore was a long way from Coruscant. "So you know all about the rapid aging sequence. Well, well."

"I identified it. Not the same thing."

"The next thing I really want to hear you say is that you can switch it off."

Uthan was still waiting for the real game to emerge. Nobody would go to all this trouble and amass so much commercial data for sentimental reasons. It was worth billions. Cloning companies would pay that simply to stop their customers being able to bypass built-in senescence in the clones they'd bought.

"What's Skirata really going to do with it?" she asked. "This whole operation, the planning, the risks—that's not just for the welfare of a few clones."

Gilamar's expression changed. His facial muscles slackened, and for a moment he actually looked as if he pitied her. For some reason, this cynical man—he was too intelligent to be otherwise—seemed not to be expecting that question.

"Have you never loved anyone so much that you'd do anything to save them?" Gilamar looked down at his armor for a moment. Uthan still wondered why it was that same dull sandy gold as Skirata's. It might have been regimental, but Mandos didn't seem the uniform kind. "Do you understand how much Kal loves those boys? Because if you don't, then you won't understand just how far he'll go to get what he wants for them."

"But this is worth *billions* . . . Mij."

"Is that why *you* do it? Material gain?"

"No." Credits had one purpose for her; to enable her to enjoy her life, and what gave her pleasure and purpose was her science. "I'm sorry. I assumed mercenaries would want to maximize income."

"Well, even mercs have other motives. Besides . . . Kal's already worth a lot more than a few billion creds. Think again, Doctor. This is about obsession, and consider me obsessed, too."

"Call me Qail," she said. She didn't believe Skirata was a billionaire, but Kyrimorut had to be costing a lot of creds, and he seemed able to afford any number of weapons and vessels. Nothing flash, nothing conspicuous—but enough to equip a strike force. "We can't keep calling each other Doctor, because that'll get tedious."

"Okay, *Qail*. And now I know the genes have been identified, I'm really looking forward to working with you."

Uthan loved a challenge. She was certain she could switch off the accelerated aging. She wasn't sure that she'd still be alive after she did it, but there came a point where she couldn't stall any longer, and she knew she'd reached it. Gilamar had her pegged. The Kaminoan tissue samples removed her last excuses. If she could understand the techniques that the Kaminoans used to engineer extended life, then she'd have most of the missing pieces of the puzzle.

"Let's get on with it, then," she said. "If only I had some control samples of ordinary Kaminoan tissue."

Gilamar laughed. "I think we can manage that. Just don't ask me how."

Uthan recalled what Skirata had said about Ko Sai, and thought of Jaing's elegant gray gloves.

And Jaing seemed such a charming young man, too. The more she knew of Mandalorians, the less she understood them.

3

Good news. Niner's okay, and so is Darman. Well, they're both in good health, at least. Don't say we never do you favors, Mereel—it took a lot of maneuvering to get that servicing work for the Imperial Army, and if you give us a little time, and make it worth our while, we can get you a secure link . . .
—Gaib, of Gaib & TK-0 Inc., high-tech bounty hunters—obscure data and hard-to-source hardware procurement a specialty

Landing pad, Imperial special forces HQ, Imperial City

"**S**pook," said Bry. "Definitely a spook."

Bry nodded in the vague direction of the Imperial agent walking toward the shuttle. The man's name—if it was his real one, which Darman doubted—was Sa Cuis, and he didn't look much like a holovid action hero.

They never did. That was what made them dangerous.

Darman watched him carefully, something he could do easily in a helmet with wraparound vision.

"There's no reason to brief us on the launch pad," Ennen said. "We're not short of time, and we're definitely not short of troops now. So all this last-minute briefing means they don't trust us not to leak stuff."

"Why, when we've been specially selected for this?" Niner stood with one boot on the ramp, looking impatient to leave. "The rest of the old commando brigade is on routine duties."

"Maybe," Bry muttered, "we've been picked because Palps thinks we're soft on Jedi and he wants to weed us out. Or that we know where they are. Because we got on well with some of the Padawans."

Darman didn't want to talk about relationships with Jedi. "Why don't you zip it and wait for the briefing?" he snapped. "Things leak and we know it. Jedi escaped. They had sympathizers. And anyway, there are guys in the unit who didn't much like Jedi."

The two newcomers—Darman definitely saw them as outsiders coming into *his* squad—went quiet for a moment.

"Just saying, that's all." Ennen sounded peeved. "What's your problem, pal?"

"I'm not used to serving with *shabuire*."

"Oh, yeah, you're one of the Mando boys, aren't you? All mouth. Knuckle-dragging savages."

Not all the commandos had been trained by Mandalorians. Jango's handpicked sergeants included some *aruetiise*. Darman braced his shoulders for a fight, but Niner stepped between them.

"*Udesii*, Dar . . . take it easy."

"Yeah, he was trained by a Corellian. No wonder he sat the war out, painting his nails."

"*Whoa*. We never had divisions before, and we're not going to have them now. Okay? Cool it, both of you—and you, too, Bry, 'cos I can hear you making *dissenting* noises."

Very little escaped the scrutiny of the helmet audio systems. Niner had always tried to be Sergeant Kal to his squad, and he slid right into the role now, smacking them back into line for their own good. Darman felt lost. He was torn between needing that solid sense of family and security that he got from being Mandalorian, and trying to forget what else went with it: a dead wife and a son he couldn't be with.

But that wasn't happening to *him*. It had happened to

some other Darman. He hung on to that detachment to get through the day. At night, though—when he shut his eyes he couldn't stop thinking about what had happened to Etain's body. He simply didn't know. It wasn't the Mandalorian way to fret about remains, but he had nothing left of her, not even a scrap of armor.

I just want to know where she ended up. Then I might be able to cope.

"Spook Boy isn't coming with us, is he?" Bry said. "That's all we need."

Head direction was never any guide to what a guy in a helmet was actually looking at, let alone what he could detect with sensors. So there was no reason for Cuis to know he was being stared at, discussed, and mistrusted. The squad could chat on their private link without being heard. They always folded their arms or hooked their thumbs in their belts to avoid the temptation of automatic gestures, so a casual observer wouldn't even know they were having a conversation.

Niner didn't join in. He was paranoid about bugged comlinks. Nothing would persuade him otherwise.

"So what can the spook do that we can't?" Ennen asked. "He's a bit on the *plump* side."

"Maybe he's a good shot," said Bry.

"Maybe his uncle put in a good word for him."

"Maybe he didn't, and this is the punishment run."

Darman was more interested in observing Cuis. Something about the man bothered him beyond the usual level of healthy suspicion. Anyone in that line of work would have assumed he was the subject of speculation and gossip when he was around troops, but Cuis seemed to be *reacting* as if he was listening to the chat—subliminal, near-invisible reactions, but reactions nonetheless. He looked uncomfortable as he walked across that lonely stretch of ferrocrete. He was a man with the power to make citizens vanish, no questions asked, and yet he walked self-consciously.

Darman was pretty sure he wasn't going to break into a jog.

It was hard to hide small detail from a clone. Darman lived his whole life attuned to the tiniest variations in facial expression and body language—and voice, and smell—because like all his brothers, he'd spent most of his life among men who looked almost identical. They weren't. Every clone learned to spot the small distinguishing features and behaviors that marked each man. And that skill carried over into the observation of the entire world around them. Detail mattered. Lives depended on it.

Darman decided that Cuis could either hear the comm circuit, or . . . he *felt* the tone of the conversation. Ennen and Bry were dismissive and contemptuous, not hostile. Maybe . . .

"Maybe," Darman murmured, "he's a Force-user. So let's not give him anything to notice."

"You reckon," Bry said. "Really."

I know Force-users. I know them in ways you can't imagine. I know their reactions, the way they deal with the things that we can't detect, the things that sometimes give them away to us ordinary folk. Because I've been as close to a Jedi as an ordinary guy can get.

"Yes," Darman said. "I do."

Darman didn't think of himself as ordinary folk, though. He'd been raised to understand he was *optimized,* the best raw material trained in the best way to be the best at his job, and now he fell back on the most important childhood lesson that Sergeant Kal had taught him. He could do anything he set his mind to; not because he started with the advantage of the genes of one of the toughest fighters in the galaxy, not even because he was fed and trained to a peak since childhood, but because he had acquired the right mental attitude. Skirata called it *ramikadyc*—in a commando state of mind. It was a soldier's unshakable belief that he or she could do anything, endure anything, take any risk, and succeed. It was stronger than muscle. It made the body do the impossible.

I'm not in pain. Any pain that I feel is temporary.

Nothing can touch me. This is happening to someone else. I just observe it as I pass.

That mantra kept Darman going when all he wanted to do was lie down and die. He'd felt that way more in the last few weeks than he ever had in his life. Kal Skirata had taught his young commandos an armory of *ramikadyc* techniques for resisting interrogation, a way of shutting out reality to become someone else who wasn't in that terrible place you found yourself in.

Some visualized putting their pain and fear in a box, or concentrating on its physical reality so minutely that it fragmented and ceased to register; some simply imagined they were somewhere else. And pushed beyond the breaking point by hunger, thirst, or exhaustion, Darman had been taught to focus only on the next moment that he could bear to think about—the next second, next step, next hill, next meal—time after time, until he'd come through the ordeal.

Darman wasn't in physical pain, but he hurt more than he could stand. Until he worked out the best way to stop that for good, he shut down.

I know what happened. I see it every night when I close my eyes. But it didn't happen to my Etain, and it didn't happen to me. It was some other couple. It was a holovid. It wasn't us.

Cuis walked straight up to Niner and handed him a datachip. It was impossible to pick out the squad sergeant from four identically armored men, so Darman decided he was right. He'd work on the assumption that Cuis was a Force-user. There were probably a lot of them he didn't know about. It made him feel distinctly uneasy.

I don't like your type. I don't like your type at all.

Of course he could just be reading Niner's body language. Niner moves forward a fraction, Spook decides he's in charge . . .

Cuis turned away from Niner and stared right at Darman. Then he walked up to him and held out his hand for shaking. Nobody had ever shook clones' hands, except the decent Jedi officers. It was unmilitary, for a start. And when Darman did the instinctive thing and gripped that hand, the feeling he got was . . . unsettling.

He's testing me out. I've seen Jedi do that. Felt Etain do it. I know that feeling. Yes, he's a Force-user.

Darman wasn't sure if he disliked the sensation in his mind because he felt spied upon, or because it was another painful reminder of *her*. Cuis let go quickly and shook hands with the others as an obvious afterthought.

"Jilam Kester is confirmed as being on Celen." Cuis's eye movements—or lack of them—told Darman that he was trying very hard not to look at him now, so he had *felt* Darman's reaction, all right. "This contains your charts, building plans, and informant contact details. Bring him back alive."

Niner inserted the chip into his datapad. "What is he, then? Padawan? Minor Knight?"

"He's not even a Force-user. But he knows where they are, and he's been getting them out via a refugee network. He's an Antarian Ranger."

"Never heard of them."

"They're one of the Sector Rangers groups. Antarian Rangers are ordinary law enforcement officers who worked with the Jedi."

Darman was instantly fascinated, especially as he'd never seen them tasked to do any jobs in the war. That in itself was odd. "If they worked for the Jedi, then why didn't we come across them? They weren't even on our briefing list."

Cuis nodded. "The Jedi Council didn't *acknowledge* them, but they certainly used them. Rangers want to be Jedi but have no Force powers. So they tag along when Jedi need extra support, or do the dirty jobs nobody else wants. None of the glory, all of the danger. Sad little creatures. What a miserable existence, putting your life on the line for those who don't even admit that you exist."

"Disgraceful," Niner said. Only Darman knew him well enough to wonder if he was being literal or sarcastic.

"What others abandon, we protect," Cuis took out a datapad from under his cloak. "That's the Sector Ranger motto, you know. I often wonder if they're being deliberately ironic."

"So you definitely want him alive," Ennen said. "Despite general orders."

Cuis nodded, looking more distracted by his datapad. "Yes. Even I can't get answers out of a dead man, although I know some who think they can."

Darman thought briefly of Fi and then stifled the image. There was no reaction from Cuis. If he was a Force-user, and not on the hit list, then what was he? Jusik had mentioned dark Jedi and Sith, although Darman had never paid much attention to the conversation. Now he wished he had. He wondered if there were Force-users who didn't have to take sides at all.

Then he remembered why he was wondering that, and reminded himself that the son he thought about wasn't *his* son, but another Darman's, and it didn't break his heart not to see him, and he wasn't terrified that he might not be able to raise him. He felt nothing. He didn't dare.

Why am I doing this? What if the Jedi I go after are just like Bard'ika?

They wouldn't be. They'd be like the ones who killed that other Darman's wife. They'd be like the ones who had rules so callous that Jedi weren't allowed to have families, and the ones who tried to had to live a lie. So he had nothing to search his conscience for.

He didn't ask himself how he would feel about hunting down his brothers, because he knew that they would never be found. It was academic.

"Now, when you detain this man, there's no need to be discreet," said Cuis. "We want even the most obscure cesspits in the Empire to know that there really isn't any place we can't keep an eye on."

The shuttle lifted off. It wasn't a LAAT/i, and its distinctive noise wasn't yet burned into Darman's subconscious as the promise of immediate extraction or welcome supplies. That would come in time, he was sure.

He settled back in his seat and tried not to think beyond the moment. If he thought ahead—asked himself what he was doing here, asked why he didn't desert now that Niner had recovered and could leave, too—then he'd have to think about his future, and that was impossible now without having to face his immediate past.

His past hurt too much. It hurt so much that he wasn't even sure he had what it took to be a good father.

But that was another Darman.

Kyrimorut, Mandalore

It was saliva, *strill* saliva—a puddle of it in the flagstone passage outside the central living room, the *karyai.*

Ordo saw it a fraction of a second too late when he glanced up from his datapad as he walked. He skidded. Walon Vau was back, and so was his strill, Mird. Ordo could smell its pungent musk everywhere.

"*Shab.*" He doubled back to the kitchen to grab a mop, cursing to himself. "Disgusting *shabuir.*"

"You don't mean that, *Ord'ika,*" said Vau. He was filling a bucket from the faucet in the kitchen. "You know you're glad to see Mird back. I'll clean up the mess."

The drooling culprit sat with its head in Ny's lap, grumbling happily. Ny indulged it with a handful of cookies, apparently oblivious to the volume of slobber a happy strill could generate.

"I got you a bantha bone, *Mird'ika.*" Ny bent over to whisper in its ear. Ordo admired her ability to inhale that close to the creature. "But the bad men took it. Yes, they *did,* they took your bone! Their akk ate it. Naughty akk! I'll get you another one, shall I? Nice big bone?"

Mird rumbled approvingly. Ordo forgot nothing; he recalled every detail of the times the strill terrorized him as a child in Tipoca City. He'd come close to shooting it.

So had *Kal'buir.* But now Mird was as much an ally as anyone else at Kyrimorut, and even Skirata admired its intelligence and devotion. Ny seemed to dote on it almost as much as Vau did.

But it still stank. Nothing would ever change that.

"So stormies are *bad men,* are they, Ny?" Vau asked, soaking a floor cloth and wringing out the water. "How bad?"

"If they'd spotted the Jedi, I'd have found out the hard way," she said. "Can Mird have pups?"

"Mird can bear pups *and* sire them." Vau headed for the passage with the cloth. "But don't ask me how hermaphroditic reproduction works in practice. All I know is that if Mird meets the strill of its dreams, then they end up with a litter of little strills."

"And I bet they're *adorable,*" Ny said, ruffling the loose skin on Mird's jowls. "Little balls of wrinkly golden fluff. Just like you, *Mird'ika.*"

Mird yawned, showing off a fearsome mouthful of teeth. Strills were possibly the least adorable animal on Mandalore, and Ordo struggled to see what Ny found so appealing. Mird had six legs, lethal claws, a massive square head with a huge jaw that could bite through skull bone, and folded skin that looked several sizes too big for its body. It could fly, too, provided it had some high point to launch from. The animal was admirable—and loyal—but beauty and fragrance were two qualities it lacked. Human males found its scent offensive; Ordo certainly did. Human females and other species didn't seem to notice it, which probably explained why such a smelly animal could be such an efficient hunter.

"You boys having a crisis meeting?" Ny asked, still making a fuss of Mird. "Anything I can do?"

"Just a routine briefing," Ordo said. "One of Mereel's business contacts located Dar and Niner, so we have work to do."

"Is Niner okay? How about poor Darman? How is he?"

"Back on the job. Both of them. Beyond that—we have to find out."

"At least Kal can relax now."

"Not until we get them home."

"That should be easy for you, though. Shouldn't it? You're the extraction and retrieval experts. No door closed to you, and all that."

"In theory, yes."

"You're a very cautious lad, Ordo."

"That's because I watch plans go to *osik* every day."

Ordo was desperate to ask Ny a more personal question, but Besany had forbidden him to raise the topic of her opinion of *Kal'buir*. Trying to marry them off was *premature,* Besany warned, and there was a chance it would scare Ny away.

Ordo couldn't see why everyone was skirting around the issue. A'den had decided the two of them were a good match, the rest of the brothers agreed, and *Kal'buir* needed a wife. If he didn't get a move on, Vau might move in. Ordo had never known Vau to show the slightest interest in another living being, but he'd watched enough holovids to know that romance sprang from the most unlikely shared moments, and Mird was in danger of becoming one of those.

"Something on your mind, Ordo?" Ny asked. "You look like—"

She was cut short by a yelp from Mird. It threw up its head and trotted to the kitchen door, tail whipping. Ordo heard footsteps—light shoes, not Mando *cetare*—and Scout appeared in the doorway. After a few sniffs of the girl's robes, the strill slunk back to Ny as if disappointed.

"What's *that*?" Scout edged into the kitchen and stared at Mird from a cautious distance. "Is that the strill?"

"Lord Mirdalan," Ny said. "Mird, meet Scout."

"Wow."

"It's okay, it's safe to touch him . . . her . . . it. Whatever. Sorry, Mird, it just feels *rude* to call you *it* when you're such a sweetie."

Mird basked in the attention. Scout didn't look convinced that the strill was harmless—a wise girl, because it wasn't—but she squatted down and petted it anyway. Mird rubbed its head against her face, stopping short of slobbering over her. Ordo got the feeling it was working out who this stranger was that had upset *Kal'buir* so much.

"He's very friendly." Scout rubbed Mird's ears and got a long rumble of delight. "Kina Ha will be fascinated."

"It," Ordo said. "And it might be a good idea to keep it away from Kina Ha. Mird doesn't like Kaminoans."

"Well, looks like Vau left me holding the baby." Ny waved Ordo away. "Go on. Get to your boys' club meeting."

"Females aren't excluded. You can join in if you like."

"Someone's got to get dinner on the table."

Ordo wondered if the strill had sensed Scout as a Jedi and thought Etain had come home. It was hard to know what went on in a strill's head, but Mird was intelligent enough to know Etain was dead because it had seen her body. Perhaps, like a grieving human, it thought it saw her now, even when it knew that couldn't possibly happen.

Is that what Darman's going through, too? Does he keep seeing Etain in crowds? Does he forget for a moment, see something that would make her laugh, then remember she's dead?

How does he go on? How does anyone go on?

Ordo couldn't get the idea of bereavement out of his head since escaping from Coruscant. He'd never lost brothers in combat, not like the other clones had, and he found himself trying to imagine what life would be like if he lost the people he loved. The idea of life without *Kal'buir* or his brothers was almost too much to think about. And now he had a wife, too, another person to fear for and fret over. The more you loved, the more pain lay in wait. Vau seemed to have the right idea. If you didn't love anyone, you couldn't be hurt or be-reaved. Life was a trade-off between loneliness and in-evitable peaks of joy or agony.

Ordo walked into the main room that formed the hub of the Kyrimorut complex, the living area where the clan ate, argued, and generally entertained themselves. The usual war council was assembled—Skirata, Vau, Gila-mar, Ordo's brothers, and Jusik. Fi, Corr, and Atin obvi-ously had better things to do, probably with Levet, who was teaching himself to farm with the aid of an instruc-tional holobook and some very confused nuna.

"*Ord'ika*—take a seat, son." Skirata nursed a steam-ing mug of *shig*. The tisane smelled like *behot* herb. *Kal'buir* was in need of comfort, then. "We've got a lot to catch up on."

Skirata wasn't a man who liked formality, but Ordo could see why Ny thought he'd suddenly caught a dose of organization. She hadn't lived in barracks; she didn't know the routine. Even Mandalorians needed a little structure in their lives, however anarchic they looked to *aruetiise*. The day had to start with a *din'kartay*, an as-sessment of what was happening and what everyone needed to do next, and sometimes that was just a chat over breakfast. Sometimes—like now—it was much more serious, an operational planning session.

Gilamar sat on a veshok stool, warming his hands by the log fire that burned in the center of the room. "Who wants to start? Walon, I take it you had no luck finding leads on Sev."

Vau didn't even shake his head. It was hard to read the man, and if Ordo hadn't known better, he might have thought that Vau didn't care much about the missing member of Delta Squad.

"Nothing," he said. "It's near impossible to do any-thing on Kashyyyk at the moment anyway, now that our beloved Emperor's crushed the Wookiee clans and let the slavers in. Enacca's still on Togoria organizing a re-sistance. But she's made finding Sev her personal mission, and I feel a little . . ." Vau trailed off. "Shall we move on?"

"Hard to do that when we're going to be working out how to get Dar and Niner back, Walon. Can't ignore Sev."

"But we know where they are." Vau's tone was very final. "First things first."

"Okay." There was a long silent pause. Gilamar didn't sound convinced. "Uthan's started analyzing the *kaminii*'s samples. I think we should get her to create an antigen for the FG thirty-six virus, if she hasn't already worked that out, which she probably has. It's too dangerous— Palpatine's got it, even if he doesn't know what it'll do when dispersed."

"And you trust her?" Vau said.

"As much as I trust anyone who's not one of us and makes weapons of mass destruction for a living."

"Do you trust her to create what she says she's going to create, and not just poison us all?"

"I don't know," Gilamar said. "But I don't think she knows, either. I'd like to give her a reason for working for us beyond being scared we'll shoot her if she doesn't."

"I don't think she's going to be won over by our rough Mando charm," Skirata said. "Or the justice of our cause. Or even credits. This is a psy ops job."

"Well, I'll start working on her for an antidote. She can re-create that original virus anytime. She's got all her research with her. We ought to have control of that, just in case."

Skirata nodded, still subdued. He'd been that way for a couple of days, ever since he set eyes on Scout. "Jaing, finance report?"

At least Jaing looked happy. He radiated satisfaction. "Even at the lowest interest rate in the galaxy, we're making fifteen billion creds a year," he said. "That's about two hundred million a week, even without compound interest. *A week*. Not a bad return for a paltry credit skimmed off every bank account in the system."

They were unthinkable numbers, so far beyond the personal needs or imagination of anyone in the room that they were almost meaningless. Ordo could only think of the things that credits could never buy.

Jusik was a natural optimist, though. He applauded. "*Oya!* We can do a lot with that."

"I bet even Walon can't imagine that much *waadas,* and he was born stinking rich." Skirata drained his mug. "But isn't that going to get noticed sooner or later?"

Jaing winked. "Not split across thousands of separate accounts and invested in companies across the galaxy, no . . ."

"Ah, my clever boy. My *very* clever boy."

Nobody seemed particularly excited about so much wealth. Ordo, like all the clones, had never needed credits until he left Kamino, and even then all his needs had been met by the Grand Army's budget. And men like Skirata came from a frugal culture. Nobody was about to rush out and buy a stable of racing odupiendos or a luxury yacht. It was all *ret'lini*—just in case, a Plan B, the classic Mando mind-set of always being ready for the worst. The fortune was insurance against a rainy day, intended to be spent on whatever it took to resettle as many clones as possible.

So far . . . it's just us, Yayax Squad, and Commander Levet. But it's early days yet. More will come.

"So we can afford to buy a lot of loyalty," Skirata said. "Mereel, you think this Gaib is reliable?"

"He hasn't let me down yet," Mereel said. "He works with a tech droid called Teekay-O. They're the ones who led us to Ko Sai, remember. They know who's selling, who's buying, and who's shipping what and where, and how much. So they did a bit of digging for us, and what better way to spy on the Empire than through its procurement contracts?"

"What do they want?"

"Credits, like any mercenary."

Skirata didn't even have to ask how much. It didn't

matter, as long as it wasn't anything that drew attention to Kyrimorut. "So Dar and Niner are Five-oh-first Legion. Vader's Fist, my *shebs*. Who is this Vader, anyhow? Never heard of him."

"Palpatine's right-hand man. Red lightsaber, Teekay-O says."

"*Shab*, another Sith. Same old feud. Why don't all the Sith and Jedi move to some planet nobody's ever heard of and slug it out in private, and leave the rest of the galaxy in peace?"

Skirata didn't even glance at Jusik, not even to say that present company was excepted. He seemed to have erased the idea that Jusik had ever been a Jedi. Ordo wondered how Jusik saw himself, though. He never did things by half. Ordo wondered if Jusik put so much effort into being Mando to atone for some sense of guilt at having been a Jedi. He really seemed to reinvent himself.

"Anyway, saber-jockey infighting apart," Mereel said, "Vader's set up a special assassination unit of former Republic commandos and ARCs within the Five-oh-first solely to hunt Jedi, deserters, and sympathizers."

"That's us, I think," Jusik said. "Now we know where Dar and Niner are, though, it's just a matter of collecting them, isn't it?"

Skirata shrugged. "It shouldn't be too hard, but we don't have the freedom to come and go that we used to have. We're the enemy."

"And how does that stop us, exactly?" Vau asked. "It's not as if Zey ever gave us his blessing to do what we did. He didn't know about most of it, for a start."

Skirata studied his datapad. "If we work out what missions they're tasked for, we might not even have to land on Coruscant. Just show up and tell them their taxi's arrived."

"I don't think the Empire's seen me before," Prudii said, deadpan. "Or Kom'rk. Eh, *ner vod*? The great thing about being a clone is that we've got literally millions of places to hide. Grab the right armor, and no mongrel's any the wiser."

"Son, you know how many times we've pulled that stunt?" Skirata asked.

"Yes. You know how many times it's worked?"

Kom'rk inspected his fingernails. "Well, that's another problem they've brought upon themselves—it's not like they can take our DNA to prove who we are. Or stick us in a lineup."

"Well, they *could*," Mereel said. "Because we devlop differences but—"

"Okay, point taken." Skirata didn't start the paternal lecture about not taking risks. This was possibly the most straightforward operation they'd ever faced. All they had to do was locate their missing brothers and show up on the day with transport; no guards to slot, no doors to blow open, no hostiles to battle through. By the time the Empire realized Dar and Niner were gone, they'd be home and dry at Kyrimorut.

And Darman would be reunited with his son.

"Any other business?" Skirata asked.

"Yes, what are we going to do about Dred Priest?" Jusik said. "Not that I know the man, but *you* do."

Gilamar looked as if he was going to spit. "He's a *hutuun*. I don't care how good a soldier he is. He talks that supremacy *osik*, and we don't need his kind on Mandalore."

"Shysa would never listen to him, anyway," Skirata said. "He's too smart. Everyone knows Mandalore's never going to be a galactic empire again. *Shab*, we haven't been a major power for millennia."

"And we don't *want* to be." Gilamar was on his favorite topic now, unstoppable. "Empires are doomed from day one. Whatever happens, however well they start out—they get too big and go rotten. They *all* fall. They're *all* overthrown. It's the cycle of nature. Let's stay on the margins, moving in the gaps the big boys leave."

"Too right," said a voice from the doorway. It was Ruu. "Can I come in?"

"Of course you can, *ad'ika*." Skirata made room for

her on the bench. "We must be bored. We're arguing about politics."

"I'm not arguing," Gilamar said. "Just making it clear that if I run into Dred and he starts on that bring-back-the-good-old-days garbage, I'll gut him. And his crazy girlfriend."

"No reason to run into him," Ordo said. "Unless you're in Keldabe."

"Don't you think it's time we started fighting for our own interests?" Ruu took the mug out of her father's hand and peered into it as if checking up on him. "I'm not saying this guy's right, but being at every *aruetii*'s beck and call and doing the dying for them doesn't sound smart to me. Look at this world. It's dirt-poor. That's not much to show for the lives we've spent on shoring up other governments."

"Good point," Vau said. "You're definitely a Skirata."

That was an odd thing for Vau to say, seeing as no Mando cared much about biological parentage. It was a culture of adoption and blurred lines between offspring and in-laws.

He just means she says the same things as Kal'buir. *That's all.*

Ordo scrutinized Ruu, still not sure how he felt about her. She'd fallen instantly into the role of dutiful Mando daughter, even though she hadn't seen her father since she was five. As far as Ordo was concerned she was Corellian like her *aruetyc* mother. Yes, he knew that wasn't fair, and it wasn't the way Mandos did things. She had as much right to leave her past behind as Jusik, to walk on *cin vhetin*, the virgin snow of a new life, judged only on what she did from the moment she threw her lot in as a *Mando'ad*. She hadn't even asked to be rescued.

But Ordo had fought alongside Jusik. *Bard'ika* had put his life on the line for the clones time after time. He was as much a brother as Mereel.

Am I jealous? Is that it? I'm an adult. I'm a married man. I'm too old to be jealous of new siblings.

Ordo was thirteen in calendar years, going on twenty-seven biologically. He knew he'd grown up too fast to get some things out of his system or even experience them to begin with. Sometimes the small stuff hurt a lot more than he knew it ought to.

Skirata could sense Ordo's mood as well as any Force-user. He got up and walked across the room to sit next to Ordo and ruffle his hair.

"You okay, son?"

"Fine, *Buir*."

"I know things are a mess at the moment, but it's going to work out. I promise."

It was a lie, because Ordo knew they'd probably spend the rest of their lives on the run with bounties on their heads, never able to drop their guard. *Kal'buir* had lost count of the number of death warrants out on him. Now they all had one. But a lot of Mandalorians—and others—lived their lives that way, and seemed happy enough. Ordo decided he would be happy with it, too.

"What are we going to do about the Jedi when Uthan's finished with Kina Ha?" Ordo asked. "We're going to have to deal with that sooner or later."

Skirata put on his don't-worry face that said anything but.

"I'll think of something, son," he said. "I always do."

Whatever he thought of, it wasn't going to be easy— or without a price. Ordo was going to make sure that nobody here would be the one to pay it.

Chelpori, Celen, Mid Rim

Chelpori was a nothing town on a nondescript planet, the worst place to hide as far as Niner was concerned.

The easiest place to vanish without a trace was a big city. That was where Niner would have gone to ground, anyway. A fugitive could merge into the mass of anonymous faces, and the more urban it was, the more shifting the population, so nobody really knew their neighbors. It was perfect.

And what am I planning to do? Hide in the middle of nowhere, or wherever Kyrimorut is. Nowhere, Mandalore.

The CR-20 set down in an empty landing pad on the outskirts of Chelpori, just a sprinkling of streetlights and a couple of illuminated cantina signs in the darkness. It wasn't going to take long to cover it, even if they had to search every building. Niner handed out the PEP attachments, a deuterium fluoride laser bolt-on for the Deece that came in handy if you didn't want a lethal outcome. It still hurt something fierce to be brought down by one.

"So do we have to ask him to come nicely?" Ennen said.

Niner checked that his PEP attachment was charged. The indicator light glowed bright red. "Cleaner and faster than clubbing him senseless."

"This intel better be reliable," Darman said. "It's all come from their civvie police force, by the look of it."

Niner almost reminded Dar that Jaller Obrim was a civvie cop, and he hadn't done so badly. But mentioning Obrim would open a door onto that terrible night at Shinarcan Bridge. He let it go. Bry began walking to the rendezvous point with Ennen. The squad was definitely split into two pairs, not a four-man team like Omega at all. Niner wondered if he was going to hang around long enough to need to worry about that.

"The Antarian's just a civvie cop, too," Bry said. "It's not like he's going to outclass them."

Niner trailed after the others, listening in on the local police comm net. Eventually, the patrol speeder came into view, parked on the dirt road into town. Nobody got out to talk to them, so Bry went up and knocked on the side screen. He jerked back a step, then laughed to himself.

"You didn't see us coming, then . . . ," he said as the screen opened.

An enforcement officer got out of the speeder, mopping his tunic and pants. The light from inside the speeder showed a big dark patch on his uniform as if he'd dropped something wet in his lap.

"No, we didn't," he said sourly. "Which is how come I spilled my caf. You scared the living daylights out of us."

The officer's buddy opened the other door and slid out. "Very stealthy. You going to sneak up on Kester like that?"

"If you've found him," Niner said.

"We've been keeping tabs on a guy who fits the broad description. Well, up to a few days ago."

"How broad?"

"Hair's different, and he's got a beard now. Hard to tell from his ID chip, 'cos it was a little out of date. Solid guy with scruffy white hair."

"Look," Niner said, "a few weeks ago, this man was still a serving Ranger. Are you telling me that's the best personnel ID that law enforcement agencies keep on record?"

"I'm not in charge of workforce resources, buddy." The cop shook one leg carefully, looking increasingly uncomfortable in his wet pants. "Anyway, he's rented a house, and we've picked up bursts of transmissions from comm equipment, but the frequency changes every few seconds."

"And?"

"What?"

"Transmissions." *Country yokels. We're on our own here.* "Want to share?"

"It didn't make much sense."

"Share anyway. We're good at making sense of big words."

The cop gave him a look of thin-lipped disapproval. The name tab on his jacket said NELIS P, and he had lieutenant's insignia on his helmet. "Something about kids. Moving youngsters to the well, whatever that means."

The cop was right; it didn't make sense. It sounded like some crude code. The target could have been a smuggler or some stim dealer, of course. But there were no rich pickings in illegal trade to be had here. There was nothing much to do on this kind of planet except hide.

Niner had his orders, and he was going ahead with them. "Okay, let's pull him in."

"We've got the place surrounded." Lieutenant Nelis took out his datapad and flashed up a street plan. Niner had seen bigger floor layouts for Galactic City shopping malls. "I've got six teams on surveillance outside. Kester hasn't left the place since yesterday morning."

Oh boy. If Kester hadn't noticed that he had an audience, then he must have been in a coma. "You sure of that?"

"This isn't the big city, soldier. We'd *notice.*"

When they got to the house, an anonymous-looking permacrete cube on the outskirts of a small industrial zone, Niner could see the police speeders parked behind dense bushes. They were pretty easy to pick out with his helmet optics; he could even see the fading heat of the drives as a dim splash of amber in his infrared filter. He wondered if Antarian Rangers had night-vision goggles or other fancy kit, because if they did, the squad had already lost the element of surprise with Kester.

Niner assumed the worst. The house was in darkness, and it was too early in the evening for the guy to be asleep. "What's the layout of the building? Is it the same as the data we were sent?"

"From what we know—central staircase, four rooms upstairs, three on the ground, front and back doors." Nelis drew an imaginary rectangle in the air, miming the long narrow shape of the windows. "And eight windows, although he'll have a tough job exiting through *those.*"

Darman didn't seem to be listening. His POV icon, offset to one side of Niner's HUD display, showed a fixed scene of the town, as if Dar was staring absently at the lights in the distance. Maybe he wasn't up to the job today. They'd all find out soon enough. But it was only an arrest, not full enemy contact, and the worst that could happen was if Kester got in a lucky blaster shot. Even this new armor could withstand that.

No, the worst is if we end up killing him. We answer to Vader now, not good old Zey. Vader won't just sigh in exasperation. He'll do that Force thing, grab our throats, and—

"Alive," Niner said, motioning the squad forward with a gesture. "We need him *alive*, Lieutenant, so even if he opens fire—leave it to us. Just duck. Now, let's all stay on the same comm channel, shall we?"

"What's that?" Darman pointed in the direction of what looked like a gasholder a couple of hundred meters behind the house. "Tibanna gas? It's not on our local map."

"That's because it's a new one." Nelis, pants now dried out, braced both elbows on the roof of his speeder to steady his electrobinoculars. "It's local bio-gas—produced from waste to power houses and generating stations. We *farm* here, see. Want me to draw you a diagram? Nerfs and banthas eat grass, and then they digest it, and—"

"We get it," Bry said. "Thanks."

"What are the adjacent buildings?" Niner asked. One side of the house nestled against a row of single-story buildings. "Industrial?"

Nelis fiddled with his helmet comm receiver as if it was playing up. "Accommodation for construction workers. They're building a new gas pipeline out to Orinar. They come and go—not local folks, normally."

"And they haven't noticed your patrol speeders hanging around."

"If they have, they haven't knocked on Kester's door to tell him."

Everyone waited. Niner wasn't sure why a few more minutes or hours would make any difference, but the cops were still trying to intercept transmissions. He worked through the frequencies in his helmet comm, trying to pick up something, but he could only hear sporadic voice traffic on the police network and the sound of Bry letting out an occasional sigh.

Eventually a voice cut in. "Lieutenant, he hasn't transmitted anything for hours. We're picking up movement at the back door, though."

"Visual?" Nelis asked.

"GPR scan."

"Is he still alone?"

"Haven't seen anyone else go in or out since we tracked him here. Days."

"Stand by." Nelis looked at Niner as if he was waiting for instructions. "It's as good a time as any."

"Okay. And minimum damage. We want his equipment and anything we can extract information from."

Nelis seemed satisfied and moved his headset mike closer to his mouth. "Okay, stand by—riot guns only, lads."

Niner wasn't leaving anything to chance. "Bry, Ennen— take the rear exit." He signaled the squad to split. "I'll go in the front with Dar. Okay?"

If Kester didn't surrender with four Deeces shoved in his face, then he'd feel the persuasive force of the PEP laser. Niner suspected the man might decide he'd have been happier dead once Imperial Intelligence got its hands on him.

Bry and Ennen vanished into the darkness. Niner waited until the police were in position, then worked his way along the row of gas workers' homes with Darman. They took up position, one on either side of the front door.

Niner switched to the commandos' secure comlink. "Bry, can you get a strip-cam under the door? See what's going on inside."

"Keep your bucket on. Just placing the frame charge." Bry sounded breathless. He was sticking detonite on the back door to blow it. Like the front entrance, it was a single hinged door. "Okay, wait one . . ."

A small image flickered into life in the margin on Niner's HUD. The image-enhancing holocam, reduced to the thickness of a sheet of flimsi, transmitted an image of an untidy house with crates stacked everywhere, as if Kester was in the process of packing to leave. Niner couldn't see movement yet, and he couldn't hear anything. Strip-cam audio was pretty limited.

It was at times like this that he really needed a Jedi to sense what was going on and who was where. Darman pressed a strip of explosive down the hinge side of the door, top to bottom, wired the detonator, and gave Niner the thumbs-up. They flattened themselves against the wall. Debris would fly out in a straight line for fifty meters or more, lethal as projectile rounds.

Niner took a breath. "Okay, on my mark."

"I don't like the look of those crates," Ennen said. They could all see the same image relayed to the HUDs. "They're like an obstacle course. And—hey, I think I saw movement. I think he's gone into the room adjoining the party wall."

"Stand by." Niner's stomach tightened. It wasn't a dangerous mission, not compared with the last three years, but he couldn't shake the adrenaline reflex every time he stacked to enter a building. "In three. Three, two—*go!*"

Darman pressed the det.

A split second of white light, smoke, and raw noise reduced Niner's attention to whatever he could see right in front of him. He wasn't aware of the rear-door charge going off, or what the POV icons were relaying from everyone else's HUD. He rushed through the gaping hole where the door had been, jumping over shattered wood, while Darman covered the room on the left.

"Rear hall *clear*," Ennen yelled. Niner heard ragged breathing as Ennen raced up the stairs—a straight flight to the landing, no ambush-friendly turns—while Bry covered him. There was a pause. "Upstairs—front room left, *clear*—back room left—*clear*."

" 'Fresher, right back—clear." That was Bry. "Room, right front—clear."

Kester couldn't have missed the fact that his house

was being stormed. He was holed up in one of the downstairs rooms. It would have been so much easier if Vader had wanted Kester dead. *Dead* would have taken seconds.

"Dar?" Niner smashed open the interior door to his left, Deece raised, and swept the tactical lamp's beam around. Nothing. He turned; Bry and Ennen were back in the downstairs passage that ran from front to back. "Two rooms to the right."

"Kitchen at the rear," Bry said. "The boiler vent's on the rear wall."

"Okay, either he's a *very* heavy sleeper or he's open to suggestions." *Or sitting in one of these two rooms with a heavy blaster trained on the door.* Niner gestured Bry to the kitchen, stood to one side of the door to the front room, and switched his audio to external so Kester could hear him. "Kester? There's no way out. Why don't you surrender, and then we can all go home."

Silence. Ennen brandished the strip-cam to indicate to Niner that he was going to take a look. It wasn't without its risks, seeing as Kester would have been staring hard at the door if he was in there. Niner moved to let Ennen slide the device under the gap.

"If he's in there," Ennen said, "he's hiding behind more crates. Not sure what he's moving out of here."

Antarians were cops. Cops throughout the galaxy had a healthy attitude when it came to risking their necks, and they tended to know when to call it a day. Niner cut to the chase.

"Kester, the Jedi never thought of you Rangers as anything more than latrine cleaners. It's not worth getting fried for them now." Niner realized he actually believed what he was saying. Yes, he *did*. He had no illusions about the Empire, but he didn't have any left about the Republic, either. "Take it from fellow cannon fodder, buddy."

Still silence, apart from the tinkle of broken transpari-steel as if one of the cops was treading on debris from the shattered windows. Ennen edged back toward the kitchen and eased the strip-cam under the door a millimeter at a time. The kitchen looked as chaotic.

Niner switched back to helmet comm. "Let's check the front room, just in case."

He leaned on the door, then kicked it wide open. A quick scan showed the room was just full of empty crates. That was weird. Niner couldn't imagine Jedi and their sympathizers needing all that storage.

Weapons? Are they shipping arms?

He'd let someone else worry about that when he was debriefed. He was only tasked to bring back Kester for interrogation. With nearly twenty cops outside and a heavily armed commando squad inside, storming the house had suddenly plummeted to an anticlimax. Kester hadn't even opened fire.

Neither had the commandos, of course. But explosions at both doors should have provoked *some* reaction. Niner's big fear was that Kester would blow his own brains out rather than be taken alive.

Because that's what I'd do. I'd end it.

"Let's get this over with," Darman said, flicking the control on his PEP laser. "Let me drop him. This is overkill for one lousy Ranger."

Niner counted down with a hand gesture. *Five, four, three . . .*

"Maybe Vader doesn't trust us after all," Bry said.

Bang.

Darman put his boot through the flimsy latch and sent the door slamming back. Niner was first in, Deece aimed. The commandos all started yelling at once, a disorientation technique to get the Ranger to surrender—or step out where they could stun him.

"*On the floor!* Get down, Kester, get down on the floor where we can see you!"

"Kester, *drop your weapon!*"

"Get down on the floor! *Arms away from your sides!*"

Tactical lamps swept the kitchen in a silent split second, picking out a landscape of crates, containers, and—weird, this—the reflection of a computer screen. There was a faint smell, maybe decaying food. Just as Niner was about to start booting boxes out of the way, a figure rose slowly from behind them.

Niner could see white or gray hair tied back in a tail. He didn't see hands raised in surrender. He shone his lamp in the guy's face, catching sight of one arm half raised to block the light, body turned so the right arm wasn't visible.

"Whatever you've got, buddy, lay it down nice and slow," Niner said, flicking the Deece's charge button so that it whirred audibly. "Dar, you ready?"

Darman seemed to be itching to laser Kester. Niner could hear his teeth clicking as he clenched his jaw.

"Hands above your head, Ranger," Niner said. "You really don't want to feel the—"

And then the guy straightened up and turned full-on to face them. Niner saw the streak of blue energy just as he heard the *vzzzmmm* of a lightsaber, and the face suddenly illuminated by it was one he knew all too well.

And because he knew the man, he froze for just half a heartbeat, and that was too long.

Oh, shab . . .

Jedi General Iri Camas, former Director of Special Forces, took advantage of the split second that gave him and batted the PEP laser bolt aside.

"*Force?*" Camas said, raising the lightsaber for the kill.

4

*Son, Ruu's fine. We found her. You won't hear from her
again for a while, or from me, and I can't tell you
where we are. Look after yourself. Tell Ijaat I'm sorry I
never got to talk to him. It's safer for you both if you
don't try to contact me again.*
—Kal Skirata, in an untraceable message to his es-
tranged sons to let them know the outcome of the
search for their sister

Kester's base, Chelpori

Jedi Masters were to be shot on sight, and Darman was
surprised how little that bothered him.

He switched his rifle to lethal rounds just as Camas—
a man he *knew,* a man who'd been his boss—leapt high
into the air, wholly unreal in Darman's green-lit NV filter, and came crashing down on top of him.

If Ennen hadn't been in the right place for just that
fraction of a second and brought his Deece up hard into
the general's face before he steadied himself, Darman
knew that lightsaber would have taken his head off.
Niner went flying back against the wall, Force-thrown.
Camas swatted away Bry's hail of blasterfire and burst
out into the passage.

Nelis's voice broke into the comm channel. "Four-
zero, what the stang's happening? We're coming in."

"Stay back," Niner barked. "It's a *shabla* Jedi."

Darman hoped the cops had the sense not to open fire

when they didn't know who was coming out the doors
next. He almost knocked Bry over in his race to get to
Camas first. Camas's boots thudded on floorboards—
not out of the house, but into another room.

Insane. Why not run for it?

Maybe Camas knew how many police blasters were
waiting outside for him. Not even a Jedi Master could
fend off scores of bolts from all directions. They were
far from unkillable.

"Trap," Niner said. "The *shabuir*'s playing us. Let's
finish this."

"What trap?"

"Dunno, but Camas never *panics*."

Darman almost expected Niner, good old loyal Niner,
to find it hard to shoot at Camas. He didn't. He blasted
the door of the front room from its hinges and laid
down fire. White bolts of energy shot back out at him;
Camas knew his way around a blaster, too.

Darman dropped to one knee as rounds went over his
head, but Ennen was right behind him, and didn't. Two
bolts smacked into his visor. Ennen went down. Bry was
nowhere to be seen. Darman turned to drag Ennen clear
and check him out while Niner pinned Camas down
with blasterfire.

Why is Camas using a blaster?

Jedi usually didn't. They trusted their lightsabers,
dumb and cocky as that was.

"Ennen? Ennen!" Darman pulled off the man's helmet.
He was alive, just stunned for a few moments. "You
okay?"

Ennen scrambled onto his knees to grab his helmet
back. It seemed to be working despite the damage.
"Where's Bry?"

"Heading him off at the pass," Bry's voice said. "I'm
coming in via the front window."

Niner ducked back to one side of the door to reload.
"What's that smell?"

"I think it's—"

Adrenaline seized Darman. He'd fought close-quarters

battles so many times that this felt like blissful release—
no caution, no take-him-alive, no fancy rules of engage-
ment, just kill or be killed. He pushed into the room
behind Niner to see Camas Force-smash a hole through
the wall into the kitchen. Bry swung through the narrow
window and cannoned into Camas as the Jedi clam-
bered over the rubble. He brought his gauntlet vibroblade down hard but it skated off the general's back as
if it had hit armor plate.

*Why doesn't Camas make a run for it? Why is he
going around in circles?*

"Gas," Niner said. "Shab, it's *gas.*"

They didn't encounter bio-fuel often. It took them a
few seconds too long to piece it together. Camas brought
his lightsaber up into Bry's chest plate and then sent him
crashing back through the exterior wall with a massive
Force throw.

Darman didn't have time to think anything but *stop
Camas.* The Jedi was through the hole in the wall now,
and suddenly Darman could see why he was so keen to
get back into the kitchen: the general stood by the cook-
ing range, frozen for a moment as if something hadn't
gone to plan, and Force-pulled the pipes from the wall.
Darman heard the loud hiss of venting gas.

"Looks like I timed this all wrong, didn't I?" Camas
said.

Camas raised his lightsaber and Darman opened fire.
It was the last thing he should have done, but it was pure
reflex. He couldn't stop his body responding. A sheet of
fire ripped across the room from the ruptured pipe like a
flamethrower. Camas just ducked. He didn't try to run.
Darman had a fleeting and time-wasting thought that
the old *chakaar* had something else up his sleeve. But he
was so eaten up by vengeance and a reflex to fight that
even when Niner grabbed him and tried to pull him
clear, he carried on firing at Camas point-blank. The
whole place was now on fire. The plastoid surfaces were
starting to melt and the wood and drapes were ablaze.

"Dar! *Out!*"

Darman pushed Niner aside. "I'm not letting him get away."

"He's not trying to, Dar. Out—*now*."

"We're all going to die," Camas yelled, lightsaber in one hand, blaster in the other. "But I'd hoped more of you would come and die with me . . ."

Darman realized none of them had identified themselves to Camas as his old commando cadre. He wondered if it would have made any difference if they had.

Camas dropped his blaster and stood with legs apart, one hand reaching down to the floor as if he was pulling on some invisible trapdoor.

"Run!" Niner yelled.

He grabbed Darman by the strap on his backpack and jerked him away with such force that Darman found himself almost running backward. He had no recollection of how he ended up outside the front door, only that Niner pulled him to his feet when he stumbled. One moment he was staring into flames licking out of a side window; the next, an exploding ball of flame blinded him for a second.

"That's the gas main," Lieutenant Nelis said. "Somebody get that thing shut off. Hey, Berila—call the gas company. Get that main shut down."

The scene around Darman now was chaos—the house burning steadily with its roof gone, flashing red and blue lights, med speeders, a fire crew, frantic cops, some of the neighbors staring in horror. And there was Ennen—Ennen kneeling next to Bry, pumping his chest with both hands until a civilian med tech pulled him off. Ennen walked away a few paces then came back again. But Darman knew what *too late* looked like.

"It's not going to blow again," Niner said calmly. He seemed to be shaping up to do something, rocking back on one heel as if he was going to take a run at it. He was. "Got to salvage that computer."

Darman was flooded with hardwired animal dread at the thought of going back into the flames. He'd been okay standing his ground when the fire had started around him, but somehow walking through it even in heat-resistant armor was a different matter. His animal instincts said no. He'd been caught in fires before, and it brought him as close to blind panic as he'd ever been.

"It's a waste, otherwise," Niner said.

"Bry's dead. Niner, Bry's dead—"

"A *waste.*"

He ran back into the burning house. Darman went to follow, but there was Bry down, Ennen pacing around close to losing it, and Corellia's Nine Hells breaking loose, and for a few seconds Darman wasn't sure where he was needed most.

Niner. That's who needs me.

Darman took a deep breath and ran after him. If he didn't think, he'd be fine. He wouldn't feel the heat—not for a good thirty minutes—and his plates would protect him from any falling debris. But it still scared him. His gut still froze.

"You never listen." Niner felt around for the computer in the fog of flame and blackened debris. The conversation felt weirdly surreal, and got worse when Darman found what had been Iri Camas. The blast had embedded the general's lightsaber in the opposite wall. "I said *stay put.*"

"Just in case you get into difficulties," Darman said.

He wouldn't leave Niner at Shinarcan Bridge, and he wasn't about to leave him now.

"That's it, there." Niner wrenched a burning shelf clear of what had been a counter. "It's welded itself to the worktop."

Flames licked across what was left of the ceiling joists as the burning gas vented like an oversized torch. Melting kitchen shelves dripped onto the floor; the computer's screen was shattered and its plug fused into the wall outlet by the heat, but all they needed was the base unit. Niner wrenched the cable free.

"Let's move," he said.

As they made for the doorway, Darman pulled the lightsaber hilt from the wall and found that his gauntlets were sticky with near-liquid plastoid. The melting floor tiles dragged on their boots like glue. When he finally stumbled outside, he walked into a wall of water jets. Firefighters moved in behind them.

"Idiots." One of the firefighters stopped to berate them. "If that stunt had gone wrong, guess who'd have to go in and save your sorry butts."

"Yeah, but it didn't," Darman said, ungrateful for the prospect of rescue. He didn't need saving. Commandos looked out for each other. Brotherhood hadn't saved Bry, though. "This is what we came for."

Niner was still clutching the buckled computer in both arms. He couldn't put it down because the plastoid was stuck to his armor. "Come on. Let's get out of here."

It took Darman some determined work with a vibro-blade to separate the melted material from Niner's plates. But this *wasn't* what they'd come for. They'd come for Ranger Kester, and they'd found General Camas and a computer instead. And they'd lost a man in the process.

Simple police job. Right. Me and my big mouth.

"Sorry about your lad," Nelis said. "Just when you think the war's over. Rotten shame."

Luckily, he said it out of earshot of Ennen. No soldier needed that pointed out to him. Losing buddies was bad enough, but there was something even worse about losing them on the margins of combat—fate's cruelty, lulling you into thinking you'd all made it okay through the worst, not knowing that the worst was just dawdling around the corner, and just late for its appointment.

Niner snapped back into sergeant mode. He went up to Ennen, who was standing by a med speeder with his forehead resting against the vehicle's durasteel side, and reached out to put his hand on the guy's shoulder. But Ennen shook it off and walked away. Darman couldn't see Bry's body. He stopped a med tech in passing. This was probably the entirety of Chelpori's emergency response team. It was a small place.

"Where's our buddy?" Darman asked. "What have you done with the body?"

The med tech jerked his thumb over his shoulder. "One of the officers is looking for a body bag. Won't be long."

Nobody said a word about the destruction all around. Maybe they were too scared to argue with the Empire, or at least with heavily armored armed commandos. The houses next to Kester's base—and where *was* Kester?— were still intact except for their windows. The blast looked as if it had been directed upward rather than sideways. The gas workers from the houses stood outside and stared, as if they couldn't believe the whole row of homes hadn't been demolished with them inside.

Darman tried again with Ennen. It was harder to comfort a guy you didn't actually like much. Friends and brothers—that was instinctive. Darman struggled for the right words. He'd lost brothers, and he'd lost his wife. He just wasn't sure if it was a good idea to tell Ennen that he'd seen someone who mattered to him cut down by a lightsaber, too, and that he understood completely.

Ennen glowered at him, turning his helmet over and over between his hands. Darman wasn't sure what they were going to do with the body. Burial hadn't been an option for most clones killed in action, and Mandalorians generally didn't go in for cemeteries or memorials. A piece of armor for commemoration, that was all.

But Ennen and Bry had been trained by a Corellian sergeant. It showed. Their attitudes were Corellian; they'd have fitted in seamlessly in any Corellian town.

"Cremation," Ennen said. "I don't care how we do it, but I want him to have a proper cremation."

It seemed an uncomfortable parallel with the burning house behind them. "We'll get it done."

"Yeah, screw the regulations. Whatever they are now." Ennen wiped his nose with the back of his glove, his face soot-stained. "*Jedi.* Our own general, too. You think he knew it was us?"

There were so few commandos compared with the main army—fewer than five thousand after Geonosis, maybe only three or four thousand now—that it seemed reasonable to think Camas still knew who his men were even after Zey had taken over. But chances were that he hadn't known more than a couple of hundred by sight, and then Darman didn't know if the general could tell them apart like Etain and Jusik or Zey did. They were probably still just numbers, strangers. Camas couldn't have known them all. Darman didn't know if that made the whole thing more or less poignant.

"Who cares?" Darman said. "Camas doesn't matter anymore. None of them do."

"Did you or Niner kill him?"

"Camas? Neither, not exactly. He was fried on the spot when my Deece ignited the gas."

"Good enough for me," Ennen said. "Thanks."

They left Lieutenant Nelis and the emergency crews to their task. Ennen and Darman carried Bry's body back to the shuttle and Ennen took the controls. Darman and Niner sat in the crew space behind him, salvaging what they could from the computer, and tried not to think about Bry and how they hadn't bonded with him. Darman could see it all on Niner's face when he took off his helmet.

"So what was going on there?" Darman said. "Crates. No Kester. Camas sending out coded transmissions."

"Escape route."

"Yeah, I know that, but . . ."

"Let's see if we can get any clues from this."

Niner chipped away at the plastoid for ages and finally managed to pull out a few circuit boards. The datachip was still inserted in one of them.

"Might as well try," he said. He pried out the chip and slid it into his datapad. "Atin would have had this all sorted by now."

When Niner turned the chip reader to show Darman the display, there was nothing on it. Camas must have wiped it before he made his last stand, which was still the dumbest death that Darman could imagine.

But we wouldn't let ourselves be taken alive. Would we?

Camas could have tried harder to escape. Okay, he wasn't Jusik or Kenobi, and he'd spent too long sitting on his backside before the war, but he seemed determined to stay put.

"I think he was a decoy," Darman said at last. "I think he was keeping us busy for as long as he could while something else was going on."

"Shame this thing won't tell us what." Niner took out the chip and stared at it as if a frown could reboot it and restore the data. "But who knows? Jaing always said it was really hard to wipe data completely. Maybe someone can recover something off this."

If there was anything recoverable on the original chip, then the commandos would probably never be told. Darman knew that. Even when Skirata was involved, they hadn't been told everything.

But he couldn't bear the thought of Bry dying just to take out one Jedi, not even a Master and general like Camas. He wanted the chip to be the key to a dissident network. He wanted it to be *pivotal*.

Darman knew it was guilt for giving Bry a hard time until it was too late to befriend him.

Kyrimorut, Mandalore; week four of the new Empire

The ice-glazed trees at Kyrimorut shed a slow, steady rain on the ground, the first sign that the thaw had started.

Jusik stood at the window and listened to the faint trickling of water in the gutters and down-pipes. The world outside still looked frozen solid, but spring was coming. He could smell it; he could sense the life underground waiting to wake. There was a marvelous feeling of hope and anticipation that he'd never detected on Coruscant. The global city was choked with permacrete and its weather controlled artificially, leaving almost nothing wild to stay in touch with the natural cycle of the seasons.

I love this. I feel alive. Is this like the world where I was born? I don't remember it. But this feels like home.

Kad seemed to be aware of it, too. Jusik held him on one hip as he stared wide-eyed through the transparisteel at the dripping plants in the courtyard, pointing occasionally and saying, "Reesh! *Reesh!*" It took Jusik a while to work out that he'd learned a new word—*piryc,* wet—and the best he could manage was the last syllable.

"It's wet because it's melting, *Kad'ika,*" Jusik said. "It's getting warmer. You'll be able to play outside soon. That'll be fun, won't it?"

Nobody called the child Venku anymore. Darman had preferred Kad, but he hadn't known the baby even existed until more than a year after the birth, so the name had been dropped. This was Dar's boy; Jusik reminded himself of that every day. Jusik was just one of an army of willing foster parents taking care of Kad until his father came home, and the fact that he had a special bond in the Force with him didn't accord any extra privilege.

He's not my son. I mustn't mean more to him than his dad just because I'm around and Darman isn't.

It wasn't the Mando way, this fixation with biological parentage. Every *Mando'ad* had a duty to look after the children of the clan, and adoption erased a kid's past—or even an adult's. But Jusik felt like a usurper every time he connected with Kad and felt him in the Force.

"Hey, *Kad'ika,* look what I've got." Jusik took his holoprojector from his belt-pouch one-handed and switched it on. He couldn't bear to show Kad the images of his mother yet, and left that task to Laseema, but he could cope with reminding Kad about Darman. "Look. That's your dad. Dada. *Buir.* He's coming back one day soon. We know where he is. We're going to bring him home."

Kad chuckled and pointed at the holoimage. "Boo! Dada!"

"That's right. *Buir*'s coming home."

Jusik felt Gilamar approaching. He could usually pick out everyone's impression in the Force as clearly as seeing them. Vau was a strange pool of calm; *Kal'buir,* whirlpools of passion, from violent hatred to selflessly devoted love. Ordo was another contradictory mix—a ferociously agile mind and complete physical confidence coupled with the wild emotional swings of a teenager. And Gilamar . . . Gilamar was mostly acceptance, a little loneliness, and pain so deep that it seemed an essential part of him. Jusik had no idea when Gilamar's wife had been killed, but he got the feeling that it would always be yesterday for the man.

"What's it like?" Jusik asked, not turning around. Kad put his palm flat on the window and banged it a few times to get Mird's attention. The strill was in the courtyard, nose pointing into the wind, inhaling intriguing scents on the air. "How does it feel to have a Force-user around all the time? Does it ever bother you?"

"What, that you might be doing mind tricks on me or something?" Gilamar made faces at Kad. "Or that I can't hide emotions from you? Not really. It's no different from the strill. It can sense things I can't. I don't resent it for that."

"I hope I smell better . . ."

Gilamar studied him. "If you were Force-sensitive and didn't train, would you develop powers anyway? Would you even *know* you had powers?"

"Probably not." Jusik could feel the next question developing. "The Jedi Council wouldn't have needed to test for midi-chlorians otherwise. You'd just find you understood people better than most, or had better hunches than your buddies, or terrific visuospatial awareness. You'd end up as a psychologist. A successful gambler. A pilot. A sports star."

"So . . ."

"Okay, you're thinking it might be a good idea not to develop Kad's skills. Am I right?"

"I thought the idea was to teach him how to control them so that he didn't attract the wrong sort of attention. If he can just let them lie fallow and be none the wiser, that's an interesting dilemma."

"You're full of those."

Gilamar looked at him with distinctly paternal tolerance. "And so are you."

"I don't think it's different from encouraging any talent in a kid and then letting them choose how they use it."

"Except with the way Palpatine's going, it's a talent that's going to mean a death warrant. So carry on teaching him to keep it under wraps."

Kad would know the truth about his mother in due course, but Jusik didn't feel any need to teach him Jedi lore. Kad could have his own personal link to the Force with no Masters or lords to intercede or dictate the form it took. Didn't every living creature connect to it in some way? It was simply a matter of degree.

"I'm going to see what I can do for Arla today," Jusik said. "You know I'm guessing my way through this, don't you?"

"Welcome to the adventure of practicing medicine." Gilamar patted his shoulder as they walked away down the passage. "You guessed your way through repairing Fi's brain damage pretty well, so I shall watch and learn, *Bard'ika*."

Jusik didn't need to see Arla Fett to work out how she was feeling on any given day. He could feel her in the Force. He sensed her much as he had at the Valorum Center for violent psychiatric patients: a deeply troubled soul that manifested itself as jagged lines and harsh primary colors in his inner eye, confused and in pain, defying him to walk by and leave it to its misery.

I rescued her. She's my responsibility. What's the point of swapping one locked ward for another?

He paused in the corridor outside her room, still holding Kad on one hip. Gilamar stood well back.

"I'm scared to see what happens if we stop her meds," Jusik said. "But I can't help wondering if they were more about keeping her docile for the center's benefit than to help her."

"Well, if I were dealing with homicidal patients, I admit I'd probably use the zaloxipine cosh, too." Gilamar shrugged. "We could try tapering off the dose. But I'm not a shrink. Your Force senses can tell better than any doctor how she really feels."

Jusik had tried to use the Force as little as possible when he left Coruscant, as if he could shrug off every trace of his Jedi past. It seemed an unfair advantage to have gifts that his clan brothers didn't. But he couldn't do it. It was like shutting his eyes to pretend he couldn't see to fit in with a community of the blind, temporary and artificial, always with the knowledge that he could open his eyes at any time—not so much equalizing the situation as trying to imagine what it might be like to lose that sense. He couldn't shut it off. The best he could do was be conscious of the ways he used his Force senses, and never exploit them.

"Some days she's calmer than others, whatever the dose," Jusik said.

"Well, it'll be a case of trial and error, then." Kad reached out for Gilamar's hand and shook it with the grave politeness of a diplomat. "You think *Kad'ika*'s going to help things?"

"If I go in there with a small kid, it's clear I'm not going to hurt her."

"What if he reminds her too much of Jango?"

"Is that going to upset her any more than seeing his clones?"

"She wouldn't remember Jango as an adult. But he was a kid when she last saw him, so she might recall looking after him at Kad's age."

"Well, let's see."

Jusik knocked on the door. Nobody had locked it since Arla had arrived. The alarm system would kick in if she left the building, and—apart from Vau—nobody seemed concerned that she might harm anyone. She never wanted to come out anyway. Sometimes she tried to barricade the door from the inside with a chair or table. Whatever had made her kill didn't seem to make her go out looking for victims.

"Arla? It's Bardan." He waited. Kad slapped his palm

on the door a few times. "Would you like to come out
for a walk with us? Get some fresh air?"

Silence. Jusik felt her wariness and confusion. The latter might have been put down to the mind-numbing
dose of zaloxipine, of course.

"Okay, can I come in and see how you are? I've got
Dr. Gilamar with me."

Jusik opened the door. The internal doors at Kyrimorut were wooden and hinged, an ancient design that
needed no power to operate them. In the most isolated
parts of a largely rural planet with unreliable power supplies, that mattered. Arla Fett—forty-something, faded
blond, thin, so unlike her brother as to make her unrecognizable as a Fett—sat on the edge of the bed with a
pillow clutched tightly to her chest. The bed was so
neatly made, the sheets and cover so tightly tucked in,
that it looked as if a soldier had done it. Jusik didn't
even try to guess what had happened to her in the thirty
or so years since her parents were murdered by the
Death Watch for aiding Jaster Mereel.

*Does she know about Jango? How do I even broach
the subject? Good news, Arla, your brother survived the
massacre. Bad news, he saw everyone he cared about
slaughtered, he spent years in slavery, and he got killed
by a Jedi in the end. Sorry about all that, Arla.*

No, he couldn't do that yet. The medcenter records
he'd sliced on Coruscant said she'd been committed to
the Valorum Center ten years ago, no next of kin, no
personal details beyond *no fixed abode.* And that was
all long before the Clone Wars started. He doubted that
the staff even knew she had a brother, let alone that he
was Jango Fett.

Gilamar waited by the door. Even out of armor, he
looked like a bruiser, and armor definitely upset Arla.
How could she tell the difference between one Mando
and another, anyway? To her, they probably all spelled
grief and trouble.

"Hi, Arla." Jusik stood back a couple of meters and
made a fuss of Kad, taking the boy's hand and waving it

at her. "Say hi to Arla, Kad. Arla, you've seen Kad before, haven't you? He's a . . . distant relative of yours."

"Careful, *ad'ika* . . . ," Gilamar murmured.

Arla studied Kad's face with a slight frown. Kad gazed back at her, mesmerized, and for a moment Jusik couldn't work out if the kid was sensing something in the Force, or if he was just a curious kid like any other.

"What *are* you?" she said at last, looking straight at Jusik. "You're not a doctor."

Jusik was surprised to hear her speak coherently, and in Basic, too. She had a slight accent. And she made eye contact for a few moments, as normal as anyone.

"No, I'm a . . . well, I don't know what I am, actually. A soldier, maybe." Jusik took a breath. "I'd like to say I was a friend of your brother, but I never knew him. I'm just doing what I think he would have wanted, which is to get you well and help you make some kind of life for yourself."

Arla stared at Kad, then glanced up at Jusik again. "Where are you from?"

"I don't know." *She's asking every question I can't answer.* "I was taken from my folks when I was a baby."

"Are they dead?"

Oh boy. "I don't know. I wouldn't even know where to start looking."

Actually, that wasn't true; the Jedi Council records were now reduced to ashes, but his family name was probably real, and so Mereel or Jaing could run a few searches in moments and track down worlds where the Jusik name was common.

Jusik suspected he didn't *want* to know. He didn't need another conflicting identity. Clan Skirata was his family now, and he could shut out everything else. He *had* to. He could only handle one allegiance at a time, all or nothing.

But he wondered if some spark would be struck if he ran into his own flesh and blood by chance. Biologists said closely related humans really could recognize one another by scent even if they didn't realize it, just like

Siolans and Kemlans. Maybe Arla knew deep down that the clones and Kad were her kin.

Arla looked right through him. "Well, *my* folks are dead."

"Tell you what," Jusik said. "Put a coat on, and come out for a stroll with us. If you want to tell me about yourself, and your family, that would be good."

She still stared. All things considered, this was an improvement. "When are you going to make me drink that stuff?"

"What stuff?"

"The medicine. Not the capsules. The liquid that makes me have nightmares."

Gilamar kept his voice very calm, very quiet. "They gave you something else at the Valorum Center, then? Not just zaloxipine. Do you know what it was called?"

"No."

"Are you still having nightmares?" he asked.

"Not the same ones. More like bad dreams I can't understand. Most of the time I don't remember them, but I know I dreamed them."

Gilamar moved forward two slow steps. Jusik couldn't believe Arla was talking this lucidly. When she first arrived she'd either been totally silent, or made no sense at all.

"If you were prepared to give me blood and hair samples," Gilamar said, "I could test it to see if any other drugs were still left in your system."

"You can't make me drink that stuff."

"*Ner vod,* we don't even have any to give you, whatever it is. All we've got is the zaloxipine the center gave us."

Ner vod. Arla might have been familiar with the words. In Concordian, the Concord Dawn dialect of *Mando'a,* the phrase—brother, sister—sounded very similar. She frowned at Gilamar as if she was trying to focus on him rather than disapproving of what he'd asked.

*She's medicated out of her skull. We're going to have
to be careful how we reduce that dose.*

"Okay," she murmured. She rolled up her sleeve and
held out her arm with the fold of her elbow uppermost,
as if she'd had blood samples taken a hundred times.
"Get it over with."

Jusik began to hope. Arla was already improving simply for being out of that asylum. When he first met her,
she cowered from all men; now she was letting Gilamar
draw blood from her arm.

"Now, you want to take that walk?" Gilamar asked.

Arla shrugged. "Maybe tomorrow."

They didn't even have to send the samples away for
analysis. With the small lab that Mereel had set up for
Ko Sai, and the assortment of medical equipment that
Gilamar had stolen from Republic medcenters, Kyrimorut could do most of its own lab work.

The lab was situated opposite the roba pen, where a
huge sow stood guard at the entrance to her shelter.
It was a very Mando juxtaposition of high tech and
manure-scented agrarian life that hadn't changed since
Canderous Ordo's day.

Gilamar shook the vial of black-red blood as he
walked down the passage, pausing to hold it up to the
sunlight slanting through one of the windows.

"Funny stuff, blood," he said.

"Chemically, or spiritually?"

"Both. And it's not thicker than water, whatever they
say."

"She seems better this week. The other medication
must be wearing off."

Gilamar opened the lab door. Uthan's perfume wafted
out, a subtle herbal scent that might have been sham-
poo. "I'm wondering why they had her on two antipsy-
chotics like that. Just saying that there might be a good
reason."

"We'll find out, won't we?" Jusik said, and left with
Kad to ponder how little blood meant to him.

Derelict hunting lodge, Olankur; the southwest coast of
Mandalore's north continent

"You're a suspicious man, so you are, Kal."

Fenn Shysa brushed a layer of dust from the rough table and set a bottle of *tihaar* and two glasses in front of Skirata. The layer of dead insects on the windowsill suggested the hunting lodge hadn't been used for some time. Olankur was an awfully long way to come for a drink.

It was a long way from the Imperial garrison, too, and that was the whole point.

"Keeps me alive," Skirata said.

"We could have had done this in Keldabe. Don't you trust your *Mand'alor*?"

"We could have done this by comm, too, but you're the one who wanted to talk face-to-face."

Skirata trusted Shysa as much as he trusted anyone outside his family, but he didn't want to be seen with him too often. The *Mand'alor* was known to the garrison commander. Skirata had to assume that one of the stormies—or the mongrel officers, or even that inbred chinless *di'kut* of a commander—would get lucky and find out something sooner or later.

Mandalorians were tight-lipped around outsiders. But nothing stayed a secret forever.

Shysa pulled the stopper from the bottle and poured two small glasses of *tihaar*. Skirata could smell the colorless liquor from the other side of the table, a wonderful velvety aroma of the ripe varos fruits it had been distilled from. Every tihaar was different, made from whatever local fruit was available. Varos grew in the tropics, so this bottle was a rare treat.

"Your boy doesn't have to wait outside, Kal."

"Ordo just likes to keep an eye on things."

"Sensible lad." Shysa sipped, frowning in concentration. "But you could always change your *shabla* armor. Imperials can't tell one Mando from another as long as you keep your *buy'ce* on."

Skirata raised his glass and gulped the liquor down in one. *"K'oyacyi."*

"K'oyacyi." Shysa went to pour top-ups but Skirata placed his palm over the top of his glass. "Ah, you think I'm buttering you up for something, Kal. Don't we know each other better than that?"

"I don't think fast with a few drinks inside me."

"You don't need to think fast. You need to listen."

"You still want me and the *Cuy'val Dar* to train your resistance, is that it?"

"Resistance sounds a bit too romantic and hasty for my tastes. I'm thinking of it more as . . . an *intention to respond in kind* if the Empire doesn't turn out to be the reliable and reasonable tenant any self-respecting *Mand'alor* would want. But that's not why we're talking."

Shysa was a reluctant Mandalore, which was a healthy attitude as far as Skirata was concerned. He'd stepped up because he had to. After three years without Jango Fett, without a chieftain of chieftains, the clans were getting too used to the idea of having no compass, and there was a fine line between freethinking independence and chaos. But Shysa wasn't there to run the place like some *aruetyc* bureaucrat. He was there to provide focus, and he had plenty of that. He was a determined man when he found something worth pursuing. Skirata was still waiting to find out what it was.

"Okay, I'll have that second *tihaar* if you're still offering," Skirata said.

Shysa smiled to himself and poured two more glasses before taking a datapad out of his belt pouch and shoving it across the dusty table. Skirata picked it up.

"Business is good, Kal. The Empire wants to spend. It's just the nature of their shopping list that's giving me a few concerns, so it is."

Skirata sipped the *tihaar,* scrolling through the messages and purchase orders on the 'pad, noting the usual bounty-hunting business and contracts for mercenary units. Nothing surprising there; that was how Mandalorians had put food on their tables for generations. What caught Skirata's eye was the document addressed to MandalMotors, closely followed by the offer of eight hundred million credits for *beskar* mining rights in the Tokursh region.

Initially, we require three hundred operational prison ships with beskar *enhancements. The contract will be for refurbishment of those vessels mothballed since the last action against the Jedi, as well as construction of new vessels. We also wish to place orders for specialist equipment made from beskar, including manacles, holding cages, security doors . . .*

"So Palps wants *beskar,*" Skirata said, sliding the 'pad back to Shysa. "But unless he's up against Force-users, why does he need it? Mundane creatures like us can be kept in check pretty well with heavy-gauge durasteel at a fraction of the price."

Shysa raised his glass and winked. "It's a serious case of overkill. And a lot of creds for the privilege."

A few hundred million. A few weeks' interest on the Skirata Clone Resettlement Fund. But you don't need to know that, Fenn, much as I like you. Even if you are *my* Mand'alor.

"You're worried. Please tell me you're worried."

"Cautious, let's say."

"Who's he afraid of?"

"Maybe just us, on account of us having the *beskar* and knowing how to use it."

"We haven't fought the Sith for millennia. You know the *chakaar*'s a Sith, don't you?"

"I'd guessed as much from the word I'm hearing about some big fella with a red lightsaber. Vader."

"But he's wiped out . . . pretty well all the Jedi." Skirata hoped that Shysa put his pause down to the alcohol. Shysa could have had no idea that Etain had been a Jedi, or that Kyrimorut was now crawling with Force-users. "Some Sith feud?"

"If Palps was having a misunderstanding with other dark side folk, we'd have known about that by now.

Maybe he's buying up *beskar* to stop anyone else from re-arming against *him*."

Apart from mercenaries, Mandalore's only exports worth a cred were its unique iron, and the secret metal-working skills to make the most of its resistance to lightsabers and Force tactics. Even Skirata wasn't privy to what went on in the forges, and he prided himself on being able to get hold of any information he liked. He only knew that without Mando artisans, Palps wouldn't get his creds' worth for the *beskar*. That was starting to look more like a liability than a trump card.

"Remember the royal tomb-builders on Belukat? The ones the kings enslaved and shot so they wouldn't tell anyone how to rob the tombs?"

"I hadn't missed the similarities, *ner vod* . . ."

"If the whole Jedi Order couldn't stop Palpatine, there can't be many Force-using threats left to worry him."

Shysa held his glass up to the light slanting through the grimy window, squinting with one eye to examine the clarity of the *tihaar* before inhaling the aroma like a connoisseur.

"Ah, there's a little list, so there is, Kal." He sipped appreciatively and shut his eyes for a moment as if the bliss of the flavor had overwhelmed him. Maybe he just realized how big a job he'd taken on. "A few escaped Jedi . . . his own dark side minions, if they get out of line . . . all the little sects that went underground to avoid the Jedi . . . and the unlucky individuals who just happen to get born Force-sensitive. Oh, and folks in places like Haruun Kal, where *everyone's* got the talent. I wouldn't be buying any real estate there if I were you, not unless you like your front yard all charred and glassy."

"Suddenly you're the expert on midi-chlorians."

Shysa paused. "There's an interesting word."

"There's no point trying to wipe out Force sensitivity." Skirata tried to brazen it out, worried that he'd now revealed he knew a little too much about Force-users. "Where do you think Jedi come from? They don't have families—for the most part. Force stuff just shows up. He knows that."

"The point isn't whether it's true, but whether he believes it is."

"Maybe he wants to stamp out the training. If a sensitive isn't trained, then they can't do all the clever stuff like telekinesis and mind-bending."

"You know quite a bit about this midi-chlorian business, yourself, then, Kal."

Skirata felt his scalp tighten. He'd played this game of verbal sabacc with too many beings over the years, and it made him assume the worst rather than anything at face value. He was usually right. When he was wrong—well, it was safer than the alternative, and he was prepared to lose a few friends rather than risk something far worse.

"I've worked with enough Jedi over the last few years," Skirata said carefully. For a second or two, he felt regret for General Zey, who'd had the makings of a decent human being if only he could have been cured of that Jedi *osik*. "You pick it up as you go along."

"Ah, that'd be right. So you would."

Shysa went quiet and poured a third *tihaar* for himself. He tilted the bottle at Skirata in a mute offer of a top-up, but Skirata shook his head. If he wanted to get completely *haryc b'aalyc*—tired and emotional, as *Mando'ade* called it—then he'd wait until he got home. He really needed his wits about him now.

The silence was seductive. It was all too easy to fall into it and fill the gap by volunteering information. But Skirata had played that game before, too. He could sit it out in silence.

What kind of Mando am I? A Mando with a Force-sensitive grandson, and an ex-Jedi who's as dear to me as my own sons, that's what. And a Mando who isn't going to drop his boys into another war they didn't volunteer for.

Shysa let the silence go on for a while, then tipped his chair back on two legs to put his boots up on a nearby stool. It was always a matter who could sit and wait the longest.

"See, Kal, I recall meeting an unusual young fella in the *Oyu'baat* not so long ago," he said at last. "One of the Jedi generals who loved our stylish *beskar'gam* so much that he left the Jedi Order for a *beroya*'s way of life. Ah, there's dedication to fashion." He tapped his datapad and held it for Skirata to see. The screen showed an Imperial bounty list with a grainy security-cam image of a very young, bearded, long-haired Jusik in his Jedi robes. "This dashing wee warrior."

So that was what Shysa *really* wanted to talk about. Skirata couldn't deny it. The wanted list had been widely circulated among the bounty-hunting community so Jusik was hardly a secret. But Jusik had an altercation with Sull right under Shysa's nose. It was hard to dismiss.

"Yeah, that's General Jusik," Skirata said. The glow of the *tihaar* vanished from his gut and ice took its place. "He objected to using clones and told the Jedi Order where to shove its conscience."

"Now, if he were on your comlink speed dial, for the sake of argument, you'd let me know, would you not, Kal?"

"No." Skirata stayed genial, but he couldn't lie now. He could only stall. "I would not."

Shysa paused, but the faint smile never left his face. "We don't get too many Mando Force-sensitives, which is a bit *unlucky,* given how many worlds our fine population's drawn from. Imagine how handy it'd be to have some *Mando'ade* who could use the Force."

"Imagine," Skirata said. "But one Force-user in armor isn't going to help us much against Palpatine. The whole Jedi Order couldn't stop him."

"I was thinking longer term. Maybe young General Jusik will have plenty of kids who take after him."

"No."

"I didn't ask a question, Kal."

Shysa knew. He *knew.* Well, it didn't take a clairvoyant

to work out the association, just a friendly chat with the staff in the *Oyu'baat*. Skirata stood his ground. "If anyone knew how to breed for Force sensitivity, they would have done it by now," he said. "We've survived well enough against Force-users for five thousand years without it. It's not a deficiency. It's what we are."

"Fine sentiments, but they won't be much comfort when the Empire decides we're a problem. And they will."

"We'd be better off relying on Verpine tech and a bit of honest sweat than on genetics. Makes us no better than *aruetiise*—than Jedi, with their genetic *superiority*. No thanks."

Shysa wore his patient look now, a slight but well-meaning frown. "I hate to spoil that fine illusion, Kal, but take a look around you at the *Mando'ade*. A mixed bunch, and no mistake, but don't you think we've self-selected and bred a hardy, stubborn type? What's the difference?"

"That's not the same as trying to produce Force-users," Skirata said, trying very hard not to lose his temper. He was angry with himself, not Shysa. He knew he'd already lost the argument. "We've bred an *attitude*, Fenn—self-reliance, tenacity, guts. That's not in the genes." He tapped his temple. "It's available to anyone who is willing to work for it. It's up *here*."

"I'll be sure to tell Palps that when he rolls in with a whole fleet of warships. We'll just *think* hard and see him off."

Skirata waited for the inevitable question, and knew that if Shysa asked it then it would be the last time he spoke to the man. That scared him. It told him that he put his own wishes above his people. This wasn't how Munin Skirata had raised him. *Communal* responsibility. That was the watchword. A Mandalorian who thought only of himself wasn't a *Mando'ad* at all.

But I look out for my clan. Clans build the people. Can't have one without the other.

"Kal, I'm just asking you for *Manda'yaim*," Shysa

said. "If you ever run into this Jusik, and he still thinks of himself as one of us, then he's got skills we'll need in years to come."

Skirata felt his world shrink. His focus shifted so that the rest of the shabby hut was a blur but Shysa was so sharply vivid that Skirata could see every pore and hair.

We could sit out this trouble. Go anywhere. Jusik's earned some peace, every bit as much as my boys. But if I mention this to him—he'll think it's his duty.

"I can't help you, *Mand'alor*," Skirata said.

"Ah well, I was just asking, just in case you ever saw him." Shysa shrugged. "Anyway . . . if any of your fine clone boys are minded to do a little bit of observation, seeing as they can pass for stormies easy enough, then I'd be grateful."

Skirata knew that Shysa couldn't have guessed just how much espionage the clones could do. He hoped it didn't show on his face. But he still couldn't bring himself to commit them to Shysa's fledgling resistance. Everyone thought the ends of their own cause justified its means. But that was where Skirata had to draw the line, even when he didn't want to. If he made that choice for the clones, he was no better than a Jedi general. He wasn't even sure that he could face asking them. They'd say yes, just like Jusik; he knew it. They'd do anything for him.

"It'll be their decision," Skirata said. "If I've struggled to give those *ad'ike* anything, Fenn, it's a *choice*."

Shysa looked at him for a long time, not a trace of frustration or disappointment on his face, and then pushed the bottle toward him.

"I appreciate your time, Kal," he said. "Keep the *tihaar*."

It was a clear glass bottle. No tracking device could have been hidden in it, but Skirata was too wary to accept it.

"Save it for next time," he said, knowing there might never be one. "I'll keep you supplied with intelligence.

Just accept that I'm dealing with things you're better off not knowing about for the time being."

A terrible feeling of finality almost overwhelmed him. He was tempted to offer Shysa some concession out of sheer guilt that he hadn't leapt to offer everything he had to protect Mandalore against the Empire.

How can I fail the Mand'alor *at a time like this? What would my father think of me?*

Skirata had vast resources at his disposal now, from wealth to bioweapons to . . . Jedi blood, whatever use that would actually be. The *resol'nare,* the six tenets of Mandalorian identity, said he was obliged to look after his kids, his clan, and his culture, and to rally to the *Mand'alor* in times of need.

Shysa smiled. "I trust you, Kal."

It was one hell of a knife to twist in Skirata's gut. He clasped Shysa's forearm in farewell, the traditional Mando grip with the hand just below the elbow, and left.

The speeder was parked nearby. The hatch popped as he got closer, and he could see Ordo sitting in the pilot's seat, arms folded.

Ordo raised one eyebrow a fraction. "What's wrong, *Kal'buir*?"

"Let's get out of here and I'll tell you. Nobody's been near you, have they? Nowhere near the ship?"

"If you're asking if anyone's had the chance to slap a tracking device on us—no, they haven't. The place is deserted."

The drives started up, rising from a low rumble to a high-pitched whine before the speeder lifted into the air.

"It's a bad sign when you don't trust your own *Mand'alor,*" Ordo said, confirming Skirata's guilt. "What did he want?"

Skirata wrestled with his divided conscience, knowing which part would win but not feeling proud of that.

"Too much," he said.

5

Controlling a population is an economical business. We have twenty-six Imperial enforcement officers over-seeing Oznar, a city of a million beings. Ninety percent of the reports of anti-Imperial activity and crime comes from the good citizens themselves spying on their neighbors and denouncing them. The biggest task we face is sifting that information. Far from having to be coerced, far from struggling under the so-called yoke of Imperial oppression—the average galactic citizen is only too happy to seize the opportunity to settle scores or merely make a show of being loyal. And I guarantee that in years to come, they will deny all knowledge of doing so.
—Armand Isard, Director of Imperial Intelligence

Imperial City

Ennen didn't accompany Niner to Imperial Security to deliver the datachip. He stayed in the shuttle, hunched in the pilot's seat.

"I'm waiting here until I get an answer about Bry," he said, answering the unasked question. He picked up the comm mike from the console. "I want them to treat him right. Ops, I want to speak to the Special Unit duty officer. *Now.*"

Treating Bry right meant cremation, the traditional funeral for Corellians in exile. Ennen and Bry seemed every bit as Corellian as Omega Squad and the Nulls were Mandalorian. Niner was reminded just how central the *Cuy'val Dar* training sergeants and the cultures they brought with them had been in shaping the clones they raised.

Niner ushered Darman off the shuttle. "Let's get this chip off our hands."

"Who are we delivering it to?" Darman looked back over his shoulder as they walked away from the shuttle. "Don't we just give it to Cuis?"

Niner consulted his datapad again. It definitely said to deliver the material personally to Imperial Security's IT division, part of the Anti-Terrorist Unit, and not to deviate. The last thing he saw as he walked away from the landing strip was an Imperial commander, a tall thin guy, jogging toward the vessel. Niner hoped he was the sympathetic type. Ennen wasn't in a negotiating mood.

Niner took a waiting speeder bike, and they headed for the IS offices. Someone could get some data off that chip, he was sure. If only he could make contact with Jaing—or Mereel. Those two could do just about anything with information technology, most of it illegal and dangerous. But he'd lost contact with them. The Imperial comm codes and firewalls had all changed, and as far as he knew the Nulls were safe and well on Mandalore with Fi, Corr, and Atin.

He missed them all. He tried hard not to dwell on that. It left him churning over the whole idea of desertion, which had seemed totally wrong at first, and then started feeling a lot more right as the war reached its final days. He'd psyched himself up to go at last, and then—the moment was snatched away.

He still wanted to go. He hadn't changed his mind. And neither Jaing nor Mereel would have been much interested in helping the Empire catch renegades even if they'd been around to help.

"They let us out without a spook," Darman said. "They trust us more than I thought."

Niner measured every word carefully, still not sure if

his helmet comm kit was bugged. It was starting to get to him now. He felt under siege, uneasy, violated. Maybe he was paranoid in the medical sense, though, not just over-careful, and this was how *really* crazy people felt. He just didn't know.

He took off his helmet and switched off all the comms. "Replacement for Bry," he said, changing the subject. "Ennen's going to have a hard time of it. Let's help him along best we can, Dar."

"We've got to work with a new guy, too. As long as it's nobody from Reau's squads, that's fine by me."

"Might get one of the cross-trained meat-cans instead, like Corr." Changing the dynamics of a four-man squad was never easy. Omega had worked out fine in the end, but losing a brother and absorbing a new one always upset the harmony for a while. "Don't worry about it."

We won't be here long enough, Dar. We're leaving. Soon.

Darman was having one of his it's-not-happening days. Niner could see him straining to be the normal Dar again. Most of the time he managed it, but when his attention wandered, the pain was visible in his eyes. His expression didn't match his tone of voice.

"Amazing how fast they can change things when they want to." Darman nodded at signage on the walls as they passed. IMPERIAL SECURITY, it said. "Shame they couldn't have managed that speed and efficiency during the Republic."

Imperial Security was another new label on an old box. The information technology center was an old Coruscant Security Force divisional HQ. The new organization had swallowed up chunks of the old CSF, mostly the detective and counter-terrorism side, but Niner wasn't sure why Palpatine needed both the civilians in IS and the military Imperial Intelligence to do a similar job. Maybe he wanted them to spy on each other to stay sharp. Perhaps he was just such a dyed-in-the-wool politician that his instinctive way to deal with anything was to create new departments with confusing titles.

Niner didn't think there were enough shady characters, revolutionaries, and terrorists to keep two big departments busy. They'd be fighting over suspects.

Ah. I get it now. That's why he's doing it.

They reached the turbolift lobby through another set of key-coded doors. The sign said PLEASE REMOVE HELMETS FOR SECURITY PURPOSES, a remnant of the time when folks thought manners mattered.

"I already did," Darman said. "I bet they don't get many Mando visitors."

Niner made a conscious effort to play down his associations with Mandalore now. He wasn't ashamed of being Mandalorian, and he had no reason to think that Mandalore was regarded with suspicion, but something told him to keep his mouth shut about it and *go gray*— the intelligence services' phrase for not drawing attention to yourself. His wariness was about more than the secret he had to keep. He had a feeling that Mandalorians would eventually be regarded as trouble, because they didn't like belonging to anything—republics, empires, or anything with rules they didn't have a say in making. Sooner or later, that was going to make Mandalore a liability. He could see it coming.

Darman looked back at the doors as they snapped shut behind him. "I hope this isn't where we find out we're enemies of the Empire and get banged up for life."

"Don't be daft," Niner said. A couple of droids whirred past him and ignored both commandos. "They'd send us to Imperial Intelligence for that."

"You always make me feel so much better."

Niner stepped into the open turbolift and consulted the floor directory on the control panel. "Fortieth floor."

"Nice view."

The turbolift left Niner's stomach at the ground floor. He wanted to talk to Darman about Sa Cuis, and how the agent gave him the creeps, but he didn't dare. All the little safety valves a clone had—grumbling, off-color jokes, outright dissent—were denied to him now.

If anything finally tipped him over the edge, it was going to be that.

When the 'lift doors opened again, Niner stepped out into an even more deserted lobby, without even droids wandering around, only a muffled carpeted *quiet* with the faint trembling sensation of a million machines simmering just under the threshold of his hearing.

The view from the wraparound windows wasn't all that great, unless you liked staring at the headquarters of the Capital Reclamation and Sanitation Company. Niner turned to his left, following the signs on the wall, and pressed the entry button on yet another key-coded security door. It slid open and he stepped inside, Darman right behind him.

"My, don't *you* two look spiffy," said a familiar voice from somewhere behind a server rack.

Darman spun around, looking for the source. Niner peered around the rack.

"Captain?"

"No rest for the wicked, Niner." Jaller Obrim held out his hand with a sad smile. "Good to see you again, son. And you, Darman."

There was no reason to be surprised to see Obrim here, but he was a face from the recent and dangerous past. Niner's first thought was to pray that he could keep his mouth shut.

It was a crazy thought. Obrim had as much to lose as they did—maybe more. The man had bent every rule in the book for Skirata, and probably a few that weren't in the book at all. Obrim had turned more blind eyes than an Alderaanian argus, leaked classified information, gone selectively deaf, made inconvenient bodies disappear, and generally supported Skirata in whatever scam he had going. He'd diverted CSF resources to spring Fi from the medcenter, and sheltered him while Skirata arranged to get him off Coruscant. That was probably only the tip of the iceberg in terms of the stunts he'd pulled to cover Skirata's backside.

The two veterans were best buddies, and CSF—the old CSF, at least—had been so close to Skirata and the Nulls that it had been hard to tell where one ended and the other began.

Yes, Obrim had a lot to lose. Niner was surprised that he hadn't disappeared in the Purge. He definitely didn't have the right stuff to be one of Palpatine's men, that was certain, but then maybe Palpatine still thought of him as the good old reliable Captain Obrim of the Senate Guard. He didn't realize just how much Obrim enjoyed being a cop.

Niner took Obrim's outstretched hand and shook it. His knuckles turned white from the pressure. "You don't fancy the new red armor, then?"

"I'd look a complete idiot in it." Obrim patted his gut, which was straining a little under a plain tan tunic. "No, the Imperial Guard can do without me. I'd never fit in the suit now. Besides, the Emperor wants fit and dedicated young stormtroopers to do the job, and I'm an old street cop at heart. How about you?"

There was so much unsaid at that moment, so much tension in the air, all born of shared guilt and a lot of memories that ranged from the best times ever to pure abject grief. Niner glanced at Darman to see if meeting Obrim again had rubbed on that ever-raw nerve.

Obrim was there when Etain died. Is he going to mention it? How can we not?

"We're called Squad Forty now," Darman said. "Dull, isn't it?"

Obrim looked as if he'd had a reprieve, but only a temporary one. "Great for picking lottery numbers." He gestured at them to follow. "Let me show you what the tech boys can do with that datachip you rescued."

There was no mention of Skirata, no questions about Fi, and not even a mention of Niner's paralyzing spinal injury, none of the friendly routine chat that might have been expected if Obrim hadn't known what had really gone on in the latter months of the war. And he'd almost certainly seen the death warrant list, but he didn't mention that, either.

The techs—who might have been droids for all Darman knew—weren't around when Obrim opened the inner lab door, and it definitely wasn't caf break time. He punched in another security code and led Niner and Darman into a room full of test benches with chip readers, scopes, meters, and probes at every workstation. He sat down at one of them and tapped the controls. The screen filled with prompts to insert a new chip.

"Now," Obrim said. "I'm not good with this kind of thing, but the techies tell me *proper* erasure can take hours, even a whole day if it's a big-capacity chip. Can't just hit the delete button like they do in the holovids."

"I couldn't find any visible files on it," Niner said. "But then we don't usually carry forensic devices."

"Well, maybe your Jedi managed to erase everything, or maybe he didn't, but even if he did—there are *mechanical* ways of reconstructing data on files. Stuff that software can't even do."

Darman's eyes flickered between the screen and Obrim's face. Niner watched them both struggling to ignore the unsaid thing on their minds. He also saw Obrim reach casually into a drawer and pull out a stack of new datachips in a flimsiplast wrapper. The captain opened it like a packet of candy and threw the balled wrapper into the bin under the desk.

"Well, Camas wiped it, all right," Obrim said. Niner leaned over his shoulder; the screen looked a lot like his chip reader—empty. "Why don't you grab a cup of caf, lads? I'm going to be a while. Now, do I remember Camas? Don't think I ever met him . . ."

Obrim gestured to a seating area in the far corner of the lab. There was a caf dispenser there, and the second most seductive lure in the galaxy for any clone—a plate of cookies, cakes, and nut bars. Darman seemed distracted by the promise of sugar-laden calories and drifted in their direction. Obrim crooked his finger at Niner.

"Is he okay?" Obrim's whisper was barely a breath. Niner strained to hear even this close. "He doesn't look it."

"No, he's not himself."

"Okay. I talk to *you*, then. Got it?"

Niner had to think about that for a couple of seconds. Then he got the idea. This was, after all, *Kal'buir*'s confidant and occasional quartermaster. Deals were done under tables.

Niner went to claim his free snacks, but kept an eye on Obrim. He could just about see his screen from the seating area if he leaned at the right angle. He caught a glimpse of something suddenly scrolling down the screen that looked like a list of files. It could have been diagnostics, of course. Niner wasn't Jaing. This was a magician's trick to him.

"I never knew Obrim was all technical," Darman said, topping up his cup.

"Neither did I."

"He wants to ask, doesn't he?"

"What?"

"He wants to ask me how I am. To say how sorry he is. But he's too embarrassed."

So Dar was having a lucid moment, admitting to his grief. "I think he doesn't want to upset you, *ner vod*. Or talk about things that might be overheard."

"You and your surveillance conspiracy theories," Darman said, but his tone sounded as if he thought it was a reasonable doubt to have.

Niner's eyes never left Obrim. He could only see the top half of the screen, not the surface of the desk, and he tried to guess what was going on that he couldn't see. Eventually Obrim stood up and nodded to him.

"Dar, stock up on the freebies, will you?" Niner pointed at the pile of delicacies, not the kind of treats the Empire laid on for clones. They were worth filching. "I'm sure IS won't mind feeding the starving of the Five-oh-first."

"On it," Darman said, and began slipping food into his belt pouches.

That would keep him distracted for a couple of minutes. Niner had shared every thought and fear with Darman since their first mission on Qiilura, but right now he felt, just as Obrim seemed to, that Dar was safer not knowing something.

What, exactly?

Skirata trusted Obrim with his life—with everyone's life. So Niner would, too. He leaned over Obrim and listened. On the desktop, datachips lay fanned out with some sheets of flimsi. Obrim fidgeted with them, frowning at the display.

"He managed to wipe nearly everything except the operating system, and then he had a try at trashing that." Obrim showed Niner a list of confusing file names that could have been anything. "He's really mangled it."

"Useful?"

Obrim had that look, a hint of a twinkle in his eye that Niner had seen before when he was up to something. "I was hoping it would have information on a rebel escape network, maybe like the Whiplash underground. It could have led us to all kinds of folks trying to evade the Empire. Jedi . . . civvie pilots . . . mercenaries . . . their arms deals, their finance routes . . ." Obrim sighed and rattled the datachips in his cupped palms like he was at a casino. "But Camas erased it completely. They say a Vorandi scanning microscope can detect deleted data in the actual chip structure and recover it, but I think that's complete *osik,* personally."

Obrim had picked up the odd *Mando'a* profanity from Skirata. Niner took another second to catch on again, and realized he had to stop being literal. This was *Jaller Obrim,* for goodness' sake. He'd defied Palpatine to get Skirata off Coruscant, and he was still here to tell the tale. And he was still watching Skirata's back, even now.

Jedi, civvie pilots, deserters, mercenaries.

Yes, I get it, Captain.

Niner had no idea what was accidentally hidden on that chip—maybe not accidentally at all—but he knew that whatever was coming next, he needed to contact Jaing at any cost.

"Sounds like a myth to me," Niner said. "Vorandi, you say."

"Yeah. And you'd need a *phenomenally* gifted techie to make anything of it, even if it could be done. I don't think we've got anyone like that, even in Imperial City."

"Shame," Niner said, gut churning. "Nothing else you can do with the chip now, then?"

He got the fact that this was a message. The trouble was that he didn't know what it said or how to transmit it. Then Obrim shrugged, pulled the chip from the docking port, and stared at it.

"Not much," he said. And he palmed it. He palmed it so skillfully that it vanished for a moment among the other identical chips he was fiddling with on the desktop. "But I'll log it as evidence anyway. Chain of custody and all that."

Obrim shook Niner's hand again—with both hands—and nodded a few times. Niner felt something rigid press against the palm of his glove. Instinctively, he closed his fingers around it as he withdrew his hand, and folded his arms.

"You did well to even salvage this." Obrim put the datachip—no, *a* datachip—back in the docking port and tapped the screen. "See? Just part of the operating system left. I'm really sorry about your buddy. But please, Niner, don't feel his sacrifice was wasted. Something positive can come out of this."

That wasn't Obrim, not at all. He was a man who could silence a room just by walking into it. He didn't get sentimental with people. He was a hard-nosed cop, even by CSF standards, a man with nerve. Niner adjusted his gauntlets, slipping the chip inside the right one with his left thumb as he did so.

"Thanks, Captain," he said. "We're looking forward to working with you again."

Obrim slapped his shoulder. "Me, too, lad. You know you can count on us. Anything for our boys."

"Dar's nicked all your cakes, Captain . . ."

"Like I say, *anything*."

Darman gave Niner an odd look as the turbolift shot down to ground level. Niner was busting to tell him what had gone on, how he now had some vital data that he needed to get to Jaing if only he could find him, but his gut reminded him that the safest thing for everyone was to keep it to himself until the last minute.

"I'll give Ennen some of the stash." Darman opened one of his pouches and checked his haul of goodies. "Not the warra nut slices, though. I call dibs on those. You reckon they've got hidden surveillance cams up there?"

"We'll find out if they raid the barracks tonight and confiscate your warra nuts."

Obrim must have assumed there was constant surveillance as well, or at least the serious risk of it, if he'd gone through this charade so carefully. It made Niner feel a lot better.

He wasn't paranoid, not in a crazy way. The Empire really *was* out to get him.

Kyrimorut, Mandalore

Besany held the sheet of *haarshun* dough up to the light with both hands.

"Ny, is that thin enough?"

Ny peered up at it. Besany was as tall as Ordo, a head taller than Ny and Scout. "Can you see through it? Rav says you have to be able to see your betrothal ring through it."

"Sort of."

"Well, it looks okay to me."

"If it's supposed to bake hard, then how do they use it

as dry rations?" Besany held up the sheet of dough between her fingertips like laundry. "They couldn't get that in a backpack."

"You roll it up before you cook it," Ruu said. "Then you soak it in water to make it soft again."

"Wow. Fascinating."

They were making unfamiliar food to mark the start of the thaw. It wasn't a festival as Ny understood one, just an impromptu meal taken outside because the weather was no longer cold enough to weld skin to metal. It still felt freezing to her. But she could definitely sense what Skirata and the others could smell on the air: spring.

Besany plowed on making more *haarshun* bread. She wasn't one of nature's chefs, but she tried so hard that it hurt. Ny felt sorry for her. She was a clever, strikingly beautiful girl from the city who didn't really fit in this frontier kind of life, but she was determined to be the perfect Mando wife for Ordo. She threw herself into the culture. She was learning to cook the food, wear the armor, and even fight.

Either the culture attracted those who needed identity, or it was so overwhelming that it swallowed those it touched. Ny wondered how long it would be before she, too, was dragged in by its gravity. It might have been partly down to Skirata, of course. He had a talent for gathering people around him—even the most unlikely beings—and making them feel like family.

While Besany wrestled with dough, and Scout and Ruu sliced the haunch of shatual that Mird and Vau had hunted, Ny made igatli from scratch, following a recipe on a datapad propped on the kitchen table. The coin-sized crumbly cookies weren't a Mandalorian recipe; they were Kuati, fiddly and insubstantial, nothing like the practical and filling cuisine here. Skirata came from Kuat. She knew that. He'd mentioned it just once, and that had intrigued her, because she hadn't realized just what a mixed bag Mandalorians were. Until they took off their helmets, they all looked the same to her.

She knew better now. Beings—humans, Togorians, Weequays, Twi'leks, all kinds of species, but mainly humans—came in at one end and emerged as Mandos at the other. Ny still couldn't work it out. There was no enforcement, no rule book beyond some very basic stuff about language, armor, and making kids—*everyone's* kids—the center of your life, but somehow they all ended up essentially Mandalorian, just with fascinating variety in accent and food. Everything else was jettisoned. One day, she'd understand it. In the meantime, she worked on the principle that Skirata recalled enough of his very early childhood in Kuat City to appreciate a homemade delicacy he probably hadn't tasted for more than fifty years.

Scout kept looking out the window. "What are they doing?"

"*Meshgeroya,*" Besany said. "The beautiful game. That's what they call it here. Bolo-ball. Limmie. The ground's thawed enough to play."

"They haven't got enough players for two teams."

"Oh, that won't stop them."

"Good grief, is Laseema going to play?" Scout seemed horrified. "And Jilka?"

"I think they're going to be line judges. Parja's refereeing."

"What line? It's just grass and mud out there."

Besany and Ruu laughed. *Meshgeroya* was a Mandalorian obsession and certainly seemed to get a lot of boisterous energy out of their systems. When Ny looked out of the window, she was surprised to see Kina Ha and Uthan sitting in the shelter of the courtyard wall, shrouded in scarves, chatting. Skirata had a told Ny that Kaminoans didn't like sunlight and preferred endless rain and permanently overcast skies like their homeworld, but Kina Ha didn't seem bothered by the weak late-winter sun. She did, however, have a peaked cap to shield her eyes.

She's doing well. Kal hasn't pulled a knife on her yet. Even Mereel's being icily polite.

"Shame," Besany murmured.

"What is?"

"Wouldn't it be perfect if Etain was here?"

All Ny could do was nod. In the last few weeks, Etain's absence hung over every meal and conversation. Mandalorians tended to talk openly about dead loved ones as if they were still part of the clan, but it was clearly still too raw for anyone here to keep mentioning her name as often as they thought it. Ny was pretty sure that it overshadowed every happy moment. She could see it on their faces every time they looked at Kad.

I never knew her. I can't join in.

"Okay, let's get this stuff in the oven, and it should be ready by halftime. Or full time." Ny checked the chrono. "Whenever that is."

Kad kicked the ball around under the watchful eye of Kom'rk. It was more like running at the ball, colliding with it, and then chasing it, but he was giggling happily. Ny was relieved to see him behaving like a normal toddler. Sometimes he seemed so serious and grim that she wondered if a carefree infancy had passed him by somehow, and that all Force-users were doomed to be plugged directly into the awful reality of existence from birth whether they wanted to be or not. She could see it in Jusik and Scout sometimes. Their eyes could make them look older than time. She couldn't define it. No doubt Kina Ha's gaze gave away her Force-user status too, but Ny had no idea what a normal Kaminoan's eyes looked like, and anyway—Kina Ha *was* ancient.

"Bolo-ball hadn't even been invented when I was young," Kina Ha said. "Not that anyone played it on Kamino when it *was* invented, of course."

Ny couldn't tell if she was being deliberately funny or not. Mereel's expression suggested he'd never met a Kaminoan with a sense of humor he could recognize, and the jury was still out.

"Come on, *Kad'ika.*" Ny lifted Kad onto her hip. "Let the big kids play with the ball now."

Fi tossed the ball in the air and headed it as if he was

checking that he could still do it. "Love us, love our game."

"I'll get used to it . . ."

Even Vau joined in. Ny watched, waiting for the crunch of old bones whenever Skirata and Gilamar were tackled by one of the clones. The lads were big, fast, and exceptionally fit, far too fit for the veteran sergeants. Ny could see a little midlife crisis raising its graying head there. But maybe the crazy old barves just loved playing *meshgeroya*, and the risk of a painful trouncing from the youngsters wasn't enough to stop them.

The shouts and indignant appeals for penalties sent Mird into an excited frenzy. The strill slapped its whip-like tail on the ground and squealed to itself, occasionally racing around what seemed to be the edge of the pitch in its imagination. Kad watched the game intently, fist held to his mouth. Vau went for a high ball and headed it down between two bushes that seemed to be the only goal. He roared truimphantly.

"Offside!" Corr protested. Ny had no idea how he worked out where the goal was, let alone whether Vau had broken some rule. She didn't really get the game at all. "Ref, that was offside."

Parja allowed the goal, pointing imperiously toward a nonexistent center spot. "Wasn't. Play on."

"Devious old men *one,* fit young upstarts *nil,*" Vau said smugly. But he looked seriously out of breath.

Kina Ha seemed more engrossed in the strill than the game. But Jilka was paying more attention to Corr than keeping up with the play, and Uthan was watching Gilamar. It was interesting to see how fast relationships of all kinds were beginning to form.

It's a closed world here. No strangers. We stick to the folks we trust.

She realized that meant herself, too. Did Skirata even need anyone? He was completely obsessed with his kids. It was hard to see a gap where she might fit in. She'd always feel like an intruder.

"I'm going to check on those cookies," she said to Besany. "It's all too complicated for me."

As she turned and walked back toward the kitchen doors, she caught sight of a face at one of the slit windows. Arla was watching. She didn't look quite as blank and lost as she had when she first arrived. If anything, she looked increasingly baffled and agitated, and Ny wondered how anyone was going to be able to explain to her what had happened to her brother, and who the clones really were. Would she see them as nephews? From what Ny knew of Mandalorians, there was no reason to suppose she would, but then Arla wasn't a Mando. She was Concordian. They weren't the same thing at all.

Ny smiled and waved, but Arla just looked startled and fluttered her fingers, as if she was mimicking a foreign language. It must have been a long time since anyone had shown any personal concern for her.

The igatli cookies were evenly browned and looked pretty good, Ny had to admit. She slid them off the tray onto a plate and tried one. Was this how the things were supposed to turn out? She had no idea, but the vital touch was a spice, the seeds and dried stamens of a Kuati plant, and she'd bought the ingredients on her last cargo run to the Kuat shipyards. That had been before the night of the Jedi Purge, long before she was even conscious of the fact that she had a very soft spot for Skirata.

Insane. Completely insane. But we're all a longtime dead, right? Life has to be lived. Especially when all we've known for too long is bereavement.

Ny arranged the cookies on a tray with a few other treats—uj cake and cubes of herb-flavored local cheese—and composed herself before walking out into the yard again. She'd never felt this foolish in her life.

Try telling them you're just passing through now. Folks who pass through don't do this sort of thing.

"Hey, halftime!" Jaing called.

Ny checked her chrono. "You've got another ten minutes," she said.

"Food," Fi said. *"Ori'skraan!"*

The clones had impressive appetites, and everything stopped for food—even the beautiful game. Ny placed the tray on an old ammo crate in the yard and batted Fi's fingers away from the cookies.

"Your dad has first call on those." She ruffled Fi's hair and shoved a slice of uj cake in his mouth to appease him. "This is a special surprise. Come on, Kal. Tell me what you think of these."

Skirata stared at the cookies for a few moments. Maybe she'd made them the wrong shape. But Jusik, Scout, and Kina Ha all looked toward him at the same moment, even though he hadn't moved a muscle. They could sense something.

Oh boy . . . I've got something seriously wrong . . .

Kuat was a strange world. On one hand, it was heavy engineering and the height of modern technology. On the other—it was feudal and caste-ridden, with its merchant noblewomen relying on servant consorts to father their heirs. The society repelled her. Skirata must have been a small child when he left Kuat, too young to know about that kind of thing, but she wouldn't have been surprised to find that his loathing of nobility, privilege, and exploitation had its roots there. It was everything that Mandalore wasn't.

Skirata leaned over the tray a little and inhaled. Then he picked up a cookie, bit into it, and closed his eyes. Kad reached out to him with both hands, squirming in Jusik's arms to touch his grandfather. It was then that Ny saw the tears beading along Skirata's eyelashes.

He swallowed with difficulty. *"Shab,* that takes me back."

"I'm sorry," she said.

"Don't be. They're perfect."

Smell brought memories back faster than anything. Ny knew Skirata had been adopted by a mercenary who found him living like a little wild animal in the rubble of a war zone. It was a big mistake to assume that everyone's childhood was one long sun-warmed idyll. For most of the clan here, their early years had been full of fear and the threat of death, so making anyone recall that kind of past was asking for trouble. Skirata turned and walked around the courtyard, head down, while everyone else ate. He wasn't usually self-conscious about tears. He wept openly, and often. This had to be something different.

Eventually, he came back to the tray and took another cookie.

"I can remember my mama," he said. "You know, I haven't thought about her in years."

Skirata had never mentioned his mother, or even his adoptive father's wife. Everything in his life revolved around fathers. Ny wasn't sure if she'd ripped open an old wound or enabled some long-overdue catharsis, but either way, she'd never intended to make him weep. She felt terrible.

Skirata didn't return to the game with the others. He gave Scout a gentle shove to take his place, and Ny was sure that the kid would be reduced to splinters in seconds. But she had a remarkable ability to dodge and weave, as if she could predict what was coming next. It looked like another Jedi talent at work. Ny saw Jusik give her a knowing wink.

Skirata watched from the sidelines, subdued again. Mird settled down beside him, red-rimmed golden eyes fixed on the cookies in his hand.

"Sometimes I wish I could wipe my memory," he said. "Just the bad parts."

"Jusik can do that for you, can't he?"

"I'm not sure I'd be a better man for it."

"I'm sorry. I didn't think it through, Kal. I didn't realize it'd hurt."

"I think *bittersweet* covers it. *Aayhan*. It's a Mando thing. The painful memory of loved ones at otherwise perfect moments. Can't have one without the other, really." Skirata crunched another cookie, then gave one to Mird. "Then there's *shereshoy,* and *aayhan* inevitably leads to *shereshoy,* and so the wheel turns to joy again."

"What's *shereshoy?*"

"A lust for life. Grabbing it and living it for the day, because you don't know if you'll be around tomorrow."

"*Shereshoy.* I like that word."

"If you ever see a Mando in orange armor, that's what the color means." Skirata held the last chunk of cookie to his nose and inhaled again. The aroma was obviously evocative. "You're a good woman, Ny."

"You're not so bad yourself, Shortie."

So this was *shereshoy* in action. The snow had melted, the sun was struggling to get noticed, and that faint promise of winter's end had sparked an impromptu game of *meshgeroya* and modest feasting. Ny liked that. Her life had always been spent deferring gratification, waiting for that mythical *one day* to come when she and her husband could spend good times together, but now that day had passed a few thousand times and would never come again.

Ordo, sweat-streaked and visibly pleased with himself, halted the game to hand out mugs of *ne'tra gal.* Ny decided now was a good time to learn to enjoy the Mandos' sweet black beer, their crazy obsession with bolo-ball, and their eccentric hospitality that could, in the same heartbeat, take in both friends and traditional enemies. There would also come a time when she would have to come to terms with their ruthless, more brutal side. But that time could wait.

Now was the very best time to do most things. It was better to discover that late in life than not at all.

"*K'oyacyi,*" she said. There was no better toast than that. It was a command—"stay alive, come back safely"—but it could mean anything from "hang in there" to "live life to the fullest." If anything summed up Mandalorians for her, it was that word with two poignant meanings. "*K'oyacyi.*"

Staying alive was the one thing none of them could count on.

Laboratory, Kyrimorut, later that day

"No wonder Arla's perked up," Gilamar said. He sat at the workbench, half a mug of ale in one hand, and seemed to be reading test results. "The quacks at the Valorum Center were giving her sebenodone. Over a long period, too."

Uthan wasn't a physician, but she'd kept up to date with general medicine by reading every scientific journal the center would allow her. There hadn't been much else to do for three years in solitary confinement except read and theorize. At least breeding soka flies for genetic variations had given her some respite. She wondered if Gilamar would have thought she was crazy for giving the flies names.

"That's another antipsychotic drug, yes?"

He took a pull of his ale. "Right. A tad heavy-handed, I'd say. It's amazing she was even conscious when *Bard'ika* found her."

"They might as well have hit her over the head with a mallet."

"Well, it takes some time to metabolize and excrete completely, so she's still sedated, but that explains why she's getting more responsive."

"Isn't that dangerous, stopping a drug like that?"

"Could be. You should always taper it off. Given how persistent sebenodone is, though, she's probably still dosed up."

A doctor working with an ale in one hand wasn't exactly the kind of professional discipline that Uthan was used to, but Gilamar seemed to get the job done. This lab had suddenly become her refuge, a faint echo of her life as it had once been before the war started, and she liked to come here to savor both the familiarity of equipment and the novelty of relative freedom. Perhaps Gilamar liked recalling a time when he didn't have to fight for a living.

It was good to talk shop again, too.

"So how did you get all the equipment?" she asked.

"Not just this lab. All the medical facilities. The portable diagnostic kit. The monitors. The operating table. I couldn't help but notice the Republic Central Medsupply security labels on it all."

"Ah," Gilamar said. "That'd be because I thieved the lot, although we did buy this lab fair and square—but I think the creds we used were stolen, too. Oh, you know what Mandos are like. Light-fingered and dishonest, every last one of us."

Uthan found herself laughing. She thought he was joking for a moment, but even when she realized he wasn't, she still thought it was funny. Most criminals stole easily fenced, high-value objects, or trinkets that amused them. But this man stole entire *hospitals*. That took a certain panache.

"I make the population of Kyrimorut thirty at the moment, if you include the strill."

"And I do, Qail, I *do*. I don't care how many legs my patients have."

"So . . . I know we're a long way from decent medical facilities, a whole *sector* away in fact, but isn't your medical facility *excessive*?"

"Not if you need to handle any injury a clone trooper might arrive with."

"Skirata's serious about resettling deserters, then."

"Some of those lads are going to be pretty damaged. You know what happened to Fi. Well, look at him now."

"Temporary coma?"

"Brain-dead. I mean *really* brain-dead. They switched him off and he went on breathing, but his brain scan flatlined."

"You're sure about that?"

"Oh yes. Fi's our little miracle."

"Don't tell me you're a neurosurgeon. Either that, or you stole a neuromed droid."

"No, Doc Jedi to the rescue. *Bard'ika* put Fi back together again. Astonishing."

"So they're good for more than just being Republic stooges."

"Some are. Anyway, he's not a Jedi now. Never use the J word to him."

"They can switch it off, Jedi-ness, can they?"

"Are you mocking me, Dr. Uthan?"

"Why, the very thought, Dr. Gilamar . . ."

Uthan enjoyed the cut and thrust of conversation with a smart man. Gilamar spoke her jargon, understood her profession, and—despite that prizefighter's nose, or maybe because of it—she found him attractive company. The last thing she'd expected was *not* to want to kill every Mandalorian she met, given what had happened to her. Solitary confinement had changed her at a level she still didn't quite understand.

So I'm happy to mix with the scum of the galaxy. Is that it? But nobody's who I think they are these days.

Gilamar shrugged. "I don't know about other Jedi, except Kad's mother, may she rest in the *manda*, but Bardan left the Order before the war ended. He's got remarkable healing skills, very logical ones. He was influencing Fi's progesterone levels to repair brain tissue, for example. Quite extraordinary. And completely untrained."

Uthan dealt in the detectable and demonstrable, and she suspected Gilamar did, too. But everyone clutched at straws when science failed them. Perhaps some straws had more substance than she imagined.

"So, did you begin life as a Mandalorian, or did you join the club later?" she asked. "You all sound so different."

"Adult recruit. My late wife was Mandalorian. And I look great in armor." Gilamar's guard dropped just a fraction. "If you're asking why I ended up in the *Cuy'-val Dar* . . . some of my patients were the kind who got into big trouble and tended to spread it around. The good news is that Mandos need a lot of emergency medicine and first aid with no questions asked. The bad news is that I can't overcharge patients in some fancy Coruscant diet clinic."

"Imperial City."

"What?"

"Palpatine renamed Coruscant *Imperial City*. It was on the holonews."

"Nothing says *I am an insecure maggot* quite like renaming cities to reflect your own imagined importance."

"He never struck me as that—insecure, I mean. Maggot, yes." Uthan got up and switched on the holoreceiver. Skirata had made sure there were plenty of things to entertain her, at least. He wasn't a total brute. "When did you last watch the holonews?"

"I get headlines from the datapad. It's all garbage. It was garbage under the Republic, too. Nothing changes."

Uthan needed the news, garbage or not, because it was her only glimpse of her homeworld, even if it was filtered through the spin of a regime that treated it as a dangerous enemy. She hadn't been back home for years. She caught sight of her own reflection in the holoscreen, superimposed for a moment on the scenes of devastation on remote worlds like Nadhe, Cel Amiin, and Lanjer. All she saw was her failure to stop Palpatine's power grab when she'd had the chance. She'd been so close to perfecting the FG36 virus when Omega Squad had captured her that it hurt.

And they're here, aren't they? Fi and Atin, at least. Funny, now I have names for them. I can tell them apart. They have lives, wives, histories, plans for the future. Is all this their fault?

She didn't know. She was torn between seeing them as a threat she'd once tried to neutralize and young men who she knew, ate with, talked to. She watched the screen, feeling Gilamar's stare burning a hole in her, and waited for her world to appear on the list of planets that just didn't seem to understand that the Empire was their friend and only wanted the best for them.

"*Meanwhile, on Gibad, assembly leaders have refused to allow an Imperial diplomatic mission to land in Koliverin. After a four-week standoff, Gibadan forces are . . .*"

It didn't look like a diplomatic mission. It looked like an assault ship. And the troops in that ship would be exactly like the nice young men she'd just watched playing bolo-ball and pulling faces to amuse the baby son of one of their brothers.

Uthan lived by clarity, definitive answers, and—even in the still-uncertain world of genetics—predictable outcomes. Confusion and conflicted feelings weren't something she was used to. She didn't like it at all.

"You know what the final score's going to be," Gilamar said. "And there's nothing you can do to stop it. So you might find it easier to switch off the holoscreen for a week."

"You think it's that inevitable, do you?"

"Palps has to make it clear that nobody breaks away on his watch. Big show of force, start as you mean to go on, and all that *osik*."

"I just don't understand how the CIS caved in to the Republic when it had the upper hand, when it had Coruscant under attack—"

"Qail, there were never two sides in this war. Don't you get it? Palpatine was running both campaigns. He's a Sith, and he engineered the whole war to get rid of what stood in his way—the Jedi Order. Then he moved in his second army to consolidate the Empire."

"I didn't even know what a Sith was until I came here. If Mandalorians fought for them, why can't they defeat this one?"

"We fought against them, too, but that's the nature of the *beroya*'s job. You think *we'd* be any better off under the Jedi? Mandalore, I mean? It makes no difference to us. When it does—*then* we'll get involved. One thing we won't be doing is fighting an ideological war for *aruetiise* who'll spit on us the moment we win it for them, and blame us if we don't."

"That's how tyranny succeeds," Uthan said. "When folks think it won't affect them. Until it eventually *does*."

"Thank you for the tips on glorious rebellion and liberty. Me, I like clearer definitions of glory and freedom before I start a fight over them."

"The galaxy is entering the dark ages."

"Actually, most of the galaxy won't notice the difference. Some of it will even be better off. The average citizen just wants an excess of food on the table, something to watch on the holonet, and the freedom to indulge a few health-destroying habits. The individuals who'll feel aggrieved about all this are the aristocrats and politicians who lost power and want it back, the hobby revolutionaries, and the relatively few unlucky *shabuire* who have something the Empire wants and plans to take."

"I think you're in that group somewhere, you Mandos."

Gilamar just gave her a look that said he'd heard it all before. But for a moment, she wondered if she *could* do something to stop what would happen to Gibad. The question wasn't whether the Empire would subdue it by force, but how much damage it would do in the process.

The only thing she could do was perfect the FG36 virus, get it to her government, and then hope there was enough time to produce millions of vials of it. She'd also have to hope there was a way to distribute it not only across the surface of Gibad but throughout the galaxy to kill every clone soldier without a shot being fired.

She would also have to find a way to get from Mandalore to Gibad. Right now, she didn't even have a way of getting to Enceri.

She was too late. She'd been too late more than three years ago, and only just realized it.

"We'll be in the *karyai* this evening if you want to join us." Gilamar stood up to go. "Relax a bit. I know this project is urgent, but you're no use to us dead."

"Ah, Mando concern." Uthan didn't want to take it out on Gilamar. None of this was his doing. They were all in this mess together, and she was looking for reasons to like him. "The *karyai* is the big central living room, yes?"

"It is. We might get a little emotional when someone

talks about Etain, but generally we plan to laugh. The dead don't like us moping around."

He leaned over and switched off the holoreceiver, smiled sadly at her, then shut the lab doors behind him. Uthan was left staring at her reflection in the dead screen, suddenly feeling worn out and useless. Her black hair was still in the meticulously groomed style she'd worn for years, pulled tight behind her ears in a pleat and highlighted with brilliant scarlet streaks. She didn't want to be that Uthan any longer. She wouldn't be able to maintain the complex color anyway, not here. Mandos didn't seem to go in for hair fashions.

Perhaps it was frustration, or anger that had no safe outlet. It might just have been pragmatism. Whatever sparked it, she'd made up her mind. She unpinned her hair, reached for the lab shears, and began cutting.

Change was coming. She preferred to go and meet it.

6

Beskar is a uniquely resistant iron that develops a wide range of properties—and colors—in the hands of skilled metalsmiths. Depending on the alloy, it can take any form from plate, laminate, and wire to foam, mesh, micronized particles, and even a transparent film. Mandalorians jealously guard their beskar-working skills and refuse to sell the formulas for any price; attempts to reproduce finished beskar elsewhere have been disappointing. The ore is found solely on Mandalore, and only Mandalorians know how to work it to maximize its extraordinary properties. Therefore if you want beskar, you must take Mandalore. But that inevitably proves easier to say than to do.
—From *Strategic Resources of the Galaxy,* by Pilas Manaitis

Main living room, Kyrimorut

Only a Mando would create a musical instrument that doubled as a weapon.

Wad'e Tay'haai had shown up with his *bes'bev,* an ancient flute made out of *beskar,* playing tunes that Jusik didn't recognize. He thought he didn't, anyway. It was only when he tried to hum them to himself that he realized what they were. The marching song "Vode An"— learned by all clone troopers bred on Kamino, the only *Mando'a* language that most of them ever heard— sounded totally different played as a lament.

Tay'haai held out the flute to Jusik. It was painted a deep violet, like the man's *beskar'gam*. "Want a go?"

"I'm not musical." Jusik took it anyway, held it as Tay'haai demonstrated, and blew across the lip plate. The *bes'bev* remained stubbornly silent. When he balanced it in his hand, it had a pleasant heft to it. "So you can use this as a club. Which is probably the only use I'd get out of it."

"It's made for stabbing." Tay'haai ran his fingertip along the end to indicate the diagonal cut, like a quill stylus. "Bleeds out someone very efficiently."

"Why have a flute that's a weapon?"

"Maybe we just don't like music critics."

Tay'haai began playing again, and Mird didn't so much as howl along with the music as whine to it. Astonishingly, the strill managed to hit at least half the notes, sounding like a drunk who couldn't remember the words but was doing his best to join in. A'den only made matters worse by howling along, too, which drove Mird into an operatic frenzy. It was the first time Jusik had ever seen Vau laugh uncontrollably.

If only . . .

The *karyai* was almost full to capacity this evening; Cov and his three brothers from Yayax Squad were demonstrating—with Levet—how they'd learned to plow a field. The joy of simple achievement radiated from them. Rav Bralor—Parja's aunt, another member of Jango Fett's *Cuy'val Dar*—showed up with a crate of her special throat-searing *tihaar*. She'd trained the Yayax Squad back on Kamino, and they seemed to spend as much time at her clan's farm a few kilometers away as they did at Kyrimorut.

She's like Kal'buir. *She treats them like her own kids.*

Jusik, pleasantly tired from an afternoon of *meshgeroya*, full of food, and slightly numbed by black ale, felt that he could sink into the sense of well-being contained in that room like a deep mattress.

If only . . . Etain could see this now.

Beneath the vague sense of celebration, though, Jusik

could sense the absence of Dar and Niner nagging at everyone. They should have been here making plans for the coming year about what to grow on the farm and how the various business interests would be run.

And Dar should have been here for his son.

Kad played with Laseema on the floor, retrieving toy animals that Atin had carved out of veshok. Laseema named the animal—nerf, bantha, *shatual,* nuna, jackrab, *vhe'viin*—and Kad had to go pick out the right toy. Jusik watched, fascinated both by how fast Kad learned words, and by what a great mother Laseema was turning out to be. Atin joined them. As the three of them played, they looked like a perfect family, and Jusik sensed the slight sadness when Laseema caught Atin's eye.

A human and a Twi'lek couldn't have children. That didn't matter to a Mando, of course, and adoption was common for all kinds of reasons, but it obviously mattered to Twi'leks—even those who'd joined the clan. Laseema had raised Kad while Etain was away; the kid still ran to her like a mother. Jusik would have given anything right then to see Atin and Laseema with a baby of their own, but there was nothing whatsoever he could do about it, and in this isolated place, in hiding from the world, where could they find a child who needed a home?

Skirata sat down beside Jusik on the cushions. "Well, this is fun, *Bard'ika.* All this talk of grain yields and nerf calves makes me positively giddy with excitement."

"Levet's taking it very seriously. The fewer supplies we buy in, the less traceable we are."

"So is everyone happy? As happy as they can be, anyway."

"You really want to know?" Jusik asked.

Skirata could read moods pretty well, especially within his family. He didn't really need Jusik to sense things for him. Perhaps he was opening up the conversation to tackle something else. "Tell me."

Jusik took a breath. "Ordo's a little wary of Ruu.

She's trying hard to fit in, but feels lost. Scout's scared of clones—all of them. Jilka's scared and confused, but Corr makes her feel better. Besany worries about everything. Ny is . . . Ny likes you."

"I need to get Ordo and Ruu sorted out, don't I?" Skirata looked weary again, and didn't seem to take any notice of the comment about Ny. "Is he worried she's going to rob me or something?"

"Even adults feel disoriented when a new sibling shows up—not just children."

"Ordo, jealous? Never. Six brothers, and not one of them ever showed any signs of jealousy."

"I think it's his compulsion to protect you."

"I'm not much of a father if I can't make my kids feel secure, am I?"

"You're a terrific father. It's just been a very traumatic time. Not even Ordo's immune to that."

"No, I'm not a good *buir,* because I make decisions for my *aliit* without asking their opinion," Skirata said. "*Bard'ika,* I owe you an apology. I made a decision for you. I shouldn't have."

"It can't have been that bad," Jusik said. "But tell me anyway."

"I turned down an offer to put you out to stud."

Jusik burst out laughing. "But I'd sire winners, *Kal'buir.* We'd make a fortune."

"I wish it was a joke. Shysa got an idea into his head that *Mando'ade* would benefit from your abilities. He even mentioned a genetic line."

"I suppose I'm the worst-kept secret on Mandalore."

"Sull's probably told him all about you."

"Does Shysa realize midi-chlorians show up when they feel like it? And even if we *could* breed for it, it'd take—wow, *centuries* to populate the place with Force-users. And—"

"Yes, *yes,* he does. I told him so. And that it was un-Mandalorian anyway."

Jusik was speechless for a moment. He'd never seen himself as a strategic resource. He *wasn't*: he was only one Force-user, and one against an army of millions was useless. But he understood what Shysa had been thinking, and why, and suddenly he felt guilty. He had a duty to his adopted people.

"Put your trust in trained troops and reliable weapons, because an army of better Force-users than me couldn't take Palpatine," Jusik said. He could feel the doubt radiating from Skirata. "But if you want me to step up, *Kal'buir*, just say."

"Yeah, that's exactly what I thought you'd say."

"And you feel guilty for saying no."

"Got it in one. Shysa's recruiting. You and the boys have enough of a struggle ahead without getting into a new war. Am I a bad *Mando'ad* for saying so?"

Jusik tried to lighten the mood. He had a duty, all right, but he'd think of better ways to fulfill it that wouldn't upset Skirata.

"Never," he said. "And for all Shysa knows, Mandalore's full of Force-sensitives anyway, but they don't know it. They'll just seem unusually athletic, or perceptive, or lucky. If the Jedi hadn't signed me, I'd probably be a professional gambler or sports star now."

Skirata looked grim for a moment. Then his face split into a wide grin and he ruffled Jusik's hair. "It's never too late. Break out the pazaak cards."

"Never play cards with Force-users."

"I like a challenge." Skirata looked up. "Scout? Kina Ha? Can you play pazaak?"

It was an unusual peace gesture for Skirata. He seemed to be bending over backward to treat the ancient Jedi as a guest. Jusik felt Skirata's painful memories of Kamino and the resentment on behalf of his clones crashing up against a strange sense of bewilderment, as if he still didn't know where Kina Ha fitted into all this.

"Why do you care if the Jedi are happy?" Jusik asked.

"They're going to be here for a long time, and I don't want to turn this into a prison camp. It's not good for anyone. And we've never been much interested in taking prisoners."

Jusik considered what *no prisoners* actually meant. It was pretty final. "And she's not like the aiwha-bait you knew, right?"

Skirata got to his feet and set up a small card table. "She had nothing to do with the Tipoca government or the cloning program."

"You don't have to feel guilty, *Kal'buir.*"

"Who said I did?"

"You feel you're going soft on Kaminoans, and that it's letting the clones down."

"Maybe I'm just asking myself if I am."

"We should judge others by what they do, not by what they are. That's the Mandalorian way. You taught me that."

Skirata pulled up seats as the Jedi joined them, and laid the pack of cards on the table.

"Usually," he said.

Scout obviously disturbed him, and she seemed to know it. She kept looking at Jusik in a mute plea for explanation, but that would have to wait. She knew about Etain. That was explanation enough. She didn't need to know that Skirata was in constant torment about the way he believed he'd treated her.

"Do you know exactly where you are?" Skirata asked, not looking up from his cards.

"A long way from anywhere," Scout said.

Jusik knew why he was asking. If they could pinpoint Kyrimorut precisely, then they were a security risk if they ever left. Everyone had known that from the start. It was just one of the things that had to take second place to getting a look at Kina Ha's genome.

But anyone could guess that Skirata had fled to Mandalore. It was just a big, wild planet to search, and the natives kept their mouths shut. That bought time.

Kina Ha checked her cards with an expression of baffled amusement, then peered at the hand Skirata had laid down.

"I do believe I've lost, Master Skirata," she said. "So you see that Jedi are neither omniscient nor invincible."

Scout laid down her hand. "Count me in the vincible camp, too."

Skirata looked at Jusik and tapped on the cards. "Can you beat those?"

"No," Jusik said. "See? You don't need midi-chlorians."

Gilamar wandered over. "Never play for creds with Kal," he said to Scout. "Want me to show you how to beat him, kid?"

"Are you getting me into bad ways?" she asked.

"No point coming to Mandalore if you don't pick up a few useful vices. Think of it as survival training."

Kad was asleep on Laseema's lap. Skirata got up and let Gilamar have his seat. "Time to put *Kad'ika* to bed," he said. "I don't think I'll have to tell him a story this time."

Maybe Skirata had had all he could take of diplomacy for the evening. Jusik stayed to play a few more hands of pazaak. Scout seemed a lot more relaxed with Gilamar than with *Kal'buir*.

"You don't know what to do with us, do you?" she said. "You don't know how long we'll have to stay here, or if there's going to be anywhere else safe for us."

"That's about the size of it." Gilamar picked a card from the top of the pack and grimaced. "But we're not going to kill you, if that's what you're worried about."

"Even in these terrible times," Kina Ha said, "it gives me hope when beings like us, who should be at one another's throats, can sit down, cheat at cards, and unite against a common threat."

"I'm not cheating," Jusik said.

"But *I* am," said Kina Ha.

Jusik didn't ask her to define *unite*, but he was pretty sure that Skirata didn't see it that way. He was simply suppressing his prejudices, which was as much as anyone could be expected to do. You felt what you felt. There was no conscious will involved in hatred, or in love come to that; it couldn't be taught, unlearned, or reasoned with. Only the visible reactions that sprang from it could be changed. Skirata would never love Kaminoans, or see the Jedi as anything but a trouble-making sect like the Sith, but he'd decided not to take a blaster to them.

And Scout couldn't help being scared of clones after what happened on the night of Order 66. She'd just have to stop feeling and start thinking.

The game broke up around midnight, and eventually only Gilamar, Jusik, and the Nulls were left in the *karyai*. Skirata wandered back to join them again. The season had started to change that day, and now Jusik had the feeling that everyone at Kyrimorut had reached a watershed, too.

"They'll always be a risk, you know that, don't you?" Gilamar said. "They might not have the coordinates of this place on a holochart, but any competent Jedi could find us again."

"Yes, I know," Skirata said. "But I had to do it any-way."

"Then we need to have a plan for relocating this whole setup at a moment's notice," Jusik said. "Just in case."

Skirata smiled indulgently. "*Ret'lini.* Yes, we have to be ready for *ba'slan shev'la.*"

Mandalorians were good at that—strategic disappear-ance. They could scatter and vanish at a moment's no-tice, Vau had told Jusik, leaving no trace, to regroup later and strike back. It was like trying to crush mercury, he said. You could smash it as hard as you liked, but it would only disperse in a mass of droplets to coalesce again later, all shiny and renewed, as if nothing had hap-pened. It couldn't be broken. Jusik rather liked that, be-cause it reassured him that nobody could ever wipe out *Mando'ade.* Many had tried. They'd all failed.

Skirata's comlink chirped. He checked the display, frowned slightly, and answered it. Jusik sensed his mood change even before he saw the expression on his face set-tle into dismay.

"Where are you?" Skirata put one hand slowly over

his eyes as if he was shielding them from the light, trying
to concentrate. He didn't seem to be talking to anyone,
but his lips were moving slightly as if he was repeating a
chant or trying to make sense of something. Eventually,
he hit one of the keys as if he was cutting short a transmission. The lost, wistful look that had been there for
the last few days had left him, and he was the old
Kal'buir again: focused, alert, a fire blazing within.
Ordo moved in immediately, always the first to go to
Skirata if he thought there was something wrong.

"So what was that, *Buir*?" he asked.

"Someone worried enough to send me a one-way message in *dadita*." Skirata got up. "And how many *aruetiise* know that?"

It was an ancient code system of long and short tones
that spelled out words or numbers, transmitted by just
about anything that came to hand, from banging on a
metal hull to flashing a lamp. It was so low tech, so ob-
solete, and so peculiarly Mandalorian that few if any
outsiders even knew it existed.

"Jaller Obrim," Mereel said.

"Got it in one." Skirata scribbled something on his
forearm plate. Even when he took off the rest of his
armor, he still wore the plate to keep his comm and
recording devices close to hand. "He says Niner got a
computer chip that he can't read, but it could expose
us."

"Time I called Gaib and Teekay-O," Mereel said. "In
fact, time we pulled our brothers out, whatever's keeping them there."

Special Operations Unit barracks, 501st Legion HQ, Imperial City

Niner now knew what it felt like to walk around with a
live grenade in his pocket.

When Captain Obrim had pressed the salvaged datachip into his palm as they shook hands, he knew the

thing was vital and dangerous. He also knew that he had to keep it to himself, and in the tight-knit world of the squad, that was hard.

It was harder still now that Bry's replacement had been picked. He wasn't a former Republic commando, or even a white job like Corr. He was one of the new clones, the ones grown on Centax 2 in a year by Spaarti process from second-generation Fett genetic material.

Niner couldn't imagine how anyone like that could handle special operations. The Spaarti stormtrooper couldn't possibly assimilate all the training he needed— the *real* stuff, the hands-on stuff—in less than a year. *Shab,* that wasn't even enough time to learn the classroom component, or anything about the outside world. Flash learning was standard on Kamino, but it still took time. That poor little *shabuir* must have had his head pumped full of basic propaganda and all kinds of shallow, undemanding *osik*. Not training, not education: indoctrination.

It would make him a dangerously weak link.

His name was Rede. Niner wasn't sure if that was a name he'd chosen, been given at birth, or had pinned on him instead of a number so that he'd fit in better with the Tipoca-raised clones. They'd find out soon enough.

"We've got plenty of experienced commandos," Darman said. "If they wanted to backfill posts, then a regular Five-oh-first trooper could be cross-trained. But not a *Spaarti* clone."

"It's just an experiment to see how they cope."

"When we've got our hands full with real missions. Great."

"Can you think of a better time to test a guy?"

"Ennen's pretty hacked off about it."

Niner searched for clues to Darman's state of mind today. "He just misses Bry."

"Seriously—what do *you* expect from a Spaarti job?"

"Probably the same as mongrels expect from us. And just as wrong."

Dar grunted, but didn't seem convinced. "Okay. Point taken."

Niner tried to treat Dar gently these days. Sometimes the old sergeant habits got the better of him and it turned into a rebuke he didn't intend. He watched Dar cleaning his rifle, its parts spread out neatly on the table, and pondered on two things: exactly what information the datachip contained, and how he would get it to Jaing or Mereel. He understood where his loyalties lay. He wasn't any more anti-Empire than he'd been anti-Republic, or even anti-Separatist, because the politics were meaningless to him. He had no stake in whatever any of those regimes wanted to do with the galaxy. All he had was his brothers, one of them here and badly in need of his care, the others light-years away in a place he hadn't even seen and couldn't locate on a chart.

But the stormtroopers around Niner, even former Republic commandos like Ennen, were almost *aruetiise* in the most benign sense: *not us*. While he watched Darman reassembling his Deece, he wondered why he hadn't bonded with them as easily as he'd expected. They were all soldiers, just like him. They faced the same threats, and looked out for one another in the same way, but somehow Niner didn't feel at home or safe here. It was the most corroding thought he'd ever had. He could almost understand the gulf between him and the regular stormtroopers, the clones raised in a brief year by Spaarti methods and who had never seen Kamino, but men like Ennen—and poor old Bry—were still his comrades. They'd all been hatched at the same time in Tipoca City. Even though they'd been trained by different sergeants—not Mandalorians, but *Cuy'val Dar* nonetheless—they still should have felt like *brothers*.

It wasn't about them. It was about himself, and he knew it. It was the first time that he'd started to realize that Darman wasn't the only one succumbing to stress.

And I was the one who thought desertion was a bad idea. I was, wasn't I? The others had to talk me into it.

Darman looked up at him as he calibrated the rifle's optics. "What's wrong with you?"

"You really want to know?"

"That's why I'm asking, *ner vod*. You're not yourself."

"I was thinking the same thing about you."

Darman just looked at him for a moment, staring past him as if there was something far more interesting on the wall of their quarters.

"I'm fine," Darman said. "I can keep going like this."

For a moment, Niner saw another glimpse of self-awareness there. Darman knew he was a mess. He was lying to himself, playing a mind game simply to put one foot in front of the other enough times each day to function. Medication would have been more effective, but how did he report sick in this army, and how the *shab* did he explain why he felt the way he did?

It's like this, Doc, I was having an illicit relationship with a Jedi general, and she had a baby and never told me until a year or so later, and then we tried to desert and she got killed by another Jedi, and I can't see my son anymore, so all in all, Doc—I'm not feeling so great.

Yes, the Imperial Army would understand perfectly. Vader would give Darman a month's leave, and the Emperor would send him a nice box of candies to show his concern.

Right.

"You're not fine," Niner said. "But I'm here, and I'll keep an eye on you. Okay?"

Darman blinked a few times. "I'm going to the gym. Maybe we ought to get Ennen along, too, and Rede. Why don't we mix with the others?"

"Because we're not very sociable," Niner said.

Because we're not planning on staying. That's why I don't feel part of this army. I switched off, and I can't switch back on again.

"Do you still . . . want to go?" Niner asked carefully.

"Go where?" Darman said.

Niner imagined bugging devices everywhere. Sometimes that seemed ludicrous—who would suspect clones of disloyalty?—and sometimes it made perfect sense, be-cause the rest of his squad, his training sergeant, and the ARC troopers he'd served with were all on the death list. If the Empire was looking for deserters, where better to start than by waiting for their closest friends to make a slip?

"The gym," Niner said. "I meant the gym."

Darman gave him a blank look. "I'm going. It'll do you good to go, too. Come on."

Niner had always been too busy fighting to worry about keeping fit. Running for his life and hauling a heavy pack was all the exercise he needed. But now that his duties were less active—physically, at least—he had to make an effort. He changed into his shorts, tucking the datachip carefully in a sealed pocket, and left his armor stacked neatly on his bunk as if ready for kit in-spection. But Darman shut his armor in his locker and secured it. Niner wondered if he'd kept some incriminat-ing keepsake of Etain, like a letter or something.

That could get both of them killed.

What had Darman done about the data stored in his old helmet? He'd proposed to Etain via the messaging system, and she'd accepted the same way. He never saw her alive again after that, except for the short minutes on the bridge before she was killed, just meters and sec-onds away from escaping with him. It still seemed mas-sively cruel—newly wed, unable even to touch before they were separated forever.

He must have had the sense to erase anything stored in the helmet's memory. Dar's thorough. If he hadn't, we'd be in big trouble now, wouldn't we?

Niner realized that he was behind enemy lines. Sud-denly, life seemed simpler.

Fine. I'm trained for that. I can handle it.

He played pairs-slingball with Darman, smashing the ball against the wall as hard as he could and not even thinking about the score. A game that intense took his mind off everything except the fast-moving, rock-hard ball that gave him no time to think. It purged all the pent-up anger and frustration from anyone's system. Nobody interrupted a game like that. That was the plan; Niner had seen Darman lose it with Skirata once, and if he could take a swing at a man who would have done anything for him, his adoptive father, then he would do a lot worse to some hapless stormtrooper who rubbed him up the wrong way in a game.

The less attention Dar drew, the better.

Niner couldn't return half of Darman's shots. The ball was coming back off the wall like a missile. Sweat stung his eyes, and Darman collided with him a couple of times without even seeming to notice. Eventually Niner slowed to a standstill and bent over with his hands on his knees, catching his breath.

"Good game," Darman panted. Sweat dripped off his nose. "Want another?"

"I'm done. I'm going to clean up."

This was where things started to get complicated. Niner had to keep the datachip on him at all times, and when it came to using the 'freshers, that wasn't easy. He didn't dare leave the thing in his locker. The chip was about three centimeters square, wafer-thin, so he racked his brains for all the places he could hide the chip while showering. The choices weren't fun. He opted for wrapping the chip in a layer of waterproof plastoid and tucking it inside his cheek.

Just don't swallow it. That would be . . . awkward.

It still took a conjuror's dexterity to slide the chip from his shorts and then find a private moment in the communal changing room to slip the thing in his mouth before taking his clothes off. He was lucky that the chip was too thin to create a telltale bulge in his cheek and make him look like a foraging profogg. All he needed now was to avoid getting into a conversation. Concentrating on the tiled wall was the best way to do that.

Darman switched on the spray head next to him.

"I don't know when I'm going to be Dar again." He seemed to be having another lucid moment, able to stand back and see that he wasn't quite right. "I'm sorry, *ner vod.*"

"It's okay," Niner mumbled. He felt like an idiot with the chip lodged in his mouth. "You don't have to explain yourself to me."

Niner dressed, hid the chip in his pants again, and went back to the room to do his laundry. He found the doors open and his helmet missing. For a moment he was ready to go find Ennen to tell him exactly what he'd do to him if they tried to pull some stupid stunt with his bucket, but as he checked the other lockers, he heard the rattle of a droid in the corridor.

A tech droid with a polished dome and a cylindrical body, like a taller version of an R2 astromech unit, rolled into the room carrying Niner's helmet in both arms. He knew it was his. He recognized the scrapes and charring on the cheek piece.

"Servicing complete." The droid placed the helmet back on Niner's bunk in exactly the position where he'd left it. "But I've been unable to service your colleague IC-one-one-three-six's helmet. It wasn't left for collection. Have a pleasant day."

The droid spun 180 degrees to leave, but Niner tapped it on its dome. It turned back to him with a slight pause. He could have sworn it was exasperated.

"Yes, IC-one-three-zero-nine?"

"I didn't ask for helmet repair."

"I know. This is routine maintenance under contract. A number of helmets have developed comm problems due to component failure. I suggest you test the audio systems at your earliest convenience and report back to Equipment Maintenance if problems persist. Is there anything else I can help you with?"

Niner hadn't had any problems with his bucket. He didn't like it much, but that wasn't going to be solved by servicing, and there was no point arguing with a droid.

"That's all, thanks," he said.

"How nice to receive courtesy from a *wet*," the droid said, and left.

Skirata had brought up his young commandos to say please and thank you, even to Kaminoans and droids. Niner still found it funny to hear a tinnie call him a *wet*, though.

But now he was alone. He'd been waiting for relative privacy to examine the datachip again, and this was as good a time as any. He removed the transmitter unit from his datapad to make sure that anything he viewed wouldn't end up being relayed to prying eyes. Then he sat on the bunk and hunched over the datapad so any hidden surveillance cam wouldn't see what showed on the screen.

Well, until I know this place isn't bugged—I'll assume the worst. Enemy lines, remember.

When he slid the chip into the port on his datapad, the device told him that it was empty. For a moment he wondered if Obrim had slipped him some other chip, but nothing was precisely what he should have expected to see. Only Jaing could coax information from the chip. But he had no idea yet how to contact him, and in the new army, he couldn't just put in a comm call to Mandalore or cadge a ride with some unit heading for the Hydian Way.

Shab. If he messed around with the chip too much, he might end up corrupting the data. After a few minutes staring pointlessly at an empty dialogue box, he gave up and hid the chip carefully again.

There has to be a way to do this. Whatever's on here matters to Kal'buir and my brothers. Obrim wouldn't have taken a risk like this if it wasn't crucial.

Niner checked his helmet, working out how he would locate Jaing if he could reach the Mandalore sector—just theory, mind, not a plan at all. He flipped the helmet over in his hands and looked at the tight-packed interior, every space lined and studded with suit environment sensors, displays, and interfaces. When he lifted it and inhaled, he could smell unfamiliar scents: the incense-like perfume of solder, a faint whiff of cleaning fluid on the mike and earpiece adapter, and something else he couldn't identify. Singed plastoid, perhaps.

There was only one way to fully test a helmet, and that was to suit up and close all the seals to make the armor soundproof. He dressed, distracted by the thought that Dar knew that he was behaving oddly, and imagined how scared that made him. It was bad enough to grieve. It had to be even worse to watch yourself coming apart at the seams as well.

As soon as Niner closed the neck seal, he was back in his own one-man world of silence and perfectly controlled temperature and humidity. He blinked to activate the HUD and sound systems, selecting the diagnostic icon to test that everything was working. The ambient sound of the room flooded in, then the calibration tone, and lines of readouts cascaded down the HUD like an overlay on the world around him.

Fine. Working just fine.

He commed Control to check his mike, and got confirmation from a droid that it could hear him perfectly.

What do I do now?

Imperial Command wasn't as free and easy as the Grand Army's special forces setup. There was no way of vanishing for a few days on a whim if a target looked promising. There was no *Kal'buir* to cover for them while they did as they pleased, or an indulgent General Jusik to task them as he saw fit.

Or Etain. Poor Etain.

How the *shab* could he get a chance to go to Mandalore? How much more could he ask of Jaller Obrim? The man would be watched as closely as anyone. One thing was clear to Niner, even if he didn't care about politics: in the new galactic order, Palpatine was checking who was with him and who was not.

"*Ner vod . . .*"

Niner turned, expecting to see Darman, but he was still alone in the room. He adjusted his audio, cycling through comm frequencies and picking up channels he didn't know he could access. They were all Imperial military channels. He was entitled to use some of them, being special forces, but he hadn't been able to get this many before. The droid had screwed up.

And now he kept hearing a voice.

Niner couldn't make out the words, but it was definitely a man's voice, very faint, very broken up, buried in radio interference when he switched comm channels. He wondered if he'd picked up a holonet transmission or even a taxi frequency. Then the voice came in loud and clear.

"Niner, *ner vod*," it said. "You didn't think some *osik'la* Imperial encryption could keep us out forever, did you?"

The voice almost made him lose control of all sphincters. It wasn't Darman who was going crazy. It was him. He didn't dare reply. He activated the signal locator in his HUD, but it told him the transmission was coming from inside the barracks, and he didn't believe that for one minute. He knew that voice. He was just too scared to say the name, in case it was a setup, and he was wrong—fatally, finally wrong.

"Niner, cut the *osik* and respond," the voice said sharply. "Can you hear me?"

"Identify yourself," Niner whispered.

"The galaxy's gift to women. The best data slicer this side of . . . well, anywhere. Financial genius and all-around modest *ori'beskaryc vod*. Jaing Skirata. Who'd you think it was—Mereel?"

"You wish . . . ," said Mereel's voice.

"*Shab*," Niner whispered. Was he hallucinating? He answered anyway "They'll pick you up and trace you. *Shut up*."

"You always were a worry-guts, Niner. Trust Teekay-O. He's done a lovely job on your comms. I await his invoice with interest."

"The droid."

"Inorganic colleague, please." Jaing sounded chipper. Niner was relieved that he wasn't hallucinating, but now he had an extra risk to worry about. "Niner—

you're coming home. And I hear you have something for me . . ."

Kyrimorut, Mandalore

"Who's for more eggs?" Corr yelled over the hubbub. He'd volunteered for kitchen detail with Ny this week, probably to impress Jilka, and Ordo decided it was working. She watched Corr when she thought he wasn't looking. "Make the most of these. The nuna can't keep up with you greedy *shab'ikase*. It'll be boiled mealgrain until they start laying again."

"But we're trillionaires," Fi said. "How come we've got an egg crisis? We should be brushing our teeth with Daruvvian champagne."

"It's all Levet's fault. He's not farming fast enough."

Levet looked up from his plate. "I'm only halfway through the livestock manual. I'm still on chapter ten— nerf husbandry."

"You know there's a law against that, don't you?" Fi said. "Hurry up start on the chapter about roba. I like smoked roba."

"Let's admit temporary defeat and ship in extra eggs for the time being," Levet said. "We can glory in our gritty self-sufficiency later."

Ordo watched Uthan and Ny with interest. Neither woman was aware—as far as he knew—that Fi wasn't joking about being worth trillions. Ordo wasn't sure that Ruu knew or understood the details, either. Uthan definitely seemed to be taking it as a joke. He wondered how they'd react if they knew just how much wealth the clan was sitting on.

But creds didn't solve every problem.

Skirata tapped the end of his fork on the table. "Okay, *ad'ike*, what's the drill today?"

"We're tracking Niner via his helmet systems," Jaing said. "So we rendezvous with Gaib and Teekay-O off Coruscant, they supply us with ordinary stormtrooper armor, we swap out the electronics, land in Imperial City or whatever it's called this week, pick up Niner and Darman, and bang out."

"Just like that," Fi said. "Can I come?"

"Nulls only," Mereel said. "And before anyone else asks—no. It's going to be just us and Ny, because her ship's been passed and inspected at Imperial checkpoints."

"We never needed to worry about that before," Atin muttered. "Bogus transponder signal. Don't leave the barracks without one."

"But it's a one-shot trick. We might want to drop in again. First rule—don't make things any more complicated than you need to."

Ny watched the discussion with her arms folded, lips pursed in apparent disapproval. Ordo thought she was the perfect cover. She was used to contraband runs—and, *Kal'buir* said, after a certain age women were invisible, just like clones. She was the wrong gender and the wrong age to look like a gang courier. Females who did that kind of work were expected to be young and dangerous looking, because most beings watched too many holovids with glamorous actresses playing blaster-toting heroines, and so they believed that was how things were in the real world. Men like Jaller Obrim weren't fooled that easily. But the galaxy wasn't full of men like him. It was full of fools.

Ordo thought of mentioning that by way of explanation, but he knew Ny wouldn't appreciate the candor.

"Okay, I'm up for it," Ny said. "Shall we pick up some eggs at the store on the way back?"

It was hard to tell if she was joking, deadly serious, or scathing. Her expression seldom changed. She rarely looked happy, but sometimes she smiled—at *Kal'buir,* at Fi, at Kad—and became a different person. Ordo held out hope that she would stop sleeping in her ship as if she was on a cargo stopover, and accept that this could be her home, too.

"Okay, let's do it," Skirata said. He bounced Kad on his knee. "This boy needs his *buir*."

"And I really will stock up on supplies," Ny said. "Get your grocery list together, folks. No point wasting fuel. Might as well make the best use of it."

Skirata fumbled in his belt. Kad tried to help him find what he was looking for. "How many creds, *Kad'ika*?" Skirata asked, laying cash chips on the table. "Tell me, then give them to Ny."

Kad studied the chips. "Lots. Five." That was as high as he could count. "Six?"

"Clever boy, close enough," Skirata said. It was a lot more than that. "Now, what's special about them?"

Kad looked up into Skirata's face for a prompt, then shook his head.

"If you spend these, nobody knows who you are," Skirata said, holding one up. "You can spend them in secret. Nobody knows where you live or what you've bought." Skirata turned the chip over to show Kad the holoimage on the back. "That's important, *Kad'ika*, because there are bad people out there who want to find us and hurt us. That's why we use these, so they can't."

Kad looked as if he understood, but then he always did. He nodded gravely.

"Now give them to Ny."

Kad slid off Skirata's lap and delivered the chips. Ny took them with a show of mock formality, suddenly the other Ny again, and gave Kad a cuddle while she counted the credits.

She lowered her voice. "Kal, that's a little excessive for groceries."

"It's for fuel and parts, too." Skirata shrugged. "You can't keep thrashing that old crate around the galaxy on your own budget. And you brought supplies this time."

"It's not necessary. I eat your food, so I pay my way."

"Ny," Skirata said, "let's you and me go for a walk, shall we? There's something you need to know."

He gave Ordo a meaningful look as he ushered her out of the room. So he was going to tell her what she'd walked into, then, as if volunteering for Palpatine's hit list wasn't crazy enough. She was another passerby sucked into the vortex of *Kal'buir*'s grand plan who had to leave her life behind. Nobody escaped unscathed. Even Parja's engineering business was now a sideline. She spent most of her time servicing the vessels and equipment at Kyrimorut.

Uthan turned to Ordo. "Kad's just a baby. Is it right to teach him that the galaxy's full of beings out to get him? He'll grow up paranoid."

"He's the son of a Jedi and a commercially valuable clone, his family are deserters and enemies of the Empire, and there's an occupation force on his home-world," Ordo said. "How would *you* describe the world to him?"

"Do you see the Keldabe garrison as an occupying army?"

"You would, if this was Gibad."

"But your leader let them come here and rent land."

"We're in no shape to fight that big an army. If Shysa had told them to get lost, you know what would have happened next. Better to watch and wait. Build our strength."

"And steal their kit," Gilamar said. "Just a little. Here and there."

Uthan should have known better than anyone what it meant to cross Palpatine. There was no holoreceiver in the *karyai,* because Skirata felt it stifled conversation— and carousing—but Ordo knew that as soon as break-fast was over, Uthan would retreat to her laboratory and switch on the news to see what was happening to her homeworld. Gibad didn't have a history like the Man-dalorians'. They hadn't learned to live with war and fight a hundred different ways.

Gibad was going to be brought into line as an exam-ple to anyone else thinking of arguing with the new management. It was only a matter of time, and that time depended on what worked best for Palpatine. The assault wasn't being delayed to allow negotiations to take place.

"You always play the long game, you Mandos," Uthan said.

Gilamar smiled. "It's cheaper in the long run. Your hair looks great, by the way. Very lower-levels street gang."

"Flattery *is* effective, Mij." She put a self-conscious hand to her head. "But you'll have to work harder on your analogies."

Now that Skirata had left the table, everyone else took it as a cue to go as well—except Ruu. Ordo wondered why he couldn't immediately accept her as a sister, another *vod* like his brothers. She was *Kal'buir*'s flesh and blood, wasn't she? How could he *not* find some kinship with her, then, some common bond?

Besany leaned over him as she cleared the table. "Sweetheart," she whispered, although the clattering plates made it hard to hear her anyway. "I nearly acquired a stepsister once. Hated her guts on sight. It takes effort and time."

Ordo couldn't imagine Besany hating anyone, not until he recalled how fast she bonded with this clan. For an apparently rational woman, her emotional reactions were powerful and instant. *"Nearly?"*

"Dad didn't marry her mother. Thankfully."

"So you didn't stop hating her guts."

"No, but I only mildly resented them in the end."

"Uplifting thought, *cyar'ika.*"

"Keep on thinking it."

Ordo wondered why nobody wanted to extend that same tolerance to Skirata's sons, the ones who had formally disowned him, but Ruu—Ruu had constructed an entirely different image of her absent father in those years. Ordo could see it on her face. She seemed to be permanently awed by *Kal'buir*, as if he fully measured up to the hero she'd expected him to be.

Boils were there to be lanced, Mereel always said.

Ordo prepared to trade a few painful seconds for long-term comfort.

"So, Ruu, is *Kal'buir* as you remembered him?"

"Pretty well. I thought he was taller, I admit." She gave Ordo a careful smile, as if she were being interviewed for a job and wanted to make a good impression. "But everything else—yes, I remember the gold armor and how he was always going off to war, or coming back from one with all these weird and exciting gifts. A real warrior, like in the holovids. I always thought he wasn't afraid of anything or anybody, and how *dashing* he was."

Prudii laughed. He was like Mereel and Jaing in many ways, comfortable with everybody and happy to joke and gossip. "Actually, that's a pretty accurate description," he said. "Short people can be dashing, too. So no disappointments?"

"I always told myself he'd come back for me," she said. "And he did. How can I be disappointed?"

Ruu was in her midthirties. Ordo wondered why she hadn't got on with her life and had a family of her own, but he understood that powerful sense of salvation that Skirata could instill in anyone just by showing up. He saved people. He'd certainly saved Ordo and his brothers, and yes—he *had* been both dashing and unafraid, holostar-style, when he did it. But Ordo wondered if Ruu realized he *un*-saved people, too, for bounties, payments in kind, and even revenge. He didn't want to see that adulation in her eyes tarnished by reality. *Kal'buir* would see it, too, and it would break his heart.

Ordo wasn't ashamed of his father's past. Skirata did whatever he had to do to survive without handouts in a hostile galaxy that had never given him a break or a head start.

"*Buir*'s had to take some tough jobs over the years," Ordo said. "You'll hear some say harsh things about him, but he's a good man. The best. That's why we're very *protective* of him."

"I noticed. But there's nothing anyone can say about my dad that I hadn't heard from my mother."

Mereel looked at Ordo with a smirk that said he doubted that Skirata's late wife knew half of what her old man did for a living, even if she'd accepted his credit transfers over the years.

"Look, it's nothing personal," Ordo said. Yes, it *was*. It definitely was. Like all his Null brothers, he found it hard to be neutral about anybody. Everyone had to be assessed—a potential threat to be neutralized if necessary, or someone you would lay down your life for. There was no middle path, much as he struggled to find one. "We just don't know how to deal with you."

"It's okay, Ordo. I don't want Dad's credits, I'm not here to take your place, and I understand why you don't find it easy to trust newcomers. I'm just grateful to have my father back and get to know him again. Does that make you happier?"

The part of Ordo that was common sense and reason told the wary animal within him that it was okay. When he let his intellect run the show, and it stopped his instincts from getting the better of him, he always felt guilty for what he'd said or felt. But instincts were there for a reason.

"Yes," he said. "Much happier."

"That's good. Now, is there any use I can be on this mission?"

"Not unless you can look like a clone."

"I think I fail on all points there."

A'den, the nearest the Nulls had to a diplomat, held up a finger.

Ordo cut him off at the pass. "And you're not coming, *ner vod*, because if you have to take your helmet off, they'll see you're a little weather-beaten. I doubt that the ordinary meat-cans are going to look like that."

"I prefer *bronzed*," A'den said. "And maybe you should do something about your gray hairs, then. Anyway, I was going to say that Ruu might be able to help Arla. She knows what it's like to have your past crash-land on you. Poor *Arl'ika* doesn't know what happened to her brother yet."

"Does anyone?" Ruu asked.

"Vau knows more than *Kal'buir,* I think."

Ruu had a wary look so like her father's—slightly narrowed rabid-schutta eyes, head turned away just a fraction—that nobody was ever going to ask for a paternity test, even if Mandos cared about that sort of thing, which they didn't. "I'll do what I can."

Ruu left, taking her plate with her, and Kom'rk raised an eyebrow at Ordo.

"Don't take this the wrong way, *ner vod,* but you lack sensitivity. Poor woman didn't go looking for *Kal'buir.* We *abducted* her."

"She knows the score."

"So you're happy now."

"Less tense, let's say."

Jaing laid his datapad on the table. "Oh *good,*" he said. "I thought we were going to have a spat about Number One Son losing his place in the pecking order. Okay, what floor plans do we need?"

It had always been a joke, but Ordo wasn't sure it was so funny now. He'd been the informal alpha male of the brothers since infancy, and Skirata treated him as such. Mereel had always fallen into the sidekick role. In a family of six sons, it was inevitable that there'd be alliances and harmless rivalries. Now Ordo was starting to worry that they really did see him differently. The last thing he wanted was advantages that his brothers didn't have.

"Do you think I'm jealous?" he asked.

"More scared," Jaing said. "She's got to *prove* she's loyal and not a *chakaar* like her brothers." As he scrolled through schematics on the small screen, Ordo could see the flickering light on his hands. "Now remember that second virus I fed into the Republic mainframe?"

Mereel got up and stood behind him, hands on his shoulders. "You mean the incredibly risky and cocky demonstration of your programming skills that you performed under the nose of Republic Audit?"

"Yep. That'll be the one."

"I do recall. Has it been busy?"

"Well, now your pet tinnie and his minder have set up a comm portal, I can retrieve the data it's mined. What do you want—building plans, budgets, procurement contracts, Imperial canteen menus?"

Ordo cut in. "Plans and layouts. Keep it simple. We're not going to sabotage the Empire. We're extracting our brothers. *Nothing else.* Understand?"

"Oops," Mereel said. "Old habits . . ."

As long as the Empire left them alone, they'd give it a wide berth. That was *Kal'buir*'s plan, and Ordo was going to make sure everyone stuck to it.

This was a time to pick their battles carefully. Now they had a choice about who and where they fought— and why.

The *aruetiise* could fight their own wars for a change. It'd do them the power of good.

7

We conquered whole star systems. We had an empire. When cities heard our armies were coming, populations fled before a shot was fired. Now we cling to a pathetic sector of dirtball planets, we scramble for the crumbs that the cowardly aruetiise *throw when they want us to fight for them, and they use us as breeding stock for their clone armies. The aruetiise will always treat us like an animal species to be used for their convenience until we stand up for ourselves again.*
—Lorka Gedyc, commander of the Mandalorian Death Watch—not disbanded, merely in *ba'slan shev'la* awaiting a convenient time to return

Freighter *Cornucopia*, off Ralltiir; rendezvous point.

Ny Vollen's freighter dropped out of hyperspace just as she realized there was something in her coveralls that she hadn't put there.

Her pant-leg pocket bulged open. She didn't notice it until she reached for the controls and the fabric caught on the armrest of her seat. When she looked at what had snagged it, she found all the cash creds she'd shoved back into Skirata's hand before she left Mandalore, a stack of five-hundred and thousand denomination chips.

I do not *need your creds, Shortie. I don't care how much you're worth. Nobody's going to accuse me of sponging off a rich man. Any* man, *in fact.*

"You stubborn old barve," she muttered, staring at the plastoid chips. She hadn't even felt him put them there. The man would have made a superb pickpocket, and probably had been one in his past. "Guess where I'm going to ram *these*."

Mereel laughed. "Perfect. When can I start calling you Mama?"

"When the Kaminoans tweaked your genes, they definitely removed the one for subtlety, didn't they?"

Ordo didn't laugh, but Prudii, Jaing, and Mereel did. Four Nulls was about the most Ny could handle at one time. All six of them together—that was a *pack*. Not unruly, not undisciplined, just . . . *primed*. She felt that raw power and complete focus in them, like hunting animals waiting to be let loose. Even Mird didn't make her feel like that.

"We mean well," Jaing said. "But *Buir* doesn't meet many folks he likes and trusts, especially *female* ones his own age."

"The diplomacy gene's gone missing, too, I see."

"It's all about time, Ny. We've all got less left than we ought to have."

Jaing had a rare talent for getting to the point, not as bluntly gauche as Ordo but equally capable of saying the things other folks kept to themselves. Yes, they were all on borrowed time, and there was every chance she'd still outlive them. And so might their father.

"Things aren't always that simple," she said.

Mereel put on his I'm-just-an-innocent-kid face, which pressed all Ny's buttons even though she knew perfectly well that he was nothing of the kind.

"We like having you around," he said. "And *Buir*'s been alone for years—long before Kamino. We know he likes you because he says things to you that he'd never normally tell anyone."

"What, like he's got a trillion kriffing creds?"

"He told you he came from Kuat," Jaing said. "And he *did* admit he was a trillionaire. The night you first met him. Remember?"

Ny recalled that just fine. Yes, he had. And the Nulls never forgot anything, not with those eidetic memories the Kaminoans gave them. "I thought he was joking."

Ordo, hunched in the copilot's seat, looked up from the navigation display. "Mereel, shut up, will you?"

"Well, *Buir* doesn't have my natural charm with the ladies, so he's never going to raise the—"

"I said *shut up*." Ordo turned and reached behind him to put a worryingly firm grip on Mereel's shoulder. "Ny's lost her husband. She might not be ready for all this. She might not like *Buir* in that way. Just get off her back."

Ny had never seen clones lose their tempers with one another. For some reason, she thought they'd be perfectly attuned in some kind of mystic twin-like harmony, but she was wrong. They were like any other family with their spats and fallings-out. She felt awful for being the cause of this one.

"Hey, Ordo, it's all right." His intervention sounded like something Besany had said to him, a lesson he'd absorbed, but maybe he really did think that. "I'm not offended. Mereel's just . . . oh, c'mon, you two, truce. Okay?"

"Don't make her come back here," Prudii said.

Ny understood why Skirata indulged his sons so shamelessly. She'd give in to just about anything they asked of her.

"There's matchmaking," she said carefully, "and then there's forced marriage."

Jaing grinned. "Yes, but where's a pensioner like you going to meet another eccentric trillionaire at your time of life?"

"I haven't *got* a kriffing pension." She clenched her back teeth. If she laughed, it only encouraged them. "Just give me some thinking time. And don't bug your dad about it, either."

"See? She's got the mother thing down pat." Mereel wasn't deterred by Ordo's temper. "Next stage is *just wait until I tell your father*."

Ny knew the only way Mereel could have learned that was from holovids. These clones had a devoted father, but they'd never known a mother or anything resembling one. The constant joking about it made her wonder if it troubled them at some subconscious level, or if it was just that they loved their dad, saw their brothers settling down happily, and wanted the same for Skirata because they thought there was some universal remedy for a broken heart.

Ny wasn't immune to that. The prospect of filling the void in her life was all too easy to grab without thinking. Why else had she flung herself into this, when she could have lived out her widowed years quietly and never needed to worry about the Empire kicking down her door?

Jaing inserted a probe into the navigation console and consulted the readout on his datapad. "There you go— bogus tachometer readings all sorted. We've just come from Phindar. Did we all have a good time there?"

"Can't wait to do it again." Prudii yawned. "Wherever it is."

Ordo didn't join in. He was the serious brother, constantly on duty and checking every detail. Besany was very much like him. Ny suspected that their children were going to be beautiful but unsmiling perfectionists who had to have jokes explained to them.

Cornucopia headed for the RV point with Mereel's contacts, just one more commercial vessel inbound for a freighter way station, nothing special, nothing dangerous. Ny wondered where to dock to take on supplies on the way back. Ordo followed the transponder traces on the monitor, audio headset held to one ear.

"Mereel, can you confirm this is Teekay? Hyperdrive service vessel showing as registered to the *HealthiDrive* franchise division, showing eight-zero-five."

"That's it. Send him the code."

"Receiving confirmation." Ordo nodded a few times, eyes fixed on the screen. Whatever was happening, Ny couldn't hear the conversation. "Okay, Ny, dock at pier nine-delta and they'll come alongside there."

It was just routine, she told herself. She'd stopped here a dozen times before over the years, a handy station for emergency repairs or to break a journey if she was flying the two main routes between the Core to the Tingel Arm—usually the Hydian, sometimes the Perlemian. All she had to do was behave as she had on every trip for the last forty years. If she was boarded, she was just another pilot with four Mandalorians as paying passengers, nothing out of the ordinary at all. She let the computer take over the final approach and marveled that even after four decades of hauling freight and surrendering her ship to automated systems, she still hated taking her hands off the steering yoke.

Cornucopia settled onto the platform. Locking clamps moved to secure the freighter's landing gear with an alarming *thunk,* an almost-forgettable routine that now felt unpleasantly like being handcuffed.

Mereel put on his helmet to seal his suit, then checked his blaster. "Okay, just let Teekay dock for a repair, and I'll handle the air lock transfer," he said. "And I just want to remind you *shabuire* that I've played meat-cans before."

"Were you good at it?" Ny asked.

"Fooled the aiwha-bait, and they know clones better than anybody. Ordo's done it, too." Mereel disappeared down the aft bridge hatch, boots clanging on the ladder. "We've done it a *lot.*"

"He's not expecting trouble, is he?" Ny asked, making a blaster shape with an extended thumb and forefinger.

"Habit," Ordo said. "We're opening the door in a rough neighborhood."

"It's just a freighter stop."

"*Any* neighborhood is rough when we show up."

Prudii chuckled to himself. "You'll be *ori'mando* one day, Ny . . ."

The transfer only took minutes, but it felt a lot longer. Ny wandered down to the side doors of the cargo bay and watched as a droid and a young human male in *HealthiDrive* franchise coveralls steered a heavily laden repulsor through the inner air lock. It looked as if they'd cleared out an Imperial quartermaster's store.

"Anyone call for a fuel injector gasket?" Gaib asked.

"Good. Nice to see you in character." Mereel nodded at the dull gray plastoid crates as the repulsor came to a halt in front of him. He opened a lid. "*Four* suits, Gaib. Did you get matching sets in all the latest spring colors or something?"

"*Ten* suits." TK-0 glided in between his human associate and Mereel. "We know how you like to go in mob-handed. So we thought—why not score a few more than required? Easier than going back for extras."

"You think of everything," Mereel said.

"You can do that with a positronic brain." The droid plunged his manipulators into the boxes and began extracting white plastoid armor plates. "Did you know an organic's brain is *sixty percent fat*? Disgusting. How can you bear to keep all that *mush* in your head?"

Mereel held an armor plate against his chest for size. "This is the new design? Not bad. Not as stylish as a *kama* and pauldron, but needs must."

Jaing and Prudii clattered down the ladder and pounced on the helmets. They had to strip out the Imperial comms and interface components and replace them with their own secure systems. And they looked completely delighted to be doing it. Ny found it hard not to think of them as kids—heavily armed, battle-hardened, and lethal, but still kids. They had an endearingly child-like capacity for enjoying things.

"Anything else you might be needing?" TK-0 asked, extending an arm to Mereel, metal palm upturned.

"Oh, I think this'll keep us going for a while." Mereel placed a stack of cash credits in the droid's manipulators. Ny tried to estimate how much this had cost from the stack of chips—five hundred thousand, a million?—and then remembered that the interest on Skirata's fund for one week wouldn't even be dented by that. The numbers were just too much to take in.

I wish he hadn't told me about the fortune. It's not like I even asked.

Ny was learning never to ask too many questions in the company she kept now. It wasn't just the reaction it might provoke. It was the risk of hearing the answers and wishing she hadn't, because once she knew something it could always be beaten out of her if someone else knew she had information.

But she was curious about the suits, and asked anyway, more to calculate the chances of getting caught than to learn anything. "They won't miss ten new suits, then."

"We won the contract to service some of the suit systems," Gaib said. "So we can mark defective suits as *returns*. Only we don't. We mark them as *keep* and *sell for a reasonable profit*. And this new army is a *lot* bigger than the Republic's—millions upon millions. They wouldn't notice a *thousand* missing suits."

"Or the fact that it's costing them two hundred creds for every servodriver I bill for." TK-0 probed inside a helmet and drew out tiny chips and hair-fine gold wire. "You know we could have retrieved your *consignment* for you, don't you? You could have stayed home. Door-to-door delivery, our five-star service."

Jaing looked up from the dissected lining of the helmet he was working on. "It's not that simple. It's *people*-smuggling."

Ny wondered why Jaing had told him that much—or that little. The droid certainly knew who Niner was now, and that he had an illegal comm kit in his helmet. But in this game, nobody had anything more on their business associates than their associates had on them. Ny had learned the ecology of crime very fast since meeting A'den.

We all need to keep our mouths shut. One gets caught, we all get caught. We all have to . . . trust one another.

She enjoyed irony. There was, as the sages said, honor among thieves.

Ny Vollen, taxpayer and honest citizen, was now a criminal, and she accepted that was what she was. She saw how easily it happened, and why, and knew now that she could never sit in judgment on any being again, because she was as fallible as anyone.

"Come on, *Mer'ika*." She assembled the plates from one suit on the deck. "Let's make sure we've got the full set."

"Anyone would think you didn't trust us," Gaib said cheerfully.

"Oh, I do," Ny said. "I think it's the law-abiding folk I need to keep an eye on."

She used to be one of them. She wondered what Terin would have thought if he'd been around to see her now.

He'd have understood. She was sure of it.

Special Unit briefing room, 501st Legion HQ, Imperial City

Commander Roly Melusar was a mongrel, but Darman didn't hold that against him.

In fact, he took an instant liking to the man. He walked into the briefing room with Ennen, deep in very quiet conversation. Whatever had gone on when Ennen demanded a Corellian cremation for Bry, Melusar appeared to have done something that Ennen approved of.

Ennen sat down next to Darman and Niner.

"Well?" Niner asked.

"Good man," Ennen said. "*Decent* man. Bry's at rest now."

So he'd managed to get whatever rites mattered to him. It boded well. Melusar had sprung from nowhere in the last twenty-four hours to take over day-to-day command of the unit from Sa Cuis, who had simply vanished without explanation in the way that spooks did.

Melusar seemed relaxed about his new role as he stood on the dais at the front of the room. Darman tried not to make snap decisions about beings, but it was hard to resist. Melusar was all right. He just knew it.

"Where's Creepy?" Fixer's voice was a gravelly whisper on Darman's helmet comlink. That was his nickname for Sa Cuis, although there were others, all much less flattering. "I hope he's on a fifty-klick run to sweat some of that *padding* off his backside."

Boss cut in. "Probably in some dimly lit room, showing some forgetful citizen the value of electrodes for jogging the memory."

Darman didn't dare turn his head to look for them in the small audience. When he checked his wide-angle visual feed, they were just anonymous helmeted figures in black armor like his own. But he was reassured to know the Delta boys were still around. Nothing was said about Sev now—absolutely *nothing*—and Darman had no idea what the guy's brothers were up to.

They were alive. That was all that mattered.

"Agent Cuis has been retasked on recruitment issues," Melusar said. What the *shab* was that? The more bland the explanation, Darman thought, the scarier the reality would be. "Forgive me if I repeat anything he's said already, gentlemen. But let's take a moment to remember our comrade Bry. I didn't know him, but you all did, and I know you're going to miss him. I'm truly sorry."

Melusar leaned on the lectern—tall, light brown hair, bony—and something about his earnest face and direct eye contact reminded Darman of Bardan Jusik. The gray Imperial uniform was just a detail, not the sum of the man himself. After a brief silence, he carried on. He walked slowly up and down the platform as he spoke to the commandos, gesturing to emphasize his words—more like he was trying *not* to use his hands, nothing like the performance a politician would put on—and seemed the kind of man who believed what he was saying.

"The galaxy will be a safer place for every citizen if we eradicate Force-users," he said. "I don't just mean Jedi. I mean *all* of them. I can't blame you for dismissing this as some half-wit mongrel officer mouthing the Emperor's party line, but make no mistake—stamping out these Force cults buys us *all* stability and security. Take a look in your history books. See just how many wars Force-users got us into."

Melusar definitely had their attention now.

And he knew what clones called randomly conceived beings: mongrels. Roly Melusar wasn't like Cuis at all. He knew what his men thought, and he treated them as the cynical, weary, suspicious veterans they actually were.

"Wow," Fixer muttered. "He knows we're not like the rest of the Five-oh-first."

"That's because we wear black, and they wear white," Ennen said. "We must be the bad guys."

Niner didn't tell them to shut it. He seemed mesmerized by Melusar's no-nonsense attitude, too. Usually, he'd fidget in his seat if he had to sit still for any time, clicking his teeth impatiently, but he was frozen now—and totally silent. Darman couldn't even hear his breathing. He'd switched off his helmet-to-helmet comms. In the other rows of seats, commandos shifted position. Some leaned forward a little as if they were watching a riveting movie, and some relaxed as if they realized they didn't have to put on a show of gung-ho Imperial enthusiasm for the commander anymore. Melusar was—as far as any mongrel officer could be—one of them.

That was it. *That* was what reminded Darman of Jusik. Melusar felt he was in this fight with them, not just leading them, and it wasn't an act. Nobody could fake sincerity that well.

Melusar went on pacing, slapping the back of his right hand into his left palm to punctuate his words. He spoke like a regular Coruscanti, no airs and graces or expensively educated vowels. When he talked, he seemed to speak for everyone Darman knew and loved.

"What have I got against Force-users?" Melusar paused for a moment and seemed to be gathering his thoughts, as if he were in the middle of a debate over an ale with buddies in a cantina. "*Everything*. The Jedi held positions of power and influence for millennia, all un-elected, all unaccountable to the likes of us—the ordinary beings of the galaxy. We bankrolled them for generations. We armed them. We stayed out of their internal business, and we turned a blind eye because we thought they got the job done. Those guys *really* knew how to organize themselves to get the best meal ticket from us regular dolts—but there are still other sects out there, all capable of doing the same thing if we let them. The Force will manifest itself as the Force pleases, and we can't take a blaster to that, but the *training*, the secret organizations, the cabals that whisper in government ears—*that's* our business. *That* we can stamp out."

The commandos just watched. Darman fully expected someone to stand up and clap, or at least cheer. Melusar paused for breath, looked around, and then seemed to remember a point he'd missed.

"You know what disturbs me most? They can influence your thoughts." He looked like he meant it. "They can make you hallucinate and do things you don't want to, and you wouldn't even know it'd happened. That's the most dangerous thing of all. But it stops here, and it stops for good."

Darman had seen mind influence at work, and it hadn't seemed quite like that to him. But then the Jedi he knew were . . .

Etain always asked permission first. She used it to help Scorch calm down. And Jusik, he—

Darman managed to hold on, but only just. Etain was vivid in his mind again, not filtered by that distance he struggled to put between him and the pain, and all he could think of at that moment was how he'd reacted when she told him she'd had a baby and that it was his.

He would have given anything to change that moment. He would have rewritten history so that he'd flung his arms around her and told her how happy he was. But he hadn't done that. He'd walked away in silence.

Can't change the past. Only the future. Stop it. She's gone. Stop it. *Right now. Get back on track, find something to focus on, do something that matters.*

Commander Melusar went on talking. For a while Darman could hear every word, but the meaning wasn't sinking in. He switched off his helmet mike and let the tears roll down his cheeks. Not even biting into his lip managed to distract him this time.

When he got a grip again, Melusar was standing at the front row with one boot on the seat of a vacant chair, arms folded, discussing—*discussing*—the issue with a commando. It was Jez from one of the Aiwha Squads, one of Skirata's original hundred-strong training company. He'd taken off his helmet. Their old boss, General Zey, had been a nice enough guy, the poor *shabuir,* but there always seemed to be a moat around him that you couldn't cross even when you could see what lay beyond it. Melusar wasn't distant at all. He was right in the mud with them.

"Caf and cookies at briefings next," Scorch said, but the I've-seen-it-all tone of his voice had softened a bit. "Maybe a commando-of-the-month scheme, a crate of ale for the most mission-focused man."

"Or you could have General Vos back, if you prefer *that* management style . . . ," Ennen muttered.

Niner was still unusually silent. Darman swallowed, unable to wipe his nose and eyes without taking off his helmet. Melusar was still holding forth. Jez was listening intently. Everyone was riveted.

"Here's one scenario," Melusar said. "What happened to all the other Force-using sects? If your kid's showing Force powers, then the Jedi show up and want to take it. The other sects don't want their Force-sensitives poached by a rival. They go underground to avoid the Jedi Council. Now that the Jedi have had their butts kicked, are those other sects going to feel it's safe to come out?"

"Not if they read my task list . . . ," a voice said, and everyone laughed.

They'll take Kad. But if he isn't trained to use his powers, he'll have a quiet life, and Palpatine won't go after him. If the Jedi come back—they'll take him.

That's my reason right there. Even without what happened to Etain. Even without the war.

Darman's carefully constructed barrier between his two personas had finally crumbled. The pain was almost unbearable. If it had been any worse, he would have walked out, put his sidearm to his head, and stopped the agony for good. He hovered on the brink between lashing out at anyone in his path and destroying himself, because the misery was so blinding. But when that barrier fell, he felt something else let loose—a son, he had a son, *this* Darman, *him,* a son he loved and now had to keep safe. He had a clear view of how he had to protect Kad's future.

Stop it happening again. Make sure the Jedi never come back as a political power.

The pain left him struggling to swallow, but now he could face it head-on and survive it because he had a reason to.

"The Jedi Council did a good job of looking like the sole voice of the Force-users," Melusar went on, probably completely unaware that he'd given Darman a fresh purpose in a single casual comment. "But now we'll see who else is out there. The Korunnai on Haruun Kal— they're *all* Force-sensitives there, maybe descended from a lost Jedi mission, but at least we know where they are. Not a cult, but a potential source of one. Imagine a planet full of folks who could be trained to do what Jedi could. It's a weapon waiting to be assembled."

Darman thought of Jusik, busting his gut to Force-heal Fi's brain damage. Then he thought of some Jedi shaking hands with a Kaminoan and taking delivery of a clone army. He never knew which kind of Jedi he was going to get.

"They call us *Balawai,* don't they?" Jez said. "Anyone who isn't Korunnai is a *downlander,* and they don't think much of them."

Just like *aruetiise*, Darman decided. Mandalorians divided the world into Mando and non-Mando, although the word could mean anything from foreigner to traitor, depending on how it was said. But it never meant *welcome visitor*. Darman was always unsettled when he found that he had things in common with folks who would otherwise be his enemy, and it was usually the bad stuff, rarely the good.

The commandos were totally at ease now. Melusar had a way with him.

"Have you been putting together a dodgy dossier on our Force-wielding friends, sir?" Ennen said. "You sound like you have."

"Know the enemy," Melusar said, tapping his temple with his forefinger. "First weapon in the armory. To deal with them, we have to understand them. Yes, I've studied them over the years. But it was the People's Inquest group that did the compiling."

Ennen folded his arms. "Are they that Jedi-watch group? The ones who wanted to see details of Jedi expenditure, and the Republic kept trying to shut down their HoloNet station?"

"Now who's been keeping tabs? Well recalled, Ennen, And yes, they *did* say 'We told you so.' "

Zey could never get a laugh at a briefing. Poor old Sa Cuis; wherever he'd gone, the Imperial Commando Special Unit wasn't going to miss his guidance. Roly Melusar had made the squads his own, and it had taken him less than half an hour.

"Good old Roly," Scorch mocked. *"Holy Roly."*

"*That's* going to stick . . . ," Boss said.

Niner twitched suddenly as if something had startled him. Darman wondered if he'd been nodding off. "Nice guy, but dangerous." There was no reaction from Ennen or any of Delta Squad. Only Darman could hear Niner's voice. "But does he know Palps is a Sith?"

So Niner had finally decided it was safe to talk on private channels after all. Darman thought he sounded strained, but maybe that was the man's natural paranoia getting the better of him.

"Is that confirmed?" Darman asked. "Where'd you hear that?"

"Just . . . talk. Vader's got a red lightsaber. Jusik said Sith have those."

"If Melusar *does* know," Darman said, not worrying much about Sith, "he either doesn't care, or doesn't think the Sith are as dangerous as hordes of unlicensed Force-users. Or maybe he's banking on sitting it out until Palpatine dies."

Melusar didn't have to discuss any of this at all. Every commando in that room knew what his task was: to slot the targets on his list. Rationale wasn't required. Knowing *why* was useful, because context helped you build a picture of who you were hunting and what they might do in a given situation. But discussing policy—no, the Republic had never gone in for that kind of debate with clones, and the Empire didn't look inclined to, either. Melusar, though, explained clearly *why things had to be done,* like Skirata, and didn't fall back on push-button words like *freedom* and *democracy* that could mean anything you wanted them to, including the complete opposite.

"So, we have more scraps of intel," Melusar said, turning to a holodisplay that projected notes onto the wall behind him. He scribbled on his datapad, and the lines and words appeared on the display. "We know there are still Jedi stuck here in Imperial City. And we know some escaped the planet via Whiplash and other underground organizations. Their leadership's been almost completely destroyed, so I expect some regrouping around the charismatic ones in the remnant. One name that keeps cropping up is Master Djinn Altis."

He scribbled the name ALTIS on the display and stood back to look at it, tapping his stylus absently against his palm. Some guys in the front row shook their heads.

"Never came across him, sir."

"That's because he was never part of Yoda's Council.

Went his own way. Helped out the Republic eventually, but his group was still dissident. Old-time Jedi habits. Back to basics. Very popular with civilians, because they started out giving aid to war victims." Melusar paused and wrote the words ANTARIAN—JEDI REJECTS—JAL SHEY—FORCE-USERS OR NOT? like a shopping-list reminder to get back to those topics later. "Not sure about all their philosophy, but they allow marriage and have families, so there definitely wasn't a meeting of minds between Yoda and Altis."

Darman didn't hear the rest of the sentence.

Jedi who allow marriage. Families.

Suddenly the knife that had been lodged in his chest since Etain was killed, bleeding out his hopes, twisted and dug in deeper.

If Etain had followed Altis instead . . . none of this would have happened.

She could have been a Jedi *and* a wife, without guilt or secrecy. *Other Jedi did it.* Melusar had just told him so. Darman knew the Jedi Order had bent the rules for Ki-Adi-Mundi, but this was different, a whole kind of Jedi thinking he'd never known about, and somehow it seemed even worse for being more widespread.

He could never forgive the Jedi for keeping him and Etain apart until it was too late. It wasn't *Kal'buir's* fault at all. The Jedi had failed her.

And I failed her, too. I should have been able to keep her safe.

He couldn't let his son down the way he'd let down his wife. He had to stand between him and everyone who'd do him harm—from the Jedi who'd claim him as theirs to the Empire that wanted to wipe out Force-users.

It had to be done, for Kad's sake. The galaxy could go hang.

I know a lot more about Jedi than most clones—most mongrels, too. I'm not afraid of them. I know how to take them down. For Etain, for Kad, for everyone I care about.

"Holy Roly," Fixer chuckled to himself, oblivious of Darman's moment of clarity. "Yeah, that's about right. What a saint."

Darman didn't want a saint for a boss. He wanted a soldier, and he wanted to believe in him the way he'd believed in *Kal'buir*. Vader—Vader had a *lightsaber*. He used the Force. That meant he was a potential enemy, someone who'd have a vested interest in hunting Kad either to kill him or sign him up for the Sith club. Sith and Jedi were different sides of the same coin; Skirata said so.

But Roly Melusar was an ordinary man with no illusions about Jedi or any other Force-using sect.

"Hey," Scorch whispered. "Guess what? Word is that Vader's gone off looking for new clone donors. Maybe that's the *recruitment* Fatboy Cuis is working on."

Darman still thought that Cuis was a Force-user. And if any recruiting was being done—Kad wasn't going to be part of it.

Iri Camas was the first Jedi Darman had fought, but he wasn't going to be the last.

Kyrimorut, Mandalore

Skirata split logs in the yard, and fretted.

In the past, he had been the one who went to war and left a family behind. Now he was the one waiting for news, and suddenly he had a much better idea of what Ilippi had gone through while they were married. Waiting was hard. Even with the latest comlinks and transponders to stay in touch—a luxury his ex-wife never had—the minutes were still long and empty, begging to be filled with the wrong kind of speculation.

So this is what it's like to be the rear party. Sorry, Ilippi. I never really understood.

Every time he brought the ax down on the resinwood logs, the strong scent filled his nostrils. It was probably the smell that triggered his memories again. The sweet medicinal scent of the resin reminded him of the first months of his marriage, when he was crazy about a Corellian nightclub waitress called Ilippi Jiro and he tried to teach her some essential skills of a proper Mandalorian wife—how to build a basic field shelter, a *vheh' yaim,* and cook over an open fire. She never did get the hang of splitting logs. He didn't care. He loved her, they had a small town house in Shuror where she never had to cook over open flames, and he never believed the fire would die in their relationship.

I can go for months, a whole year even, without thinking of her at all. Now she's back as if it was only yesterday.

He couldn't see a trace of her in Ruu, though. The girl was so much like himself it was unsettling. If she started showing signs of all his character flaws, it would be like living with a rebuke that he could never ignore, and he'd know why fate had decided to throw them together again.

The crunch of boots approached slowly from one side. Skirata could see in his peripheral vision that it was Vau.

"If you're that worried," Vau said, "all you have to do is comm them."

Skirata didn't take his eyes off the log balanced on the chopping block. He'd had one accident too many with axes when he was distracted.

"If they're doing a delicate job, I might comm just at the wrong time . . ." Skirata lined up his ax, swung, and split another log in two neat halves. It was a kind of meditation—nothing mystic, just living in the moment by repeating simple and necessary actions without thought, the best way of quieting the mind. "Like just then, in fact."

"You realize that Niner and Darman could have left Imperial City under their own steam by now? They're commandos, for goodness' sake. Getting out of places is what they do best—after getting in, of course."

"Yes, but they *haven't*. That tells me they need extracting."

"That's what worries me," Vau said.

"Meaning?"

"Darman's got a son here. Even Niner agreed to desert in the end. They had every reason to get out as soon as Niner could walk again. But they didn't."

"You know as well as I do that you have to pick your moment to exfil in a situation like that."

Skirata hadn't wanted to think about it, but he wondered if he'd judged it all wrong and the two clones *wanted* to stay in the army. If they did, then it was all his fault. He'd been responsible for keeping Etain's pregnancy from Darman, not one deceit but a daily cycle of lies until the kid was a toddler. If Darman hadn't bonded with his son enough to put being with him above everything, then it was because Skirata had set him a rotten example as a father. And Niner—Niner had an unshakable sense of duty and responsibility that Skirata had nurtured.

I trained them to be perfect soldiers. Now I want them to forget all that and come and play renegade Mando here with me. What can I expect?

"Yes," Vau said, as if he'd been having an internal debate with himself during Skirata's long silence. "I'm getting too anxious. Too much idle time on my hands. They were just waiting for the right moment."

"No point fighting your way out when you can walk out," Skirata said. He glanced at the chrono on his forearm plate. "Lunch. Come on, let's spend some quality *sha'kajir* time with our highly qualified comrade."

Sha'kajir meant sitting down for a meal, and had come to refer to a truce or cease-fire. Skirata found that remarkably apt in this case. Everything could be resolved over a meal, the neutral territory where you said what you had to say and everyone was treated as kin, at least until the meal was over. He was still negotiating his cease-fire with Uthan.

Vau managed a smile. "*Mij'ika* seems like a new man

since he's found someone to discuss bacteriology and congenital urethral obstruction with him. If only everyone was so easy to please."

"Not at the table, I hope."

"It's all big words, Kal. You won't understand the really stomach-churning medical detail."

Skirata ignored the jibe without even trying. A year ago, maybe less, it would have started the old fight going again, but they both found their differences weren't worth the effort now. "You know, I can't dislike Uthan, Walon. I tried, but I can't."

"You can't dislike Kina Ha, either, and I know you feel you should as a matter of honor." Vau's expression had softened and it didn't suit him at all. Nature had selected him to be a brutal, implacable patrician, a man who beat servants and lavished more affection on his pedigree livestock. It was bred into his bone structure, revealed in that harshly aristocratic face. "Species apart, I can't help wishing my mother had been like her. Very grand, very gracious. She's more of a countess than dear Mama ever was."

Age didn't change a thing as far as Skirata was concerned. Vau seemed to think old age was a state of sainthood, life's slate wiped clean simply by being too feeble to return a punch. Skirata took off his boots at the door and stood them inside the covered lobby.

"If Demagol walked in here now, four thousand years old," he said, "what would you do?"

"Tell him to make himself useful for once and give Uthan a hand in the lab."

"Seriously."

"You're asking me if I'd take a blaster to a *very* elderly man and kneecap him for his eugenics crimes, aren't you?"

Skirata wondered if Vau would forgive his loathed father simply for avoiding death long enough. He doubted it. "I'm just a simple thug trying to explore moral philosophy, *Wal'ika.*"

"Then I'd have to face him to know the answer. But I'm sure you think you know yours."

"I do. It's okay to shoot a helpless old man. Because when he *wasn't* helpless, he did some terrible things to living beings for no other reason than scientific curiosity." Skirata took off his torso plates in the lobby. They were good protection for any job, from chopping wood to fighting Trandoshans, and they also gave aging joints some welcome support. "Don't worry, Kina Ha's safe. *Shab*, she was a defective as far as the aiwha-bait were concerned. If she hadn't been some use to them for tinkering, I doubt they'd have celebrated her differences."

Two sounds competed for Skirata's attention as he stepped into the passage. One was the sound of clattering dinner plates and the faintly buzzing audio of a holoreceiver coming from the kitchen. The other was a noise that still gave him very mixed feelings: the *vzzzm-vzzzm-vzzzm* of someone swinging a lightsaber.

Actually, it was *two* lightsabers. The insistent humming sounds overlapped, so Jusik was sparring with someone, and Skirata doubted it was Kina Ha.

He gave Vau a nod to indicate he was going to check it out. The trail led to one of the empty rooms, doors wide open, a bedroom waiting for a deserter in need of a roof over his head. Jusik, fully armored but minus his helmet, was dueling with Scout. He stopped instantly. Skirata gestured to carry on and not mind him.

"We were trying to be discreet about the lightsabers," Jusik said, holding his blade wide to his right while Scout took up her stance. "Sorry, *Kal'buir*."

Skirata shrugged. "Ignore my ramblings. I've used one, too, remember." He'd used Jusik's, in fact. He'd killed Jedi with it, just crazed shocked seconds after Etain was cut down. He wondered if it troubled Jusik to hold it now, whether the blade spoke to him of former brothers abandoned, or if it marked some kind of watershed of leaving his Jedi identity behind. "They're not snobs, lightsabers. You can swing one no matter who your father was."

"Scout has to stay sharp." Jusik seemed to need to excuse why he was doing it. "She'll have to defend herself again one day."

Jusik spun. Scout moved to block his thrust before he shifted his weight; she looked like she knew which way he was going even before he did. She did it again, and again. Jusik ended up with his lightsaber held almost like a knife, cantina-fight-style, weight on both feet, knees bent, rocking one way then the other before leaping. And she *still* blocked his blade. Then she lunged and hit his chest plate. A charred streak marked the green coating.

"Sorry!" She put her hand to her mouth. "Wow, lightsabers really *don't* do much to proper *beskar'gam*, do they?" She stepped forward and wiped her finger across his armor. "It's just zapped the paint. The metal's fine."

"That's why I'm wearing *beskar*, and not durasteel." Jusik glanced down at the mark, then winked. "Look, *Kal'buir*, this'll enhance my reputation no end. Fought with a Jedi and survived to show off the damage."

Even harmless comments could bring that image of the chaos on Shinarcan Bridge back to Skirata. But he couldn't go through life flinching at every word. He made himself face each painful syllable.

"Lunch, *ad'ike*," he said, clapping his hands together to hurry them up. "We're thin on the ground today. If we keep Jilka waiting, she'll skin us."

In the kitchen, Vau, Uthan, and Gilamar sat at the table watching the holonews, while Besany and Jilka helped Arla serve up the meals. It was the first time Arla had joined them. She looked lost, but then a kitchen was a chaotic, noisy place after years in a padded cell.

"You'll forgive me for bringing the holo in here," Gilamar said. "But things are getting hairy on Gibad."

"Fine by me." Skirata helped himself to the mealbread rolls. "Where is everyone?"

"Fi, Parja, and Corr went hunting with Mird," Besany said. "Kina Ha's meditating by the lake, and everyone else is fishing or helping Levet sow beans. Yes, Laseema's taken Kad along, but she made sure he was wrapped up warmly. Did I leave anyone out?"

"You know me too well, *ad'ika*."

Besany winked. Jilka hadn't gone off with Corr, so maybe relations with Besany were thawing. Skirata hoped so.

"Anyone want to update me on Gibad?" he said.

Uthan kept her eyes on the screen. The holocast was live from outside the Gibadan parliament, a deceptively pleasant scene of a tree-lined square with a formal fountain in the center. Skirata could see armored vehicles in front of the building, troops guarding the huge bronzium doors at the top of steps that ran the full width of the colonnaded building. Update captions edged across the screen or flashed briefly as static icons.

"They've told Palps to kiss their collective *shebse*," Gilamar said. "So they're counting down to the surrender deadline and standing by for a full orbital assault."

Gibad wasn't worth fighting over, nice as the place looked, except to teach the rest of the galaxy a lesson. Uthan probably knew what was coming. Skirata wondered if he would have had the stomach to watch helplessly if that had been Keldabe and he'd been marooned light-years away; he doubted it. But *not* watching probably felt like dereliction of duty to her.

"Doctor, have you still got family there?" Jilka asked.

"Indirect family, yes. Colleagues at the institute. Friends."

Skirata felt a sick chill in his gut. *She hasn't been able to contact her home for three years. I never thought she might want to call and talk to family, but then I wouldn't have risked it anyway. Everything's changed now. Do I let her call home?*

It already looked too late. He slid his comlink across the table anyway. She looked at him, then picked it up.

If she tried anything stupid, he could always shoot her. The comlink was untrackable. She tapped in a code and lifted the comlink slowly to her mouth.

"Sessaly? Sessaly, is that you, dear? Yes, it's Qail . . .
yes, I'm fine, I'm safe, I'm . . ." Uthan only met Skirata's
eyes for a second, then glanced away. "I can't say where
I am, but everything's fine . . . no, someone got me out,
but that doesn't matter, are *you* all right? Are you? I'm
watching it all on the news . . ."

Skirata wished he'd been more deaf than he was, because it was awful to hear that panicky edge in Uthan's
voice. She was as hard as nails—until now. That was
what made it worse. Jusik patted his arm as he sat down
next to him, and for a few minutes everyone tried to eat
and pretend they couldn't hear Uthan's increasingly
emotional conversation. Sessaly was her cousin, by the
sound of it.

Skirata concentrated on the news anchor, and realized
the reporter at the scene was the droid behind the holocam.

*Okay, send a tinnie to record a war, fine—but it's
going to get fried the moment the turbolasers start.
What kind of a propaganda show is that?*

"We understand that the surrender deadline has now
passed, with no undertaking from the Gibadan government," said the anchor. "The Emperor has now autho-
rized the use of force to restore order."

Gibad looked pretty orderly to Skirata.

Oh, shab . . .

"Sessaly, you have to find shelter right now." Uthan
stood up, raking her hair with one hand. "Please. We
can talk later. Just get into a shelter. *Please.*"

Even a woman prepared to kill millions had feelings.
Skirata glanced at Gilamar, always a more sentimental
man than most realized, and saw him suffering with her.
Skirata would never have bet on those two getting close.

"No . . . ," she murmured. The crawler caption running across the bottom of the image read DEADLINE FOR
GIBAD SURRENDER PASSES—IMPERIAL TASK FORCE BE-
GINS ASSAULT. "Sessaly, stay in the basement, do you
hear me? Sessaly? *Sessaly!*"

Gilamar let out a long breath. Uthan stared at the comlink, eyes brimming.

"I—I think the outgoing comms have been jammed," she said.

There was a chance that Sessaly might make it, but Skirata didn't spend too long working out her odds. Uthan handed the comlink back to him and stared unblinking at the screen. Scout and Jusik watched her, grim-faced, and then Scout moved across to put her hand on the woman's arm. Whatever Scout and Jusik could feel emanating from Uthan seemed to be a lot more harrowing than Skirata could see.

"Who's recording this?" Gilamar said. He looked equally unhappy. *Shab,* he was getting too fond of Uthan. "If the bombardment's started, they're missing it."

"Droid," Skirata said absently. "Until a laser barrage hits it."

Odd . . .

The holocam shot tilted up to the sky, focused on something in the clouds, and small dark dots began resolving into fighters—or so Skirata thought. Then he realized they weren't military craft but droid crop sprayers. He could see a fine cloud emerging from the undercarriages as the holocam zoomed in.

Gilamar seemed to get the idea before he did. "No, that's too disgusting even for Palpatine."

The assault had started, all right. But there was no bombardment. And now Skirata knew why the reporter was a droid, because there weren't going to be any turbolasers turned on the cities of Gibad. The place would still be standing tomorrow.

Crop sprayers only did one thing. They released chemicals. And that was what this fleet appeared to be doing now.

"Chemical weapons," Gilamar said. "Utterly gutless. *Hutuune.*"

Yes, that was a coward's weapon. Skirata wondered if it mattered how you died in a war as long as it was over quickly, but how an army fought decided if its society was honorable or a bunch of savages. Dropping chemicals on a city instead of landing troops was about as bad as it got for Skirata. Whatever the *aruetyc* world thought, Mandalorians had their code of conduct, and dragging civilians into a war—as targets, as shields, as anything—meant all bets were off. An enemy like that deserved no quarter, and got none.

But it's Palpatine. We're not going to fight him. Not now, anyway. So I'll file that for the future.

The basement hiding place wouldn't save Sessaly or anyone else. Uthan closed her eyes, put her hand to her mouth, and wept silently as the droid cam shifted position and tracked to the city itself. Gilamar took her hand and gave Scout a look that, for just a split second, made the three of them look like a family.

Skirata looked away, feeling like a voyeur, and wondered which chemical agent the Empire was using. Then he had a terrible thought. He wondered if it was a chemical at all.

8

*I see no need to lay waste to an entire world to end a
war. Gibad is intact—except for its sentient population.
The buildings are still standing. Its farmland and its
seas are untouched, and it can be recolonized in weeks.
War is never pleasant, but it can be waged in the least
destructive way, and let us not forget that this
bioweapon was created by a Gibadan scientist. It could
have been turned against any peaceful world in the
Empire. This is justice, is it not?*
—Emperor Palpatine, giving a statement to the media
on his policy on weapons proliferation in dissident
worlds

On board Cornucopia, freight terminal 35, Imperial City

"Are you getting this?" Prudii said. He stood with one
hand cupped to his ear, listening to the audio feed from
Niner's helmet via the bead comlink. "Is that Melusar
guy real? Listen to him."

Ordo eavesdropped via his helmet system while Ny
maneuvered *Cornucopia* along the traffic separation
lanes, skimming just above ground level. The rust-
bucket was just one freight vessel in an orderly line of inbound ships carrying imports from all quadrants of the
galaxy. Nobody knew any better.

And because the Empire was more worried about who
might be sneaking *off* the planet, it wasn't looking too
carefully at who was coming *in*.

Getting out would be trickier, of course. But they'd worry about that when it happened.

Ordo caught sight of one of the outbound terminals, now a sea of grounded freighters waiting for exit clearance. Every cargo vessel was being searched; nobody seemed to expect a fugitive to stroll back into the danger zone. That was just plain unimaginative. They should have known that special forces clones were compulsive risk takers, chancers to a man, raised to believe that nothing could stop them and everything was doable—one way or another.

"Maybe it's a trap," Ordo said. Commander Melusar sounded completely genuine and made perfect sense. He would have been right at home sharing a bottle of *tihaar* and arguing politics with *Kal'buir.* But he was an Imperial, and he'd hunt down Ordo and his brothers and execute them if he could. He didn't stand a chance, of course, but it was a fascinating conflict. "He'll lull the *vode* into a sense of security, make them feel they can tell him anything, and flush out the doubters and dissenters."

"We need a Jedi to sense his feelings."

"We're fresh out of Jedi, in case you hadn't noticed. Check his file when you get a chance, Jaing."

"It's not like the commandos obeyed Order Sixty-six to the last man, is it?" Mereel said. "Or some of the meat-cans, come to that. He *has* to realize he's probably still got some men who don't think the war's fulfilled their career expectations."

Jaing chuckled under his breath. "Palps should ask Kamino for a refund. He took the keys to that army thinking he'd get a hundred percent blind obedience. Sucker."

Ordo was disappointed that there hadn't been a mass exodus from the ranks. But he looked at his brothers and asked himself if he'd have made a run for it without them, if there'd been no Skirata around to tell them they had a right to lead different lives. He tried to see the galaxy from a meat-can's perspective, or even a Repub-

lic commando who didn't have Skirata to fall back on—
and there were still plenty of those serving. It was hard
enough to abandon the only life you knew without leaving your family behind as well.

*Especially if you don't even understand what else
might be out there for you. Poor shabuire. They never
had a chance.*

One thing was for sure. There wouldn't have been
many clones who stayed because they believed in Palpatine's political vision.

"I think he'll get his representatives to drop by to discuss his dissatisfaction with Lama Su," Ordo said.
"Maybe not now, but eventually. The man's got a lot of
planets to smack down before he starts on Tipoca."

Ny hadn't said a word since her last exchange with
Ground Traffic Control. She always looked like she was
chewing a saber-wasp at the best of times, not a woman
you'd approach expecting help and a kind word, but she
looked really grim now. She drummed her fingers on the
console every time the line slowed to a halt.

"Ny, are you okay?" Maybe she'd spotted something
he hadn't, an unexpected security check ahead. "It's all
going fine. You've done insertions before."

"You make me sound like the Galactic Marines." She
tapped her headset earpiece. "I'm listening to the news
feed. It's not good. They've attacked Gibad. And if it
sounds ugly via *that* Imperial mouthpiece, then you can
work out the rest for yourself."

There was only one reason for Ordo to worry about
Gibad's future, and that was the effect it would have on
Uthan's enthusiasm for her work. Skirata had done a
deal: if Uthan found a way of stopping accelerated
aging, then she could keep her research and go home. If
that home was reduced to a glowing river of molten
slag, Skirata's incentive scheme would be down the
'fresher. And Uthan didn't seem the type to be threatened into cooperation.

"*Shab.*" Mereel had obviously thought it through,

too. "We can't keep abducting top geneticists if *she* goes off the boil."

"Worse than that," Prudii said. "Uthan's the one who knows most about the aging mechanism. It's all second best after that."

"Stay on task, *vode*." Ordo tapped the helmet that Prudii had left on the seat beside him. "Nothing we can do about it now. *Focus*. We have a mission. Buckets on, and think meat-can."

Ny slowed and brought *Cornucopia* to a hover at the main exit. "And keep your heads down. We're coming up to the gate, and if anyone decides to check us out, I can't explain why I have four stormies on board."

"Copy that," Mereel said, feigning a meat-can tone of voice. "Yes *ma'am*."

"Ha ha . . . well, I'm fooled."

"They're all lousy shots, the Spaarti clones. I'm working on being mediocre."

Ny frowned at him. "That's an awful thing to say."

"Well, they're not made from fresh wholesome Jango like us. They're second-generation DNA, clones of clones. All kinds of problems, they say."

"How can you dismiss them all like that when you're the first to say you're more than your genes?"

Ny wasn't joking now. She was offended, and the frown was real, not habit. Ordo interrupted. Ny was to be kept placated, or else she might not marry *Kal'buir*, and finding someone else for his father was only going to get harder as time went on.

"They're Spaarti clones," Ordo said. "Grown in a year. It's not the raw material that causes the problems, it's lack of training time. We had blasters in our hands from the time we could walk. They've probably had a few months' training at best. We're bound to be better at everything requiring motor skills—until they've put the time in, of course. And then they'll be able to slot us with the best of them."

Ny leaned on the steering yoke and turned to look at him. She seemed to be studying his hands, as if imagining what size blaster a child of that age would need just to be able to grip it.

"Kal told me that," she said quietly. "About you handling weapons as toddlers, and all those tests and experiments. You poor little barves. It's criminal. No wonder you hate Kaminoans."

"Oh, they didn't expose us to live fire until we were two. Which is about four or five, in clone terms. We weren't *babies*."

Ordo wasn't making light of it. He was simply correcting facts, and he didn't expect to see Ny's eyes glaze with tears. Sometimes Besany had that look, too—pity, like she could see something he couldn't and that she didn't want to mention.

I don't need pity. None of us do. Not us Nulls, anyway. We control our own lives.

"*Kal'buir* saved us," Ordo said, "and after that, it was the aiwha-bait that was afraid, not us. Genetics isn't a cake recipe. They found that out fast enough."

Mereel seemed chastened. He still had to have the last word, though. He'd spent a lot of time working on the Kamino research data, and—Ordo had to admit it—he was getting annoyingly cocky about it all.

"Okay. I surrender," he said. "The Spaarti guys can be just as good as us if they eat their greens and work hard."

"Sad," Ny said wistfully, and went back to staring at the cargo doors of the freighter in front of her. "Very sad." She shook her head. "Do Niner and Dar know Palps is a Sith?"

"Yes," Ordo said. "I told Niner."

"And how did Dar take it when you told him Kal had refugee Jedi at Kyrimorut?"

"I didn't tell him."

"Don't you think he ought to know?"

Ordo had a feeling Dar wouldn't be comfortable with that. It was better to break it to him when he could see how harmless the two Jedi were. "He'll find out soon enough."

Outside the terminal, altitude was restricted, and Ny had to stick to freight skylanes. As soon as *Cornucopia* cleared the gates—no stops, no inspections, just a droid recording transponder codes for port taxes—she dropped the ship into a freight lane and headed for the nearest commercial sector of the city. Everywhere Ordo looked, there were advertiscreens exhorting citizens to be vigilant and report beings acting suspiciously. That applied to half the planet on a good day. The ad he found most unsettling was one that depicted a humanoid of indeterminate species skulking in an alley as if planting a bomb: HE COULD BE YOUR NEIGHBOR. YOUR FRIEND. YOUR BROTHER. YOUR SON. SUSPICIONS? COMM THE IMPERIAL SECURITY HOTLINE.

Imagine not being able to trust your own brother.

Ordo found that unthinkable. He had to respect Palpatine's capacity for getting the public to do his dirty work for him by sowing doubt and discord. Every citizen would be a spy, afraid of their own shadow and looking for threats everywhere.

"Palps must have more of an unhappy minority left over from the war than we thought," Mereel said. "After the cease-fire, always the purges . . ."

"New despots are always a little nervous."

"He's not exactly new at this."

"He had the Senate and the Jedi getting under his feet before. Maybe the new freedom to throw his weight around is making him a little giddy."

"I need directions," Ny said. "As in, you haven't told me where we're going yet."

"Just working that out now," Jaing said. "If you see a grocery warehouse, feel free to stop and load up while we talk to Niner."

"I know you're clever boys," she said, "but you do worry me. Whatever happened to precision planning?"

"Look at it this way, Ny. If we don't know where we're going next, nobody can plan an ambush for us, can they?"

Ordo prodded Prudii. "Monitor what that officer's

saying. Leave Niner to me. Can you separate the audio channels?"

"I can remote-launch the Emperor's private shuttle if you give me an hour."

"Yes or no?"

"*Yes.*"

Ny just snorted to herself and stuck to the skylane. She couldn't exceed the speed limit, anyway. Ordo activated his secure comlink with a couple of blinks, reassured that Ny was such a worrier. Worriers tended to check everything and not make dumb mistakes.

"Niner, are you able to talk?"

"Who's that?"

"Ordo, *ner vod.* We're clear of the freight port and we need an RV point."

Ordo could hear the hum of discussion in the background. Niner was still in the briefing. "*Shab,* that's short notice. This isn't Zey's brigade anymore, you know. We can't come and go as we please, and we're tasked at the last minute for security reasons. I need to set something up."

At least someone in the Imperials had learned from the liberties that Skirata had taken with the Jedi generals.

"We're ready when you are," Ordo said. "Got the chip?"

"Yes." Niner sounded as if he was trying not to move his jaw too much. His consonants were distorted. "And never ask where I had to hide it."

"Dar hasn't got a secure link installed, has he?"

"No, the droid couldn't get access to his helmet. But . . ."

"But what?"

"It's probably for the best. He's on a short fuse. I'm never sure what he's going to do next."

"Is he cracking up?"

"*Ner vod,* he saw his wife killed. Is he completely reliable and on top form? Not guaranteed. I haven't told him about the chip yet. Or that I'm in contact with you."

Niner was always the ultra-cautious one. "Then you have your doubts." *Great. We need Dar to stay cool. Never mind. We can extract them. Treat it like a cas-evac under fire. Or a civvie hostage.* "We'll allow for minimal self-help on this, then. Just don't feel insulted."

"We won't." Niner paused. "You know we went after General Camas, don't you? He's dead. Cost us a man, too."

"Ah, that was the *shabuir* who was going to chill us down after Geonosis, before Zey took over. Well, you got extra Palpatine Points for capping your old boss. He'll trust you more now."

"We hope."

"Now, that commander of yours . . ."

"Roly Melusar. Just took over from the Intel guy, Sa Cuis."

"He sounds keen."

"Very. He almost had me convinced that I could save the galaxy, secure lasting peace, and put an end to injustice, all before lunch."

"Almost?" Ordo said.

Niner's voice dropped to a whisper. "I want to go home before I get too comfortable here. Dar needs to get out, too. He really does."

"Consider it done," Ordo said. "We'll carry on monitoring your audio input. Try not to power down your *buy'ce* until we get to you. Ordo out."

Ordo listened to the audio as Prudii monitored it. He heard Scorch: *Holy Roly.* Ordo hoped the commandos didn't get too attached to the man. Charismatic leaders like Melusar could inspire you to do anything and feel it was a privilege to die for them. Ordo felt a little wary prickle tighten his scalp, and reminded himself that Skirata was just like that, too—pulling a knife on Kaminoan clonemasters, defying generals, instilling a sense of invincibility into any clone he trained, managing to be both uplifting and dangerous at the same time.

Men like that could wield enormous power for good or ill.

Maybe Melusar really is a decent man. But maybe he's out to entrap the security risks. I'll have to assume the latter until proven otherwise.

"Where to, then?" Ny asked.

"Do normal things," Ordo said. "Pick up supplies as per your transit sheet."

"Shopping." Ny tapped the nav computer on the console and set a skylane route. "Let's try the Core Comestibles Warehouse. It's bigger than Keldabe, and if they haven't got it, it doesn't exist."

The Empire ran a tighter ship than the Republic, that was clear. Niner would have to keep his helmet on at all times so he wouldn't attract attention as he waited for instructions. Ordo could feel a little bead of nervous sweat snaking down his spine, nothing to do with the temperature in his suit, and rubbed his back against his seat to relieve the itch.

He didn't usually get this edgy on a mission. But the memory of Shinarcan Bridge had dented his confidence a little. That extraction had been only seconds from completion, not even in hostile territory, but Etain had been killed and Darman and Niner had been left stranded.

Nothing was risk-free. And Nulls weren't omnipotent. *Just a lot faster, harder, and smarter than everyone else. We were built for this. Come on. We can do it.*

"Poor *Dar'ika*," Mereel said quietly. "Niner must think he's lost the plot completely if he hasn't even told him we're getting them out."

"Ah, you know Niner," Ordo said. His top lip itched with sweat now. He'd have to take off his bucket to have a good scratch while he had a chance. "He invented caution. He's got a secret ambition to be an accountant."

Prudii was still monitoring the briefing, recording it to extract every scrap of data and any subtle clues about the location that just might come in handy one day.

Ordo concentrated on the voices. "So they're interested in a human male, Master Djinn Altis, and they don't know much about him or how many followers he had . . . some guy called Jax Pavan . . . a bunch of Padawans—mainly human, some Twi'lek—a Whiphid called Krook or something, and . . ."

Mereel looked up from his datapad. "That'd be K'Kruhk. A Knight. The one who left the Order for a while because he wouldn't use clone troopers."

"Looks like most didn't survive the Purge." Prudii was listening intently, occasionally scribbling on his data- pad. "But it's clear that Imperial Intel doesn't have any hard numbers, and they don't know who's just missing and who's escaped. We can use that, I think."

"Can't they tally the bodies?" Mereel asked.

"You think the Jedi Order let them have a copy of the Temple payroll so they could tick-box the dead ones?" Prudii made a huffing sound. "Looks like they got most of the Masters. And the Knights. You can't fault Palps on strategic planning. Nearly a clean sweep."

"When they mention Kina Ha and Scout, start worry- ing."

"Why? I mean, why worry more than usual?"

"If Palps knows about Kina Ha's age, he'll be after her like a borrat up a drainpipe. Remember what Ko Sai said about why she went on the run? The old *shabuir* wanted her to extend his life span."

Altis. Ordo recalled one of the Altis sect Knights, a young woman called Callista Masana. Even if the Kaminoans hadn't engineered his eidetic memory, he'd never have forgotten her or her young comrades.

"I met some of the Altis Jedi," he said. "They have their own rules. Not like other Jedi."

"Are those the ones who had families?" Jaing asked.

Even Ny perked up at that. "They do like to bend the rule book, don't they?"

No, they were definitely *not* like other Jedi. Altis al- lowed attachment. They'd returned to the practices of a *less rigid and ascetic age,* as Etain had put it. They took lovers. They married. Ordo even saw Callista kiss her boyfriend, and nobody had apoplexy about it.

Ordo found the very existence of Altis's sect troubling. Their differences seemed so profound that he found it hard to believe the sect hadn't been a permanent topic of discussion in Jedi circles. Every Jedi who had to walk away from a forbidden love—and there had to be plenty, he was sure, because all beings needed someone—would have found that contradiction baffling and painful.

He did, too, but for different reasons.

There were Jedi he liked, and Jedi he despised, and then there was the Jedi Order, which was no better than the Senate as far as he was concerned. It existed for its own sake, like all institutions. After that, things got murkier. There were dissidents, the Altises and K'Krukhs of the galaxy, and there were all kinds of Force-using sects Ordo hardly knew about. They didn't seem to be one happy Force-bending family.

Commander Melusar regarded them all as dangerous. Ordo didn't have an answer to that, and uncertainty ate at him like the itch on his back. The argument was persuasive. He tried to separate the apparently unfair advantage of being able to use the Force from his own advantage of being vastly more intelligent than anyone else other than his brothers.

It was an interesting thought. He set it aside when Ny suddenly took a left turn, an unplanned one that set her route computer chiming to tell her she was lost. Ordo looked around, expecting trouble.

"Relax, *ad'ike,*" she said. She was learning the odd *Mando'a* word or two. "Just a detour past somewhere I'd rather not overfly again—not yet. One day, though."

"Where?" Mereel asked.

"Shinarcan Bridge." Ny pressed her headset closer to her ear to follow the newscast. "And Palpatine's just issued a statement about why he had to pacify Gibad . . . with a killer virus."

Kyrimorut, Mandalore; ten hours after the release of
prototype virus FG36

"I killed them," Uthan said. "This is all my doing."

She sat with her head in her hands, elbows braced on
the kitchen table. Jusik didn't know where to begin to
comfort her. He simply sat vigil with her, with Skirata
and Gilamar at the table, while the rest of the household
slept. It had been five hours since Gilamar had decided
Uthan had had enough of watching the destruction of
her civilization, brought to her courtesy of the Galactic
News Network and the generous sponsorship of Kuat
Drive Yards.

There wasn't much you could say to a scientist whose
bioweapon had just been used to slaughter millions of
her own people. Jusik willed Skirata not to make the observation that those who lived by the sword also stood a
good chance of dying by it, and had little right to gripe
if they did. Then he had a fleeting moment of panic as he
realized he'd come perilously close to mind-influencing
Kal'buir without even thinking about it.

*That's not right. You know that's the worst thing you
can do. And you know he's not susceptible.*

But at that moment, Skirata was; his guard was down.
He glanced at Jusik as if he'd felt something. Where was
the line between influencing someone the *wrong* way,
and just being able to silently divert them from saying
something because they knew you well enough to read
the subtlest of gestures? Jusik had no idea if he'd used
the Force or not. He found himself mired in guilt—guilt
at having that ability, guilt at worrying about it when
millions were dying, guilt for everything connected with
Uthan. He berated himself both for not pitying Uthan's
grief enough but also for turning a blind eye to her job,
which, at least in part, was killing at arm's length in vast
numbers.

*Moral certainty. What a joke. After all my high-minded
arguments with Master Zey about using clones, and here*

I am suspending my morals because I want Uthan to save my brothers.

But what could he do about a scientist like Uthan, other than disapprove? What did duty—ethics—demand when he came face-to-face with someone like that?

I don't know. I just don't. Should I bring her to justice? I don't even know what justice is these days.

Jusik's influence, whatever it was, didn't make Skirata pause for long. He tapped at his datapad, doing a passable act of being distracted.

"You sure it's your virus?" he asked Uthan. "There's plenty on the market for Palps to choose from."

Uthan finally raised her head. Her face was gray, utterly drained of blood. "And what do *you* think he'd use to make his point?"

"But how do you know it's your handiwork? Maybe he's so good at messing with our minds that we're doing his psy ops work for him." Skirata slipped his 'pad back in his pocket. "What have you seen that makes you think it's yours?"

Uthan looked at the dead holoreceiver's screen for a few silent moments. "It's mine, believe me."

She got up and pushed her chair slowly back from the table. Gilamar gave Skirata a discreet nod to say he'd take care of things, and followed her out of the room.

Jusik waited until their footsteps had faded and switched the news back on again. Gibad wasn't even the top headline on the hourly bulletins now. The attention span of the galactic news services was just as short as it had been under the Republic, and Palpatine's propaganda machine didn't have to work terribly hard.

One man—one Sith—can't do it alone. He needs help from the lazy and disinterested.

"Fierfek." Skirata shook his head. "The old *shabuir* picks his moments."

Jusik strained to focus on the small detail of the holo-cam shots of Gibadan cities. Disasters all had a sameness about them—cityscapes that looked almost normal, almost familiar, until the debris in the streets suddenly resolved into bodies, and the whole scene changed. Along the lower edge of the screen, brief headlines faded in and out. Some were relevant to the images, and some were totally different stories. Nobody paused and examined anything carefully anymore. Jusik could still concentrate, though, and he followed the headline as it scrolled laboriously.

FUGITIVE GIBADAN SCIENTIST BEHIND BIOWEAPON— VIRUS COULD HAVE BEEN USED AGAINST EMPIRE, SOURCES SAY.

"It's hers, all right," Jusik said. "Look. Palps has outed her."

Skirata frowned at the screen, seeming distracted. "He's a real sweetie, isn't he?"

"Why's he bothering to name her?" Jusik asked. "He doesn't need to justify himself, and there won't be many Gibadans left to bay for her blood."

"Could be plenty of expats left elsewhere, though. He might think they'll turn her in and save him some time."

"But he's got what he wants from her."

"Well, he's not got the clone-specific virus, or an extended life . . . and he's a sore loser." Skirata rubbed his eyes. "But how are we going to keep her mind on her aging research when she's just watched her own world go down the 'fresher thanks to one of her recipes?"

Skirata had his priorities, and they obviously didn't include weeping for Gibad. Jusik understood why that was a step too far for him. It wasn't the first world to feel Palpatine's fist, and it wouldn't be the last; all that mattered was that it wasn't Mandalore. But Jusik still felt a gut-level resistance to the idea of lying low, a need to do something that he couldn't define, even if he knew it was pointless.

"Is that a rhetorical question, *Kal'buir*?" he asked.

"No. I need to keep her motivated, and the best I can come up with is reminding her that we might end up being her only tool for revenge."

"You think she'll want vengeance?"

"She's human. Wouldn't you? Okay, maybe not . . ."

"It's hard to put those feelings aside, even with my training."

Jusik had come to accept his darker, unlovely side. Every being had one. Denying it was dangerous delusion. Anyone who thought it could be removed by meditation or willpower simply failed to recognize ugly motives for what they were, and gave them a perverse spiritual respectability. *You can kill without falling to the dark side if you don't feel anger or hate. That's what the Masters taught me. Oh, really? Tell that to the being you kill.* Jusik needed to know his normal, acceptable, *inevitable* human darkness, to shake hands with it and know its face, so that he could always recognize it in the shadows. He had to be able to see the brink to step back from it.

"What we need," Skirata said, eyes fixed on a point just past Jusik, "is for Uthan to work up a countermeasure for that *shabla* virus, in case Palpatine tries to use it on *us*."

"But that's going to divert her from the aging research."

"A virus will kill my boys long before rapid aging does. So we need to find a way of getting both jobs done. Maybe *Mij'ika* can soften her up."

Jusik was never sure whether Skirata—a very emotional man, without doubt—could feel much for strangers these days. There was only so much compassion anyone could expend in a lifetime without going under, and Skirata had already taken on the burden of every passing clone who needed help. It wasn't fair to see him as callous toward Uthan simply because he had other priorities. And Jusik knew it was all too easy to pity vast numbers of strangers on principle without being able to apply that to flesh and blood standing right in front of you.

I used to be so sure what was right. Didn't I?

Gilamar had been a loyal friend to Skirata for years. Jusik tried to find the acceptable line between exploitation and making the most of a friendship for mutual benefit. It wasn't easy.

"She'll want to lash out at Palpatine." Jusik knew he was complicit from that second onward. "I could feel her helplessness, and she's not used to it. She lives in a world where she does rational things and gets results from them. She's used to having control. Even in jail."

Skirata raised an eyebrow. "I know what you're thinking."

"You never needed Force senses, *Kal'buir*. I'm a lousy sabacc player."

"Yes, I *will* use her any way I can. She made the *shabla* thing. She knows she's got to do something—either to atone, or to thwart Palpatine. I don't care which, and I don't feel bad about exploiting that guilt. I might even be purging it for her."

"I'm not arguing."

"I care what you think of me, *Bard'ika*. I'm still honoring the deal I made with her."

Jusik didn't feel comfortable holding that much sway over Skirata. It wasn't the way things should have been; a son needed the approval of his father, not the other way around, and Jusik felt very much the son who had most to prove. *Kal'buir* was his benchmark of devotion, so selfless that it wiped the slate clean of his long criminal history. If he stole or killed these days, he did it for those he loved, and that included Jusik.

It's not the dark side if you don't feel hate or anger.

The old dilemma wouldn't go away. Jusik realized he applied the same self-justification as any of his former Jedi brethren. The difference was . . . *shab*, he couldn't work it out. It just felt different somehow.

"I know, *Kal'buir*," he said. "Do you think she ever tested it on humans?"

"Well, we know she never had the chance to test it on clones. I don't want to think about what scientists get up to behind closed doors. Turns my gut."

Jusik knew that the action of drugs, bacteria, and viruses could be modeled on computers, their biochemical actions predicted and plotted. But he found himself feeling worse for thinking that a virus designed solely to kill had been *tested* on anything living. It was a strange sensation. He was suddenly conscious of the weight of his lightsaber on his belt, and wondered exactly when and how some ancient Jedi had worked out that an energy beam could take off someone's head.

Nobody's hands were completely clean. All any being could do was to strive to make sure the dirt was kept to a minimum.

"I think you should just come straight out and ask her for the antibody, and tell her why," Jusik said at last. "She responds to reason."

Skirata nodded. Then he levered himself to his feet, both hands braced on the arms of the chair. "Time I got some sleep," he said. "They say you need less as you get older, but I just seem to need more."

Skirata hadn't slept in a proper bed since the night he saved the young Nulls from extermination in Tipoca City. He'd do what he'd done every night for the last eleven or twelve years: settle down in another chair with his feet up on a stool, or even curl up on the floor with a bedroll under his head as if he were still on the battlefield. He didn't talk about it. Everyone knew why he did it. It was a habit that had become a ritual, his unspoken vow that he wouldn't take it easy until his clone sons had their lives back. Jusik followed him into the *karyai* and watched him make himself comfortable—or what passed for it—on one of the upholstered seats.

He had a bedroom of his own, like everyone else. Only his clothing and his favorite Verpine sniper rifle occupied it.

"I'll talk to her in the morning," Jusik offered. "I won't even mess with her mind."

"I'll do it. Me and her, we've got an understanding."

Jusik recalled a comment *Kal'buir* had made a couple of years ago. He couldn't remember what had led to it, but it had moved him deeply, and every so often it surfaced in his memory: *Bard'ika, if you ever want a father, then you have one in me.* Yes, Jusik often wanted a father. He'd been handed over to the Jedi long before he was old enough to have any memory of his own. But he was now part of a culture where fathers and fatherhood *mattered*—not lineage or bloodline, but the long and infinite duty to a youngster who depended on you. He badly wanted to be part of this family, a real part, formal and permanent.

"*Kal'buir,*" Jusik said, "have you got room for another son?"

Skirata looked baffled for a few seconds, then smiled and held out his hand to grasp Jusik's arm, Mando-style, hand to elbow. "*Ni kyr'tayl gai sa'ad, Bard'ika.* I recognize you as my child."

Mandalorian adoption was fast and permanent, a few words to recognize someone as child and heir regardless of their age. Given the emotional weight behind it, the oath seemed almost inadequate.

"*Buir,*" Jusik said. *Father.* Everyone called Skirata *Kal'buir,* a mark of affectionate respect, but the word was now changed forever for Jusik, because it was suddenly real and literal. He was finally someone's son; someone with a name, someone he knew and cared about. For a man with no past, that sudden sense of completion was heady and unexpected. "I wonder where I'd be now if it wasn't for you."

Skirata let go of his arm. "Works both ways, *Bard'ika.* That's what makes us family."

The house was completely silent except for the crackle of embers in the *karyai's* huge fireplace and the occasional click as roof timbers contracted. Jusik made his way down the passages to his room. He didn't even remember falling asleep until he woke up staring into the dark vault of the ceiling, wondering what *that noise* was.

As always, it wasn't just a noise. He sensed a whole package of other information with it via the Force. It was dread, confusion, and a need to run. He let it wash over him for a moment.

Claws tapped on the flagstones in the passage. The door edged open.

"You heard it too, Mird?" Jusik whispered. The strill had its own kind of radar, a predator's sensitivity to every noise and smell. "How'd you know I was awake?" Jusik swung his legs out of bed and pulled on some clothes. "Come on. Let's see what it is."

Mird seemed to know where the sound was coming from. Jusik buckled his belt and lightsaber out of pure habit, and followed the animal past the kitchen to the main back doors that led out onto open country. Thaw or not, the air felt bitterly cold. Mird stood completely motionless, nose pointing into the breeze, and grumbled quietly in its throat. Someone was walking around the perimeter, occasionally cracking twigs in the undergrowth, and for a moment Jusik feared the worst—that the bastion had been found. But Mird's reaction—calm, more *worried* than defensive—told him it wasn't a stranger prowling out there, and what he sensed in the Force was a troubled spirit.

It was probably Arla, or maybe even Uthan unable to sleep. No . . . *Arla*. It was Arla. Poor woman, she was coming off those stop-a-bantha tranquilizers, and she was in no shape to be wandering around in the cold and dark in a strange place. He'd bring her back inside.

Mird trotted on without prompting, leading Jusik through the trees. They made enough noise not to startle her. Jusik tried to imagine what might have made her venture outside, and wondered if it had been such a good idea to leave doors unlocked. He spotted her standing on the bank of the stream that formed a natural boundary to the north.

"Hey, Arla," he called. Despite the racket he was making, she still flinched. "You're going to catch your death of cold. Come indoors."

Jusik ambled up to her, making a point of looking harmless. He wondered why some could live with horrific memories and others couldn't. *Poor Arla*. They'd done the right thing getting her out of that place. It

wasn't going to be easy adjusting to life outside, but it
had to be better than an institution.

He was about a meter from her now. She was radiating so much tension in the Force that he almost expected
her to panic and run, but she turned to face him almost
casually, right arm at her side, left hand in her tunic
pocket.

It was then that she raised her arm and he saw the
weapon—wood, a metal bar, he wasn't sure which. In
the stretched fraction of a second before it hit him, he
defaulted to being a Jedi, and sent her crashing backward with a Force blow that was pure reflex.

He should have seen it coming.

Mess hall, 501st Legion Special Unit barracks, Imperial City

Niner now had to think on his feet.

The longer Ordo and the others were on Coruscant,
the more they risked getting caught. He had to deliver
that datachip if nothing else. He also had to get Dar in a
position where he'd desert with him, right there and
then. There'd be no second chances or asking for a week
to think it over. If Ordo had to come back and run the
gauntlet of Imperial security checks again, the risks
would be even higher than hanging around.

It couldn't wait. He watched nervously as Darman
dawdled over his plate of noodles, and the moment he
twirled the last strands around his fork and slurped
them, Niner took the plate away and stood up.

"Practice range," Niner said. "I really need to sharpen
up."

It was stand-easy time, and they'd have the SU range
to themselves for a while. Darman just gave him a look
and didn't argue. They knew each other well enough to
gauge what was a problem and when it needed to be discussed elsewhere.

"Okay." Darman took the plate back and placed it
on the tray of a service droid as it passed on its never-

ending trawl for dirty dishes, cutlery, and spills. "Let's see what we can do. But remember the new guy's showing up in an hour."

Shab. Niner had forgotten about Rede. Well, they could get this over and done with by then, and then he could worry about how to handle Rede.

"An hour's plenty."

The interior range was soundproofed, ringed by handy booths and storage areas that were ideal for avoiding interruptions. Niner switched to his secure helmet link as he walked down the corridor, inaudible to Darman.

"Ordo? It's me. Where are you?"

Ordo was obviously standing by. There was hardly a second's delay. "Four klicks from your position, *ner vod*."

"I'm about to break the news to Darman. It'd be a good idea to give us a time and a place. Things are getting complicated here."

This time, the link went quiet for a few moments. "Where might you be able to hang around in full armor without looking too obvious, and where a freighter could lay up?"

"Is that what you're driving today?"

"Ny Vollen's crate. *Cornucopia*. It's a CEC *Monarch*, thirty meters length overall, beam ten meters, total draft fifteen meters."

Niner couldn't recall seeing the ship. He tried to visualize something that size and where it might hang around for a while without looking out of place. The first thing that sprang to mind was an industrial zone, but that wasn't somewhere a commando in full black rig could loiter without drawing attention in daylight. Then there were commercial areas, maybe the megastores with loading areas the size of small neighborhoods.

"Can we do this when it's dark?" Niner checked his chrono. "Seven hours, roughly."

"Yes."

"How about one of the waste processing plants?

They're full of vessel holding areas. Or a repulsortruck park."

"Repulsortruck park makes sense. You won't be hanging around long, anyway. Report in on the hour, and we'll fine-tune the RV time and location."

"Copy that."

"Very convincing, *Ner'ika* . . . Ordo out."

Darman nudged him. "You're up to something."

"Maybe." Niner checked that the range was clear, switched on the DO NOT ENTER safety sign, and steered Dar into the end stall. "Bucket off."

Darman took off his helmet, powered it down completely, and stuffed his gauntlets into it. "I get the idea," he whispered.

"Dar, I'm going to have to mention some painful things."

Darman looked like he was trying hard to be unconcerned. "Okay, I promise I'll stop eating things that give me gas."

"Serious."

"Yeah, I was afraid of that."

Niner hadn't spelled it out before. They both knew all too well what had happened the night of the Jedi Purge, and he thought that the less he reminded Darman of his misery, the safer it would be. Darman seemed not to want to talk about it, either. Now he had to.

"Dar, your kid needs you. We have to get out of here. Sorry. I don't know how else to say it."

Darman looked away for a few moments, focusing on the blasterproof wall. "I know," he said at last. "But I still feel like I'm running out on my buddies."

"Do you still want to . . . leave?" Niner was wary of saying the D word, even when he was sure he couldn't be heard. "We decided we would. All of us."

"Yeah. I remember."

"You want to see Kad again, don't you?"

Niner knew as soon as he said it that he'd stepped through thin ice.

Dar's eyes glazed with tears. "You know what?" he

said. "I don't know if I can look at him. When I look at him, I'll see her and everything we never got a chance to have as a family, and I don't think I can handle that."

"But he's your son." Niner understood exactly what he meant. "You'll pick him up, and all that father stuff is going to flood in. You'll want to be with him for exactly that reason—because he's yours and Etain's."

It was the first time Niner had dared say her name for ages. In fact, he wasn't sure he'd said it at all since the night she was killed. Her death hung over him and Darman like a permanent pall of smoke that they could both see but never mentioned, because its presence was so overwhelmingly obvious.

Dar shut his eyes for a moment and pinched the bridge of his nose. "How am I going to keep him safe? What if the Jedi come back?"

"If they ever do, they'll have to find him first, and then they'll have to get past Skirata. And the Nulls. And *me*."

The longer they waited to escape the less urgent it seemed, except for the fact that Kad was growing up without his parents. Niner wavered between looking forward to a new life and fearing that he'd waste it because he wouldn't know what to do with it.

"What did they do with her body?" Darman asked. A dam seemed to have burst, spilling out questions that must have been eating him alive. "I don't know where she is. Did they take her? I can't get it out of my head. I don't even know how to find out."

It seemed as good a time as any to tell him.

"I'll ask Ordo," Niner said.

Darman looked up very slowly. "You're in touch with the Nulls."

"Yes."

"When were you planning to tell me that, *ner vod*?" Darman hadn't been told he had a son for eighteen months. He didn't take kindly to being kept in the dark, and Skirata had the scars to prove it. "That explains a lot."

"No, it doesn't—"

"I knew it. You've been acting weird."

"I swear they only made contact today. That's why we're standing here now."

Darman wasn't catching on fast enough. "Cut the *osik*. Tell me."

"They've come to get us out."

Darman's gaze flickered. "They're taking a big risk."

Skirata always talked about cage-farmed nuna. It was hard to set them free, he said, because they'd been born in a cage and bars were all they knew. They'd often scuttle back to the cage when set loose, as if the sheer scale of the open fields overwhelmed them. Niner thought he saw that nuna look on Dar's face.

"That's why we need to get moving," he said. "We've got a few hours yet." He tapped his helmet. "Jaing seems to have a hundred ways of getting into government systems. The man's *inventive*."

"Okay," Darman said again. "Can I talk to him? Can I talk to Ordo? Why did he contact you, and not me?"

It didn't take a mind reader to work out what Darman wanted to ask.

"His spy couldn't find your helmet to slip the comlink in," Niner said. "You want me to ask him . . . about Etain?"

Darman put his helmet back on. "Yeah. Do that. Thanks. Look, I better go meet Rede. Ennen's not up to being sociable yet."

Niner watched him go, and realized that losing a wife was a different kind of grief. Mourning a brother killed in action was bad, and it never got any easier; commandos just found ways to cope with it day by day, and Ennen would, too. But there was no expectation of definite events in a shared life, none of the stuff that a couple assumed would happen to them—having kids, seeing those kids grow up and have kids of their own, and finally growing old together. Things that Darman had started to expect would happen to him would now never take place, even if he married again. The future with Etain had been glimpsed before a door had slammed shut. That somehow seemed even more cruel than just missing a brother in that general he's-not-there kind of way.

Niner put his helmet on and activated the comlink, still wary and half expecting to be intercepted. "Ordo, you there?"

"Receiving, *ner vod*."

"Darman needs to know what happened to Etain's body."

Ordo was silent for a few moments, as if he'd had to think about it.

"We took her back to Mandalore, and she was cremated in keeping with her custom."

"Jedi custom."

"*Kal'buir* wanted it." Ordo sounded almost ashamed. "Her ashes haven't been scattered. We're waiting for Darman to come home."

Niner felt a familiar ache behind his eyes and shut them tight until the feeling passed. "I'll let him know. Niner out."

Back at the mess hall, Darman and Ennen sat huddled at a table with a clone who had to be Rede. It was hard to explain to randomly conceived beings, but despite looking almost identical, this man was a stranger. The sameness got filtered out, leaving only the small variations—lines, gestures, tone of voice—as distinguishing features. Niner hadn't got the measure of Rede's yet.

And he was *one year old*. More or less.

Almost everything he knew, and every skill he had, was the result of flash learning. He just hadn't been alive long enough to undergo any of the basic training that took up the first years of a Kamino clone's life. He was going to have a tough time in special operations.

"*Sergeant*." Rede sat bolt-upright. "Trooper TK Seven-zero-five-five-eight, Sergeant."

"You'll probably end up calling me Niner." He sat down. "Small-squad habits. Did you volunteer?"

"No, Sergeant. Aptitude assessment."

"But how do you feel about joining us?" The lad had

to learn that he was free to say what was on his mind. "Happy? Annoyed? Upset at being separated from your old buddies?"

Rede paused as if it was a trick question.

"I'll miss them," he said. "But it's an honor to serve in the Five-oh-first, especially in the commando corps."

Honor wasn't all it was cracked up to be. Niner knew just how it felt to start over in a completely new squad among complete strangers. "Fair enough. Can you shoot better than the other Centax guys?"

"We can always use more range time."

Good attitude. Niner was aware of Ennen frowning at him. "So what do you think our overall objective is?"

"To neutralize insurgents, political agitators, and other security threats seeking to destabilize the new government, Sergeant."

It sounded like something Rede had learned. Poor kid; how could anyone cram enough into a human being in one year to make them functional but without turning them into basket cases? It still didn't sound right to Niner. And now there was a whole army of beings below him in the victims league. He wasn't sure if that made him feel better or much, much worse.

"I'll ask you that again in six months, if you're still with us," Niner said.

Ennen drained his cup of caf and got up. "If we're still alive."

Rede looked to Niner with an expression of grim anticipation, as if he was expecting some guidance. "What do we do now, Sarge?"

Sarge wasn't *Niner,* but it was a start. Niner felt a pang of guilt that he wasn't going to be around to look after Rede. He just hoped Ennen would latch on to him in the days to come. It was hard to look the guy in the eye and make reassuring noises when Niner knew he'd be gone by tomorrow morning.

"We start planning the next mission," he said. "Ennen, show Rede his locker and bunk. I've got an errand to run and then I'll join you. Dar? I want a word."

He made it sound as if he was going to give Darman a private dressing-down. Like all lies, he didn't enjoy it much, but it was temporary, because by this time tomorrow they'd be on their way to Mandalore, or even making themselves at home in Kyrimorut.

Niner had never seen Mandalore. It was weird to have a spiritual home he'd never visited, and a *real* hometown—Tipoca City—that he never wanted to visit again unless he was dropping in to bomb it back into the sea.

He walked out onto one of the barracks landing platforms with Darman and leaned on the safety rail, staring out into the forest of towers and apartment blocks whose foundations were more than a kilometer below. He'd never noticed there were so many surveillance holocams in the city before. Once they'd been a useful source of information; now they were a threat.

And he was *sure* there were more cams installed than there'd been six months ago.

"Dar, I spoke to Ordo," he said. "When you get home, there's something you'll need to do . . . something you'll want to do first, I think . . ."

Niner tried to imagine what it would feel like to hold the ashes of someone you loved, whether that gave closure or just ripped open wounds that hadn't even begun to heal. If it was him—

If it was *him*, he'd just see how little life had left him with.

9

I take nothing for granted. The Empire may well have millions of troops, but it is still a fragile thing, still in its infancy, and there will always be those who want to overthrow it. But they will look ahead to the time when they are powerful enough to do so; they have no idea that their best time to strike is now, while I have still to consolidate my power. As always, the ignorance and apathy of the populace works in my favor.

—Emperor Palpatine, to his secretary droid

Kyrimorut, Mandalore

Skirata could hear someone having a furious argument with General Zey, distant and muffled. But Zey was already dead, and that fact bothered him so much that he decided he had to be dreaming.

He was. He woke up in the chair but the yelling went on, because it was real. There was a brawl in progress. It took him a couple of moments to surface and work out that one of the voices was a woman's.

Shab, Jilka's finally snapped with Besany . . .

He scrambled to his feet and ran down the passage, nearly tripping over Mird as they met halfway. If there were intruders, the strill would have ripped them apart: so this trouble was domestic.

"Menav ni! Menav ni, taan!"

Jilka didn't speak *Mando'a*—no, it wasn't *Mando'a*, it was Concordian. That was Arla screaming blue murder and demanding to be let go. Skirata flung open the door to the rear lobby, instinctively letting his knife slip from his sleeve into his right hand. He found Jusik holding a wild-eyed Arla in an armlock.

Now Skirata could *see* she was Jango's sister. Her eyes had that same insatiable, wounded anger.

"Sorry, *Kal'buir*." Jusik's face was streaked with bleeding scratches. Arla froze, panting as if she was getting her second wind. "It was all I could do to get her back in here without breaking something."

"*Shab*." Skirata leaned out of the door and yelled. "*Mij'ika? Mij'ika*, you awake? *Medic!*"

Arla elbowed Jusik in the chest the moment he slackened his grip. "You stay away from me, Mando," she spat. "I'll cut your kriffing throat. I *promise* you. And you, Granddad, you come anywhere near me and I'll gut you."

Skirata could hear the clatter of boots approaching. Arla jerked her head back into Jusik's face with a loud *thwack*. The next second, she went completely limp and Jusik lowered her carefully to the floor, blood trickling from his nose. Skirata wasn't sure if she'd stunned herself or simply collapsed. Gilamar appeared in the doorway with his medic's bag and looked from Skirata to Jusik and back again.

"She'll be okay," Jusik said. He wiped his nose on the back of his hand. "It doesn't hurt. Ask Ruu."

"What?"

"Force stun. Sorry, but I had to do it." Mird wandered over to sniff Arla and lick her face, but she was out cold. "It's kinder than breaking her wrist."

Skirata tended to forget just what a range of combat skills Jusik held in reserve. "I don't think that would have stopped her. What happened?"

"I found her wandering outside, really agitated, and when I tried to get her to come back indoors, she went berserk and took a chunk of wood to me. She certainly knows how to scrap."

Gilamar held a hypospray up to the light to check it, then squatted over Arla to jab it into her arm. "This is what comes of stopping her meds abruptly," he said. "Now I know why they dosed her up to the eyeballs. I've got to find something to replace the sebenodone and taper the dose off properly."

"You can translate that into Basic for me sometime," Skirata said. He beckoned to Jusik and examined his injuries. His nose was bent slightly to one side. "Is this going to keep happening? I can't help but hear Vau telling me he told me so."

"Just because she's a convicted murderer, it doesn't mean this episode is her normal behavior," Gilamar said. "She's coming off a tranquilizer that would paralyze a Hutt, she's traumatized, and she's scared. There's nothing to suggest we can't get her past this stage."

"I feel so much better knowing that," Skirata said. Yes, it was his idea—and Jusik's—to spring her from the asylum, knowing full well that her file said *murderer*. He'd killed more than once himself, so he couldn't get too sniffy about anyone else's criminal record. "Just how dangerous is she?"

"Dangerous enough." Jusik submitted to a cold-pack on his nose, and stood with his head tilted slightly back. Gilamar tilted it forward again. "I can't keep wrestling her like this."

"Well, first thing we do is lock the doors, and put a lock on her room, for everyone's safety," Skirata said. This was a complication he didn't need, but he was stuck with it now. "You okay, son?"

"I'll live."

Everyone had woken up now and came to see what the commotion was about. A small crowd assembled at the door, led by Fi and Vau.

"Let's move her," Fi said. He and Parja didn't seem remotely surprised. Skirata had to admire his family's ability to take absolutely anything in stride. "Don't want her regaining consciousness with a crowd around her, do we?"

Vau shook his head. "Told you so."

"Yeah . . . so you did." Skirata had to look away as Gilamar eased Jusik's nose back into line. He *felt* that

pain as the cartilage moved back into place with a definite *shlick* sound. "But we can't dump her back on a
medcenter, and even if we find any Fett kinfolk on Concord Dawn, they won't be able to cope with her in this
state. So we need a solution."

"What makes you think we can cure what the Valorum Center couldn't?" Vau asked.

"We've got a vested interest in freeing her. They just
wanted her off the streets."

Gilamar seemed to be putting on a show of good
humor. He wasn't happy at all, though, and Skirata
didn't have to be a Jedi to sense it. "Kal, making crazy
people *un*-crazy is a long job if it's trauma that's driven
them nuts. Brain chemistry imbalances are relatively
easy. You just top up the oil, pharmaceutically speaking.
Bad experiences aren't as fixable."

"Maybe I can do it," Jusik said, his voice distorted by
his broken nose. "I'm good with brains."

"He brings Fi back from the dead, and suddenly he's a
brain surgeon." Gilamar winked at him. "Can you visualize what's happening in her brain that causes the problem? That's how you fixed Fi, isn't it? Seeing something
in your mind's eye and manipulating it with the Force."

Jusik shrugged. Skirata was suddenly aware of Scout.
She'd slipped through the press of bodies and was
watching Jusik intently, as if he was saying something
that nobody else could hear.

"It has to be possible," Jusik said. "The brain's a machine. Thoughts, feelings, memories—it all comes down
to chemical and electrical switches going on and off. I
think we manipulate that a lot, but don't realize we're
doing it."

"We?" Scout asked.

"Force-users."

Something had grabbed her imagination. Skirata could
see it written all over her face. "Show's over, *ad'ike*," he
said. "Time to get your beauty sleep."

While everyone else started drifting back to their
rooms, Scout looked back at Jusik again as if she was

going to ask him a question, but thought better of it. Besamy hung around.

"I'm going to keep her sedated until we can get some sebenodone," Gilamar said. "But that will just keep the lid on her at best, and maybe do her real harm at worst. That stuff's got a lot of *permanent* side effects. Now, I'm going back to bed, and we'll take a look at her in the morning."

Nobody had asked many questions about who Arla had killed. Skirata noted, as he occasionally did, that *aruetiise* had a different take from Mandalorians on the violent side of life. For millennia, they'd done the jobs that were too dangerous or difficult for other folks' armies, and hunted the galaxy's most violent criminals. Killing *happened.* And when you made your living that way, there was always somebody waiting to kill *you.* In the more genteel, better-fed parts of the galaxy, a single killing kept the news and the neighbors enthralled with horror for weeks. Here . . . it was simply part of existence, and only the circumstances mattered. There was no glamour to being a killer, and no stigma, unless the killing had been *ori'suumyc*—"way beyond," too far outside the rules of acceptable Mando conduct.

Arla was assumed to have her reasons until proven otherwise. But she wasn't a Mandalorian, despite her illustrious brother, and Skirata reminded himself that he knew almost nothing about her.

"What did you do to start her off?" Besany asked Jusik.

Jusik looked a little indignant. "Nothing, other than being male."

"I try not to imagine what would make a woman that scared of men." Besany fussed over Jusik's nose and made him a mug of *shig.* He drank it with difficulty. "And what would tip her so far over the edge."

"Well, she doesn't stand a chance of getting any better until we find out."

"Maybe she's always had mental problems," Skirata said. "We're assuming an awful lot. If everyone who had a horrific childhood turned into a psycho, half the galaxy would be at each other's throats."

It sounded callous as soon as he said it, and he didn't mean it that way. Besany hovered on the edge of a frown. "Has Ordo called in?"

"No. It's all on schedule."

"Oh well. I suppose he'll let us know in his own good time." Besany yawned. "It'll be good to have Darman and Niner around again. The place doesn't feel complete without them. Good night, *Kal'buir.*"

It was three in the morning. Skirata wondered what an uneventful life felt like. But his boys were coming home, and he had a brand-new son in Jusik, and that kept the hurdles he had to face in some kind of perspective.

This is who it's for. This is why it's worth it. Work through the problems one at a time. Eventually . . .

"How are you feeling, *Bard'ika*?" Skirata ruffled his hair. "You want a painkiller?"

"I'll be okay, thanks," Jusik said. "Not the first black eye I've had."

"You should spend more time healing yourself, you know. It's not selfish."

"Fi still needs therapy. And I'm sure I can do something for Arla. I've just got to work out how. *Kal'buir,* if you could feel things in the Force . . . the *misery* that just flows out of her is terrible. It's like she's permanently crying."

Skirata found it revealing that Jusik talked about his powers in such technical terms—therapy. He saw his Force abilities in terms of the real world, like a tool that obeyed the laws of physics and could be understood and explained. He'd never been all that mystic. Sometimes Skirata felt his powers embarrassed him because they weren't logical, and that he needed to nail them down and define them.

If only they'd all been like him. If the Jedi had all been like Jusik, we'd never have been at war with them.

"Get some sleep, *Bard'ika,*" Skirata said.

He walked past Arla's room just to check things were back to what passed for normal. Mird was curled up right in front of the door, one golden eye open and watching Skirata, nostrils flaring briefly as it sampled his

scent. The strill usually slept at the foot of Vau's bed. It
had either been put on sentry duty or decided for itself
to guard Arla's door.

*Ny's really got a soft spot for Mird. Bantha bone in-
deed . . .*

He missed her already. He hoped she was getting on
all right with the Nulls. Mird grumbled as if to reassure
him that everything was under control, and that he
really ought to get some rest now.

Rest wasn't easy. Skirata checked his chrono to work
out Coruscant time, and decided that Ordo would be
calling in soon. Then there was Uthan to deal with before she got too distracted by Gibad's fate to focus on
what needed doing.

I'm a real piece of work sometimes, aren't I?

For some reason, he thought of Dred Priest, probably
because he was a piece of work, too, and wondered if
the *chakaar* had heard that his *Cuy'val Dar* comrades
were around. Everyone at the *Oyu'baat* knew; Skirata
had to assume Priest did as well. He wasn't sure just
how much of a risk Priest might be.

*No, he likes being alive too much. And if he knows
Gilamar's here—he won't want any trouble.*

Skirata settled down in the kitchen with a mug of *shig*
and listened to the news feed for the latest on Gibad.
There wasn't a lot to report, seeing as most of the inhab-
itants were dead, and any expats wouldn't exactly be
rushing to the nearest offworld studio to express their
outrage.

*Am I wrong to lean on Uthan when she's just lost her
entire world?*

*In the end, we all walk over those we don't really care
about. Only difference is that I don't lie to myself about it.*

After a while, his comlink chirped. Ordo was a little
early. Skirata opened the channel, wanting to hear that
Dar and Niner were on their way back, but realizing that
it would probably take a while to slip out of Coruscant.

Imperial City, my shebs. *Corrie.*

"Sergeant?" said a voice.

It wasn't Ordo. The voice was familiar, a clone's, but not one of Skirata's boys. It could have been anyone; word was probably finally getting around that there was a safe haven for deserters. It was hard to let those who needed sanctuary know where to get help and still keep Kyrimorut's location a secret, but Skirata's old comlink code was known by quite a few, and there was now no way that the link could be traced to a specific location.

"Who wants to know?" Skirata said.

"It's me, Maze. Formerly *Captain* Maze."

Maze was on the wanted list. He was the last clone Skirata would have bet on to desert, but then ARC troopers were a funny bunch. "You need help, son?"

"I heard you were . . . running a relocation service."

Skirata felt a sudden flood of relief. *This* was what he'd set out to do. His existence was justified. "We'll get you sorted out. You want to tell me where you are?"

"How do we handle this?"

"We don't give coordinates over the comm. Pick an RV point, and we'll come to you."

Maze paused. "Fradian. The ore terminal."

"Might take a couple of days." Skirata couldn't get a location from Maze's comlink. But he would have been disappointed if an ARC captain wasn't cautious to the point of paranoia. "You okay to hang on?"

"Yeah."

Skirata wanted to ask Maze what had made him jump ship, but that could wait. The less time they spent transmitting, the better. He'd tell Maze about the Imperial garrison when he needed to, but no ARC was going to be troubled by a few Imperials for neighbors.

"Want to give me your comlink code? It's not showing."

"It's a public comm booth," Maze said. "I'll call you again when I get to Fradian."

He could have been anywhere, then, and he had his reasons for not saying. Skirata closed the link and smiled to himself. The waifs and strays were coming home at last. Everything was going to work out fine, he knew it.

"Come on, *Ord'ika*," he murmured, glancing at his chrono. "Call me. Tell me my boys are on their way."

Freight vessel park, Quadrant G-80, Imperial City

Ny wished she'd sprung for a better security system for *Cornucopia*.

The freighter's external cams gave her a limited view of the outside world, just the critical areas she needed to keep an eye on for safety—the cargo ramp, the drive exhausts, the ground immediately beneath the landing struts, and the main hatch. As she sat fretting about who might be lurking in the yard waiting to arrest her, she realized just how much she *couldn't* see.

It'll be dark in a few hours, too.

"Relax, Ny." Prudii looked engrossed in his datapad, but he had even better peripheral vision than she thought. "The eggs won't break."

In the hold, a complete pallet of assorted eggs—nuna, marlello, even meal-sized ganza eggs—was secured to the deck. Ny hoped the rest of the tasks on her list would be as easy as getting the groceries. If she'd known how long they were going to be stuck here, she'd have stocked up with a lot more supplies.

"It's not broken eggs I'm worried about," she said. "It's other broken things. Like legs and necks."

The big illuminated sign on the opposite side of the compound really bothered her. It was the only new, shiny thing she could see in the area, which still bore signs of cannon damage from the failed Separatist invasion, blast-pocked walls and gaps in the rows of buildings like missing teeth. The sign showed a kindly but serious cop and a stormtrooper, side by side, guardians of the new Imperial peace, with the words: SUSPICIOUS? OUT OF PLACE? REPORT IT. BE THE EMPIRE'S EYES AND EARS.

The posters were big, bright, and *everywhere*. It gave her the creeps.

"Cheapens the military image, doesn't it?" Jaing flexed his shoulders as if the new armor was too tight. The Nulls were more heavily built than the average trooper, and Ny wondered when the recreational eating at Kyrimorut was going to show up on their waistlines. "They'll have stormies issuing parking tickets next."

Ny reached across and twanged his belt. "I'd really recommend trying the concealed tanks for size, boys. The Jedi found it a tight squeeze. And we'll have *six* strapping lads to hide on the way out."

"Not for long," Prudii said. "And these suits are atmosphere-tight for half an hour."

Ny had visions of the clones clinging to the outside of the ship like Salgari street kids sneaking free rides on transport speeders. "You're going to have to draw me a picture."

"Means they can withstand immersion, too. Who's going to look for illegals in a *full* water reservoir? Or a full fuel tank, come to that."

"That's just mad," Ny said. The idea made her shudder. That fuel was liquid trimoseratate—not as volatile as liquid metal, but nasty enough. "You're off your kriffing heads."

"We can't help it, *Buir'ika*." Prudii stood with his finger pressed into his ear. He was just listening to the audio feed from Niner, but he hammed it up into a credible impression of a lunatic. "The aiwha-bait built us crazy."

Mereel raised an eyebrow. "As long as I don't have to hide in the waste tank."

"They might not even try to board us," Ordo said. "And your faith in Imperial procurement quality is *disturbing*."

Mereel didn't take the bait. "Everyone's a comedian . . ."

"So what's the plan *now*?" Ny asked. "We just sit here?"

She was defying an Emperor who'd wiped out a planet for arguing with him, and she was scared that she'd be the weak link that compromised the whole mission. The Nulls could stroll through this without breaking a sweat, but she was in danger of letting them down by looking like she had something to hide when they had to clear departure checks. Waiting wasn't easy. It gave her too much worry-time.

"Yeah, we just sit here," Jaing said. "Unless Niner calls for assistance."

Ordo was never chatty. He was staring at the bulkhead chrono, counting down to something else entirely—his scheduled sitrep call to Skirata. Every six hours, on the dot, he commed Kyrimorut to update him. Ny watched his gaze fixed on the seconds on the chrono display.

Five, four, three, two . . .

"*Kal'buir?* Everything's fine here. You've seen the news on Gibad, I assume."

Jaing, Prudii, and Mereel seemed to be ignoring the conversation. Prudii was listening to Niner's audio feed while he read a technical manual and made notes in the margin. Jaing and Mereel were watching something on Jaing's datapad screen.

"My," Jaing said, all smug satisfaction, "hasn't my little backdoor program been busy? It's always gratifying when your offspring come of age and branch out on their own."

"Is that the *second* one you fed into the system?" Ny asked.

"They were so trusting, the Republic. So *innocent.*"

"What's it found?"

"You sure you want to know? With much knowledge comes bad stomach acid."

Skirata had explained how Jaing had acquired the clan's vast fortune by skimming off just a cred— sometimes half—from trillions of bank accounts via the galactic clearing system. It was, by anyone's standards, a bank robbery on a grand scale; theft, fraud, a very *wrong* thing. If Jaing had walked into a branch of the Core Bank and hosed the staff with a blaster before making off with bags of credit chips, Ny would have classed him as a criminal. But when she watched him so clearly delighting in his technical genius, all she could see was a nice young man who'd had the worst imaginable start in life, and who was now redressing the balance in favor of other young men just like him.

Skirata called it social taxation. Ny tried to work out just how far the Nulls would have to go before she'd find them frightening or repellent. But they were professional killers and saboteurs, however kind to animals and polite to old ladies, unashamedly dangerous men who were bred to be lethal. Ny just happened to be within their defensive circle, not a target beyond that protective boundary.

Would they kill me if they thought I was a threat to Skirata's scheme?

She knew the answer, even if they didn't.

"Bankrupting Palps again?" she said carefully.

"More like searching through his drawers." Jaing smiled. "He keeps a lot in them, or at least his idiot minions do. Every citizen on a database, data shared among departments, clerks who use their pet akk's name for passwords . . . once you get past the first level of security, you can just wander around stripping whatever you want from the system. Treasury data, banking, personal details on Imperial employees, procurement plans, government speeder pool schedules . . . you'd be amazed how this stuff all builds a picture."

"No, I wouldn't, because I was spying on KDY for you lot, remember?" Ny said.

"So you were." Mereel smiled. "*Kal'buir* likes his ladies a bit *risky*."

Ordo was taking no notice of them, still deep in conversation with Skirata. He seemed to be listening more than talking, eyes shut occasionally as if he was struggling to concentrate. Ny heard him say, "Well . . . that's a surprise. Okay, *Buir*. Ordo out."

That was worrying in itself. Ordo had everything

nailed down and under control. He was never surprised
by anything as far as Ny could tell.

"What's a surprise?" Mereel asked.

Ordo sat down and stretched out his legs. "Guess
who's asking for sanctuary? *Maze.*"

Ny couldn't recall meeting Captain Maze. The other
clones gave her the impression that he was humorless
and lonely, although Fi said he was all right for an Alpha
plank, whatever that meant. Ordo seemed to have
grudging respect for him. He described him as *persistent.*

"Really?" said Mereel. "He must be missing you,
Ord'ika."

"*Kal'buir*'s working out how to get him to Mandalore. He didn't head straight there. Odd."

"Maybe he thought it was too obvious a location for
Kyrimorut."

"And you, Jaing—*Kal'buir* wants to know if your
program can trawl for Arla's criminal record. He wants
the details of the murders. She attacked *Bard'ika,* and
the more background they have, the better the chance of
rehabilitating her."

Ny was appalled. "Is he okay?"

"Broken nose and a few scratches. He's fine."

Prudii shook his head, clearly dubious about the
whole thing. Ny got the feeling that the Nulls accepted
Arla because Skirata's word was law, but that left to
their own devices they wouldn't have rescued her.

"If she comes after *me* with a meat cleaver," Mereel
said, "I might forget my manners."

Nobody mentioned Gibad or how Uthan had taken
the news. The only question was probably how disabling the shock had been, and whether the scientist was
able to get on with her task. The promise of being allowed to return home had been all that was keeping her
going.

Prudii suddenly held up a finger for quiet, staring in
defocus at the bulkhead as he concentrated on the audio
feed.

"Hey, Niner's on the move," he said. "Melusar's called him and Dar into a briefing."

"Just them?" Ordo asked. "Not the others?"

"Sounds like it. Maybe they're the flavor of the month for finishing off Camas. Big prize."

"We've got a few hours yet. Whatever it is, we can wait for them."

Ordo folded his arms and looked relaxed enough to nod off. The Nulls seemed to treat this level of danger as absolutely normal, and Ny envied their cool confidence. Skirata had done a great job of raising them to believe that they could do absolutely anything. The fact that she'd come here with them was proof of that. They made walking into the Emperor's front yard and scamming him in broad daylight seem routine.

Night was the best time to do this kind of op, Ordo said, but Ny had always been a little afraid of the dark. Humans had evolved with that hardwired fear for a reason. The dark was dangerous.

She adjusted her seat so that she could see all the security cam outputs on the bulkhead, expecting a rap on the hatch at any time and the sound of a loudhailer demanding that she exit the freighter, put her hands behind her head, and surrender.

"So what's on the chip, do you reckon?" Mereel said. "Names, places, codes?"

"You'd think they'd memorize things and not record them." Jaing shook his head. "They never learn."

"Good old Jaller," Prudii murmured. "But one day soon, we're going to need to get him out of here. He's going to get caught."

Ordo glanced out of the viewplate. *Cornucopia* was too high off the ground for anyone to see into the cockpit, and Ny had made sure the ship was turned away from the security cams. They seemed to be a token gesture. Nobody parked valuable vessels or cargo in this yard. It was too easy to enter. That was why she chose it.

"Just when you think that all *aruteiise* are the same,"

Ordo said, "you find another one who puts their life on the line for you."

Ny reflected on that, stomach churning, and saw herself from the outside for a few moments: a crazy old widow with a beat-up ship, smuggling enemies of the state, hanging out with a gang of assassins and thieves, trying to outsmart a dictator who killed whole planets to make a point.

At her age, she should have been knitting vests for *Kad'ika* and telling him stories.

But terrified or not—crazy or not—it made her feel thirty years younger.

501st Legion Special Unit barracks, Imperial City

Commander Melusar's small office had a dead, muffled silence that made Niner feel that his ears had blocked up.

The walls were covered in sheets of flimsi—charts, lists, calendars. A single desk lamp and a holochart projection lit Melusar's face from below and made him look cadaverous. It all felt like a dressing-down session waiting to happen. *Reasons in writing with no caf*, Skirata called it, a terse could-do-better speech from your CO. Niner held his helmet under his arm, systems still active, wondering how much the Nulls would be able to hear.

"Camas was your commanding officer, wasn't he?" said Melusar. He didn't sound in dressing-down mode, though. "Can't have been easy facing him like that."

This had to be a test, then. Niner was determined to pass it long enough to get to the extraction point. Melusar seemed like a nice enough guy, but Niner and Darman had plenty to hide, and so any figure of Imperial authority was a threat until proven otherwise.

Two of our old squad on the run. Our sergeant and everyone we know—all on the death list. Even Zey didn't trust us completely. Why should Melusar?

"We weren't conscious at the time, sir," Niner said.

Melusar looked up from the holochart. He was moving virtual markers around with a stylus, each green point of light representing the last known whereabouts of an escaped Jedi. The green lights were dwindling in number.

"Sorry?"

"We were put in stasis when we got back from Geonosis, then revived three months into the war," Niner said. "So we didn't see much of Camas. General Zey was our CO for most of the time." And there was something he had to add, because Melusar's observation didn't make sense unless he was stupid—which he clearly wasn't—or trying to entrap them. "Most troops had to take out their own Jedi officers, so it was no harder for us than it was for them. Easier, actually, sir. Camas was firing at us."

Omega hadn't carried out Order 66, of course. They'd been too busy trying to desert. Niner had a terrible sick feeling in his gut as he was reminded just how close this was becoming to a rerun of that awful night.

"But it's about doing the job, Sergeant." Melusar said. "It's about being a professional. And you're still here when others aren't."

Only a civvie would have thought of Order 66 in simple terms of either unflinching loyalty or cruel betrayal. It was neither. It was *complicated*. It was the sort of *complicated* you could only truly grasp if you were standing there with a rifle in your hands, if all your buddies were dead, if you understood exactly why orders weren't optional. And it was the sort of *complicated* you just didn't have time to debate and second-guess in the middle of a crisis.

That was why you drilled. That was why you had orders. It was to make sure situations—and soldiers—didn't fall apart when things got tough.

There were clones who liked their Jedi officers, or hated them, or didn't know them well enough to have an opinion, and there were clones who felt the Jedi had simply used up troopers' lives in their plan to overthrow the government. But most of them carried out the order, and for one reason—lawful orders couldn't be ignored when you felt like it. The army was there to do the bidding of elected governments, not to decide policy for itself. Orders came from those who had the bigger picture when you didn't.

But we didn't obey.

Nothing to do with some moral stand. Everything to do with wanting to get away, and not wanting to kill two ex-Jedi who gave up everything for us. Our buddy. And Dar's wife.

Niner didn't feel good about that. Part of him now wondered if fate was punishing him for letting the other squads down. They'd behaved like pros, whether it had broken their hearts or not, and Omega hadn't.

Darman stood to Niner's right, saying nothing.

"Got a job to do, sir," Niner said noncommittally. He could smell a fresh herb scent like tea and the metallic aroma of ink or copying fluid. "No heroics. Just the job."

"Well, I'm still impressed you got Camas," Melusar said.

"He seemed to want to be *got*, sir."

"Oh, he'd have made a run for it if he could have. But Intel's pretty sure that the Ranger escaped, possibly with some Padawans. They've been piecing together ship movements that coincided with your raid. Latest analysis says Kester's shipping escapees from planet to planet and then to a couple of Masters—Altis or Vamilad."

Niner felt the hidden datachip gnawing away at his pocket. He was so used to dealing with Jedi officers that he expected Melusar to be able to sense his deception, but Melusar was a regular guy, and that changed things.

Melusar tapped his stylus on the holochart control. One more green light winked out of existence. "You know why removing Camas was a coup, Niner? Because every Jedi Master we remove lessens the chances of the Order rebuilding itself. Without the Masters, the cult starts to die. They've learned all the tricks. If they can't pass them on, can't organize—it's over. Cut off the head and the body eventually dies."

Niner wasn't sure about that. "But the Knights are pretty smart, too. As long as there's one Jedi out there, they'll know enough of the basics to find Force-sensitives and train them."

"Exactly." Melusar looked at Darman, and then nodded to himself, smiling. "They're *all* a risk."

Niner couldn't work out if Melusar was testing him or leading up to some revelation. "We'll do whatever we're tasked to do, sir."

"Jedi don't have numbers on their side now, Niner, and they don't have the taxpayer bankrolling ships and arms for them. They'll hide for a while and lick their wounds. But then they have to do two things—contact other Jedi to regroup, and then latch on to mundane beings to mount an insurgency. They need an army to do their dirty work for them. They'll sniff out dissent wherever they can find it, ferment it, and ride it. Nobody who's that used to power can ever give it up."

Niner understood that only too well. On Qiilura, Zey and Etain had trained and organized the locals to fight the Separatist occupation; they called it a *resistance*. When the Seps did the same thing against the Republic, that was called *exporting terror*. Niner just saw it all as combat by any means available, although he knew whose side he was on at any given time.

They're as bad as each other. And we're always the meat that gets minced between the two.

"Sir, I don't understand," he said. "Are these new orders? Are we going to be tracking Jedi by looking for insurgent hot spots?"

"Everything we discuss in this room goes no farther."

"That's a given, sir."

"Not even to your squadmates."

That felt pretty uncomfortable. A squad shared everything. Niner never liked agreeing to anything before he knew what it was, but he was deserting in a few hours, so this was either intel he might be able to make use of in his new life, or something he could forget the moment Ny Vollen's ship left orbit. Darman just watched—probably doing his best not to lose it, Niner supposed. It couldn't have been easy to listen to a casual conversation about Order 66.

Did Melusar know? Did he know about Etain, who she'd been, what had happened to her? Niner racked his brains to think who might have been around and able to gossip. No clones, that was certain, but there'd been a lot of CSF cops around, and however tight-lipped they were under Obrim's command, everyone talked sooner or later.

"Understood, sir," Niner said.

"Sergeant, this office is soundproofed, and I sweep it for surveillance devices every time I open the door." Melusar was a man after Niner's own heart. "This really is between us."

Wow, he's jumpy. Or he's going to shake us down.

"Got it, sir."

"Your squad was very close to General Jusik, wasn't it? Give me your assessment of him."

Niner's gut almost tied itself in a complete knot now. It didn't show on his face, he was sure of that, because clones learned in Tipoca City how to present a bland face to the Kaminoans. For the ordinary troopers, it saved them from being reconditioned. For commandos protected by their ferocious training sergeants, it was just a habit, but a useful one.

"Depends what you mean sir. As a soldier?"

"As a Jedi."

"He left the Order, sir. He was ashamed of it in the end. Argued with the Masters, told Zey they'd lost their moral authority. Didn't want to be a Jedi anymore. If you're wondering if he'd be regrouping survivors—no, not him."

It was true. Niner just hoped he hadn't said it with too much conviction, though.

"Just curious. I'd heard he walked out, and walking away from power is pretty unusual in most species."

Melusar seemed to back off. Niner was now on full alert. "Remember that not all Force-users are Jedi, and they're not all on the run. Some of them are right here pretending to be on our side. But I don't buy that. The only side they tend to be on is their own."

Niner just concentrated on the green lights of the holochart so that he didn't blurt out something he'd regret. *Does he mean Vader? Does he know about Palpatine? If he does—he's going to be a dead man. Shame. But I can't help him now.*

Niner was now painfully aware of the chrono ticking, delaying his escape, but at least the Nulls would know why he and Darman might be running late.

"You're very quiet, you two."

Darman suddenly came to life, scaring the *osik* out of Niner. He had no idea what was going to come out of Dar's mouth next. "We haven't got a lot to say, sir."

"You know why I'm telling you all this?"

"No sir."

"Because I need a few men I can trust in *difficult* times." Melusar's understatement almost reminded Niner of Vau. "I don't doubt any trooper's loyalty and discipline, but sometimes we'll need to do things without Intel noticing. And from what I've heard over the last year or two—you fit the bill. You had a very *independent* sergeant in Skirata. You were completely loyal to him *and* to the Grand Army. By some extraordinary process, all your Republic records, helmet logs, and everything else relating to your service has now disappeared from the Defense mainframe." Melusar paused. "I know enough about you from the war. You didn't desert when you could have with the others, but you haven't betrayed Skirata now, either. That can't be easy."

Melusar had no idea just how *not easy* that was. Niner felt horribly ashamed as he hovered on the brink of making an excuse to leave. *To desert.* He still couldn't shake the feeling that this was entrapment. But then Melusar was taking a big risk confiding in them that he

was planning to sideline Intel. This was his first day as
their boss. He obviously didn't believe in hanging
around.

"What do you want from us, sir?" Niner said. He
only had to keep this up for an hour or two at most.
"Just say the word."

"I'm not convinced that Intel is free of Force-users.
They think we mundane folk don't notice, but I can usually spot them. So . . . sometimes I'm going to have to
task you without their knowledge, because they can
never be on the side of the average citizen. They're trying to recruit more of their own Force-using kind. Or at
least that's how I've interpreted their request to bring
the Z-list Jedi and other small fry back alive." Melusar
oozed contempt. "Personally, I'd rather spend the security budget on more akk hounds."

Business as usual. Omega and the Nulls had spent the
whole war keeping things from Intel, and from the senior command, too. And it wasn't because they were
Force-users.

But Melusar really had it in for everyone with Force
powers. Niner wondered what had happened to him to
make him so unusually rabid. His arguments made perfect sense, but he *meant* that distrust and dislike with
every cell in his body. It oozed from him.

"Are you comfortable with that?" Melusar asked quietly.

"We understand perfectly, sir," Darman said, before
Niner could respond.

"Excellent." Melusar seemed genuinely relieved. "Pity
that we don't have the principled General Jusik on staff.
A Force-user who doesn't want power would be very
useful."

Niner hoped Ordo picked that up. The comment could
have meant anything. It might have been an oblique offer
to Jusik, which—of course—*Bard'ika* would have the
sense not to accept. It might have been a setup. Niner
was beginning to resent everything about this world for
making him doubt and question every single word said

to him. He wanted to live in a society where *hello* just meant *hello*.

But he needed to seize his chance. Now seemed a good time. "Sir," he said, "during the war, our commanders let us go into town when we were off duty. Do you mind if we do that? It's not even mentioned in the regs, so . . ."

Melusar slapped Niner's shoulder as if his conscience had been pricked. "Of course, Sergeant. A man's got to relax and have an ale from time to time. Good for the soul. Maybe take Rede with you. I worry for these young-sters."

Niner had to get out, right now, before he dug himself in too deep. "Thank you, sir."

"Dismissed. And don't worry so much. You're still the soldiers you were, and everyone respects that."

Darman matched Niner's hasty escape down the cor-ridor, striding as fast as he could without breaking into a run.

"He's really down on Force-users," Darman said.

"Do you blame him?"

"No." Dar seemed to be chewing something over as he walked. He stared at a point a few meters ahead. "But they're all the same, aren't they? Jedi, Sith—doesn't matter who's in charge as far as most folks are concerned. The Force-users run the show, at least be-hind the scenes, and never us."

"You think the Jedi ran the Republic?"

"You said a Sith did. The Jedi were the enforcers—even before Palps."

"It doesn't matter now."

"No, I suppose not."

"Are you okay?"

"No, I'm scared stiff. This galaxy's falling apart." Dar dropped his voice as they turned into the mess lobby. "My kid. What's going to happen to my kid? You heard what Holy Roly said. He can't even trust Intel now. We've swapped one rotten regime for another."

"Welcome to the real world," Niner said. "But there's always a door marked EXIT."

They didn't need to take anything with them. They didn't have anything of value, anyway. Niner had to keep his helmet on to maintain comms to the ship.

Rede was busy cleaning his boots when they walked into the squad room. He looked up, wide-eyed. No, science couldn't possibly cram enough into these Spaarti clones in a year. Poor kid—they were walking out on him when he needed them most. Ennen wasn't around.

"Are you going to show me some vibroblade techniques, Sarge?" Rede asked. "I'm a fast learner."

"Tomorrow," Niner said. He felt awful. Now he had to lie completely. "We're just going for a recce around town. Old buddies to check up on. We'll be back before lights-out."

Rede frowned slightly, but went on cleaning. The truly weird thing was that he seemed to be changing before Niner's eyes. He really was learning by the minute. In the space of a day, he'd picked up habits and gestures. Whatever medical science tried to do to human beings to speed up their development, they still had to go through that process of learning from adults around them and then fitting in with the tribe. Rede was just doing it faster than a Kamino clone.

And we did it faster than mongrels.

"See you later," Darman said. He was pretty convincing.

Niner put his helmet back on as they walked through the main doors and headed for the perimeter gate. Beyond that lay what had been Galactic City, now Imperial City, and Niner could probably have counted the number of times he'd walked out into that civilian world on one hand.

He opened the secure comlink. "Ordo? You receiving? We're on our way."

"Nice excuse, by the way." Ordo sounded relaxed. "We picked up most of that cozy chat. What an *affable* fellow Holy Roly is."

"He's crazy," Niner said. "He's going to be running his own private army."

Jaing interrupted. "I'm shocked, I tell you. Who'd abuse their command privileges so shamelessly? And guess what—his family's from Dromund Kaas. You won't find *that* in your database, *ner vod,* because it wasn't even on Republic charts. The place is run by dark side weirdos called the Prophets. They make sure their prophecies of doom and dark destruction come true. Now, I'm no psychologist, but between the saber-jockeys and the mad monks, I think I can guess what shaped your boss's bad attitude to our paranormally gifted friends."

"Pity he's on the wrong side," Ordo said. "*Kal'buir* would like him."

"*Kal'buir*'s never going to get the chance." Niner picked up speed as they passed through the security gates. "We're coming home, *vode.*"

"*Oya manda,*" Mereel said approvingly. "I hope you two don't mind hiding in a water tank while we exfil."

They were going to Mandalore. Niner could rarely re-call being excited, but this was like nothing else he'd ever known. It was a leap into a new life, one he couldn't begin to imagine, and just not knowing was a thrill in itself. He thought that was odd for a man whose nickname was Worry-Guts.

He'd try farming. Fishing. Bounty hunting, if he got bored with the rural life. And he'd find a nice girl, just like Fi had.

Fi. He hadn't seen his brother in nearly two years.

And Darman—Niner didn't ask, because he didn't need to. Dar was going to be reunited with his son.

"What did Ordo have to say?" Darman asked. He was shut out of the secure link, but he could guess Niner was talking to the Nulls. "Everything okay?"

"It's all going fine," Niner said, regretting that he'd never get to ask Holy Roly what had happened back home to make him bitter enough to defy Force-using Intel agents. "Soon be home."

10

There's something unusual about that clone Darman. I can't quite place it, but he feels . . . different. I get an unusual sense of Force-users woven into his being, and he reacts to me as if he senses what I am, which is impossible. He may be dangerous; keep a close eye on him.

—Sa Cuis, Emperor's Hand, shortly before his death on a mission to test the new Lord Vader's resolve

Kyrimorut, Mandalore

"**H**ave you been here all night?" Gilamar asked.

Uthan looked up from her notes, elbows on the lab bench, head propped on her hands. In front of her, she had the rough sketch of the level-10 containment unit she'd need to safely re-create the virus that had been unleashed on Gibad.

"More or less," she said.

"How's it going?" He pulled up a stool and sat down next to her, laying his hand on hers with the kind of firm grip he probably reserved for his drinking buddies rather than women. It was still comforting to have someone hold your hand when your world—in every sense—was in tatters. She hadn't pegged him as the hand-holding type. "I wasn't expecting you to be working on this. But . . . yes, it helps. After Tani was killed, I think I read every paper on pituitary tumors in the Republic Institute."

"I'm working on justice," Uthan said. "And I don't mean the clones' problem. Palpatine wants to play dirty? Fine."

Gilamar glanced at the diagram. "You going to explain?"

He was a Mandalorian. He'd understand. He wouldn't spout some high-minded piety and tell her that brutal vengeance just brought her down to her enemy's level. He'd want to eliminate future threats.

She liked him a lot.

"I'm working out the fastest way to re-create and manufacture the phase-one FG thirty-six virus," she said. "And then I'm going to let it loose on Coruscant."

"Understood," he said, nodding.

"Of course, once I've got a few canisters, I'll need transport to the Core. It's a very economical virus. You can accelerate its spread by airborne distribution, or just seed a few carriers and let it progress at its own pace. Incubation period six days or so in humans, infectious for six weeks, designed to work through an entire population and defeat normal quarantine measures. Go on, tell me how clever I am for building such a stealthy pathogen."

She waited for him to explain why she should just stay home and bide her time, all comforting and sensible. But he just nodded again.

"I'd do the same, I think, except with something that made a lot more noise and flame." He picked up the datapad and looked as if he was calculating what materials were needed. "It's a really simple process, then. What did you base the virus on?"

"It's a modified version of nebellia."

"That just causes minor respiratory tract problems and diarrhea. It's not fatal."

"It is after I've done a little nip and tuck on its DNA . . ."

"Clever girl."

"All I need is a sample of nebellia and the cell culture to host the virus—preferably *Gespelides ectilis*—and I can grow industrial quantities of the strain within weeks.

Great value, bioweapons—expensive on the R and D side, of course, but dirt cheap on production."

"You could just propagate monnen spores, of course," Gilamar said. "Naturally occurring, and patent-free."

"You know, Mij, I'm not sure if you're encouraging me, mocking me, or humoring me."

"I'm just seeing the downside of this, but also wanting you to avenge your world and kick Palps so hard up his *shebs* that his eyeballs rattle." Gilamar shut his eyes for a moment. "There's only so many times I can say how sorry I am. You don't need to be told how bad it is. I think you're the kind of woman who needs to get even."

Uthan liked that honesty. She felt she could say whatever was on her mind in return, and he'd never take offense. "It'd be a great deterrent for Mandalore to hold."

"You know what? I think we'd rather have an antiviral first. Because Palps knows his toy really works now. He might want to play with it again."

Uthan had worked out that Mandos regarded biological and chemical weapons as beneath contempt, a coward's tactic deployed from the safety of an armchair. But they were too pragmatic a people to have any warrior-ethic objection to doing things the easy way.

"Would Mandalore *use* a biological weapon?" she asked.

"We prefer sharp things. Pointed things. And noisy things that we can see from about twenty klicks away, preferably resulting in a big ball of flame." Gilamar looked utterly dejected despite his chirpy tone. She found it odd to have a relative stranger mourning with her. "Trouble with the invisible stuff is that you don't actually know where it is, or what it's doing. Or what happens after you let it loose."

"If I'd had any sense, I'd have made the immunogen at the same time as I developed the virus. But even if I had—I had no way of getting it to Gibad. Fi and his friends captured me long before then."

Gilamar ignored the irony. "I think that antiviral is pretty urgent now."

"Agreed."

"What do you need to produce it?" He was a kind man, but he wasn't letting her off the hook. He was right, of course. "Ironically, developing a vaccine is the most dangerous and rebellious thing you can do to the Empire now."

"I just manipulated two genes in a naturally occurring nanoscale virus." Uthan turned her datapad back the right way up and calculated a few more dimensions. "We still need to hold a live virus, so we'd need some extra safety precautions. But FG thirty-six latches on to a single protein in human DNA, and the protein can be made resistant by one gene mutation. I can induce that gene mutation in a population with an engineered virus."

"Based on . . . ?"

"Something easily transmissible and low-grade, like rhinacyrian fever. Very few humanoids have resistance to it. A day or two of a runny nose and itchy eyes, which is far preferable to dying of internal hemorrhaging and involuntary muscle paralysis."

"How fast?"

"Weeks."

"How easy to treat the population?"

"Vaccination's best, if you can herd four million Mandos. It would probably be simpler to let it loose and rely on human carriers to spread it. Or do what Palpatine did—disperse it in the air. But that requires a lot of equipment and someone will notice."

"Okay, give me your shopping list," he said. "I'll get the stuff as soon as I can."

"And then how about wiping out Coruscant?"

"First things first."

There was a timid knock on the door. Uthan looked up to see Scout in the doorway, and hoped the girl hadn't heard the conversation. It felt indecent to discuss plans for mass murder in front of a Jedi. Uthan wasn't sure why she reacted that way, seeing as she had little respect for the Jedi Order playing enforcer for the Republic, but Scout was a scared child, and that defused Uthan at an instinctive level.

"I wondered if you wanted breakfast," Scout said. "I'll bring it here, if you like. Peace and quiet. You, too, Mij?"

"Thanks, *ad'ika*," Gilamar said. "You've got a good heart."

Uthan listened until the sound of Scout's boots faded. Then she looked at Gilamar. "What a strange little group we are, clinging together. All loss and loneliness."

"Everyone's lonely until they find kindred spirits. I think this is a community of folks who've had enough and can't run anymore."

"I'm truly grateful for your kindness, Mij. It's as if everyone's conveniently forgotten what I actually do for a living."

Gilamar shrugged. "Most folks here have taken another being's life. I think that includes the Force-users, too."

"How's Arla doing?"

"Not good. Her past seems to be coming back to her, and it sure ain't happy memories."

Scout came back a lot sooner than Uthan expected. She caught herself feeling indignant, and then plunged into burning guilt for getting too engrossed in Gilamar when there were so many dead. But there was a void in her misery, a gap in the connection to the loss of her world that translated into aching, inconsolable grief for loved ones. She was upset, shocked, horrified, enraged—but she felt her sorrow was a fraud, because her personal loss was minimal.

I have no right to sympathy.

Sessaly was a distant cousin she saw once a year out of duty, the nearest she had to a family. Somewhere, her ex-husband and in-laws lay dead, too, but she hadn't spoken to them in ten years. There were colleagues from the university. But there were no close friends. Uthan felt like a holovid fan sobbing over a dead actor, mourning someone she didn't even know, appropriating grief. Her life had been lived out in a laboratory and fixated on achievement, and now it was barren in every sense of the word.

"Eggs," Scout said, putting the plates down in a clear space on the workbench. "Last of the nuna ones until Ny gets back."

"Thank you." Uthan noted that even Ny had found a niche here. "We won't starve yet."

Some tragedies were so huge that mention of them was superfluous. Uthan could sense Scout's awkwardness, not knowing what was appropriate at a time like this, so Uthan broke the silence that followed.

"I have to manufacture an antiviral," she said. "In case the Empire decides to use the virus here. Would you be interested in helping me?"

Scout gave her a wary look. "Does it involve cutting up animals?"

"No. Not at all. I just tinker with a virus, and then put it in a plant cell culture. The more the cells multiply, the more of the beneficial virus we get."

"Back to the AgriCorps," Scout said. "I'm great with plants."

"That's what we need most," Gilamar said. "Actually, this would be a yeast. But I'm splitting hairs. Are you interested in medicine?"

Scout seemed genuinely curious. "Did Bardan really repair Fi's brain damage with the Force?"

"Watched it happen," Gilamair said. "Measured it. Truly amazing."

"It must be wonderful to be able to heal. I'm not strong in the Force, though."

"I hate to break it to you, but most medicine in the galaxy is practiced by regular dolts like me, using pretty ordinary equipment," Gilamar said. "And tinnies, of course. Med droids outnumber qualified wets. The Force is an extra therapy, that's all. You fancy learning a little first aid? Always comes in handy."

Scout nodded. There wasn't a lot for her to do here, Uthan thought, but then she realized she had no idea

what Jedi normally did to keep themselves busy. Perhaps
Scout was reflecting on a life without much personal
contact in it, too. But she was young enough to avoid
ending up like Uthan.

"I'd like that," Scout said. "I can't stand the thought
of any more killing."

Gilamar nodded. "Me neither."

"I'll teach you the clever stuff," Uthan said. "Doc
Mando here can cover lancing boils and setting bones."

*My world's dead. I don't have any stake in the future.
No children, no academic legacy, no hope, nothing.*

There was something compelling in the chance to
teach a youngster. It felt like planting trees. It was never
wasted effort. If the teacher was lucky, the pupil went on
to change the galaxy for the better. Uthan clung to that
thought.

It didn't mean she wouldn't give Palpatine what he
had coming to him as soon as she got the chance,
though. But Scout had no need to be taught about the
art of revenge.

Imperial City

Nobody looked too hard at armed Imperial commandos
walking through the alleyways of Imperial City.

Civilians seemed to be very busy *not* noticing Darman
and Niner walking briskly down the walkway that
linked the cantinas and restaurants of Quadrant G-14
with the increasingly grim sector two kilometers north
of the RV point. Factories and warehouses sat between
residential blocks and the occasional run-down alcohol
store.

It wasn't the kind of place anyone expected to see
stormtroopers of any description. Police patrolled here
occasionally, but not troops.

"They're scared of us," Niner said. Darman couldn't
see his POV icon because they'd switched off most of
their helmet feeds, except their private short-range comm.

They were supposed to be out on the town for the evening and off the chart, not wandering around somewhere they definitely shouldn't have been. "Okay, we never had welcome-home parades under the Republic, but I don't recall anyone looking *afraid* of us."

"You think they even realized he's a chakaar? As long as there's a good holodrama on the 'Net and they can afford enough ale to fall over on a regular basis, they don't give a mott's *shebs* about pounces."

"You feel it? The whole place is different. Wary. Not like it used to be."

Used to be was based on a few rare forays into this alien world outside the perimeter. Darman had never been part of civilian Coruscant, and he didn't think he'd missed much. The Empire was no different from the Republic for men like him. And civilians got the governments they deserved.

They're not my problem now. I did my duty. The Seps didn't overrun us. Now the civvies can worry about their own welfare, and I'll look after me and mine.

Darman was back being Darman now, the real Darman, the one who could feel the pain of losing his wife. Now that he'd confronted the grief a few times and let it rip his heart out, he was starting to function again without needing to detach from reality. He was still hurting. But he found a little space opening up in his mind that had room for planning, for focus, for taking *action* instead of just being swamped by loss.

I have a son, and everyone's a threat to him. Palpatine. The Intel freak show. Any Jedi or Force-user who wants new recruits. Any clonemaster who wants to use him.

I know what I have to do.

Melusar's right. I know it. We all get used.

The farther Darman walked, the more uneasy he felt.

"Would you believe Ny's done some grocery shopping?" Niner said suddenly. He seemed to be talking to the Nulls again. Darman couldn't hear him when he switched to the secure circuit. "They're doing an extraction behind enemy lines, and they *find time to shop*."

"Tell Ordo he didn't need to show up mob-handed. We could extract ourselves."

Niner fell silent for a moment. "Ordo says *Kal'buir* got fed up waiting. Your dinner's in the oven. If we're late, the strill gets it."

Darman could hear the tension in Niner's voice. The muscles tightened in his throat, and it forced his voice a little higher. And he swallowed a lot. Swallowing sounded much louder in these new helmets. Darman couldn't decide if his brother was nervous or excited, but either state was unusual for Niner.

"We're going *home*," Niner said. He sounded as if he didn't believe it. "For real. Everyone back together, like it ought to be. The rest of the squad. *Kal'buir.* Even Vau. Kad's going to go crazy when he sees you—*shab,* I bet he's grown a lot. They grow fast at that age, don't they?"

Darman tried to stifle the thought that was eating its way out of that clear corner of his mind. He wasn't winning. The thought was a voice; not a real one, nothing insane or frightening, but a voice all the same. It was his common sense, his duty, the core of reality that never let go. He'd been able to bury it for a while. But it never went away. It was the voice that had no doubts and told him to stop kidding himself. He couldn't do what he wanted. That wasn't because he was a slave, but because he was a free man. It was *responsibility.*

Can I face Kad?

I couldn't save Etain. I bust my gut saving a world that doesn't care if I live or die, and I let my own wife down.

How do I tell him? How do I look at him and not see her?

Darman had to be sure why he wasn't as excited as Niner. He didn't have time to mess around like this. In ten minutes, they'd be at the RV point.

I can't board that ship. I can't leave.

I need to stay here, inside the system, for Kad's sake.

Darman walked on another fifty meters before he stopped and faced the inevitable. He came to a halt opposite a cantina. Light spilled onto the walkway from an open door, and the illuminated sign that took up an entire wall had so many broken tubes that he had to stare at it for a few moments to realize it was supposed to be a giant cocktail glass garnished with fruit. Niner walked on past him for a few paces before turning.

"What's wrong, Dar?"

"I'm not going." As soon as the words escaped, Darman felt better. Not happier; his stomach churned, threatening nausea. That was how much it hurt to know his son was waiting for him, and that he wouldn't see him for . . . he just didn't know how long. *Maybe never.* "I have to stay."

"*Shab,* Dar, what's brought this on?" Niner didn't seem to believe him. He just sounded mildly annoyed, and caught Darman's arm as if he was dawdling and needed some encouragement. "Come on. Move it."

Darman shook him off. "I mean it, Niner."

"Spit it out. What's the problem?"

"Unfinished business."

"*What* business?"

"Jedi, Sith, any *shabuir* like that."

"What?"

"It's not over. Kad's always going to be in danger from them."

"And you're going to rid the galaxy of midi-chlorians single-handed? Dar, in case you hadn't noticed, there are millions of guys who can look after that. I think they can cope without us."

"But they're *not me.* This is *my* duty. *My* son."

"Oh, don't start that *osik* again. We all agreed. Remember? Look, I know it's not turned out as we planned, but we've got lives to lead, and Kad's waiting for you. The Empire doesn't need you like he does."

It was so painful that Darman felt himself shutting down again, doing that *ramikadyc* detachment trick just to cope with the next few seconds, and the next.

"I'll just be one more rifle on Mandalore. Kad's got an army protecting him, more firepower than anyone

needs. But here . . ." Darman noticed that Niner kept
putting his hand to the side of his helmet as if he was
cupping his earpiece, a nervous tic when he was under
stress. Ordo could hear one side of the argument. He
was probably pitching in with his ten creds' worth, urging Niner to shut Darman up and get him to the RV
point. "I'm at the heart of it. I'll never be any closer to
the threats than I am here. Melusar understands. He
knows the score."

"I don't *believe* this," Niner snarled. "*Your kid needs
you.* If I hadn't been injured that night, you'd have left
with the others and be with him now. You know how
that makes me feel? That you abandoned your boy to
stay with *me*? I feel like *osik*. Now quit the speeches and
get your *shebs* on that freighter. The Nulls are risking
their necks to get us out."

Niner turned and walked away. He got about five
paces before he realized Darman wasn't budging. Niner
was the most solid, steady guy Darman knew, and he'd
never seen him really lose it for all his grumbling and
griping, but he was definitely on the edge now. He
shoved Darman back against the wall and shook him a
couple of times.

"You selfish *shabuir*. Move, or so help me I'll punch
you out and *drag* you there."

Niner didn't mean the selfish bit, even if he meant the
rest. Darman could hear the desperation in his voice.
But he still wasn't going. He was inside the system, in a
place where he could spy and sabotage and intercept,
and that beat trying to defend Kyrimorut when it was
too late.

*I mean that, don't I? It's not that I don't have the guts
to be a proper father.*

Is it?

Darman had spent a matter of hours with his son. Not
days, not weeks; hours. He wondered if the Kad in his
imagination bore any resemblance to the real child, or if
he was just devoted to the idea of him. But that wasn't
the issue. When he thought of his own orders, knowing

that Palpatine was collecting Force-users, he knew the answers. *Nowhere* was too far away to be found. And if Palps fell, the Jedi would be back. There was no end to the cycle.

Niner shook him again. "I didn't want to do this, Dar . . ."

Darman braced for a punch. He could block Niner. But as he clenched his fist to defend himself, Niner relaxed his grip.

"Dar," he said. "Ordo says Kad asks for you. He keeps asking for his daddy. Ordo says he doesn't know how he's going to explain to him that his dad decided not to come home."

Darman's knees almost buckled. "Tell Ordo—nice try, but I'm done here. You tell Kad for me, Niner. Tell my boy that I can protect him better here."

Darman didn't think that the pain could get any worse, but it had. He turned and began walking back toward the barracks. A guy was staring at him—understandable, seeing two commandos way off their territory and having a fight in the street—and he snapped. He found his Deece in the guy's face, and the voice he could hear wasn't his, not at all.

"Who you staring at, *shabuir*? Beat it—"

Niner was right behind him again. He grabbed the Deece's muzzle one-handed and steered it aside.

"Okay, on your way," Niner said to the terrified man. "We're a little emotional tonight. Get lost."

The man didn't need telling twice. He ran. Niner walked a few more paces with Darman, suddenly quiet and placatory.

"Dar, I've got Ny yelling in my ear now. She wants to talk to you."

"No deal."

"Okay, you don't go—I don't go."

"You *have* to go, *ner vod*. Someone's got to hand over that datachip. Right? Whatever's on there, Obrim thinks it's critical. Go home and explain to Kad."

Two could play that game. Niner had a big streak of dutiful guilt that Darman could lean on, too. He heard him hiss in exasperation.

"*Shabuir*," he said. "How can you *do* this?"

Darman kept on walking. He was so numb now that all he was aware of was the feel of the walkway under his boots and unshed tears pricking his eyes. The numbness was pure reflex this time. He didn't even have to try.

He waited for the sound of running, or the impact of a body cannoning into him. But it never came. Niner wasn't making one last attempt to force him onto the freighter. The footsteps got steadily quieter before they speeded up into a steady jog. When Darman looked over his shoulder, Niner was gone.

Darman realized he hadn't actually said good-bye to him. When he tried to open the short-range comlink, there was no response. Niner had severed all links.

Darman regretted his decision as soon as he crossed the bridge back to the entertainment quarter. But he knew that regret was for the right reasons. Staying here was the best option—not just for Kad, but for all his brothers and friends being hunted by Palpatine. They needed a spy on the inside, too. And he had the feeling that he wouldn't exactly be thwarting Melusar's aims by being one.

He began working out how he'd explain Niner's absence to the commander. It wasn't going to be easy. He'd probably leave it until the morning, partly to buy more time, and partly to make it more credible if he used the excuse of a drunken evening and not being able to recall when Niner actually disappeared.

The rest of Omega Squad had deserted. Who'd be shocked by one more going over the wall? Much as Darman disliked the idea, it just made him look even more loyal and reliable to Melusar.

He'd be trusted. He'd get a lot more information. He wasn't sure yet how he'd relay that to Kyrimorut, but there'd be a way, and Jaller Obrim was still an ally.

Shab, I wish I didn't keep losing it like that. I've got to get a grip of my temper. One day, I'm going to do something I'll really regret.

Darman swallowed his shame at his outbursts and wandered around, killing time until he could slip back into the barracks. When he paused to look in a store window, a public holonews screen high on a building caught his eye, and he watched for a while.

Gibad had taken the full brunt of Palpatine's wrath. It was all the more reason for Darman to stick with the job in hand.

Niner would realize that, eventually. Darman just hoped that Kad would, too.

Freighter *Cornucopia*, freighter park, G-80, Imperial City

Ordo took off his stormtrooper armor and stacked the plates on the deck. *Cornucopia* was in darkness except for the faint illumination from the red and blue lights of essential systems, her interior looking like an Outer Rim nightclub that hadn't quite mastered the art of ambience.

"Niner?" He detached his secure comlink from the helmet. "Get in here. I need your kit."

Niner was making his way through an obstacle course of repulsortrucks and other goods vessels, directed by Prudii along a path that kept him out of the range of the security cams. Some of the 'trucks looked as if they'd been abandoned there. In the distance, the nav lights of another freighter wobbled toward *Cornucopia* as its pilot headed for a parking bay. It wasn't busy. Trade hadn't picked up again since the end of the war.

Why now? Why does Dar decide to do this now?

Ordo was going to kick seven shades of *osik* out of Darman when he finally got him on board. The man was out of his mind with grief, but this was stupid, pointless, *irresponsible*. They'd come to extract the two commandos and that was exactly what they were going to do.

Ny gave him her it'll-all-be-fine look, the lines in her forehead thrown into relief by the console lights. She never looked like she believed it herself.

Niner's voice crackled over the comm. "What are you planning?"

Prudii interrupted, calculating the range of the cams at every stage. "Niner—head down and go left at the next bollard."

"Got it. I said—what are you planning, *Ord'ika*?"

"I'm going to go back to the barracks dressed as *you* and drag Dar out by his *gett'se* if I have to." Being a clone always had its advantages. "*Shab,* I can't even contact him by comlink."

"Make sure you've got your recorder running, *Ord'ika*," Mereel said. "Always handy to have as much data as we can get on the interiors of enemy installations. I don't suppose Niner's been gathering layout data for us, has he?"

"No, *Niner hasn't,*" Niner snapped. "Not before your pet tinnie rigged my bucket, anyway. How would I explain that if anyone checked my systems? That I was afraid of getting lost on the way back from the 'freshers?"

"*Udesii, ner vod.*" Mereel rolled his eyes at Ordo. "Take it easy. We'll be out of here in no time."

Niner was a special forces soldier who'd operated behind enemy lines throughout the war, never turning a hair. It made Ordo uncomfortable to see him rattled by such a low-risk extraction. Maybe it was all too emotionally charged to be handled like combat. This should have been relatively easy. Nobody knew they were here, nobody had cannon trained on their position, and nobody would even notice them if they walked right in and took their helmets off. But it could still end in tragedy.

We've all been here before.

Niner didn't respond. Ordo could hear his ragged breathing and the occasional irritated click of his teeth, just like Skirata's.

If I don't get Dar and Niner home, it'll break Kal'buir's *heart.*

"Only those two could make a drama out of a nice safe exfil like this," Jaing muttered.

Ny jerked her head around sharply. "You call this *safe*?"

"Nobody's shooting at us," he said. "Or them. Relax, *Buir'ika*."

Ordo waited for the rap on *Cornucopia*'s hull. Ny, attuned to every sound and vibration in her ship, reacted before Ordo did, and he thought that was impressive for a nonclone with none of the genetic enhancements that the Nulls had been given. She released one of the hatch controls and Ordo heard the clatter of boots climbing a metal ladder. It felt like a long time before a black armored shape emerged from the hatch set in the deck. Niner pulled himself up through the opening and removed his helmet.

"So you can take out an entire droid base single-handed, but you can't make Darman behave and get his *shebs* over here," Ordo said. He knew it didn't help to take it out on Niner, but he couldn't bear to let *Kal'buir* down. "Get that kit off and let me sort him out."

Niner just blanked him and reached into his belt pouch. "This is all you'll be needing."

He held out his hand, palm up. Ordo could hardly see the datachip in the gloom, a wafer of plastoid and metal so small that a sneeze could have sent it flying into the air-conditioning vents.

Ordo took it carefully and passed it to Jaing. "Clue me in Niner," he said, realizing this had all gone to *osik*. "Are you planning to go back for him now? I'll do it. No offense."

"No, I'm staying here. I can't leave Dar. He's going to do something extreme and get himself killed."

Here we go again. "We do the logical thing. We drag him out."

"Look, I don't want this any more than you do, but I see his point. Or at least I see why one of us should stay here, except it shouldn't be him. He should be with his kid."

"If you're planning to use the word *duty, ner vod,* I might forget we're family and punch you into next week." Ordo could see a clean line to be drawn under all this, a final escape from Coruscant with no ties to keep dragging them back. This had to end now. "It's the same *shabuir* running the show, remember? Except instead of Jedi, he's got dark side saber-jockeys as the hired help. You don't owe this army a *shabla* thing, and if you've got a duty, it's to your clan. Your *aliit.*"

Niner took a step back and put one boot on the first rung of the ladder. "Dar's going to do some dangerous stuff, and I'm not leaving him to do it alone. I'll stay in contact and relay intel back to you. Now get that chip analyzed—Obrim said you could recover the data but you might need to use a scanning microscope to get at some of it. He made it clear that it's *important.*"

Ordo hovered on the edge of grabbing Niner and getting his brothers to hold him down. They could all apologize for black eyes and chipped teeth later. It was for Niner's own good.

"Last chance," Ordo said. "Give me your armor."

"When we're ready, we can bang out anytime we want. Okay?"

Ordo gestured to Ny to lock the hatch behind Niner. Mereel edged closer, ready to tackle him. Then Prudii swore to himself.

"Heads up, *vode,* we've got company . . . someone moving around out there."

"It's a freight park," Mereel said. "What do you expect?"

Ordo looked up at the monitors. Shapes flashed out of one screen and emerged again in another as someone darted from right to left, caught by the hull cams on either side of the freighter. Ny edged forward in her seat, head lowered. Whoever was on the ground wouldn't be able to see much in the cockpit viewplate, not even the faint glow.

"Y'know, maybe we should sit this out in another location."

"Can't you just take off?" Niner said. He put his other boot on the next rung down. Any moment now, Mereel would grab him. "You don't have to exit via the freight terminal checkpoint."

"We do if we want to keep coming back here." Ny squinted as if she couldn't see. Kitting her out with NV goggles would have been a good idea. "This ship shows up in systems as a legitimate commercial vessel. As long as I stick to the rules, we can go anywhere. The minute I drop off some flight schedule or the ship doesn't show up on someone's tote board, they'll flag it to board or detain. Hide in plain sight. That's what you lot always say, isn't it?"

Time wasn't a problem. Ordo thought they could hang on here for a couple of days, maybe a lot longer, but the less time spent here, the better. He seethed with frustration at having traveled light-years only to be thwarted five klicks from his target by Darman deciding to form his own one-man double-agent network.

I can be in and out of those barracks in under an hour. Okay, we might get spotted. Ny will have to keep the drives running. But it's madness to turn around and go home empty-handed.

"I don't want to worry anyone, but I think that's some local entrepreneurs doing a little asset acquisition," Prudii said. "Thieving *shab'ikase*. Look."

Jaing slipped the chip into the wristband of his gauntlet and checked his sidearm. Ordo watched the grainy image on one of the monitors. Three figures—two human, one Bothan—moved from vehicle to vehicle, trying hatches. There were two 'trucks and a small courier shuttle between them and *Cornucopia* now. The Bothan kept watch while the two humans rattled the manual latches on one of the 'trucks and vanished inside.

"Relax," Ordo said. He'd have to wait until the thieves moved on before he could venture out. Niner was stuck, too. For a moment, Ordo debated whether to simply lift off with Niner and come back later in another vessel for Darman. "Never seen a Bothan thief before."

"I hope nobody calls the cops," Prudii said.

"They'll move on."

Niner was wavering. Ordo could tell. His blink rate had shot up, and he kept looking down the shaft of the hatch beneath him. He was going to make a run for it. But Ordo needed black armor. The white stuff was fine for general loitering around, but to get in and out of the 501st Special Unit quickly, easily, and without fuss—the kind of fuss that involved blasters and rapid exits—he needed an Imperial commando rig.

Then he'd have to subdue Darman somehow and get him out of the compound. Doing that without being spotted was going to be a challenge even for Ordo.

Shab, they really might have to regroup and try another day. Like Ny said, they could always come back as long as *Cornucopia* didn't blot her copybook. There were millions of vessel movements around the galactic capital every day, and even with tightened security that meant the chances of slipping in and out unhindered were good. If they were really desperate, though, and they didn't want to use the freighter for cover again, they could get in and out anywhere they wanted. Not even Palpatine could lock down a planet this big and complex.

"Ten points for cheek," Prudii said. "Look. They're stealing the whole 'truck."

The 'truck edged forward out of the line and turned. But instead of speeding away, the vehicle stopped after a few meters, and the two humans jumped out to force the doors of the next one. They were in and out again in what seemed like a few seconds, carrying a packing crate between them. The booty went into the rear of the stolen 'truck. Now the gang was shaping up to work on the courier shuttle. Ordo watched them struggle with the hatch controls for a few minutes before they gave up.

There were no prizes for guessing where they were coming next. Their getaway vehicle vanished from the side cam's range for a moment, and then the underhull cam picked them up. The thieves were standing right under the belly hatch, looking up.

"Don't even think about it, shabuire," Mereel muttered. "Move along. Nothing to see here."

Ny's hand reached slowly for the console and hovered over the hatch controls.

"If you lock the hatch from here," Ordo said, "they'll hear the mechanism engage."

"Does that matter? It'll make them move on sharpish."

"If we have to stay here longer, it might also make folks curious about why a ship is sitting here in lights-out mode with a crew embarked."

"I can't see that lot calling the cops."

"You've seen the posters. Everyone has to denounce their neighbor to show how loyal they are."

Everyone held their breath. Niner slipped his helmet back on, one-handed, and stood partway in the hatch, waiting. Ordo didn't dare make a commotion by grabbing him now.

"*Osik.*" Prudii let out a sharp breath. Ordo could see the two humans trying the outer hatch. The *chonk* of metal flanges and the scrape of a hinge transmitted through the hull of the silent ship. "You really don't want to do that, *chakaare*. Okay, darken ship, Ny."

Niner jumped back onto the deck and turned to face what was coming up the ladder beneath him. Ny killed all the console lights and the monitors. Niner's blue-lit visor vanished along with the charge indicator on his Deece. The only sounds were occasional breaths and the faint clicks of weapons being aimed.

If the thieves decided to come on deck, Ordo didn't have a lot of choices. He couldn't let them leave. And there was one still outside he'd have to silence—the Bothan. They were just petty criminals, *chakaare*, not normally worth killing, but he'd let security lapse for a few minutes and now he had to clean up the mess. The risk was too high not to.

We should know better. We're elite special forces. And still we slip up on the small stuff. I slip up.

Ny was using her seat as cover, a small blaster aimed at the hatch. Ordo had no idea how she peformed under fire. His brothers knew without thinking what the other would do and how they would fight, but Ny was a wild card. Ordo snapped his fingers to get her attention and gestured to stay down.

Leave it to us, Ny. Let's make this silent.

Without infrared images from a helmet to guide him, Ordo could only see vague shapes in the darkness and follow sounds. Fabric rustled below. Something metallic chinked against a rung—durasteel toe-caps or a blaster— and he strained to see what was emerging.

Come on. Both of you. Don't want one of you jamming the hatch while the other gets away.

Ordo worked out how quickly he could exit and stop the getaway driver. The freighter's exits were all choke points. And one thing he couldn't do was use *Cornucopia*'s small defensive cannon here.

Shab . . .

The first thief scrambled onto the deck apparently oblivious that he was walking into an ambush. He even turned to give his buddy a hand up. Ordo waited two seconds for them both to stand clear of the hatch, and then Niner jumped one of them. Ordo heard a thud and the *shunk* of a vibroblade ejecting, followed by a wet gurgling noise. Ordo smashed the butt of his weapon down on the guy nearest to him. As the man dropped, he got him in a headlock and twisted sharply until he heard a crunch.

It had taken seconds, and it had been almost silent. Everyone froze. Then Ny hit the console, bringing up the instrument panel lights. It was enough to see what had happened.

"Ah . . . ," she said, staring. "Ah, *stang . . .*"

"I'll dump them," Mereel whispered. "Don't worry."

Sounds drifted up through the hatch. An engine

revved before dropping to idle speed. A vehicle door opened and closed quietly.

"Hey, what's happening?" It was a loud, nervous whisper. "Forrie? Kimm? I lost your comm, guys . . . guys?"

The Bothan didn't try to enter the hatch. *Crunch . . . crunch.* He took two steps, sounding as if he was backing off. He knew something was wrong. A metal door catch snapped shut.

Niner looked at Ordo. Everything had changed. Ordo hated to quit on this, but they had brand-new problems.

"I've got to stop him." Niner slipped the grenade launcher attachment onto his Deece. "Sorry. When I fire, just bang out, because there'll be cops here in minutes. Just get clear. Oh, and ask your tinnie to mod Dar's helmet like mine, okay?"

"Will do," Ordo said. *"K'oyacyi, ner vod."*

Niner dropped down the hatch and landed with a thud. Ordo's decision had been made for him. The last thing he heard before the belly hatch sealed was a repulsortruck engine roaring away.

"Abort," he said. "Ny, get us out. Niner, are you clear of the vessel?"

Ordo heard him panting as he ran. "I am now."

"Secure all hatches. Stand by." Ny hit the ignition and the repulsor maneuvering drives rumbled into life. "You sure he's clear, Ordo?"

A loud explosion cut her short as the grenade found its target. The vessels visible on the monitors lit up yellow for a few moments before settling back into reflected flames. Niner was a reliable shot.

"I think he's got a problem with his gearbox." Niner's forced cheerfulness didn't fool anyone. "It's just gone fifty meters into the air."

"Head down, *ner vod,*" Ordo said. "Clear to take off, Ny."

Ny took *Cornucopia* up in a steep climb, sending loose items skidding down the deck. Two of them were bodies. They'd have to be dumped, but that had to wait now.

"This is going to be bumpy," Ny said. "And if ATC spots us, we're borked."

Ordo buckled himself into the copilot's seat, catching Mereel's eye as he twisted around. He felt ashamed and useless. Things shouldn't have gone this wrong. It wasn't all Darman's fault, either.

"They'll be fine." Mereel could read his thoughts. "Besides, intel from the source is priceless. As is the ability to reach out and touch the Empire."

"You know what? I've abandoned two brothers. You can shove your intel."

"Just trying to make you feel better, Ord'ika . . ."

"Don't. I blew it."

"We *all* blew it," Ny said. "Ordo, prep to jump on my mark."

Ordo pressed the comlink bead in his ear and listened. Niner was calling in CSF and fire crews. He sounded absolutely calm, reporting a stop-and-search that had escalated.

"Isn't that going to look suspicious on the compound security cams?" Ny's voice shook. "How's he going to explain all that to Holy Roly? Is he really going to be okay?"

"He'll think of something," Jaing said. He slipped a datapad back in his pocket. "Of course, the problem with security and traffic cams is that certain antiterrorism officers have access to them, and they tend to erase the recordings. Don't you just hate it when that happens?"

"You called in another favor from Obrim."

"Fair exchange. We'll save his *shebs* when he runs out of luck and needs to vanish with his family."

The freighter had now climbed enough to safely engage the sublight drive. It streaked high over the city, as far from Niner's location as possible before Ny got Air Traffic Control's attention by climbing vertically to a safe hyperjump altitude. It was a maneuver that screamed *look at me, I'm in a real hurry to escape.* How long did it take to scramble enforcement fighters? Long enough. Ordo counted down the seconds until Imperial City ATC cut in on the ship's comm.

"ATC calling *Cornucopia,* you do not have customs or flight clearance, I repeat, you do not—"

"Shut it." Ny smacked her fist down hard on the audio control to silence it. "Revoke my license. Good luck with fining me, too. Ordo, you ready?"

"Ready."

"Okay, in five . . . *jump.*"

Cornucopia shuddered. Familiar constellations vanished instantly. And so did the chance to bring Niner and Darman home, for the time being at least. Ordo couldn't decide whose disappointment would haunt him most—*Kal'buir*'s or Kad's. He'd find out soon enough. At least jumping to hyperspace before he could comm Kyrimorut gave him time to prepare for the reaction.

"He seems like a nice lad," Ny said, staring ahead into the featureless void. She patted Ordo's knee. "Solid. Dependable."

"Niner?"

"Yes. I never met him before. I didn't even get a chance to introduce myself."

That stung Ordo. He hadn't realized. "He's *mandokarla.* Got the right Mando stuff."

"Free men make their own decisions, Ordo. Just remember that. Even if it upsets us, both of them are doing what they want to do, not what someone *made* them do."

Free men also faced up to the consequences of their actions. *I could have done this all differently. I didn't.* He'd sit Kad down and explain as best he could to a toddler that his daddy wanted to come home, but Uncle Ordo, *Ba'vodu Ord'ika,* had got things all wrong and had to leave him behind.

If Kad was going to feel let down by anyone, it wouldn't be his *buir.*

11

Here's why you can't exterminate us, aruetii. We're not huddled in one place—we span the galaxy. We need no lords or leaders—so you can't destroy our command. We can live without technology—so we can fight with our bare hands. We have no species or bloodline—so we can rebuild our ranks with others who want to join us. We're more than just a people or an army, aruetii. We're a culture. We're an idea. And you can't kill ideas—but we can certainly kill you.

—Ranah Teh Naast, Mandalore the Destroyer, daughter of Uvhen Chal, giving the Consul of Luon a final chance to surrender during the siege of the city

Kyrimorut, Mandalore

"I let you down, *Kal'buir*."

Ordo stepped down off *Cornucopia*'s ramp, chin lowered, looking as if he was expecting a good hiding. Skirata threw his arms around him and gave him a fierce hug.

"Don't you even *think* that," he scolded. "You hear? You *never* let me down. We can still get them back anytime we like. Come on." He broke off to embrace the other Nulls one by one. "Let's get this stuff inside. Eat."

Ny emerged from the freighter carrying a tray of eggs. She gave Skirata a sympathetic look and shrugged.

"He was worrying how you'd take the news," she whispered. "He's always so confident about everything else, but he's scared stiff of you."

She sounded as if she was asking what Skirata had done to make him that way. "I love that boy more than my own life," Skirata said indignantly. "He knows I'd never blame him for this. For *anything*."

"I know. It's just sad to watch it."

Ordo's need to please him always broke Skirata's heart. He'd never given Ordo any cause to fear him, but the Kaminoans had already burned the idea into the Nulls' psyches that failure was never tolerated. Failures had to be reconditioned—terminated. However many times Skirata told Ordo he was perfect, it never erased that lesson from infancy.

"You believe me, don't you?" Skirata said. Here he was, scared in turn of Ny's disapproval. "He did the right thing. Pull out, rethink, try again later."

"I *believe* you." Ny put a box down on the deck and caught his face in both hands, giving him a little shake. "You're a bad boy, Shortie, but nobody doubts your devotion to your kids."

She held on to him for a few seconds more than needed to make the point. He realized he had no idea how to respond. He'd forgotten the moves after all these years. Ny suddenly let go and picked up the box again, and he was left to wonder if he'd missed the cues and disappointed her.

"I think I over-ordered," she said, looking at the crates still to be moved. "But if everyone gets sick of eggs, we can pickle them for the store."

Fi and Atin bounded up the ramp, making a show of being cheerful. They'd been desperate to see Niner and Darman again.

"We never get sick of *anything*," Fi said, rummaging through the cargo. "Our favorite flavor is second helpings. Ooh, you got us some warra nuts! Hot 'n' spicy, *and* salt 'n' sour! *Kandosii!*"

"Ten kilos of each." She gave him an indulgent smile. Skirata noted that she fell into the maternal role with Fi without a moment's hesitation. "And if you eat them all in one go, Parja will make you sleep in the barn. On your own head be it."

"I'll ration myself."

"Hey, Fi—I'm sorry we didn't get Dar and Niner back. But we will. It'll all be fine. I promise."

"Maybe we can talk to them somehow." Fi sounded wistful, like a lost child, and he wasn't putting it on. "Niner's got a secure link. We can talk to him, right?"

"Yes, you can." Ny's eyes suddenly looked glassy. "Jaing can make it happen."

Atin stood back to let Fi move the laden repulsor off the ship. "I'm going to go with Mij to pick up the equipment for Uthan," he said. "We'll be back in a day or so. Anything else we need?"

"You might want to wander back via Keldabe and see what Dred *shabla* Priest is up to . . ." *I really don't need to collect more problems now. Priest can wait, surely?* "See if Vau wants a trip out, too. Poor old *chakaar* needs to take his mind off Sev for a while."

"That means taking Mird as well."

"So? Vent the aircon twice an hour."

Atin slapped Skirata on the shoulder. "Will do. See you later."

"That's a little miracle, too," Skirata said as he walked away. "Him and Vau—real death grudge. Vau gave him those scars. But they called a truce. Anything's possible."

Ny rubbed her nose discreetly as if she thought Skirata hadn't noticed the tears. "But not reconciliation with the Death Watch."

"That comes under the water-flowing-uphill section of possibility. No."

Skirata steered her down the ramp with the last of the egg crates and closed the hatch. Where could he start? But she had to know if she was going to truly fit in. Even without discussion, there seemed to be a tacit acceptance that Ny was a permanent fixture.

"Do you want to settle here?" Skirata asked.

Ny blinked a couple of times. "I think I already have."

"I mean become a Mando. Properly." He realized that

he'd opened a delicate topic that begged the question of what he was actually asking her. He skipped over it, unable to deal with more emotional complications right then. "I mean that there's such bad blood between us and them that you need to be aware of it."

"Of course." Ny reached into her jacket and took out something—a stack of cash credits. She opened one of his belt pouches and dropped the chips into it. Every time she laid hands on him he was rooted to the spot and didn't know how to react. "I'd hate to make any social gaffes at the Keldabe country club."

Skirata longed to be at ease with her. "I told you to keep the creds. Nobody thinks you're sponging."

"And I'm handing them back. Nice pickpocket job, though. Now, Death Watch. Tried to oust Jaster Mereel because he liked law and order, and that crimped their game. Big turf war. And they killed Arla's parents for sheltering Jaster. How am I doing?"

Skirata was glad she didn't say *civil war*. War was for soldiers, folks with discipline and honor. The Death Watch were just criminal scum who happened to share the same system, not real Mandalorians at all.

"Not bad," he said. "They dressed themselves up as patriots wanting a return to the good old days of the Mando empire, but it was just a cover for organized crime."

"But you lot don't have a proper government like other species. You've got this loose arrangement of clans, and you've got a head of state who only shows up part-time and doesn't make the rules. How can the Death Watch overthrow anything? There's nothing to overthrow."

"They can destroy our backbone."

Ny snorted. "Yeah? Good luck with that."

"We've had times in our past when we let rotten Mandalores steer us down some ugly paths. It happens, Ny. Ideas take root. Whole societies get swept up in things without thinking, because they're just ideas, right? Just harmless things. But they'd fight to the death to resist if an invading army showed up and tried to force those changes on us. We don't see bad ideas coming until they've done the damage."

It was all he needed to say for the time being. Ny had seen enough of Arla to get the idea that the Death Watch committed atrocities, and that was enough on its own.

Inside the house, the veshok table was laid with an impressive spread of *skraan'ikase,* an assortment of small fancy snacks that could be lingered over for hours. It was a spread for special occasions, from weddings to funerals, and sometimes both at the same time. Jilka, Corr, and Ruu were already munching on crisply fried meat. Skirata opened one of the bottles of *tihaar* on the table.

Ny stared at the bounty. "Won't Uthan find this a little . . . inappropriate? I mean . . . it's a bit *festive.*"

"It's how we do things." Skirata tried one of the pastries. "*Shereshoy bal aay'han.* You can't separate the two."

This should have been a welcome-home party for Darman and Niner. Skirata saw nothing odd about combining it with some respectable mourning for Uthan's people. Life was all sharp contrasts; you couldn't appreciate joy without understanding sorrow. Happy guests at this kind of meal were a reminder to the unhappy that life would be good again one day, and the mourners reminded those celebrating not to take a moment of life for granted. The act was one of assertion, of looking for the positive side of the moment.

It made sense to any Mando. Skirata wanted it to make sense to Ny. He stopped short of asking her if she'd ever attended a wake, and realized he didn't know much about her background. The better he got to know her, the harder he found it to talk about her dead husband.

Laseema came out of the kitchen with a tray of miniature pastries filled with conserves so transparent and brightly colored that they looked like gems. She was an impressive cook. "Might as well tuck in," she said. "The others will show up when they smell the food. *Haili cetare.* Fill your boots."

"Where *is* everybody?"

"Jaing went racing off to play with the datachip." She downed a pastry, looked pleased with the result, and licked her fingers. "Kina Ha took Kad for a walk to burn off some energy."

Skirata's alarm bells went off. "You let a *kaminii* go off with him?" He regretted snapping the second the words were out of his mouth. But it told him his hatred of Kaminoans was as embedded now as Ordo's fear of failure, and just as immune to evidence and reason. "Sorry. Just tell me they didn't go far."

"She's a thousand years old or something, *Kal'buir.*" Laseema took his arm like an old man and gave him a kiss on the cheek, humoring him. "How fast could she get away? They're in the yard, feeding the nuna."

And Dar and Niner are light-years away.

Skirata tried not to dwell on it. They were alive, and they'd made their own decisions. But there was Kad, and Kad still thought Daddy was coming home. As long as Darman and Niner were behind enemy lines and not *here,* then Skirata could have no sense of peace.

I left my kids to go to war time after time.

What was the difference? His wife had been there for them. Kad had a choice of mothers here, at least a dozen uncles, and a grandfather, too. *Aliit ori'shya tal'din*— family was more than bloodline. Dar didn't have to be here all the time to make Kad feel loved and secure. But it was more than that. It was all about Etain, and trying to heal that wound.

Skirata still couldn't work out whose wound it was. He suspected it was more his even than Darman's. Etain's ashes haunted him. He went to the cupboard where the funeral urn was kept, and stood looking at it as if she was trapped within.

It was a strange thought for a Mandalorian, in a society that had had to dispense with cemeteries and revered remains in fixed places; the dead weren't there, and the link to them in life was a piece of armor—or a lightsaber. But Etain was somehow in a kind of limbo in Skirata's mind, waiting for Darman to scatter her ashes and free her.

Becoming one with the Force wasn't like that. Jusik kept telling him so.

"Sorry, *Et'ika*," Skirata said. "Can you wait a little longer for Dar? He's doing it for the boy."

Ny was right behind him when he closed the door and turned. She squeezed his arm.

"I'll get Uthan," she said. "I'm starting to get the picture. *Shereshoy bal aay'han.*"

Skirata found himself slowly surfacing from the numbness of dashed hopes and entering a stage of anger. He was angry at Darman for putting everyone through this when he could have just walked away. *You've got a son here—doesn't that pull you back? How can you do this to him?* It felt a lot like the process of grieving; shock, then anger, and then the pain, self-recrimination, and irrational ups and downs before you accepted this was for keeps, and you had to live with it or not live at all. Skirata struggled with the familiar emotions, even knowing he'd go through a sequence of helpless feelings. But this time, those lost to him *could* come back. This wasn't death. He had to focus on that.

I wanted them to have the freedom all other beings have. I wanted them to have choices. Well, they have. And they chose, and if I don't like it—too bad.

His head knew that. But his heart remained stubbornly ignorant. He forced himself to concentrate on the room that was filling up with his family and . . . guests? Prisoners? Friends? He didn't know. He wasn't sure if it even mattered.

My clan. Isn't this a miracle in its own right? Not one of us should be here. Misfits, rejects, fugitives, disposable lives. Somehow we're making it work.

"Have a drink," Fi said. He folded Skirata's fingers around a glass of ale. Fi had definitely come back from the dead, as profound a symbol of vindicated hope as Skirata had ever seen. "We'll think of something to be grateful for. How's about we start with *Bard'ika*? A new brother. We can have sibling rivalry and fight over stuff and everything."

Uthan stood surveying the food, but it was clear her mind was elsewhere. Skirata wondered how many times she'd replayed the news about Gibad in her head, just to try to absorb the enormity of it: the genocide of her world, something few could ever have experienced. Scout hovered close by her like a doting daughter. Skirata bet on Gilamar leaving her with orders to look after Uthan while he was away.

"I believe in coming out fighting," Uthan said. She took a plate from the stack, none of which matched another, and placed a few morsels on it as if to show willing. "So this is the point where the Empire has to start worrying about *me*. An antigen for the galaxy, but a special surprise for Coruscant."

Skirata took a pull of the ale. *Casual. Act casual.* "Coruscant?"

"A planet of a trillion people, crowded together. The ideal scenario to spread a pathogen." She chewed, and nodded polite approval. "The heart of the Empire. Take out the heart . . ."

My boys are on Coruscant. Not just Dar and Niner. The other commandos I trained, too.

"So you've got an antidote," Skirata said. This wasn't the time for a debate. "Good work. Can we spread it quietly? So Palps doesn't know he'll be firing blanks in the future?"

"Silently," Uthan said. "But you realize that spreading it here means the garrison will be immunized, too. You'll lose your most effective weapon against the Empire."

Skirata caught himself hesitating for a second. The stormies were clones much the same as his boys, not volunteers, not conscripts—slaves. He knew he was going to have to get a grip of this feeling or the Empire would have him beaten from the start.

"*Shab*, we'll just have to shoot them the old-fashioned way, then," he said, and hoped he meant it.

"I can always engineer something new."

Skirata didn't answer. The room was noisier now, and didn't leave a ringing silence for anyone to interpret. Uthan had a cause for war with the whole Empire. All Skirata wanted was a small corner where his family could live in peace and not invite trouble to visit them.

So what do we do if Dar or Niner send us intel that's no use to us, but would help a resistance somewhere? What do we do with that information?

He put the idea to one side. It might never happen. He watched Besany standing with her arm around Ordo's waist, clearly devoted to him, and Parja fussing over Fi, and Corr whispering something in Jilka's ear and getting a laugh out of her. This was what Skirata wanted for his lads—the normal life that every other human male took for granted. Rebellion was someone else's problem.

Ny sat down next to Skirata on the cushion-strewn seat and nudged him with her elbow. "What are you going to do about the others?"

"What others?"

"How are they going to find someone to settle down with in the middle of nowhere? And what if they can't bring them home to meet the folks? Romances break up. But disgruntled exes always know where you live."

She was right, and he'd tried not to think about it. Ky-rimorut was already less than a secret. Rav Bralor had refurbished the place with local labor, and every clone who passed through would have a location that could be revealed.

"It's a risk we'll take," Skirata said, not knowing where to start to solve it. "Mandos keep their mouths shut."

"What if one of the boys meets someone he likes who *isn't* a Mando?"

"We'll have to lock her in once she gets here." He gave Ny a wink, but she just smiled as if she didn't understand. It was just as well. He couldn't worry about his own needs while there was so much to do for his boys. "We'll think of something."

Kad tottered around from person to person, getting picked up and fussed over at every stop. When he reached Ordo, Skirata watched, knowing what was coming next. Ordo scooped him up in his arms and took a few steps away into a space.

Ordo wasn't a natural with kids, but he looked determined to learn. Skirata saw his expression change as the boy stared into his face with that wide-eyed expectation that disarmed adults every time.

"*Kad'ika*, your daddy couldn't come back this time. My fault. Bad Uncle Ordo did something silly." He tapped Kad's nose with his fingertip, which usually made the kid giggle, but not this time. "We're going to see if we can make something clever that helps him talk to you. He misses you. Would you like that?"

It was hard to tell what Kad understood, because he always reacted as if he knew exactly what the grown-ups were talking about. Skirata could see his chin wobbling and a frown forming. He could have been responding to Ordo's distress rather than feeling upset about Darman.

But Kad didn't cry. He rarely did. He just took it and got on with life, even at this early age. Skirata tried to imagine the man he'd grow into.

"He'll make a great dad one day," Ny said.

"Kad?"

"Ordo. He's still getting the hang of it. Look at Besany's face." Ny smiled sadly. Besany was watching Ordo with complete adoration, oblivious of everything else. She was a striking woman anyway, but the beatific expression made her luminous. "We're pushovers for guys who are kind to kids and animals."

"We can forget the rich and powerful *osik*, then."

"Being rich really doesn't solve life's problems."

She had that right. The rapidly growing fund in the Clone Savings Bank, as Jaing called it, hadn't brought Dar or Niner home or stopped the rapid aging yet.

"True," Skirata said. "But it gives you more options than being poor."

Skirata shut his eyes and visualized the tick-list of things that still needed to be sorted out. Jusik could now go to retrieve Maze, and maybe take Ruu or Levet with him. They both deserved a break. As soon as Gilamar and Atin got back, they could start building Uthan's virus factory, then get her back on track with the anti-aging research. Then there was Arla. What the *shab* was he going to do about her? And the Jedi; they couldn't stay here forever, and they couldn't leave.

I'll think of something.

He shut his eyes and half dozed, soothed by all the relaxed conversation around him. Kad scrambled onto his lap, smelling of sticky preserves and baby powder, and fell asleep.

I'll think of something . . .

"Buir?"

A hand gripped his shoulder gently. He opened his eyes and stared up into Jaing's puzzled face.

"I'm not dead, son. Just rehearsing."

"I've recovered a fair chunk of the data from that chip," Jaing said. "It looks like a gold mine. I've still got to bypass the encryption on some file contents, but from what I've skimmed, it looks like the complete guide to how to hide escaped Jedi. Safehouses, sympathizers ready to give aid, ships, locations, comm codes, arms caches—the whole shebang. Obrim must have got that far with his recovery program and realized what he had."

Skirata sat up slowly, trying not to disturb Kad. "Sure it's not a decoy to throw Palpatine off the real trail? Even Jedi aren't naïve enough to risk recording all that on datachips."

"Slicers like me rely on naïveté, *Buir*. It might only be a small part of their network, of course, in which case it's not as dumb as it looks."

"So why was Obrim sweating bricks about getting it to us? No offense to our guests, but I really don't give a mott's *shebs* how many Jedi the Empire catches. I'd happily pay my taxes if it got all of them."

"There's a file on there that might be closer to home."

Skirata was wide awake now. "How close?"

"Ships and names. Friendlies. You'll know at least one of them."

Skirata felt slightly queasy. He knew what was coming next. He really should have let his natural suspicion have the upper hand. It was his fault for not asking a very obvious question months ago.

I was blinded. Grief and greed. Etain dead, the chance of a genetic break right in my lap. Grief, greed, and . . . getting too soft.

Skirata looked slowly around the room to see where Ny was. She was talking to Cov, the sergeant from Yayax Squad. It was nice to see the Yayax boys joining in. They tended to keep themselves to themselves, rarely coming in for meals with everyone else.

"It's Ny, isn't it?" Skirata said quietly.

Jaing nodded. "Yes, *Buir*. It is."

Commander Melusar's office, Special Operations, 501st Legion, Imperial City

"I'm sorry, sir. Things got a bit out of hand."

Niner took the fact he was sitting in Melusar's office rather than standing to attention in front of the desk as a good sign. But then Melusar was a hearts-and-minds kind of officer. And this was just a routine report about discharge of weapons in a public place. A grenade round versus a repulsortruck, and the grenade won. Holy Roly didn't need to know more.

"Meaning?" Melusar said.

"I should have alerted the police." Niner found it hard not to say *CSF* every time. "I used lethal force to stop a vehicle thief."

"I don't think that's going to be a capital offense under this Empire, Sergeant. But I'd like to know why you did it. You're experienced. Special forces. Not some trigger-happy security guard."

Niner reached for an outright lie. It was easy. He hadn't realized just *how* easy. "I think I'm overreacting, sir. I'm finding it hard to switch off from the war. Everything starts me off. Ordinary stuff."

Melusar just looked at him, not with that I'm-waiting-for-the-truth expression Zey would have worn, but with concern. *Real* concern, not an act he'd learned on leadership courses.

He might just have been a great actor, of course. Niner wasn't about to abandon caution.

"I'd be surprised if it didn't," Melusar said at last. "And I don't think there's a quick cure, because it's a part of what makes you a fine soldier. You've been in life-and-death situations. You react instantly to stay alive. It doesn't come with an off switch."

Niner felt terrible. He was getting sympathy he hadn't earned. There was nothing wrong with him, nothing at all. He wasn't like Darman, erupting and lashing out when things got too much. Was he?

I'd know. I'd know if I was losing it. I'm sure I would.

But an insistent little voice reminded him that he always felt pursued, spied upon, *threatened* these days. The Empire kept an even tighter watch on its citizens than the Republic had. Conspicuous new public holocams were springing up everywhere, so he knew he wasn't imagining all of it. But it was not knowing where to draw the line between the real and the imagined that was eating away at him.

"I know Darman wasn't with you at the time," Melusar said. "I want to talk to both of you, though." He got up and opened the doors to summon a droid. Niner heard him. "Five-em, get Trooper Darman, please."

The doors stayed open for a change and Melusar sat down. Niner hadn't seen Darman since he'd walked back through the main gates and reported the incident. It wasn't concealable from his end, whatever Obrim might have done with security holovids, and he decided against discussing it with Darman and dragging him farther into it.

Does Dar even know I came back?

There wasn't a lot that escaped notice in a small

closed world like this unit. Niner kept his gaze fixed on the wall, wary of making eye contact with Melusar and falling into conversation, because the guy was just too easy to talk to. Anything might spill out in that state, Niner thought. Eventually he heard brisk footsteps in the corridor. Darman marched in, helmet under one arm, and came to attention as if he hadn't even noticed Niner was there.

"At ease, Darman." Melusar gestured to the chair next to Niner. "Take a seat."

Darman sat with his fingers meshed on his stomach, elbows braced on the arms of the chair. For a second, his eyes met Niner's. All Niner could see was quiet disappointment, not surprise or anger.

Melusar closed the doors from the desk control, sinking the office back into that soundproofed, padded silence.

"I've not been entirely honest with you," he said. "But I think you know that."

Niner tried to stop himself from guessing where this was leading, but he couldn't help it. He evaluated threats fast. He'd been drilled to do that since infancy. Only he and Dar were here; that meant it wasn't about Squad 40, and it wasn't about former Republic commandos, because Ennen was absent, and Ennen had a Corellian training sergeant. Common factor: two men from a Mandalorian-trained commando company. Narrow it down: Darman hadn't been involved with blowing the truck up, so it wasn't about the incident.

Niner could have just waited to see what was coming, but he couldn't switch it off.

"You probably noticed that my first move on taking over this unit was to single you out," Melusar said. "It wasn't all about being dazzled by your dispatch of Camas. Darman, you *really* bothered Agent Cuis. I like that in a trooper."

"I haven't had much contact with Agent Cuis, sir." Darman seemed to be playing it dead straight. "I'm sorry if I gave him cause for concern."

"I'm not. You knew he was a Force-user, didn't you? And he *knew* you knew."

Darman's larynx bobbed as he swallowed. "Can't help but notice the past tense, sir."

"Agent Cuis was killed on duty. I don't get to hear every detail, but I hear enough. Intel is riddled with these mystics and their little cliques. At the risk of being exposed by telling you this—I want you two to report direct to me, *only* to me, and not deal with our other-worldly chums. Are you up for it?"

How did anyone say no to that?

"Define *deal with*, sir," Niner said.

"I don't mean neutralizing them. I'm eccentric, but not nuts. I mean to gather intel on them, maybe even de-rail their schemes when need be."

"Isn't that . . . treason, sir? For us, I mean."

"Depends on your lawyer. Me, I think of it as keeping tabs on the enemy within. They're not on the Empire's side. The Empire belongs to its ordinary citizens. I won't see it bled dry by these mumbling hand-wavers. Otherwise we've just swapped the Jedi for another secret cult."

Melusar was definitely *not* putting on an act. He was as enthusiastic and affable as ever, but Niner watched his hands on the desk. He held his stylus in a white-knuckled fist, thumb scraping rhythmically up and down the metal clip and twanging the end with the nail. His other hand was flat on the polished wood as if he was going to stand and slap it down hard.

"We're not the only commandos who could do this, sir," Darman said. Good point; and Niner wasn't sure why he was included in this conversation, other than being part of the double act. "I can spot Force-users. So can you, obviously. No magic to it."

"I know what they used to say about Omega Squad. *Overrated Mando-loving weirdos.* Sergeant Barlex was a little more neutral—*born-again Mandalorians.* Mandos aren't awed by Force-users. Some Mandos really hate them."

"Plenty of men left from the Mandalorian-trained

squads," Niner said. "Quite a few from Kal Skirata's and Walon Vau's, in fact."

"But nobody left who's been so close to the Null ARC troopers and so steeped in Mandalorian nationalism—except you two. Skirata's own."

Niner didn't take the bait. "We're good, sir, but even two of us aren't the army you seem to need."

"The smaller the circle, the lower the risk," Melusar said. "But just as the Intel Force-users can't keep everything secret from us, because they can't avoid contact with common beings, your comrades got to know a fair bit about you. And I think you're as motivated as I am in your own way to *reduce* the dominance of Force-users in galactic politics."

He didn't elaborate. Maybe he knew something, and maybe he was fishing, so Niner didn't rush to fill the silence that followed. Neither did Darman. Melusar waited a little longer, then seemed to accept he was dealing with expert stonewallers.

There might well have been speculation in the ranks about Darman and Etain. But the chances of Melusar knowing about Kad were remote.

Darman stared at him a little longer, then put on his harmless voice. "Your family's from Dromund Kaas, aren't they, sir?"

Melusar seemed caught short for a moment, lips slightly parted. "The Dromund system is just a myth."

"If you say so, sir."

Neither Niner nor Darman knew anything more than where Holy Roly came from, but it was a big card to play. He hadn't a clue how they'd know anything about an obscure Sith world that wasn't even on the Republic charts. The look on his face told Niner that he felt he'd bitten off more than he could chew with Darman. Niner decided it was a good place to park the sabacc game for the time being. Melusar seemed to take the hint, too.

"*Beskar*," he said, not so much changing tack as skipping some preamble. "It all hinges on Mandalorian iron. You know all about *beskar*, don't you? Well, Imperial

Procurement's done a deal with the Mandalorians to mine it. *Beskar* is overkill given the existing size and punch of the Imperial Army, so this is for dealing with Jedi and other Force-users. Ever seen it in action?"

"You mean have I seen *beskar'gam* deflect a lightsaber blow?" Niner couldn't recall. Skirata swore by it, though, and the Nulls all had genuine *beskar* armor. "Most of the Mando training sergeants wore it. It beats durasteel and other alloys hands-down."

"*Beskar'gam,*" Melusar said.

"Armor. Means *iron skin.* Mandos live in their armor."

"Anyone who wanted to put Force-users in their place would do well to have a supply of this stuff, wouldn't they?"

Niner could follow the logic. Melusar wanted to find some edge over Palpatine's dark side Intel operatives. But did he know Palpatine was a Sith too? If he did, he was biting off a lot more than anyone could chew. If he didn't, then—it was all the same in the end. Niner gave Holy Roly a life expectancy of a couple of months.

But isn't that why we're still here, and not on Mandalore right now? Because Dar wants to protect Kad from all this? And our whole clan? Common cause.

"And a supply of Mando ironsmiths who know how to work *beskar,*" Niner said. "You'd be needing that, too."

Melusar looked as if he hadn't considered that—a quick flash of the brows, a glance to one side for a fraction of a second—and seemed to chew something over. "You can walk away from this and we can forget anything was ever said."

Darman unmeshed his hands. "You can rely on me, sir."

He didn't say for how long. Niner hated these discussions made up of double meanings and inferences. Ordo called it ambiguity. Niner just saw it as being given enough rope to hang himself, but he nodded anyway.

"I don't have any memories of Dromund Kaas, for what it's worth," Melusar said. "I grew up without my father. And one day, you can tell me how you even know the world exists."

"That'll be interesting for both of us, sir."

Melusar paused for a beat. "Dismissed, men."

Niner just took the revelation with a nod, and left with Darman. They walked in silence until the doors to the central lobby closed behind them and they reached the parade ground, as private a place as any. Dar didn't even look at him. They had about two minutes' walk time to deal with the unsaid stuff before they were back within walls that might well have had ears.

"Sergeant Barlex," Niner said, trying to make his peace with Dar. "Second Airborne, Two-hundred-and-twelfth Battalion. Remember him? Miserable *di'kut*. He called us born-again Mandos, and his loadmaster said they'd been up against Mandos fighting for the Seps, and he called us—"

"You should have *gone*," Darman said. "Why the *shab* did you come back? What did you actually do? I told you to *go*."

"It all went belly-up. Stupid bad luck, and I had to finish off a *chakaar* who saw a bit too much."

"That's not why you came back, though, is it?"

"No, it's not."

"I don't want this guilt. You can't dump it on me."

"Hey, I'm not being a martyr, okay? My choice. I wouldn't have had a second's peace on Mandalore worrying what was happening to you here, and now that I know what Melusar's got in mind, I'm glad I stayed."

"Well, dropping the det about his homeworld got his attention, so *he's* got to live with some uncertainty, too." Darman slowed down. It had been raining. Small puddles had formed on the parade ground, and the night air smelled of damp permacrete. "But I like the guy. Him and *Kal'buir*—shame they're on opposite sides. They're both at war with the Force for the same reasons."

"I think they both just want the Force to leave them alone, actually."

"You know the killer question I forgot to ask?"

"What?"

"Whether Holy Roly thinks Mandalore should be part of the Empire. He does believe in the Empire, you know. Just not its management team."

"Does the garrison at Keldabe scare you? For Kad, I mean."

Dar shook his head. They had ten slow strides to wrap this up. "Not with the whole clan there. No."

"Good."

"I'm going to try to send holovid messages to Kad, so he doesn't forget who I am."

"That's the spirit. *Oya*."

Darman reached out to tap the security key code to the barracks block door. "And thanks, *ner vod*. It would have been hard here without you."

The doors parted, and the evening's dramas were over. Darman was on an even keel again.

Sooner or later, though, the question of when to make a run for it would come up again. All Niner knew now was *not yet*.

Freighter *Cornucopia*, next morning:
inbound for Fradian, Mid Rim

"It'll be good to see Maze again," Jusik said. "He's not a bad sort when you get to know him."

Ruu gazed around the cockpit of the freighter. A quick change of transponder codes had given Ny's ship a new identity for the time being, at Atin's insistence, and *Monarch*-class vessels were some of the most common sights around Fradian. Nobody would be looking for a specific one here, not yet, if they were looking for it at all.

"I'm impressed that Ny trusts you with her transport," Ruu said.

"I'm a safe pilot. Goes with the extra midi-chlorians."

Everything living had them in its cells. The more you had, the more able you were to exploit the Force. *Nothing special. Just the way I am*. Jusik had always treated it as a knack he happened to have, in much the same way that Jaing had a flair for data technology. The knack used to be labeled *Jedi,* both explanation and identity. Now Jusik found he had expunged his sense of Jedi-ness simply by changing a word in his head to *midi-chlorians.* He was a Mandalorian who simply happened to have more midi-chlorians than other *Mando'ade,* and had been trained to use them.

I'm still finding out who Bardan Jusik is. Now I've peeled off the label, I can see what's actually in the bottle.

"Have I got midi-chlorians?" Ruu asked.

"Every living cell has them. The more you have, the more potential you have to use the Force."

"Even animals and trees."

"Yes." A thought struck him. "So what happens if you're a nerf with a high midi-chlorian count?"

"Is this a quiz?" she asked.

Jusik was appalled that he'd never asked that question before. He didn't have an answer, and from that moment he knew he'd always be plagued by the idea. "No, it's me thinking out loud."

"Well, latent Force-user or not, I bet someone ate it. Nobody assessed its potential except for stew and cutlets."

Ruu was an oddball. Jusik couldn't think of her as an older female in the way that he did Ny or Uthan, although being at least ten years older than him should have moved her into the category of folks he expected to know more than he did about life. Instead, she came across as a restless teenager who'd seen too much, too fast. It was the way she switched between utterly open questions and weary cynicism.

"I'm not sure I'm ever going to eat nerf again," he said.

"Or sorris greens. Veggies have midi-chlorians, too."

"Now you're just winding me up."

"No. Illustrating a point about our inability to fence ourselves off completely from causing pain. Being alive has a price."

Ruu scared him sometimes. This was his brand-new

sister. He recalled how excited Fi had been to acquire an instant family by adoption rather than blood, and now he understood how important those formalities were to folks.

"So you don't trust Maze," she said. "You didn't give him the coordinates to Kyrimorut."

"Just in case he's compromised. It's nothing to do with trust. Even ARC troopers can be tracked down. We found Sull when he was in hiding, remember?"

"One day, the Empire's going to send a *loyal* clone to infiltrate."

"Don't you think *Kal'buir's* thought of that?"

"That still doesn't deal with the problem of what happens when it does."

Jusik felt a brief pang of vague, formless fear, an animal reflex that cramped the muscles in his throat. But that was exactly what Palpatine traded on. Fear kept beings in line. Fear—shadowy things, unspecified things, things that you couldn't actually see and grab hold of—made you mistrust and suspect everyone. It separated folks. Everyone retreated to the sanctuary of their own head, unable to trust even those closest to them. And divided people didn't form up into groups to rebel.

Fear was a cheap and easy pathogen to unleash on a population, every bit as destructive in its own way as Uthan's viruses.

"We're ready for it," Jusik said. "And until then, it won't stop us helping brothers in need."

Ruu just shrugged and sat back in the copilot's seat, arms folded across her chest. "Dad's a bit jumpy at the moment. Did he have a fight with Ny or something?"

Jusik had noticed. Something had shifted slightly at the gathering yesterday, and *Kal'buir* gave off a distinct anxiety in the Force. It could have been the fallout from the aborted rescue, because everyone was struggling to put a brave face on that. But Jusik knew him too well. Something else had upset him, and he was still on edge when they left.

"Maybe." Jusik checked the nav computer; half an

hour to reentry to realspace. "He might be feeling the pressure from A'den trying to marry them off." Jusik realized that might have been a little insensitive. "Sorry. I forget that you lost your mother."

"It was years ago," Ruu said. "And Dad's more than earned the right to move on."

"Do you miss Corellia?"

"I never miss anywhere. I never fit in."

"Not even in Kyrimorut?"

"That's different. It's Misfit Central."

Jusik didn't ask if she missed her two brothers. If she wanted to discuss that, he had the feeling she'd tell him in no uncertain terms. He activated the holochart and studied the street plans of Fradian's ore terminal.

Maze had carried out Order 66, more or less. Jusik hadn't yet met a clone who had, and for a moment it made him feel odd.

Ordo said Maze had actually arrested General Zey, but that Zey had asked him to finish the job, to spare him whatever Palpatine had lined up. Zey got a blaster bolt to the head, but on his own terms. And Jusik still felt guilty for the unkind thought that never left him: that the Jedi Order had sowed what it had reaped, and that its acceptance of a slave army had set up its own punishment. The Force had balanced the books.

He avoided the discussion with Scout. She was a Jedi. He wasn't. He wondered if he would ever swing back to the middle ground and see his former allegiance more neutrally.

Cornucopia dropped out of hyperspace on schedule, and Jusik landed with all the other ore carriers and supply ships. There were no Imperial troops patrolling the port, just local security, but he decided to change out of his armor. Mandalorians were highly visible. If a security holocam caught them, it might prove to be one more piece in a puzzle that some Imperial agent was putting together. Ruu watched him transfer his comm kit from his helmet to his *aruetyc* clothes.

"We could do with some discreet body armor," she said.

Concealed armor was one of the few things that was hard to come by on Mandalore. Everyone wore *beskar'gam,* up front and in your face. Hiding it just wasn't in the Mando mind-set.

"I'll acquire some," Jusik said. "But we'll be okay today. Just in and out, and home for dinner."

Ruu checked the power level on her blaster. "That's what I said just before I ended up in a Republic prison camp."

"What did you call us?"

"Carbon-flush, barves, kriffing—"

"I mean how you referred to the Republic. We called you Seps, Separatists, but you called yourselves the Confederation of Independent Systems. What was your nickname for us?"

Ruu looked as if she was running through a long list in her mind's eye. "Jackboots," she said.

"Logical."

"Control. Surveillance. Checks. Every movement and comm message logged. All for your own good, all to protect you. And you all fell for it." Ruu pulled the power clip out of her blaster with a loud snap and swapped it for another. "The only thing Republic citizens ever really needed protecting from was their own government. And now they've got what they deserve."

She was Kal Skirata's daughter, all right. Jusik marveled at the similarities in outlook, even though *Kal'buir* hadn't been around to influence her view of the world. But Corellia and Mandalore had one big cultural thing in common: they didn't take kindly to being herded.

Jusik secured the freighter and they walked through the loading yard toward the gates, dodging loader droids ferrying pallets to the ships. "You including me in that?"

"No," she said. "You were institutionalized, and you still managed to tell them to shove it."

Institutionalized. Brutal, but true. "All families are institutions. As far as I was concerned, the Order *was* my family."

"Liar. You must have known there was something missing, or you wouldn't have latched on to Dad, and you certainly wouldn't have hung up your lightsaber." Ruu, ambling casually as if she did the Fradian ore run every day, glanced at his belt. "Where is it, by the way?"

"Somewhere I can't draw it without thinking."

"Smart."

"I'm getting used to thinking *blaster first*. Verpine pistol, actually."

"Yeah, I noticed Dad loves his Verps."

The security guard at the gates was reading a holozine, arms folded on the countertop in his booth. He looked up as Jusik and Ruu inserted their identichips in the scanner, squinted at the readout, and waved them past with a grunt. For a moment, Jusik completely forgot which bogus identity he was traveling with today.

Something odd was distracting him, and he wasn't sure yet what it was. It was like his Force sense of danger in some ways, an urge to look over his shoulder, or a compulsion to pay attention to a specific place; but he didn't feel under threat. He just felt that there was something he'd missed.

This was all down to Ruu going on about surveillance and Jackboots, nothing more. She'd made him jumpy.

"Better check your buddy's there," she said.

Jusik opened his comlink. "Maze? How you doing?"

Maze took a couple of moments to answer. He sounded tense. "Welcome to Tin Town. Picturesque, isn't it?"

The terminal looked like it had been designed by an architect who hated his job and wanted to get fired. Some industrial landscapes held their own stark, utilitarian beauty for Jusik, but Fradian was just plain ugly.

"I *must* buy a holocard to send to the folks," Jusik said. "Okay, shall we meet up at the tapcaf with the least food hygiene violations?"

"I've borrowed a speeder. Let's not."

"The lawful owner's unaware, of course." Jusik felt reassured that he could still tell when someone was under stress. Poor old Maze. He'd been tied to HQ as Zey's aide and rarely got out to do all the stabbing, stealing, and sabotaging that the other ARC troopers did. He wasn't used to taking vehicles. "Okay—"

"What transport have you got?"

"Freighter."

"Can it take a small speeder? Two-seater?"

Cornucopia's cargo doors were full-width. "Sure. But you don't need to hang on to it. We'll kit you out with everything you need."

"I'm in the speeder now, and getting out will be . . . awkward." Maze didn't elaborate. "Can you get to the waste processing area and park up ready to open the hatch for a quick exfil?"

Jusik consulted his datapad. "Give me ten minutes to walk back to the ship. I'll land on the junction with the service road."

"Good plan, sir."

Maze still thought of him as General Jusik, then. "I'm just *Bardan* now, *ner vod.*"

"So you are," said Maze.

Jusik closed the comlink and caught Ruu's arm to turn her around back to the ship. "That explains my weird feeling," he said. "Maze got himself in a spot. He's a bit out of practice."

"*Now* you tell me about the feeling. Force stuff, I assume."

"Yeah."

Ruu strode at an impressive pace. "And he wants to bring his speeder on board."

"Yeah."

"I think *that's* weird."

Jusik recalled all the abandoned vehicles that Skirata's illicit activity on Coruscant had left in its wake. It had been a full-time job for Enacca the Wookiee to make sure they were all recovered, disposed of, or put back in the transport pool with new ID and livery. Abandoned vehicles made cops suspicious and left trails of evidence.

"It's only in holovids where nobody worries about basic logistics," Jusik said. "And Maze *is* pretty weird."

"*Bard'ika,* I don't like this."

"Look, you got caught." He hated himself for saying that the moment he said it. "Nobody's ever caught *me.* Relax."

As they walked back through the gates, the security guard looked up from his holozine and frowned.

"ID," he said, looking Jusik over. "Left something behind?"

"Change of itinerary. I need to move the ship."

"You're booked in for three hours."

So he wasn't that unobservant after all. Jusik drew his ID chip. "I'm an annoying pilot who's going to mess up your day with extra admin work. You decide to turn a blind eye because it's not worth the trouble I'm going to turn into. You'll forget us the minute we take off."

Jusik handed the guard both chips, his and Ruu's. The guard sighed and handed them back.

"You're just going to mess up my day with extra admin work," he said. "Beat it. And no refunds for unspent time."

Jusik just smiled and walked on. He hated using Jedi mind influence, but he'd made a deal with himself to do it only when his family or another clone was in trouble. This was *justified* mind messing. He wouldn't make a habit of it. *Honest.* But sometimes it really was the kindest thing to do.

Ruu didn't say a word until *Cornucopia*'s cockpit hatch sealed behind them.

"So what the stang was *that,* spoon-bender?"

"A persuasive technique they taught us at the academy." Jusik started up the drives, one eye on the bulkhead chrono. "We weren't the miscreants he was looking for. Something like that."

"Something like when you knocked me out cold without laying a hand on me?"

"I never left a bruise, did I?"

"Sometimes you creep me out, *ner vod*."

"I promise I'll never use Force tricks on you without your consent."

"Make that just *never*."

The freighter lifted clear and skimmed low over kilometers of elevated conduits strung between air shafts and processing plants. The waste facility glittered below it like a lake in the barren, dusty landscape, but as Jusik brought the ship in to land, the surface of the water resolved into a sewage treatment reservoir. Nothing could remain a lovely illusion for long here. He could see a speeder parking area with rows of vehicles, and a few plant workers standing around a mobile generator, chatting and drinking from flimsi cups. He commed Maze again.

"Maze, have you got a visual on me?" Jusik said, keeping the repulsor drives running. "*Monarch*-class crate. Flashing my nav lights *now*."

"Got you. You're hard to miss. Cargo doors open?"

"Come on in." Jusik could now feel something very odd in the Force, almost as if something had swept in with the grit and hot air when the cargo hatch opened. He tried to concentrate on the task in hand. He still didn't know where Maze was. "Have you nicked one of the waste company's speeders?"

"They'll notice when I start the thing. I've been holed up here since daybreak."

"I still don't see why he can't get off his *shebs* and *walk* out to us," Ruu muttered. "They won't stop him. They probably won't even know *what* he is, let alone *who* he is."

"I'm moving *now*," Maze said, voice tight and strained. "Just hold position until I'm in."

Maze was clearly under a lot of stress; Jusik didn't need to be told that. He couldn't pick out the speeder in the rows of vehicles and waited for movement to catch his eye. Then one speeder, bright red with white markings, lifted and began moving slowly out of its bay, crawling at regulation safety speed along the row toward *Cornucopia*'s position.

It had to pass a knot of workers.

"Ah, stang . . . ," Ruu said.

"Get a move on, Maze . . ."

Maze sighed audibly. Jusik still had his eye on the plant workers, and as the speeder slipped past them, one looked around casually as if to check which of his buddies was moving out. Jusik couldn't hear his shout, but he saw the pointed finger, the way the rest of the workers all whipped around, and then the billow of dust as Maze hit the accelerator and sped toward the freighter. The workers started running after the speeder.

"Buckle up, Ruu," Jusik said. "It's going to be a fast exit."

"Hundred meters," Maze said.

Jusik felt sweat prickle on his top lip. He had to sense where Maze was in relation to the ship, and his speed, and build an instant three-dimensional moving picture in his mind. Every other bad feeling in the Force that was clamoring for attention had to wait. Jusik shut his eyes.

"Remember you've got brakes, Maze . . ."

"Fifty meters."

"Start braking, *ner vod*."

"Whoa . . ."

"I said *brake!*"

Jusik felt the speeder as a disturbance in the Force that was about to crash through the back of his skull. The airframe shook. Ruu swore. Maze's voice said "Clear!" and Jusik hit the hatch control, shutting the cargo doors. He didn't think about anything else until the freighter was hurtling into a sky getting darker by the second. He headed for the jump point as soon as they were past the upper layer of Fradian's atmosphere.

"So what if that *isn't* Maze?" Ruu said at last.

Jusik breathed again. "Maze?"

He could feel something *very* wrong now. He took out his Verpine. He was sure that it was Maze he could feel in the Force, but there was someone with him. Jusik sensed a Force-user, and a presence he thought he knew but that shifted and wavered like a bad comm signal.

Maze was an ARC trooper, and he followed his orders like a pro. He had one of Palpatine's Sith agents with him. Jusik knew it.

"Ruu, when the nav computer indicates, hit the jump button," Jusik said.

"We can't dump things out the air lock in hyperspace . . ."

"Just do it."

Jusik scrambled down the ladder and made his way cautiously down the shoulder-wide passage that connected the forward cargo hold to the cargo bay itself. He reached for his weapons—Verpine in his right hand, lightsaber in his left. The blade sprang to life, green and humming. Ambidexterity was a useful ability.

In the dim deckhead lighting, he could see a dusty speeder vibrating slightly in tune with the ship. One hatch opened, very slowly. He aimed the Verp.

"Maze, *get out.* Hands on your head. Stand clear where I can see you."

The hatch opened far enough for Maze to step out. Yes, it *was* Maze. He was wearing a grubby brown tunic and a couple of days' growth of stubble, but it was him all right.

Maze put both hands on his head, fingers locked. "It's not how it looks."

"And your buddy." Jusik looked to the left-hand hatch. If Maze tried anything, he could drop him with the Verp, but the Force-user would need the little extra persuasion of a lightsaber. "Get out on deck. Hands on your head. Just *freeze,* or you won't *have* a head."

Jusik felt that wavering presence in the Force change from something vague and shifting to something he knew very well indeed. He wondered if it was a trick. There was no telling who or what Palpatine had signed up to work for Intel these days. And even if the shabby form that squeezed out of the speeder hatch was hard to recognize, the suddenly clear presence in the Force wasn't.

"General?" Jusik said, aghast. "*Master Zey?*"

The man who stood before him obeying his instructions was a lot thinner than the Zey he'd known, and looked as if he'd been through each one of Corellia's Nine Hells.

"I'm not armed," Zey said. "Maze took my lightsaber."

Jusik looked to Maze, still keeping Zey in his view and ready to take his own lightsaber to him if he moved. He was shocked by his own reaction. "You *shot* him. Ordo said you *shot him*. The night of Order Sixty-six."

"Ordo's not half as smart as he thinks he is," Maze said. "Well, he is, but he got this one wrong."

"You lied to me, Maze. You set us up."

"I just left out a detail."

"You want us to save him, too? Is that it? Or is he a peace offering for Kal to play with?"

"Yes," Maze said. "I'm asking you to help both of us."

Ruu must have been listening on the ship's system. "Sixty seconds to jump," she said calmly. "Last chance to dump them out the air lock."

Jusik looked at Maze. The man deserved better. But he had no idea what to do about Zey, or even how he'd concealed his presence. This wasn't a Jedi rescue operation. This was for the men they used and discarded.

He only had seconds to decide.

He did the compassionate thing, but he didn't lower his weapons. He made himself a promise that he'd use them later if this all went wrong. And he'd have some explaining to do to Skirata.

"Thirty seconds, *Bard'ika*," Ruu said. "I say flush Maze for being a lying barve and flush the Jedi *just because*."

Fifteen seconds. Ten.

"Jump," said Jusik.

12

Everyone's got some serious dirt in their history, ma'am. In the days of the Old Republic, we Mandalorians wiped out at least one sentient species just to prove that we could—the Cathar. Are we ashamed of that? I hope so. But if anyone tries to wipe us out again, I feel better knowing we once did something to deserve our fate. It's easier to take than just being spotless victims.

—Wad'e Tay'haai, historian and mercenary, in conversation with Kina Ha

Kyrimorut, Mandalore

"But I was never part of this," Ny said. "I never joined anything, signed anything, or agreed to anything."

There was a helplessness about being innocent that left Ny floundering. What could she say? Some Jedi had added her name to a list of pilots who could be contacted to move fugitives. They hadn't asked; she didn't know.

All she knew now was that people she loved and trusted were looking at her as if she was a traitor, a traitor who could have brought the Empire to their front doors. A'den, ever the loyal friend, leaned on the back of her chair with his hand resting on her shoulder.

"It's okay, we know," he said. "We just want to backtrack a bit so we can work out *how*, because *how* might tell us what else the *shabla jetiise* have lumbered us with."

It felt like an interrogation even if she was surrounded by friends—Skirata, Ordo, Mereel, and A'den. Ny felt guilty of being gullible. She'd never thought of herself that way. What scared her more than anything wasn't the Empire, she realized, but being despised by the only friends she now had.

"Kal, you believe me, don't you?"

Skirata sat in a chair by the door, occasionally rubbing one hand over his face as if he was tired and trying to focus. His gaze wandered back to her and he fixed her with that implacable blue stare that could have been hatred or just distraction. No, he was thinking about something else. He blinked, and suddenly he was *really* looking at her.

"Resources." He snapped his fingers. "Everyone and everything is a resource for them. Take a ship, take a pilot, take an army. All in their holy cause, all justifiable, and they don't even think about what they leave in their wake, because they *mean well.*"

Ny thought that sounded a lot like Skirata's approach, but she was in no position to lecture him at the moment.

"Well, we got to it before the Empire did," Ordo said. "Thanks to Niner and Obrim."

"That man's saved my *shebs* way too often." Skirata went to get up, but Ordo motioned him to sit down again and refilled his cup. There seemed to be a kind of telepathy at work between them. "The question now is who else has this information. Because the chances of them keeping it on one chip are zero."

Mereel sucked his teeth contemptuously. "Along with their chances of learning that the safest place to hide something is in your *shabla* head."

"It's not chaff, then," A'den said. "Not planted as a decoy."

"Not with Ny's data on it," Ordo said. "They couldn't have known it would end up here."

"You sure?"

"If they'd been able to plan *that* far ahead," Ordo said, "Palps wouldn't have been able to pull off the Purge, would he?"

"Well, we can sit waiting for the other shoe to drop, or we can get out and manage this," Skirata said. "Let's see what else Jaing shakes out of it. Then we can work out who might have what."

"I'm sorry, Kal," Ny said. She felt like a naughty kid, with the grown-ups talking over her head about what should be done about her. "I'm really sorry."

She expected Skirata to tell her that it wasn't her fault. She needed to hear that. All the sweat, all the pain, all the *lives* that had gone into creating this safe haven, and now she might be the cause of its downfall because she was gullible. She could hardly bear to think beyond the next terrible second.

"It's my fault," Skirata said. "I never stopped to ask the obvious. You told me there were Jedi looking for somewhere to hide. Once you mentioned Kina Ha, I never stopped to ask why *you*, why out of all the pilots they could have picked, they ended up with *you*."

Ny tried to reconstruct the sequence of events. Freight pilots and illegals went hand in hand. Some pilots did it for credits, some did it out of pity, and some didn't know they were doing it at all, because they didn't secure their ships or check their holds well enough. She did it out of pity. And she even did it for A'den to get whatever information she could about her husband's ship, transporting the ARC trooper Sull off Gaftikar to save him from being shot as a deserter.

"I knew Ny would help refugees," A'den said. "The other freighter pilots used to say she was soft. That's how I got to know her, and why I asked her to run errands for us. The Jedi worked that out, too. Like it or not, *Buir*, we have way too much in common with the Jedi when it comes to exploitation."

Ny had no idea she was seen as such a soft touch. She wasn't sure if she felt insulted or not.

"Well, I never dumped a stowaway out of the air lock

or called the port cops," she said. "Some I just kicked out when I found them on pre-launch checks. Some I felt sorry for. Scout approached me and I couldn't say no to a starving Jedi kid so soon after Etain died. So I said maybe."

Skirata slurped his caf and got up to wander around the kitchen. "We're already vulnerable. Palpatine's got saber-jockeys of his own, all kinds of foot soldiers who can sniff out other Force-sensitives. They *could* detect Kad and *Bard'ika* if they got within range. I'm making a dangerous assumption that having Kina Ha and Scout here doesn't add to the problem, and it's a trade-off against the benefit we can get from Kina Ha's genetic material. But as soon as Uthan's done with her—"

Skirata stopped dead, but Ny continued his train of thought. "You want them gone," she said. "But they know about this place. And even if they won't give that information away, they can have it extracted from them the hard way. Which leaves you with one option. Tell me you're not going to take it."

He looked brokenhearted. He often did these days, but she knew what was going through his mind this time: *You're not one of us, you're not the woman I thought you were.*

"Ny, I swear that *not one more clone* will die to save a Jedi's hide," he said. "*Not one.* Do you understand? If you ask me to choose between a Jedi's life and a clone's, I'll choose the clone's. The Jedi had it easy for centuries, and now they're not special or privileged anymore, they're expendable just like my boys were. We owe them *nothing.*"

He tipped the dregs of his caf down the drain and left the room.

"It's okay," Ordo said. "*Buir* knew it was a risk from the start. He's just angry with himself. If he'd told you to get lost and refused to hide Kina Ha, he'd be beating himself up now for passing on a chance to get her DNA."

A'den squeezed Ny's shoulder. "Even if Palps had that

datachip, how's he going to identify you, or the ship, or even know where you are? Anyone looking for Mandalorians knows where to start anyway. Even a Weequay."

They were nice boys, *kind* boys. She couldn't bear to see anything happen to them. "Tell me what I need to do to put this right, and I'll do it. Whatever it is."

"Nothing you can do," Mereel said. "Nothing *anyone* can do. I think we learned a long time ago that there was never going to be a point where we could shut the door, put our feet up, and say, 'Well, it's all going to be plain sailing from now on.' We don't live in that kind of world. We're always going to be fighting."

Skirata came back a few minutes later with a few sheets of flimsi in his hand, reading as he walked. "Jaing thinks he's got about ninety percent of the data, or he will have in a couple of hours. Then it just needs someone to sift through it and evaluate it."

"Me," Mereel said. "Seeing as I don't have a date tonight."

"Yeah, you need the rest," Ordo muttered.

"Altis crops up a lot." Skirata seemed to have forgotten his near argument with Ny. "He's a busy boy. Looks like he's running at least a couple of escape routes. Somebody find me some intel on Plett's Well."

"Never heard of it, but that's a challenge I can't resist," Mereel said. "Any clues?"

"Jedi safehouse, by the sound of it. Maybe that's where all the survivors headed." Skirata looked up and caught Ny's eye. She hoped he wasn't thinking the worst. He said he wasn't getting involved in anyone else's wars now, just looking after his own. "That'd be dumb, huddling in one place. You think they'd have learned from us. *Bas'lan shev'la.* Scatter. Don't present a single target."

"Coordinates?"

"If Jaing can find them, that'll come in handy."

Ny didn't dare say a word. This wasn't the time to provoke Skirata. She knew him well enough by now to realize that he switched into a savagely protective mode when he thought his family was under threat, and in that state of mind he'd think nothing of destroying whole planets, let alone individual beings. She wasn't even sure he'd regret it afterward.

He's not like the men you knew back home. He grew up without rules. He's always been on the edge of survival. He's not Papa Kal all the time.

"Hasn't *Bard'ika* called in yet?" Skirata asked.

"Not yet. Give him a couple of hours."

Skirata seemed placated. He walked over to Ny's chair, eyes still fixed on the flimsi sheets, and patted her on the head just like he did the clones.

"They used you up, Ny," he said, still not looking at her. "Now it's *our* turn."

He settled down in the chair again and went on reading. Occasionally, he snorted to himself, or said *"Shab . . ."* and shook his head. Eventually Jaing came into the kitchen with a thick sheaf of printed flimsi and dumped it on the table.

"There you go, and that's just a third of it," he said. "Poor old Camas. It would really tick him off to know we were pawing through all his data. Can I have a caf break now?"

"Son, you're a genius."

"And modest with it. No *Bard'ika* yet? Maybe Ruu got him back for that Force punch at the POW camp. She's a chip off the old block, *Kal'buir*—never forgets a grudge."

"Munit tome'tayl, skotah iisa." Skirata winked. "That's *long memory, short fuse,* Ny. The Mandalorian character."

She didn't know what to make of that. "I'll leave you lads to it," she said, getting up and passing his chair. "Time for my rounds."

"Ny, it's no big deal." Skirata caught her arm, as if he did that all the time. "We're pretty sure you were just a name on a list. Nothing else."

"I know," she said. But she also knew he'd corner

Scout and ask her why she'd approached *Cornucopia*, just to double-check, and that in his position she'd have done exactly the same.

Ny wandered around the house, checking who was where, as if the place was her ship and she was securing hatches for launch. Habit was comforting. Scout was with Uthan in the lab, deep in a conversation that looked as if it was doing both of them good, two lost souls whose societies had been wiped out in an instant. Kina Ha was dozing in her room—or maybe she was meditating. Besany was trying to get Kad to stand still to measure him for clothing. He was growing fast.

Parja stood outside Arla's room. The door was slightly open, and Ny could hear Laseema talking. Parja tapped her blaster in its holster.

"Not taking any chances," she whispered. "The sooner *Mij'ika* gets back with something stronger for her, the better."

Outside, Ny could see Jilka and Corr ambling arm in arm along the edge of the stream. That was definitely a romance in progress. In the distance, she could hear the sound of vibrosaws and occasional shouts as Levet and the Yayax boys built a fence. Or maybe it was a barn. She really didn't know what they got up to most of the time, but they seemed happy enough doing it.

Whatever was happening in the rest of the galaxy, life here was making a ferocious effort to get back to normal.

Her rounds took her the full distance of the perimeter, enough of a walk to clear her head and put things in perspective. As she completed the circle and walked back through the yard, dodging the nuna as they squabbled over mudworms, she spotted Fi sitting on the wall, staring across to the woods.

He didn't notice her for a moment. He looked utterly dejected, shoulders sagging, and he hung his head for a moment as if he was crying. When her boots crunched on some gravel, he looked up and instantly transformed into cheerful, wisecracking Fi again.

"So, are you going to call the cops and report your freighter stolen?" he said. "*Bard'ika*'s probably wrapped it around a tree by now. He's as mad as a box of Hapan chags when he gets into a pilot's seat."

Ny sat down next to him, wincing at the sharp edge of the brick under her backside, and put her arm around his shoulders.

"Cut the act, *ad'ika*," she said. "What's wrong?"

"Nothing."

"I'm not stupid."

"Okay, I'm upset about Dar and Niner. I really miss them. I really need to see them again. Am I going to live long enough to see them come home?"

He looked at her for a while as if he was expecting her to tell him to get a grip. She hadn't realized how rapid aging would start to trouble the clones. Maybe they all felt a sense of life racing past them now, faced with the changing seasons on a rural planet. Time was visible here.

Yes, Kal. I do understand. *I understand why you'd do anything for these boys.*

"Of course you will, Fi," she said. "It's not going to be forever. And everyone beats the odds here, right? Look at you. Good as new."

"Not quite. But good enough."

Ny kept him company, pulling up her collar against the chilly spring wind. She hoped he was joking about Jusik's piloting skills. Liability or not, that freighter was her last link to her old life. There were memories of Terin in it. She wasn't sure when she'd be ready to let go of them completely.

Kyrimorut, Mandalore

Cornucopia settled on its dampers, and Ruu leaned back in her seat. The silence in the cockpit almost throbbed.

"Okay, I'll head Dad off," she said at last. "You know he's going to go nuts, don't you?"

"I'll deal with him." Jusik unbuckled his seat restraint and turned to fix Maze and Zey with a warning stare. "Not a word until I've placated him, okay?"

Maze, arms folded, looked more intimidating now than he ever had in his smart white armor. Jusik wasn't sure if it was just the stubble or the look in his eyes.

"I'm not afraid of the old barve," Maze said. "I did this. I'll be just fine telling him why."

Zey looked crushed. He was a big man, a big personality, but all Jusik could feel from him was a sense of guilt that dwarfed him.

"I could just turn around and disappear again," Zey said. "It'd be better for everyone."

Ruu leaned across the console and pressed the hatch controls. "Not now you know where we are. You're not going anywhere until Dad says you can."

Maze gave Jusik a mock bow of the head. "After you, *Bard'ika.*"

It had to be done. Like all awkward things, it was best done quickly and without prevarication, Jusik decided. He wondered if he should have warned Ordo before the ship landed. But that just meant someone else had the task of breaking the news to *Kal'buir.* Jusik couldn't dodge his responsibilities like that. The hatch ramp beckoned like a condemned man's last walk to a scaffold.

What made it worse was Skirata's warm welcome when Jusik stepped off the ramp onto Kyrimorut's soil. Ordo stood right behind him.

"Good to have you back, son," Skirata said.

"You might change your mind when you see what I've brought back with me."

"Ah, never." Skirata, all smiles, looked past Jusik into the open hatch. "Maze is okay. Isn't he, *Ord'ika?*"

"I don't mean him." *Say it. Just spit it out.* "*Buir,* Maze had someone with him when we picked him up. And it was me who decided not to dump him out the air lock."

Skirata half smiled. "As long as it's not some Death Watch *shabuir.*"

"No. I brought back Arligan Zey."

Somehow, Jusik had managed to forget what would be the biggest shock for Skirata; the fact that Zey was still alive at all. Skirata just stared into his face, blinking, as if he knew he hadn't heard right and was trying to guess which words his failing hearing had mangled. But the news didn't stop Ordo in his tracks.

"Maze *shot him,*" Ordo said. "I heard the blaster discharge. I left them both in Zey's office."

"Well, whatever—Zey's alive, and Maze saved him." Jusik stepped forward and caught Skirata's shoulders. "*Buir,* I'm sorry. I had to make a snap decision. It was probably the wrong one."

Skirata looked ashen. That was worse than seeing him erupt into a rage. He looked slightly to one side of Jusik, probably not believing that Zey really would come out that hatch.

"Why, son?" His voice was a whisper. "Why didn't you comm me first?"

Jusik wanted to die of shame. His first substantial act after Skirata adopted him was a moment of madness, dangerous madness that made everything worse. He didn't deserve a father like this.

"Stupidity," Jusik said.

And maybe I'm not as Mandalorian as I think I am.

Ordo stepped in and took over, as he always did when he sensed things were about to get out of hand. He stormed up the ramp and vanished into the ship. For all Jusik's extra senses, he wasn't taking in the feeling in the Force because he was so fixed on the shocked pain on Skirata's face. He heard raised voices—Ruu, Maze, Ordo—and he was aware of movement in the background as Fi, Besany, and Ny came out of the house to see what was going on.

Jusik knew that the quieter Skirata was, the worse things would get. *Kal'buir* found it easier to let off steam about smaller matters. His silence had begun as shock and was now turning into a logjam of fury, resentment, and hurt. Jusik sensed it all in the Force. At point-blank range it was like standing in front of an open furnace.

A real Mandalorian wouldn't even blink about ditching Zey. Am I still a Jedi deep down? Is Kal'buir having doubts about me? Is his hurt coming from me?

Skirata seemed distracted by what was happening behind Jusik. When Jusik turned, Zey was stepping down from the ramp, flanked by Maze and Ruu. Ordo was right behind them as if he was shoving them out of the ship.

"I didn't think you'd be pleased to see me," said Zey. He held out his hand uncertainly, but Skirata didn't take it. "Thank you, anyway."

"Nothing personal." Skirata's voice was hoarse, as if the conversation was choking him "But if any Jedi's going to come back from the dead, it ought to be Etain."

"I heard," Zey said. "I'm so sorry."

"I just can't believe you're *jare'la* enough to stroll in here. That's nerve. That's *arrogance.*"

Ordo gave Jusik a look of pure ice and turned Skirata around bodily, facing him back toward the house. "Get inside, *Kal'buir,*" he said firmly. "We can't sort it out here. Ny? Ny, get the ship under cover. Come on, inside. *Now.*"

Jusik felt Skirata's anger swallow him whole, a great red tunnel where sound and light were instantly an infinity away. There were times when Jusik became so attuned to another being in the Force that he almost felt what they felt, and this time it scared him. He fell into that red vortex for a second. Skirata's pounding pulse shook his whole body and Jusik's with it. It took all Jusik's will to jerk himself back out of it and stand apart again. *Kal'buir's* frustration, three years of a hated war underpinned by decades of resentment, was looking for a valve to vent from. It would spurt out in the direction of Zey. Skirata stormed back inside.

Scout and Kina Ha appeared at the doors but stood back as if a speeder had nearly run them down. Jusik held out his arm to stop them following Skirata and Zey into the *karyai,* but Kina Ha drew herself up to her full height and withered him with a glance born of centuries.

"I would never abuse your hospitality," she said. "But this man is a Jedi, and so he is *my* business as much as yours."

"I was his Padawan," Jusik said, as if it was an answer.

"Are you sure you still aren't?"

It was hard to hide doubt from another Force-user. Jusik was so wounded by the comment that he didn't bar the door. An angry little group gathered in the *karyai.* Maze stared at Kina Ha and Scout, almost ignoring Skirata. The captain had never seemed the shockable sort, but it was clear he hadn't expected to see Jedi here.

"So you didn't have the stomach for it, then, Maze," Skirata said. "Or did he spin you some *osik* about his respect for all life and what a great little clone you were? How dare you bring him *here.*"

Jusik tried to get the situation back under control. "It's *me,* Buir. It's my fault. Don't blame Maze."

"No, I want to know why he thinks it's okay to bring a Jedi here, especially now that there's an Imperial garrison on our doorstep. Whether he shot him or not is his business, but when he wants to bring him here, it's *mine.*"

Maze seemed distracted by Kina Ha and Scout. "Well, looks like it's Jedi Night at Kal's, if you don't mind my saying so. And a *Kaminoan*? Going soft, Sergeant? So you're going to lecture me on consorting with the enemy, are you?"

"Kal, let's discuss this calmly," Zey said. "I don't blame you for being angry."

"This place is for *clones,*" Skirata said. "Get it? They're the ones who need help. Not *shabla* Jedi whining how tough things are and how they need protection. Is this some experiment to see how much insult you can add to injury without the whole galaxy imploding?"

Zey didn't even try to defend himself. Jusik tried to gauge who was going to snap first. He bet on Ordo.

"I'm not proud of what we were party to, Kal," Zey said. "I'm not claiming innocence or that I was only following orders. But don't you think we got our punishment for that?"

"So what do you want from us? We're collecting so many Jedi here that we're going to show up like the *shabla* Jedi Academy on Palpatine's Force radar."

"You know he's a Sith, then."

"Of course we know he's a Sith. We did business with them for generations. We know stuff about Sith that the Jedi Order erased from the records. You just can't hide history from everyone, Zey—there's always some other source. Our only problem is spotting the difference between you two gangs of crazies."

"Kal, you *know* that the Sith are bad news. They're evil. They've always been the cause of endless war and carnage across the galaxy."

"Oh, that's a good one," Skirata said. He mimicked Zey's baritone growl. " '*My* decapitations are more morally valid than *your* decapitations.' Only difference I can see is that they *plan* to end up with trillions dead, and you do-gooders manage it by accident."

"I'm not asking you to save the Jedi Order, Kal. I'm not even asking you to save me. I can leave. I should never have come here."

"The only way you're leaving here is dead, Zey. Because I wouldn't trust you not to shop us filthy Mando savages to the Empire."

It was pointless telling *Kal'buir* that Zey was genuine, and broken. Skirata would find no pity. He even seemed torn about Maze. Jusik felt the conflicting waves of sympathy and anger when Skirata looked at the man.

Skirata stared up into Maze's face. "Just tell me," he said quietly, "that you didn't do this out of loyalty."

Maze leaned over just a fraction. No, he wasn't intimidated by Skirata at all. "I did it because I thought he should get a fair trial. And because he used to make the caf in the office. It's funny how the little things tell you all you need to know about the man."

"So, give you a pot of caf—no sugar, splash of cream, maybe some nice cookies—and it's okay to send men to their deaths without asking them if they mind."

Ordo hovered, ready to intervene. Maze wasn't scared of him, either, even though the Null had once punched him out. Maze stabbed a finger at Skirata but stopped short of jabbing it in his chest.

"Zey's here," he snarled. "I'm responsible for that, the war's over, and you need to change the recording, Sergeant, because it's getting kind of monotonous."

"He'll get you killed."

"So? It'll be *my choice*. I'm not one of your poor dumb victim clones. You didn't free them from the Jedi. You just brainwashed them for Mandalore. When are you going to let them think for themselves?"

"Right *now*," said Ordo.

Just as Ordo's fist came up, Jusik reacted instinctively and Force-pushed him backward. Maze staggered back a few steps as if the aborted punch had landed; the wake of another Force-push tugged at Jusik as it ebbed. For a split-second both clones looked disoriented, and Zey grabbed Maze's arm.

"That was you, was it?" Maze asked.

"Sorry." Zey shook his head. "Don't fight over this. Please."

"Come on." Jusik stepped between Skirata and Maze. "*Buir,* go for a walk. Everyone, get out and leave us to talk. You two as well."

Ordo herded Skirata to the door, somehow forcing Kina Ha and Scout ahead of them. Maze scowled but looked to Zey for a nod to go.

"Just remember what you are, *Bard'ika,*" Ordo said.

It was one of those moments when Jusik felt he was broadcasting his innermost fears. The doors closed and he was alone with his old Master. The truly odd thing was that he had no sense of the past now, no memory of how it actually *felt* to be tied to Zey in apprenticeship.

He recalled all the details. He simply couldn't reproduce the emotions.

"Some things can't be undone," Zey said. "I should have known Skirata would react like that. And he's right. He owes me nothing, and all I can bring him is more trouble. I'm sorry, Bardan."

Jusik struggled. He wanted to be a good *Mando'ad*. "So where will you go?" *Why am I asking him that? Am I shaking him down for information?* "What are you going to do?"

"I don't know. I can't run forever."

"And Maze?"

"He put his life on the line for me. As an equal, in case you were wondering. I've got to consider his welfare."

Jusik decided not to mention Altis. "I need to know something." He didn't feel right calling Zey by *any* name now—Master, General, Zey, Arli, anything. He didn't know what Zey was to him any longer, only that the man had been instrumental in his youth, and that had to count for something. "Are you going to try to re-build what the Jedi had before?"

"Is this a trick question?"

"I need to know if anything I do to help you will end up cutting my brothers' throats one day."

"What did we ever do to you, Bardan? What did *I* do to you to drive you away like this? It's not just a princi-pled stand about the degeneration of the Order—much as I respect that."

"I'm still working it out." All or nothing; that was how Jusik was, and he knew it. He was raised in one cult and he moved seamlessly into another. He *knew* all that; he understood why the bond of combat tran-scended even family, too, but that didn't mean he had any control over it. He'd settle and find an equilibrium in years to come, but not now. He couldn't face his Jedi past for so many reasons. Mandalore represented un-questioning acceptance and space to work it all out. "This is my family. I need to be here for them. I'll do what I can for you, but not at their expense."

"Was it losing Etain that tipped you?" Zey asked. "We all lost too many friends. There's nobody left."

"Maybe there is." Jusik felt Zey's pain. Maze must have been the only person left that he could trust. "Did you think Maze would shoot you?"

Zey ran his huge hand through shaggy graying hair, eyes shut. "Right up to the moment the blaster bolt hit the wall a meter from me. I didn't even sense his emotions."

"Good man, Maze."

"Good friend. Yes."

"Come on, I'll show you to a room. We've got plenty. Kal will calm down, and then we can talk sensibly."

"*Buir* means father, doesn't it?"

"Yes. He adopted me."

Zey didn't say another word. He just put his hand on Jusik's shoulder as they walked down the passage, diverting via another corridor to avoid the kitchen. Jusik could hear the voices there. He showed Zey into one of the spare bedrooms still waiting for deserters in need of a new identity, threw him a towel from the cupboard, and left him to clean up. Then he went in search of Jaing.

Jaing was in the small workshop that he'd set up in another bedroom. Screens and scopes covered every shelf, and a thick wooden plank of a workbench stretched across the width of the wall. Kom'rk had claimed a corner to himself and was hunched over a 2-D holochart, tapping numbers into a datapad, completely absorbed in the calculation.

"Who'd have thought it, *Bard'ika*?" Jaing said, not looking up from the screen in front of him. "Saucy old *di'kut*, showing up like that. Moral of the story—always go back and check for a pulse."

"Ordo's never going to live that down," Kom'rk muttered. "Ha . . . ha . . ."

Jaing printed out some more data. "Is it hard for you? Zey, I mean. The Master-Padawan relationship must be pretty close."

"No different from families. Or marriages." Jusik
didn't want to be dissected. "Some are great. Some
aren't. Some don't get on at all. Me and Zey . . . I don't
know. More managerial than paternal."

"But he's not an innocent bystander like Kina Ha or
Scout. Command rank's got to mean something." Jaing
paused, smiling to himself as if he'd found something
juicy in the files. "Still, it's hard to cap someone who's
just standing there looking pathetic, even when you
know you'll regret it one day if you don't."

"I'll do it," Kom'rk said. "Nothing personal. Just necessary."

"Or we could use them to our advantage." Jaing
tapped his finger on the pile of flimsi. "Because one day,
the Empire's going to really tick us off, and we'll need
the skills of some saber-jockeys who owe us."

Kom'rk laughed. "They've owed a lot of people for a
long time. Don't see much of them repaying their
debts."

"Yes, but there are ways of enforcing moral obligation." Jaing grinned. He always did. He enjoyed problems and had complete confidence of his own ability to
solve them. "Like by keeping a firm grip of their *get-
t'se*."

Jusik could see the logic. And he found it telling that
Jaing could think of him as both an ex-Jedi and a non-
Jedi in the same breath. "*Buir* wants the Jedi out of our
lives, advantages or not."

"Let's not be too hasty. We know where their bolt-
holes are, and with a little ingenuity we can track their
movements. They step out of line—the Empire gets a
treasure map with *here be Jedi* on it."

Kom'rk laughed again. "That boy's sick."

"You got that location yet?" Jaing asked. "Chop-
chop. Get a move on."

"In a minute. It's looking like the Plawal Rift."

"What is?" Skirata asked.

"Their main safehouse for their kids. I think they call

it Plett's Well. Some of the data on here is from the Jedi temple archives."

Blackmail; it sounded ugly, but having dirt on others and others having dirt on you was a glue that bound folks together across the galaxy. It was as much a power for balance and harmony as the Force.

"Of course, if we know where they're holed up, we could just wipe out the rest of them now," Kom'rk said. "Or even do a deal with the Empire. But I don't trust any of them."

Jusik took to heart the Mandalorian saying that an enemy's enemy wasn't always your friend. If they were, then it wouldn't be for long.

"Ordo thinks I'm going soft on my old associates," Jusik said. "I can't blame him."

"Are you?"

"Do *you* think I am?"

"Nah. Do you want me to shoot you if you are?"

Kom'rk had that kind of deadpan humor. But humor had its serious purpose in life.

"Yes," Jusik said, half-meaning it. "Make it before I do any real damage."

Jaing just looked up at Kom'rk, the slightest pause as if it wasn't funny.

"You got it, *ner vod*," Kom'rk said, and went back to his holochart.

501st Special Unit barracks, Imperial City

"The droid came in to fix your helmet," Rede said, strapping on his belt. "It's over there. He said there was nothing wrong with it and you need to read the manual."

Darman draped his towel around his neck, rubbing his wet hair with one end, and stared at the helmet sitting on the bunk. He couldn't recall reporting a fault. Then it dawned on him; the droid was Jaing's buddy, the one that had modded Niner's bucket to give him a secure route to the Nulls. Jaing didn't hang about. The audio link was installed.

I can talk to Kad. I can talk to Fi and Atin, too. And Corr. And Kal'buir.

Darman's mood lifted instantly. It was almost as good as being there. He checked the chrono on the wall and tried to work out what time it was at Kyrimorut, then realized he had no idea because he didn't know where the place was. Without a reading for longitude, he couldn't work it out.

I'll call anyway. Whoever answers won't mind being woken up.

"We haven't *got* a manual," Darman said.

"Maybe he was joking."

Maybe Rede was, too. It was hard to tell. The kid soaked up experience and knowledge like a sponge, and Darman found it a bit unnerving. He found himself saying things that Skirata used to say back on Kamino, when he was surprised by how fast clones assimilated things, and how they changed before his eyes.

They grow up too fast.

Is that Sergeant Kal's voice, or mine? And who am I talking about—Rede, or my son?

A month was nearly a couple of years in terms of Rede's development. Darman watched him going through the checklist on his DC-17, with none of the unconscious ease that years of using the rifle had given the Kamino commandos. He wondered if that meant Rede would carry on aging at that same rate. It was a pretty depressing thought. The new clones might be even worse off than Darman's generation.

He knew that *Kal'buir* had Dr. Uthan working on a way around that. But he wasn't going to bank on it.

Niner was still in the 'freshers, but Ennen was sitting on the edge of his bunk, half dressed in his undersuit and lower body plates. He was staring at the floor tiles. The squad was supposed to muster at 0600 hours, which didn't leave any time to slob around. Darman rapped the chrono on the wall to get Ennen's attention.

"Hey, look sharp, *ner vod*. Doors to kick down, stuff to blow up."

Ennen took a few moments to react. "What's the point? Where's the peace and freedom and all that garbage we were supposed to see when we got the job done? What *is* all that, anyhow?"

Darman knew it was about missing Bry. He'd seen it before with other men. They would go on coping with losses for a long time, and then one death—not always their closest brother, but usually—would hit them hard enough to knock the stuffing out of them. Ennen had fought for three tough, bloody years alongside Bry, and now Bry was gone.

Dar and Niner had something to look forward to. It might have been out of reach at the moment, but it was there; it was full of promise and potential that he could still see, even through the daily pain of thinking of all the ways Etain wouldn't be there to share it with him.

I've got a son. I've got a home to go to one day. So has Niner.

"You want to talk, *ner vod*?"

Ennen glanced at the chrono on his wrist. "We got to go now." He stood up and attached his chest and back plates. "The war's over. It's over, and Bry made it, and then he gets killed *when it's over*. If I thought there was a purpose to it, something more than this, I think I could take it. But it's just going to be this day after day, isn't it? Until we're all dead with nothing to show for it."

The sound of running water stopped. Darman could hear Niner whistling as he dried himself. In the sergeant's absence, he had to deal with this.

"Ennen, you just have to get through this bad patch." How could Darman tell him he *knew* how pointless life could feel, because he'd lost his wife? "We've all been there. Even Delta, remember? Look, Holy Roly doesn't mind us going to cantinas. When we get back, how about we go and get an ale, and work all this out?"

Ennen stared at him for a moment as if he was looking for the catch, then nodded. "Yeah. Let's do that. If I had something to make sense of this, some end in sight, it'd make a difference. I just can't see anything."

Is he asking? I don't know how guys get to find out about Kyrimorut. Shall I tell him?

It was a tough call. Just mentioning the place was a big risk, because it revealed what Darman knew and suggested he knew a lot more, which he didn't. Ennen hadn't been raised by Mando *Cuy'val Dar* anyway. But neither had Levet, and Niner said he'd deserted to Mandalore, too.

I'll find a way to tell him, but not now. I need to ask Ordo how to do this.

Niner reached for his undersuit. "We all okay here?"

"Ready to roll," Ennen said, putting on his helmet. He switched completely. All a guy could do was get a grip and carry on for the moment. "Still the lower levels sweep?"

Niner nodded. "The cops did a routine stop on a human male with a stolen speeder and he pulled a lightsaber on them. Wisely, because they're not total *di'kute,* they pursued him at a safe distance and now they've got a wall of squad speeders surrounding the place he holed up in. Why they always bolt to the lower levels I'll never know. Too obvious."

Mandalore was an obvious bolt-hole, too. But, unlike Mandalore, the lower levels of Imperial City were still a place where people could vanish.

"What's *di'kute*?" Rede asked.

"Don't encourage them, kid," Ennen said. "They'll turn you into a Mandalorian. You wouldn't want that."

Rede paused. Darman could always tell when he was consulting the head-up display in his visor because he wobbled a bit as if he'd lost his balance for a split second. He wasn't used to the mass of images and telemetry filling his field of vision while he was trying to look past it at what was in front of him. He just hadn't had enough time alive to get used to it. It was still disorienting. Darman and Niner had worn HUDs almost every day since they were old enough to hold a spoon to feed themselves.

"I know now," Rede said. He'd obviously digested the data under M for Mandalore. "Yeah, I know what a Mandalorian is now."

Niner leaned close to him as they filed out. "That database," he said, "will tell you *nothing* worth knowing about Mandalore."

Rede didn't answer. Maybe he couldn't yet read his HUD, watch his environment, and talk at the same time.

There was a LAAT/i gunship waiting for them on the landing pad. Darman hadn't expected to see so many still in service, given the speed with which the Empire had rolled out new hardware, but they were brand-new vessels by military standards and the Empire wasn't stupid enough to junk everything from the old regime. Like the metamorphosis from Chancellor to Emperor, the change from Grand Army of the Republic to Imperial Army was often a lick of paint and a new name. The gunship had the new Imperial livery and symbols.

It's still a larty.

Darman was secretly pleased to see it. He jumped in knowing where everything was. In pitch blackness and upside down, he could find every switch, handle, and safety device. It was a little bit of what he used to think of as home, and the engine's noise was—as it always had been—a soothing voice speaking of rescue, resupply, and safe haven. Rede stood beside him in the crew bay and grabbed a deckhead strap.

"You ever done this in the city before?" Niner asked him. "It's like nothing else. Just seeing as much of a building below you as above you is weird."

"Yeah, and the neighbors love us flying by and gawking through their windows," Ennen said. "You'll be amazed what you can see. Use your infrared filter for a real laugh."

Poor Rede; Darman doubted his flash training—flash training ten times more rushed and compressed than any Kamino clone's—helped fill in the gaps there. The pilot had the cockpit door closed, so there was no opportunity for banter. The gunship lifted off high over the barracks, making Darman's teeth vibrate with that familiar frequency, and wove its way between the towering city blocks.

Fi loved this. He really got a kick out of the city. I can talk to him now. It's been—what, best part of two years? He's married. He'll have kids by the time I get to see him.

Niner's voice cut in. The lack of an audio icon in Darman's HUD told him this wasn't an official comm channel.

"So you're wired, Dar . . ."

"Can they hear us?"

"No. But Ordo or one of the others probably can."

That was fine. Darman had no secrets from them. "When we get back, I'm going to ask to talk to Kad. I want to tell him why I'm not there for him."

"Yeah, we can do that from time to time."

"Have you spoken to the others?"

"Not yet. You know what I'm like, Dar. Still got to be careful."

"I think we should let Ennen know about Kyrimorut."

"He's pretty down, isn't he?"

"He needs some light at the end of the tunnel."

"Okay, but clear it with Ordo or *Kal'buir.*"

The gunship darted through a forest of glass highrises, and for a few moments it ran level with a vast advertiscreen urging Imperial citizens to keep an eye on suspicious newcomers to their neighborhood in the upheaval that followed the war. THEY CAN LOOK JUST LIKE US, it warned. Darman wondered who *us* was on a planet of a thousand different species, but he got the idea.

Is Ennen a safe bet? Will he shop us to the authorities if we let him know he can desert anytime?

Darman just didn't know. He'd have to talk to Ordo. Niner was right. Ordo would have a sensible answer.

Rede, looking a little nervous judging by the way he

edged to the sill of the larty to look below, pointed down. "Wow, they've cordoned off a lot of skylanes for one guy."

Darman leaned out to look. The ship was flying a few levels above the target area, and the cops were taking no chances. They'd blocked off every intersection for four levels, and in a three-dimensional street grid, that meant a lot of police speeders making sure that nobody wandered into the cordon area as well as stopping anyone trying to get out.

Darman hoped they'd evacuated the immediate area. It really crimped his style when he had to worry about blowing up the neighbors as well.

"He's a Jedi," Niner said. "Got to take precautions."

"I've never fought Jedi," Rede said. "Is it as tough as they say?"

Darman doubted if Rede had fought at all. It wasn't the time to embarrass him by asking.

"They're definitely not invincible," Darman said. "They make mistakes like everyone else. And they die like everyone else."

He knew that better than anyone.

13

Mandalore's beskar *reserves far exceed its domestic
needs. The population is four or five million—a village
by our standards. They earn revenue from the shipbuilding and equipment contracts we place with them,
they have enough ore to equip a moderate fleet of their
own—limited, mind you, because they're a trouble-
some people—and that will keep them happy while we
concentrate on the business of stockpiling beskar. A
material that's effective against Force-users must never
be sold to any other government. Of course, we'll need
the cooperation of Mandalorian metalsmiths to produce the finished* beskar *... but we'll address that
problem when we come to it.*
—Churg Anaris Hej,
Deputy Head of Imperial Procurement

Imperial City, lower levels

The gunship dropped through ever-narrower skylanes
until it reached the nearest landing platform to the cordon.

It was a few meters longer and wider than the average
police vessel, but Niner doubted that the escaped Jedi
had factored that in when he went to ground down here.
The squad jumped out of the larty and jogged for the
knot of police officers taking cover behind their speeders
at the perimeter of the cordon. Niner glanced back at
the ship to see the pilot tap the chrono on his forearm
plate with an exaggerated gesture. *The meter's running.*

Niner didn't know him, but at least he had a sense of humor. A job like this could take minutes or hours.

"Where is he?" Niner asked, looking for a name tab on the nearest cop's uniform: ANSKOW. He didn't know any of these cops. They weren't any of Jaller Obrim's officers. The blue strip on their badges showed they were part-time community cops, usually drafted for crowd control at big events or traffic duties. "Have you got remote surveillance operating?"

Anskow pointed at a shuttered cantina. It was flanked by a grocery store, and a lingerie boutique whose window contained items that Niner decided didn't look sensible or comfortable.

"You'll laugh," he said, "but for all the holocams in this city, we don't have anything watching down here. Which is where most of the crime is. Funny how they're spending like crazy on snoop devices for up top, but not here."

"I think the Emperor's more interested in a different kind of crime. Got a floor plan yet?"

Anskow took out his datapad. "Best we can do is this one from the planning authority, but it's old. There might be some changes to nonstructural walls."

Niner took the datapad from him and transmitted the plan to the squads' HUDs. "Okay, that looks pretty straightforward."

"We don't think he's got hostages. Place doesn't open until the evening. The cook's normally first in."

"Jedi don't take hostages." Niner glanced at the cops standing behind the protection of their vehicles, some with blaster rifles resting on the roofs. "I've never known them to indulge in a shoot-out, either, but they're running for their lives now. What have we got, then?"

"What do you mean?"

"Padawan, Knight, Master? Any clues? Padawans wear a skinny braid, but they'll have cut those off unless they're idiots."

"Just a guy maybe twenty-five, thirty. The lightsaber

was about all we had time to notice, on account of it taking one of my guy's hands off."

"Probably not a Padawan, then."

"Does it matter? They're all dangerous, right?"

"It matters to *us*." Niner glanced at Darman, who'd gone back to the walkway above and was strolling along to get a better look. Niner could see the POV icon in his HUD. "Orders. Padawans, we take alive. Masters, we shoot on sight. Knights—depends, but *probably* lethal force, too."

Anskow gave him a long, dubious look. "Okay. We've evacuated the stores and the residential units up to this line. Area at the back of the cantina is industrial—repair shop, fuel storage, and so on. We've shut that off, too."

"We'll try not to hit it. They make a mess when they blow."

Anskow gave Niner a look that said he didn't know if he was joking or not, then motioned his officers to take up position. Darman, now accompanied by Rede, stabbed his finger down at the entrance to the cantina.

"He's not going anywhere unless he can fit down a sewage pipe," Darman said. "He's stuck in there. He'll have a reason, of course."

Jedi could get out of some pretty tight corners. Niner took nothing for granted, and reminded himself what had happened to Bry; even the most high-minded Jedi was likely to fight dirty when the entire sect was being exterminated. It looked like a dumb place to get cornered.

It had to be a setup, just like last time.

"No unnecessary risks, *vode*," Niner said. "I want everyone coming back with their head still attached. And he knows we're all out here waiting, so . . ." He upped the volume on his helmet's external speaker to loudhailer level. "*Jedi!* This is the Imperial armed forces." It just didn't *sound* right—not yet. "Come out—lay your weapons on the ground—hands above your head." He kept an eye in the POV icons on Darman's position. "Last chance, or we come in."

Predictably, there was no response. Darman took out a roll of detonite tape from his belt pouch and tossed it in his hand. "Knock knock."

"Okay, stick a charge on the front doors." Niner signaled to Rede and Ennen. "Ennen—on my signal, stick a flash-bang through the lower floor window. Rede, you place one through the roof light. Can you reach it from there?"

"Yes, Sarge."

"Okay. It's going to be quick. Simultaneous doors, flash-bangs, then *in*."

Niner looked up for a moment. Above him, beyond the cordon ceiling, he could see the undersides of stationary speeders hovering for a better look. He was sure the operation had an audience, and whatever they did would be on GNN sooner or later. He needed to get this over and done with fast.

"He's too old for a Padawan." Niner moved closer, twenty meters from the doors. "Shoot first, worry about Intel's recruitment needs later."

"What?" Rede said.

"Never mind. Everybody—in position."

Niner watched Dar drop down from the walkway on his rappel line and hug the wall as he made his way to the cantina doors. It took him seconds to slap detonite on the weak spots and take cover. Niner checked the POV icons: Rede was lined up on the skylight in the cantina roof, and Ennen was fixed on the big transparisteel window. Fired from the Deece attachment, the stun grenades would punch a hole in anything before exploding in a harmless but disabling ball of deafening, blinding light.

"Go!" Niner said.

Dar could always rig a spectacular detonation for rapid entry. He hadn't lost his touch.

Boom.

Niner ducked as the det went off and sent the doors crashing in. They rushed into smoke, tactical lamps raking the unlit counter and reflecting off bottles and mir-

rors. Niner could hear boots clattering and shouts of
"Clear!" Then wood splintered somewhere. He found
himself face-to-face with Rede. He gestured left; Ennen
appeared and pointed behind them to the kitchens. But
they didn't get that far, because the familiar *vzzzm* of a
lightsaber cut through every other sound and made
them all turn at once. The mirror behind the bar was lit
with soft blue light.

"Counter," Ennen said. "Under the counter."

He dived for the open end of the bar and opened fire.
Niner was still waiting for the booby trap, the ambush,
the feint. From his position, it looked as if everything
was happening simultaneously: a figure rising from behind the counter, the white flashes of a Deece emptying
its magazine, a blue shaft of energy that left an afterim-
age and tumbled to the floor.

Ennen kept on firing. It seemed like minutes before he
stopped. It could only have been seconds. The silence
was sudden and complete.

"That's for Bry," he said. He stepped over something,
crunching on broken glass, then grunted.

Niner braced, expecting him to trigger a device. That
was the kind of stunt a smart operator would pull, a sac-
rificial act to take Imperial troops with them just as
Camas had tried to do. Maybe the Jedi who'd been
stranded here had been ordered to do maximum damage. It didn't sound very Jedi-like to Niner, but then neither did trying to overthrow Palpatine by violence, and
they'd done that, too.

But he's a Sith. Does that make it okay, or not?

"Can't detect any explosives," Ennen said, standing
up again. "Let's see who this joker is."

The noises sounded as if he was rifling through the
guy's clothing. Less than three minutes from entry to finish; something to impress the locals. Imperial stormtroopers didn't mess around. Niner opened his comlink.
"Anskow? Building secure. We'll check for booby traps,
just in case."

"Maybe we should have done that first." Rede peered over the counter. "Did they leave just the dumb Jedi behind? Or are they all that useless?"

Ennen stood up, fanning out a sheaf of identichips one-handed. "Stang," he said. He tossed the chips to Niner and strode out. *"Stang."*

"What's up with him?" Darman asked.

Niner looked through the IDs. They were all taxi pilot licenses, each with the same image but with different names. He turned over the body and shone his lamp in the face. There was enough left for a positive ID.

"I think we just got a random thief," he said. "Which explains why he didn't put up a fight. Probably all he could do was to switch on the lightsaber and wave it around."

He searched for the hilt and found it in the carpet of shattered bottles.

"How could he get hold of it?" Rede asked.

"Were you around for Order Sixty-six?"

"I wasn't deployed then."

"It was chaos. Jedi cut down everywhere. Buildings on fire. It wouldn't take a criminal genius to grab a lightsaber from the debris, just an opportunist."

"Okay, job done," Darman said, and walked out. "Well done, anyway, Rede."

Anskow looked at the IDs and spent some time on the comm checking with someone. He even took fingerprints from the body. His embarrassed expression told Niner what information he was getting back from his control room.

"Well, he took a guy's hand off with that saber thing," he said at last. "What were we supposed to think?"

Niner shrugged. "Better safe than sorry. We won't bill you."

It was an anticlimax, but it wasn't the first foul-up Niner had been involved in, and it wouldn't be the last. There'd be some questions about how the guy might have come by the lightsaber, and someone—not them, he was sure—would be tasked to check the man's contacts just to make certain there was no real Jedi connection somewhere. Niner put it out of his head and climbed back into the LAAT/i. He'd file a report later.

Lawful warning given, suspect failed to surrender, drew lightsaber, neutralized by Trooper IC-4447 Ennen.

What a dumb way to die, all for a stolen speeder and a dangerous souvenir. *Idiot.* Did he have a family? What a rotten pointless end for his folks to have to live with.

It was just a speeder. A couple of months in jail, maybe. Not worth losing your life for. Some people just ran, even though it must have been obvious they wouldn't get away. The LAAT/i lifted off the platform and they headed back to barracks.

"You okay, Ennen?" Niner asked.

Ennen was sitting on the starboard side bench, arms folded tight across his chest, head tilted back so that his helmet rattled on the durasteel panel of the bulkhead.

"Yeah. Fine."

He wasn't. Niner knew it.

Darman took off his helmet and scratched his chin. "Ennen, if that guy had really been a Jedi, it would have been a good take. Don't beat yourself up."

"Kriffing moron," Ennen muttered. "He was asking for it. What kind of carbon-flush thinks it's a good idea to wave a lightsaber around at a time like *this*?"

"A moron who wasn't carrying a blaster?" Rede said.

Darman turned on him. "If you don't take a lightsaber seriously, *ner vod,*" he snarled, "you're going to end up dead."

"*Udesii,* Dar," Niner said. "Let's all relax. Nothing we can do about it now."

Niner kept an eye on Ennen's POV icon all the way back to base. It stayed fixed, as if he was staring at the deckhead, although that was no guide to where his eyes were directed or even if they were open. When the gunship landed, Ennen was the first man out, and he stalked off as if he had something pressing to attend to. Niner knew he'd have a tough job ahead of him to knit this squad together as tightly as he had Omega. He let Ennen go. The doors to the 'freshers slammed shut behind him. There, at least, a guy could have a few minutes of privacy.

He'd come out when he was ready. Maybe Dar could take him out for that ale later. The open invitation to the old Coruscant Security Force staff club still stood for all Skirata's squads, and it was as good a place as any.

"Let's hang around and wait for him," Darman said. "So he knows we don't go off and leave a brother when he's in a mood."

"What's *udesii*?" Rede frowned at the scratches gouged in his armor by the broken glass. "I'm trying to keep up with your slang."

Poor kid. "It's Mandalorian," Niner said. "It means take it easy. Calm down. Relax."

Rede looked to Darman. *"Ner vod,"* he said. "Buddy?"

"Brother," Darman said. "My brother. Or my sister, come to that." Rede just gave him a puzzled look. "Ennen's been a long time."

Yes, he had. Niner walked up and down the corridor a couple of times. "Nobody takes *that* long in the 'freshers. I hope he hasn't fallen in."

"I'll go see how he is." Darman walked in and called Ennen a couple of times, but the doors closed before Niner heard any reply.

He waited, watching Rede fussing over his armor. Before long, the kid would be only too happy to see damaged plastoid as battle honors.

"You'll never keep that pristine," Niner said helpfully. "In fact, the more—"

Bdapp.

The crack of a discharged blaster stopped him dead. The 'fresher doors muffled it, but the sound was too loud and too distinctive to be anything else. Niner pushed through the doors before he thought about it. Darman was hammering on one of the stalls.

"Ennen? Ennen! Open the *shabla* door, will you?"

Niner tried to smash the locked door with his boot while Darman scrambled over the top of the partition. He froze as he looked down into the stall, gripping the top of the duraplast panel.

"Fierfek."

"Is he breathing, Dar?" Niner knew the answer. Darman had seen enough casualties. If he froze, it was because there was no point in doing anything else. "Please—don't tell me he's done something stupid."

Darman dropped back, saying nothing, and rammed his shoulder against the lock. This time it gave way.

Ennen would probably have felt he hadn't done anything stupid at all. For him, it was the right thing. The man sat there, staring sightless at the ceiling, helmet on the floor, no visible marks on his face but clearly dead. His DC-15s sidearm had fallen halfway under the stall partition.

"Rede, get the med droids," Niner called. Obvious or not, someone medically qualified had to pronounce him dead. "Tell them to bring a gurney."

Darman didn't say a thing. A suicide was unusual in the commando ranks. Niner couldn't recall another one, but then he wasn't sure he would have been told about it. He didn't know how often the meat-cans decided they'd had enough, either. All he knew was that he'd failed one of his men, and that he'd never forgive himself for letting Ennen struggle on without realizing how close to the edge he was.

What tipped him? Capping a civvie? Or not capping a Jedi?

More commandos started showing up. You couldn't discharge a weapon in the barracks without drawing attention.

"Beat it," Niner snapped. "He's gone. Ennen's topped himself, poor *shabuir*. Now get back to whatever you were doing. It's not a kriffing cabaret."

Rede seemed uncertain whether he was in the get-lost category or not, and hovered until Niner beckoned him back with a jerk of his thumb. Two med droids whirred into the 'freshers with a repulsor gurney and emerged minutes later with Ennen's body covered by a sheet.

"Well, he's not miserable anymore," Niner said, not sure what was appropriate at a time like this. "It's terrible, but at least it's over for him."

"I didn't know he was that far gone." Darman sounded numb. He stared at his hands. "I was going to take him out and get him to talk about it all."

"Yeah, well, I don't think he was the talking type." Niner had to report the incident to Melusar now. What happened in these cases? He'd never dealt with a suicide before, and he couldn't even recall if there were any regs to cover it. At least they had a commanding officer who'd make sure Ennen got the funeral rite that he wanted, though. "I should have sorted him out a lot sooner. *Shab,* I should have . . ."

Darman kept taking one of his gauntlets off and sliding it back on his hand again, over and over. He wasn't really paying attention to Niner.

"That's the last time," he said, "that I ever put off doing something until *later.* There's never going to be a *later.*"

He picked up his helmet and made for the doors. Niner had thought Dar was doing okay and surfacing from the worst of his despair, but anything could tip him over the edge again now. There were only so many times you could lose those close to you before you snapped. Even if Ennen had been hard to get to know, he was still a squad brother.

"Dar, where are you going?" Niner went after him. "Hey, hang on—"

Darman slowed and turned. "It's okay, *ner vod.* I'm not going to top myself. I've got something to live for." He went to put on his helmet. "And I'm going to call him the first chance I get."

Kyrimorut, Mandalore, ten hours after Zey's arrival

Vau was back, and he was mad.

Ordo watched the conversation between him and *Kal'buir* skid downhill without brakes. Vau's expression of smug good humor evaporated two steps down the cockpit ladder of Gilamar's shuttle, and Ordo was pretty sure the words *Zey's turned up alive* had something to do with it. Gilamar and Atin carried on unloading the lab supplies as if they'd seen these fights before, which they had. The Skirata and Vau Show had been a staple diversion during the off-duty hours on Kamino.

"Are you out of your *mind*?" Vau boomed. He never shouted. He was an Irmenu aristocrat, heir to Count Gesl before his father disowned him, and the gentry did *not* yell like common folk. They could be loudly disapproving, though. The entire homestead could hear the two veteran sergeants letting rip. "What do we need Zey for? Do you understand the risks? You *lunatic*."

"You think I invited the *shabuir* to drop in for caf and cakes?" Skirata had no problem with yelling. "He's here. I don't like that any more than you do. But he *is*, so deal with it until we solve the problem."

Skirata stormed off. Ordo gave him a couple of minutes to cool from a rolling boil to a slow simmer, then went after him.

Vau didn't dislike Zey as far as Ordo knew. He'd almost seemed to enjoy the verbal sparring necessary to get one over on the general, even knowing that Zey was aware he was being conned somehow. But there was a place for Jedi, and that was not Kyrimorut.

I agree. We all do. But we don't seem to be able to avoid them.

Skirata leaned on the wall by the roba pen, throwing his three-sided knife into the thick veshok gatepost a few meters away. One of the roba, an old boar with an impressive beard of reddish hair dangling from his multiple chins, stopped rooting in the mud with the others and stood on his hind legs with his front trotters on the wall to see what was going on.

"It's okay, *ner vod*," Skirata said to the animal. He sent the blade thudding into the same spot on the post everytime and took three paces to retrieve it. "It's not time for the butcher yet. Just venting steam."

"Vau will see sense." Ordo had an unnerving feeling that the roba was following the conversation. "Look at it logically. Zey has as much to lose as we have by revealing our location."

Skirata retrieved his blade again and flicked the sharp point with his thumb. "More. And I'd see to that personally."

"Jaing's right. There's always an advantage to be gained from these situations."

"Only out of necessity. I never wanted to see another Jedi as long as I lived. But I can't seem to get away from them." Skirata inhaled, held his breath, and let the knife fly again. Ordo often wondered what went through his mind when he did that. "And if you think Vau's mad now—watch what happens when I tell him we're thinking of doing a deal with Altis."

Skirata patted his arm and went back into the house, leaving Ordo leaning over the roba pen wall. The dilemma was painful. The general principle of putting an end to Jedi influence in the galaxy—or Jedi dominance, depending on how serious a threat Mandalorians considered them to be—was always based on anonymous Jedi, or at least Jedi who were disliked. But faced with poor little Scout, the venerable Kina Ha, and a fairly pleasant man they knew well, *putting an end* to anything became brutally hard.

That didn't mean Ordo wouldn't do it, of course. He just wasn't sure how badly he might feel about it afterward. But he'd been trained to kill dispassionately because threats had to be removed, and he could see no real difference between a threat you didn't know and a threat with a familiar face.

And what was known—the location of Kyrimorut—

couldn't be erased any other way, unless Jusik had more
Force tricks up his sleeve.

Ordo realized he was now standing almost nose-to-
nose with the roba boar. The animal looked up into his
face and grunted. In that moment of eye contact, he felt
a connection to the animal much the same as looking a
human being in the eye, and wondered how he'd feel
when he eventually came to eat it.

Is that it? Is it just not knowing that makes killing okay?

Ordo shook himself out of the mental debate and
went to see how unloading was progressing. Cov and
his brothers had volunteered to convert an outbuilding
into what he called a "bug farm" for Uthan, and the
four clones were puzzling over a plan sketched on a
sheet of flimsi.

Only a few months ago, Uthan would have cheerfully
unleashed a pathogen specifically designed to kill
them—and Ordo, and all his brothers. Now she was
treating them like favorite nephews. Yes, knowing did
seem to make all the difference to some folk.

Uthan certainly seemed pleased with the haul of equipment and lab supplies, managing a smile whenever she
pried open a crate. She might have been pleased to see
Gilamar back, of course, and Ordo took heart from that;
everyone knew there was a burgeoning romance there,
and nobody minded. Somehow, the sheer impersonality
of her mission to wipe out clones took the sting out of it.
The matter of mass slaughter was closed. She had her
comeuppance before she even got around to her crime.

Vau could come to terms with Jedi made safe by mu-
tually assured destruction, then. Some fights to the death
could be stopped and turned around. *Kal'buir* certainly
seemed to have overcome his ingrained hatred by placing Scout and Kina Ha in a slot marked *Not Really Jedi*.

Ordo wondered if it was ever possible to explain to an
outsider—*aruetii* in the most literal sense—how deep an
enmity could run. More than four thousand years of
wars, betrayals, and massacres; how could the two sides
ever trust each other? It was as deeply embedded in both

factions as the religious schism of Sarrassia, except there was a third side in the hostilities, and that was Sith. Sometimes they were lumped in with the Jedi as a variation on the Force-user theme. Sometimes they were enemies, uncomfortable allies, or even employers of the *Mando'ade*. Ordo doubted that many of the Grand Army's clone troopers could have seen it this way, but there was something timeless and inevitable about a Sith Lord using an army effectively made up of Mandalorians to attack the Jedi yet again. Only the date had changed.

"Oh, *thank you!*" Uthan bent over an open crate to examine the contents, then straightened up looking as if she'd been given a birthday present. "Mij, you *remembered.*"

Ordo expected to see something exotic and wonderful in the crate. Instead, there were just packs of woodpulp sheets, the kind of absorbent material used in medcenters.

"That's because I wrote it down," he said, smiling. "And if you look in the cool-pack . . . I always say the way to a woman's heart is with a lovely box of noxious pathogens. Nebellia and rhinacyria virus samples. Knock yourself out, Doc."

Uthan positively glowed. "I'll find a home for them right away," she said, making the viruses sound like a bouquet in need of a vase. "As soon as I've modified them, we can make a start on the cell cultures."

Gilamar turned to Ordo. "Where did Vau go? Is he still arguing with Kal?"

"I'm hanging around in case they come to blows," Ordo said.

"Well, it's a bit of a shock—fancy old Maze pulling a stunt like that. Can't wait to hear how he got Zey off the planet."

"I'm sure it'll be riveting," Ordo said. "Although I'm not sure why he felt the need to dupe *me* into thinking he'd shot Zey. If I'd wanted the man dead, I'd have done it myself."

Ordo didn't have to look hard for Vau and *Kal'buir*. He just followed the angry voices drifting on the air. Skirata seemed to have decided to lance the boil early and tell Vau the whole plan. Everyone else had found something pressing to occupy them, except Jusik, who looked ready to part the two of them if it came to blows.

"I'm going to do the deal," Skirata said. "It's not like Altis is the kind of Jedi who's interested in political power and building big temples. Is he, *Bard'ika*?"

Ordo ambled around the *karyai* as casually as he could. Jusik caught his eye and gave him an almost-imperceptible shake of the head. Vau still looked livid, jaw muscles twitching. Mird, always a reliable indicator of its master's mood, was lying flat on the floor in absolute silence, gaze darting from Vau to Skirata and back again.

"They say half of his followers aren't even Force-sensitives," Jusik said. "And apparently thousands of Padawans trained at his academy—based on board a ship. If he was really into power, we'd know all about it by now."

"No wonder he got away," Skirata said. "Keep moving. Smart *shabuir*."

"Are you taking any of this in?" Vau snapped. "Have you completely forgotten the last three years? The whole point of the war? Not Palpatine's war. *Jango's* war." Vau turned and stabbed a finger in Ordo's direction. "Why do you think *he* was created? To fill some emotional void in your sorry life? *No.* Jango did it to put an end to the Jedi because *we can't trust them.* We've *never* been able to trust them. He banked everything on letting Dooku use his DNA to build the only army that had a chance of taking these *hut'uune* down. And now you're talking about *making concessions to them.* You make me sick."

"In case you hadn't noticed," Skirata said, suddenly unnaturally calm, "the winning side doesn't like us much, either. We're still under the heel of Force-users. Just one with a red lightsaber."

"So why put us at risk? Why not just shoot Zey and have done with it? Kina Ha—that I can understand.

She's a lab specimen. Scout—part of the package. But Zey? Let him go, and he'll search out his pals and try to rebuild the old Order. You don't need to do a deal with Altis to take them off your hands. You need a Verpine rifle and some guts."

"Okay, *mir'sheb*, *you* go and finish them off. An old woman and a child. *Ori'jagyc*. Big man."

"You think I wouldn't?"

"If you don't—then what are we going to do with them?"

"We get *this far*." Vau spread his arms. "We get *this far*. We finally get rid of the Jedi and its groveling lackeys. And what do you do? You *help them survive and regroup*. You, of all people. One minute you hate their guts and see them as the enemy, the next you go soft on them. Oldest trick in the book—put children and old folks and pitiful wrecks in the line of fire to shield a cowardly army. You know how we despise an enemy that tries to exploit that."

"It's . . . not about that, Walon."

Vau made a sweeping gesture of disgust. "If Fett were alive today, he'd spit on you, you know that? What did all those clones die for, Kal? So we could give the Jedi a second chance? *Sheb'urcyin . . . aruetii.*"

Butt-kisser. Traitor.

Ordo waited for Skirata to swing a punch. He didn't. He just took it in silence. Vau turned and stalked off, snapping his fingers at Mird to follow him. Jusik shuffled his boots and looked embarrassed.

"I think everyone revises history under stress," Jusik said. "He's forgotten that nobody knew Jango had set this up until the Purge happened. None of us had any idea what the clone army was really for, beyond something the Jedi Council didn't ask enough questions about."

"He's right, though, isn't he?" Skirata still stood staring down at the floor. "I go out of my way to do the decent thing for Jedi. But I won't help my own *Mand'alor.*"

"You make it sound as if you had a plan that took account of all this, *Buir*," Ordo said. "Your only plan was to save as many of us as you could. You never set out to smash the Jedi Order, *Fett* did. It's a separate issue."

"Sure it is," Skirata said. "I better see what Zey's up to, just in case he's rebuilding the *shab'la* Jedi Temple here and Maze is helping him." He got halfway to the doors and turned. "It's not them being Force-sensitive that gets to me. It's the *organization*. The way they trample us all in the process of keeping power."

Jusik waited until Skirata was out of earshot and shrugged. "I hate it when they're both right. Come on. Better stand by to stop him throttling Zey."

Vau had been far closer to Jango Fett than Skirata ever had. He understood—perhaps too late, but eventually—the depth of Fett's loathing of the Jedi. They'd cost Fett everything he held dear; the Death Watch had robbed him of more—a family and a surrogate father—but Fett still bided his time for years and saved his supreme act of revenge for the Jedi. That told Ordo everything.

And you won, Jango. Shame you didn't live to see it.

"*Bard'ika*, you know Zey at . . . *a different level* from me," Ordo said. "What's he likely to do if we let him go?"

Jusik took a long time to reply. "Zey's a pragmatist," he said at last. "He thinks in terms of living beings with faces and names, not spiritual concepts. That's why Maze gets on with him."

"That doesn't answer my question. I know he wouldn't rush to turn us in to Imperial Intelligence, but would he try to rebuild the Jedi Order along the old lines?"

"I don't think he would, even if he could."

"This might upset you, but I'm prepared to execute him."

"Yes, it upsets me because I know him too well to turn my back on him, and yes, I understand completely."

Ordo expected that from Jusik—honest, compassionate, but ultimately pragmatic, as pragmatic as Ordo himself, as pragmatic as the Jedi Order spending the lives of the clone army for an imagined greater good.

We're all the same. Except Jusik and I say it out loud. We all decide that one life is worth less than another.

"If it really needs doing," Jusik said, "I'll be the one to do it. Okay?"

That was typical *Bard'ika*. Always taking responsibility, almost to the point of martyrdom.

"The last thing we want Kyrimorut to become is the Jedi remnant's worst-kept secret," Ordo said. "That's a security measure. But you see Vau's point. Ever cleared groundthorn weed? If you leave so much as a centimeter of root, it sprouts again. I think the lives of our clone brothers should buy more than a temporary reprieve."

They wandered out into the lobby, one of the circular hubs of the complex from which passages sprouted like spokes of an eccentric wheel. The house was a chain of redoubts connected by surface corridors and underground tunnels, but the quaint charm was coincidental to its purpose. This was a bastion built to withstand a siege. Ordo never forgot that.

"I can't shut off my Force senses any more than you can think stupid," Jusik said. "And I get these . . . premonitions. Jedi call them certainties in the Force. I don't accept fixed futures, but I've got the feeling that the Jedi will rebuild one day, just like the Sith have. The best we can do is to stay away from both factions for as long as we possibly can—and definitely never fight their wars for them again."

That was the most sensible idea Ordo had heard all day. They found Zey and Skirata watching the construction work for Uthan's virus kitchen, no visible trace of any animosity between them, just two tired men of a certain age wishing things had turned out differently.

Zey didn't turn his head. He seemed focused on Cov and Jind, who were sawing lengths of wood and cutting interlocking joints into them. These were men he'd commanded.

"Where did you learn carpentry?" he asked.

"From a manual." Jind almost said *sir* but stopped himself. "Same way that Levet is learning to farm."

"So what are you building?"

Cov glanced at Skirata for his cue. "Storage," he said at last.

Skirata took over the conversation. "Dr. Uthan is reversing the clones' accelerated aging. She needs more lab space."

There was no point telling Zey that Kyrimorut was about to handle live pathogens. But once he settled down and started talking to Kina Ha and Scout, even if that was when they were all long gone from Mandalore, he'd hear it all; the FG36 virus, every detail that would be of interest to the Empire, and not in a healthy way.

"So the Imperial garrison confines itself to the Keldabe area?" Zey asked.

"Far as I know," said Skirata.

"Doesn't that worry you?"

"Not half as much as you do."

"Kal, I swear that—"

Zey stopped dead. He looked over his shoulder, then turned and stared toward the door behind him. Ordo wondered what had stopped him in his tracks until he saw Kad trot out and stand on the doorstep.

There was no hiding him now. There was certainly no way of hiding him from a Jedi Master.

"Oh my," Zey said. "I can *feel* who that is. I had no idea . . . oh, poor child . . ."

Jusik spared Skirata the burden of answering. Maybe he could sense things in Zey now that nobody else could.

"Yes," Jusik said. "That's Etain's son. Darman's son. Now do you understand the stakes a little better?"

Zey's eyes filled with tears and he squatted down to toddler height. Kad edged up to him, wary and grim-faced, then looked to Skirata for reassurance.

"Yes," Zey said. "I do."

Uthan's laboratory, Kyrimorut

"So how are you going to test this?" Scout asked. She looked very different in a laboratory coverall, gloved and booted like a technician with a cap over her hair. "How do you know if it works or not?"

Uthan opened the conservator door and took out the sealed virus samples. Gilamar's resourcefulness amazed her. She wondered where he got his medical and lab supplies, and how the vendor reacted to a Mandalorian in full armor showing up and presenting him with a shopping list like that. But a man who could steal an operating table from a medcenter wasn't easily daunted.

"Well, I'd need to infect a test subject with the modified rhinacyria virus and then expose them later to FG thirty-six." Uthan placed the samples in the biohaz safety cabinet and sealed it. "But we'd need a human. So I'm planning to test it on myself. If I live, it works. It's too important to trust computer modeling or isolated cells."

"But then how would you know that both the FG thirty-six virus *and* the other thing are actually working?"

"That's a good question."

"And that means you're going to have a deadly virus sitting in a bottle here . . ."

"Not quite a bottle, but you got the deadly bit spot-on."

"Kal and Mij must trust you a lot."

Uthan lined up the containers of enzymes and chemicals ready to modify the rhynacyria's DNA, and thought that over. Yes, they obviously did. She hadn't actually thought of it in those terms, because . . . well, that was how she did the job. She handled dangerous pathogens. It was the first time that she'd stopped to think how much faith these people had placed in her not to kill them or wipe out their entire world. Given how she'd first met the clones, she felt uncomfortably guilty for a moment.

My world's gone. They might think I've got nothing to lose. That I'm still determined to wipe out the clone army.

The more she thought about it, the harder it got.

Scout was a smart girl, learning fast, and remarkably dexterous. She followed her instructions to the letter—preparing the electrophoresis gel, sterilizing vials and containers, and lining up the various enzymes, reagents, and nutrient solutions in exactly the right place. She didn't fumble or drop things like so many technicians Uthan had trained at the university. Uthan hadn't noticed until now how precise and sure Jedi were in their movements, that extraordinary visuospatial ability. But Scout's expression told her that she was less interested in the techniques of gene splicing and switching than in Uthan herself.

"Would you use it?" Scout glanced sideways at her. "Knowing what it does, what it *really* means—would you use the FG virus yourself?"

If you'd asked me a few days ago . . . a few weeks ago . . .

"I never thought of myself as a monster," Uthan said. "I'm not. Am I? I'm no different from most beings, I think. But there's part of me that wonders if I have a blind spot about this. And then I think—does the weapon matter? Does the number of dead matter? If I shoot one enemy with a blaster, or you cut down an enemy with your lightsaber, nobody would think we were *monsters*. How many more do we have to kill, and how, and why, before we cross that line into becoming . . . monsters?"

Scout chewed her lip thoughtfully. "That's one for a Jedi Master."

"We don't need Jedi Masters to define morality for us."

"I suppose I'm saying I don't know."

"Have you ever killed anyone?"

"No."

"But you're armed. You'd use your lightsaber if threatened."

Scout seemed to be scanning Uthan's face for proof of lack of monsterhood, and Uthan found herself regretting that she'd not seen Scout grow up even though the girl was a stranger. It was the oddest feeling, like having a daughter who'd only reappeared in your life after too long an absence.

Like Kal and Ruu. That must hurt him sometimes. And her. All that lost time that can never be recovered.

"I'd probably think I didn't have any other choice,"

Scout said at last. "But it wouldn't be much different from what you did—thinking you had to kill in self-defense. It's just a *feeling* that it's different. Not a *reason*."

Uthan smiled at her. "I enjoy our conversations. After nearly three years of having no company except soka flies and third-rate doctors who thought I was a lunatic, you have no idea how good it feels to have a challenging conversation."

"So the soka flies thought you were crazy, too?"

Uthan had moments when the sheer weight of Gibad's destruction left her unable to think straight. She wasn't sure whether to hate herself for the other moments, the ones when she got on with life and even took pleasure in it.

She let herself laugh anyway. "I gave them names. Flies. What do *they* know?"

From the window, she could see the herd of roba rooting on the edge of the woods while Mird watched them at a cautious distance. Rural life went on around her, an existence that hadn't changed much in perhaps five thousand years.

"If it ain't broke, don't fix it," she said to herself.

"Pardon?"

"Nothing."

"Doctor, do you think it's right to infect everyone on the planet with this?" Scout asked. "It's just a bug that spreads like any disease. Nobody can avoid it. They don't get a choice once it's set loose."

"Let's put it this way," Uthan said. "It's a lot more ethical than watching Palpatine use FG thirty-six on the population and knowing I could have saved them."

Mama knows best. Isn't that always the way? But once everyone knows there's a countermeasure for the virus, Palpatine will simply use something else.

It kept Mandalore a few steps ahead of the worst the Empire could do to it. If she couldn't bring down Palpatine, the next best thing was to look after a planet that could be a severe pain in his Imperial backside.

"It's a bit like baking cakes." Scout looked up from the curved transparisteel cover of the small biohazard cabinet where the DNA samples would be replicated and broken up into their component genes. "Wow. Can you hear that?"

Uthan stopped shaking the transparisteel flask in her hand. The homestead's acoustics and the quiet of this remote place meant that sound carried, but all she could hear was the faint up-and-down buzzing of voices. It didn't sound like an argument. She'd heard plenty of those in the last few days. A female voice. Not Besany or Jilka . . . not Ny . . . Arla, maybe. Definitely not Laseema or Kina Ha.

"Let's go and see once this batch is set to run," she said. "Whatever it is, the antigen comes first. What's wrong?"

"It's Arla. She's getting worse."

Arla was living with horrific memories. Maybe the medication shut them out, or maybe it simply trapped her with them but left her unable to scream or flee. Trauma did different things to different minds. Skirata had been galvanized to survive, Ordo had learned to shut it away most of the time, and Arla simply couldn't handle it. There were no rules in psychology that Uthan could follow, not like the more predictable and orderly world of microbiology. It bordered on shamanism.

Gilamar seemed to be getting more frustrated each day, almost blaming himself for not being able to fix the problem. He was a man with pain in his past, too. Had *anyone* in this place escaped some kind of tragedy or suffering? Uthan didn't think so. It was a colony of the damaged and dispossessed.

And me. Pain has found me, too. None of us is normal. But then, normal people never do anything of note, nothing magnificent or world changing or on the knife-edge of risk. I belong here.

"Okay, let's leave this batch and come back later," she said. She placed the flasks in the cabinet and set the heat cycle to run. "Three hours. Check your chrono. Now let's go and be sociable."

After years in solitary confinement, Uthan found it hard to get used to a house full of the activity of thirty-odd Mandalorians, Jedi, clones, and assorted beings who'd thrown their lot in with them. Even back on Gibad, she'd never lived alongside more than three or four people. She wondered how Skirata kept track of them all. But then this was a small family by his standards. Somehow, he'd looked after and trained not only the Nulls but an entire company of more than a hundred commandos as well. So had Gilamar, and Vau. She found that astonishing.

Gilamar was standing in the corridor near Arla's room with Jusik and Jaing, all three of them muttering as if things weren't going well. Gilamar held a hypospray in one hand, filling its reservoir from a plastoid vial.

"Anything I can do?" Uthan asked.

Gilamar held up the hypo. "Just debating whether to use this or not. Stop-a-bantha juice. I'm really not happy topping her up with sebenodone, but she's doing herself damage now."

Uthan could hear the sound of thudding coming from inside the room. The doors were slightly open. It sounded as if someone was hammering plaster with a soft mallet.

"Is that her?"

"Yeah." Gilamar took a breath and lowered his chin like a nerf ram about to charge, steeling himself for the fray. "I like a shoot-out. Or a good old-fashioned fist-fight. But overpowering ladies just doesn't sit right with me."

"Why don't I do it?" Uthan said. She was very conscious of Scout standing to one side, eyes closed. Jusik was doing the same. This Force business unnerved her. "She's much calmer around women. I don't look threatening. And I do know how to use a hypo without rupturing soft tissues."

"No," Jusik held out his hand, eyes still closed. "You're going to think I'm a callous *shabuir,* but I say leave her for a while. Withdrawal's pretty unpleasant, I know, but there's something surfacing in her. It feels . . . rational. Sharp-edged. Real. Scout, can you sense that?"

Uthan fought an embarrassed urge to laugh. Scout, eyes screwed tightly shut, tilted her head back to concentrate. She was a skinny little thing, and Jusik was a small man alongside Jaing and Gilamar; they looked like two starving waifs sniffing the aromas of someone else's dinner. But this was serious. The scientist in Uthan rebelled at the idea of diagnosis by communing with the invisible. She wanted lab results, numbers, reagents that changed color.

"Yes," Scout said at last. "It's like another presence, almost, but it's her. It's more solid. It feels to me like . . . oh . . . this is going to sound dumb, I know, but I'm feeling . . . a big block of dark granite tearing through thick drapes."

"Mine's all sharp edges, black-and-white contrast," Jusik said. Uthan wondered if Jedi were all synesthetic. "Like something's forcing itself back into her conscious mind, her old self, and it's not what she wants to see." He opened his eyes. "Suppressed trauma, obviously. I hate doing this to her, but I feel it's better if we find out what it is."

"I think we know that, don't we?" Uthan said. "The Death Watch slaughtered her family and kidnapped her."

"We need to be more specific than that to help her."

Gilamar looked riveted. He was still clutching the hypospray in the filling position. "Has anyone ever done a brain scan on you?" he asked. "I'd give anything to see your brain activity while you're sensing this stuff."

"Agreed?" Jusik said, lips set in a grim line. "We let all this stuff come out?"

"Might as well." Gilamar put the cover back on the hypo. "Because it's that or just keep her drugged to her eyeballs until the day she dies. If you're going to try psychotherapy, this is the only way."

"She's not scared," Scout said, eyes still shut.

"What?"

"Usually, she's scared. I could feel it. Not so much now. She's . . . full of hate and guilt."

"Well, that fits her memory resurfacing." Gilamar shrugged. "Hate for the Death Watch, guilt that she survived and her folks didn't."

"No, that's not it. It's about her. She hates being herself."

Uthan watched, fascinated and horrified. Psychologists were all the same, even amateur ones like Jedi. It was all so *nebulous*. "Well, I'm still going in to talk to her. Isn't Laseema around?"

"She's taken Kad to visit Rav," Jusik said. "With Besany and Ordo. Until *Kal'buir* relaxes a bit about having the kid in the same space as Zey."

"Okay." Uthan took off her lab tunic. She didn't want to look like a medical orderly. "How hard can this be? At least I know what survivor's guilt feels like."

Uthan opened the doors wider and stepped into Arla's room. It was big and airy enough not to feel like a cell at the Valorum, with a pretty view of open countryside, so at least the poor woman wouldn't feel she'd swapped one prison for another. Arla had pushed her bed into one corner, and was kneeling on it facing the wall. She was banging her fist on the wall, pounding her hand against the plaster. Uthan edged around until she was at the head of the bed and could see better.

"Arla? It's me, Qail." She risked getting a little closer. She was a meter away, just out of range of a punch if Arla snapped. For a moment, she took a panicky glance at what might be in reach that Arla could use as a bludgeon. But she was sure that a male wouldn't have been able to get this close. "Arla, my dear, you must feel wretched. Would you like me to get you some caf, or sit with you?"

Uthan thought Arla was using the heel of her fist. But

she wasn't. Uthan could see now that she was using the knuckles, the bones covered by paper-thin skin, and there was a wet patch of blood on the honey-colored wall. Two thin trails of blood ran down and vanished behind the bed.

"Arla," she said. "Can you stop that for a minute so we can talk?"

Uthan put her hand out—slowly, nervously—and just got a fingertip to Arla's shoulder when the woman wrenched away and scrambled to the other end of the bed.

"Don't touch me!"

"Okay, I'm sorry. But your hand's a mess. That's got to be painful. I'm a doctor." *Well, not a physician, but it's worth a try.* "Let me take a look."

"Don't!" Arla stared at her hand for a second and then dug her nails hard into the inside of her opposite forearm. She drew blood. Uthan could only stare in horror. "I'm *filth*. I'm *filth*. Stay away from me."

"Nobody thinks you're filth, Arla."

"You don't know."

"I know that's got to hurt, and that you need a doctor to see to those wounds."

"You don't know what I am. *You don't know what I've done.*" Arla started rocking, arms tight around her knees, head buried. The blood was now everywhere. "I'll be okay in a minute. Leave me alone. You don't want to be near me. Get away."

Uthan had never been so scared in her life. She could handle privation, danger, any extreme that came her way, but watching someone else so devoured by despair and self-loathing was terrifying. She had no control over the situation. And she didn't know how to begin to make Arla Fett feel better.

I know everything about the fabric of life. How cells work. What makes us what we are. What drives the living machine. But I have no idea how to reach out to another being in purgatory.

But she was going to try.

"Nobody's judging you, Arla," Uthan said kindly. How could she? She had no idea what had driven Arla to kill, only that she'd lost her family in the most horrific circumstances. Uthan knew plenty of killers who never so much as lost their appetite for their next snack. And here was this unlucky woman, institutionalized for years, harming herself in the agony of guilt. Uthan decided to say whatever might soothe her. "I'm sure you had reason to kill . . . to defend yourself . . ."

"Not *that*," Arla spat. "Not *them*. They were *nothing*. I mean *bad* stuff. *Disgusting* stuff."

Arla rocked herself a little longer and then her breathing slowed, and she seemed to be calming down, or at least she'd exhausted herself. She shuffled into a cross-legged position, braced her elbows on her knees, and rested her head in her hands.

It seemed as good a time as any to slip out. Uthan backed away to the door, and Gilamar peered in.

"Oh, *shab*."

Jusik craned his neck. Uthan ushered them back a little way along the corridor and closed the doors. Jaing was engrossed in something on his datapad.

"Well, I'm getting a better picture of why the Valorum docs kept her so heavily sedated," Gilamar said. "She doesn't even need anything sharp to self-harm."

"Mij, I don't know what she was talking about, but she blames herself for something."

"You said you wanted me to hack into the criminal justice database," Jaing said, brandishing his 'pad. "Well, here you go. Arla Vhett, spelled right, three counts of murder, and at least six more thought to be down to her but the court ruled there was insufficient evidence. Convicted, but transferred to a secure mental unit after serving a year or two in a normal prison. That's our girl."

"So is any of that of use to us?" Jusik said.

"Ah, but it's who she whacked that makes it interesting. Assuming that the six they couldn't convict on are hers, then they don't look random, but they don't look logical, either. At least not serial-killer logical, if you know what I mean."

Gilamar took the datapad from him and read, brow puckered in concentration. "All male, all business owners—one tapcaf, one haulage firm, one catering supplies, and . . . hey, that name rings a bell. *Vargaliu*. He was a bounty hunter, way back."

The three men looked at one another. Uthan had the feeling that they would have felt better if Arla had been the kind who only killed males with red hair, a consistent lunatic. Scout tugged at her sleeve.

"I just get the feeling of the most awful guilt," she said. "The poor woman's tearing herself apart with *guilt*."

"And not over her victims, judging by what she said," Jusik muttered.

"So what can we do for her?" Uthan asked.

Jusik looked guilty himself. "We could hire a proper psychiatrist, except that we don't want any more visitors than we already have. It's getting like Galactic City spaceport here. I say we let her surface some more, and see what we're dealing with."

"And then?"

Jusik shrugged. "I have no idea."

"Me neither," said Gilamar. "But if it's insoluble, we've always got the meds."

Jaing didn't say anything. Jusik had insisted on rescuing Arla, but nobody had imagined the form that her psychosis would take. It was naïve and well meaning, a spur-of-the-moment reaction that any compassionate being would have had about someone in torment. But now it looked as if Arla could never lead a normal life or return to Concord Dawn.

"It was my idea," Jusik said, "and so she's my responsibility. One way or another—I'll get her out of this."

Compassion was a burden. Uthan realized she'd avoided it for most of her life, and Jusik had made a vocation of it.

She wondered which of them was the happier.

14

A betrothal token should be portable, capable of easy
conversion into credits in case of emergency, and, if
worn, should not impede the wearer in combat. Ear-
rings are out. So are long chains. Gems in rings should
be in a rub-over setting and shallow enough to be worn
under gauntlets. You really don't want to see what happens if you catch a ring in a moving cable or machine
part.
—Purchasing advice for Mandalorian suitors from
Tsabin Dril, jeweler and artillery specialist

Coth Fuuras space station, Expansion Region

Darman knew better than to trust anyone as much as
he'd trusted Skirata, but Roly Melusar was an all-right
kind of officer. He asked how they wanted to play things
now that Ennen was gone.

Yes, he said that. His very words. *How do you want
to play it, men? Can you handle a replacement for
Ennen yet, or would you rather operate as a three-man
squad for a while?* Nobody had ever done something
that *simple*, that thoughtful for them before—except
Kal'buir, of course.

Darman didn't want to replace Ennen yet. It was hard
enough bonding with Rede. If the squad had been ordered to, he'd have done it, of course, but at the moment
it felt less painful to stick to the tight circle he knew,

brothers who had lost a buddy in a particularly awful way.

Niner said it would be easier to operate as a smaller squad while they had a wild card like Rede to train. Dar didn't think there was very much wild about Rede at all. He just absorbed everything at a frightening rate, and he knew more about them than they knew about him.

Rede was just over a year old and he'd spent nearly all that time in a gestation tank. What was there to know about him?

"You know what makes this business with Ennen worse?" Niner said, chin resting on folded arms as he watched the station's security monitors. "Not just that he killed himself. It's that we didn't get on with him. He didn't like us, and I'm not sure we liked him. And I never thought I'd say this, but—well, it feels even worse in some ways than losing a brother you loved."

Darman tried to look as if he was more interested in the assorted views of the space station's main thoroughfares. He sat watching the bank of screens, running his thumbnail down his chin. It probably didn't fool Niner.

"Guilt," Darman said. "Guilt eats you alive."

Niner couldn't say it in front of Rede, but they both knew what Darman blamed himself for *not* doing. "I don't think *that* would have stopped him, Dar."

Oh, yes, it would. If he'd known there was somewhere he could escape to and start his life over again—he wouldn't have stuck a blaster in his mouth and pulled the trigger. It wasn't just Bry dying that tipped him. It was not having anything else to make surviving worthwhile.

"What would have stopped him?" Rede asked.

Niner filled the gap without a blink. "Us trying to understand his Corellian thing."

"I liked him," Rede said. "He was pretty good to me. Is it that much of a problem, you guys all having different cultures?"

"We weren't *all different*," Darman said. "Most of us had Mandalorian sergeants, and that's what we grew up as. Only a quarter of commandos had *aruetyc* sergeants."

"Yeah, I know what that means."

It wasn't Rede's fault that he wasn't Fi, or Corr, or Atin. Darman made a conscious effort to remember that. He tried to imagine what it was like to reach adulthood without any real contact with other beings, having everything you knew piped into your brain while you floated in some nutrient soup. That was Darman's definition of a nightmare. He couldn't believe that Rede could behave so normally under the circumstances.

"Tell us if you feel we're shutting you out," Niner said. "We don't mean to."

"You were Omega Squad, weren't you?"

"Yeah." Niner sat up a little. Something had caught his eye. "The Boys in Boring Black. That's what Delta called us."

"How do you feel about your buddies deserting and leaving you behind?"

Niner put his hand on Darman's arm in less time than it took Darman to inhale in preparation to give Rede an earful. Darman took the hint.

"We miss them," Darman said. *But I'm going to talk to them soon, and to my son.* He willed Rede not to say something insulting about them just in case he lost it with him. "You always miss your brothers. All of them."

"Dar, I think that's our boy." Niner tapped his finger on the monitor screen, then jumped up and went into the adjoining control room. A crew of droids and three Sullustan security officers were keeping an eye on the public areas of the station. "See this guy? Follow him. Keep a cam on him at all times and we'll take the feed in our HUDs. Now lock down the departure gates and seal off sections A-nine through A-fifteen. Emergency escape routes, too. I want that part of the station watertight."

"Airtight," said one of the guards. He ran a practiced eye over the crowds milling around on his screens. "With that number of bodies moving about—safest thing is to run a routine fire evacuation. Bring down the internal bulkheads. It's triggered a dozen times a week by vessel emissions anyway. Way too sensitive. Thinks everything is a fire or a fuel leak."

"Whatever it takes."

"Who *is* this guy, anyway?"

"Borik Yelgo. A Jedi Knight."

"Stang—are we going to have any station left when you lot are done fighting?"

"We promise not to breach the hull," Niner said. "But it's going to mean getting the civvies out of the way first without alerting him."

Those weren't their orders—not the ones from Palpatine's command, anyway. Once you let Jedi know they could hide behind civilians, that you wouldn't risk collateral damage, they'd exploit it. Darman knew that Palps was right for once. But Niner had always been uneasy about that kind of thing.

All the civvies had to do was turn in Jedi and stand clear of them when ordered to do so.

And when this job's done, I'm going to find a quiet corner before we head back to base, and call Kyrimorut.

Somehow, being light-years from Imperial City made that call feel safer. Darman veered between nerves and excitement as he planned what he was going to say and who he'd talk to. It pushed the capture of the Jedi into an insignificant second place.

"Okay, if we cut through the service passages, we'll end up the other side of alpha-fifteen," Niner said. "Then we can move back through the sections as they shut the bulkhead behind us."

Darman shoved Rede ahead of him as they followed Niner down the service area corridor, a dimly lit canyon of polished durasteel walls strung with cables, ducting, and pipes. Indicator lights and the glow of control panels provided the only illumination. As Darman jogged along, he could see the alarm system repeater panels flashing: the sensitive atmosphere monitors had detected particulates and ion emissions above a certain level—thanks to intervention by the station security team—and the automated system had shut down all traffic movements. It was routine, like setting off a domestic fire alarm by toasting breadmeal sticks a bit too long.

"Aren't the civvies going to rush into another sector and take Yelgo along with them?" Rede asked.

"All we need do is corner him so he doesn't end up in the service ducts," Niner said. "Don't worry. Keep an eye on him in your HUD feed. You can run and watch that at the same time, can't you?"

"I'm working on it," Rede said.

It took them minutes to run through the service area of the station and emerge into section A-15. The schematics said it was a *passage,* but Darman found himself in a wide, brightly lit plaza flanked by stores, tax-exempt boutiques, and eateries. Coth Fuuras was a popular stopover for passenger vessels as well as freighters. He could tell which beings were regular visitors and which weren't by the level of anxiety as the public-address system told them to evacuate the section in an orderly manner. The pilots and stevedores in scruffy coveralls ambled along, munching snacks and slurping caf, and the tourists—regardless of species—all seemed to be trotting, not wanting to look panicked.

A fire on a space station was as bad as things got. He couldn't blame them for being worried. Nobody seemed to take any notice of three black-armored commandos. Maybe the civvies just saw them as more folks in uniform, part of the fire-control team. It was hard to tell.

"Okay, find him," Niner said. "Fan out."

Darman kept one eye on the HUD feed from the security cam, trying to work out where he was in relation to the shop fronts that Yelgo was passing. The Jedi—maybe twenty, human, with a distinctive break in his nose and a scattering of freckles—was walking at a brisk pace like everyone else, not looking over his shoulder. He didn't need to, after all. He could sense his surroundings.

"Isn't his sense of danger going to kick in?" Rede said, keeping up with Darman.

"Sometimes they can't pick out one source of danger from another—like on a battlefield."

"But there's no real danger here."

"Yeah, but the civvies don't know that, and I bet they're generating enough fear or whatever it is he picks up on to put him off his game."

Darman could see individuals pausing to try emergency doors and finding them locked. He was coming up to a crossroads in the station, where one passage crossed another like a street. The curved shape of the space station—a ring rotating around a central gravity core, like a giant fiber reel—created a weird horizon. It made Darman feel as if he were constantly running down a hill, and he could see farther than he would have been able to on the flat. In his HUD image, he saw Yelgo pause at one of the departure areas but turn away when he found it shuttered.

He was a hundred meters from him, maybe less. Niner picked it up before Darman could.

"Tapcaf," he said. "Turn right at the intersection, follow the overhead sign for Departures Green Six, and look for the Cheery Traveler franchise. That's where he is."

The crowd was walking briskly toward the A-5 bulkhead, which would seal behind them while the fire was contained—or so they thought. It wasn't going to open. Shops were pulling down their shutters, staff filing out with irritated expressions that said they did this way too often and would have to work late to make up for lost time. Darman slowed to a fast walk so that he didn't catch Yelgo's eye.

The evacuating crowd were all facing the same way now. They knew where they were going. Darman, lost in the sea of bodies, realized he had lost Yelgo. But he had to be close.

"Come on," Niner said. "Where's he gone?"

"He knows." Rede appeared on Darman's far left, moving ahead and looking back into the approaching stream of civilians. "He knows we're here."

"Come on . . . c'mon, c'mon . . ." Yelgo couldn't get off the station, but he could cause a lot of strife while they hunted him. If only he'd turn around. If only . . .

It was worth a try. Darman decided to give him a tap

on the shoulder via the Force. If the Jedi's senses were on alert, then he should have been able to feel hostility this close—targeted hostility. Darman visualized Yelgo's face from the mug shots he'd memorized and the security cam images he'd seen, and concentrated on *hate*.

It wasn't hard.

He thought of Etain, and what she'd been robbed of— a future, a normal life—and imagined Yelgo being responsible for that. He thought of Geonosis, where the rest of his first squad and half the commandos deployed had been killed in the first few hours of fighting, because Jedi had never had to fight an infantry war before, and squandered lives through sheer ignorance and panic.

I don't have to be reasonable. Or realistic. I just have to radiate hatred. Make it personal. Ugly, savage, and personal.

It wouldn't get any more personal than what was about to happen to Borik Yelgo.

You shabuir . . .

Darman didn't even know him. It didn't matter.

Die, Jedi. Whoever you are.

And a head turned. Just for a moment, someone ahead in the crowd looked back over his shoulder, and a moment was all Darman needed. The nose, the freckles; him, it was *him*—and if Darman hadn't been wearing a helmet, they would have made eye contact for a split second.

"Got him!" Darman charged through the crowd. It was better to knock folks aside and give them a fright and maybe a bruise than let them get in the way of blasters. "Rede, you got him?"

"I see him."

"Got him," Niner said. Suddenly his voice boomed from his helmet's loudspeaker. "Armed Imperial forces! Get down! Everybody *down*!"

Predictably, almost everyone froze and dropped. Most folks here had just lived through a shooting war. They knew what *down* meant. It gave the commandos a second or two as Yelgo bolted and everyone else dithered, not knowing where to go next. In those few moments, the crowd—like a flock of birds, like a shoal of shanji-fins—reacted as one animal, saw the moving threat, and then moved away as if they'd taken an instant vote on the best place not to be when the shooting started.

Darman, Niner, and Rede ran into the gap. Most of the civvies were behind them: Yelgo was in front. And the only exit he could reach was now being cut off by the safety bulkhead, dropping from the deckhead like a guillotine. In the holovids, the hero always managed to skid under the thing in the nick of time and escape, but that was just fiction, and this was reality. The Jedi didn't make it. He came up a couple of meters short and turned to face the commandos, eyes scanning for a way out.

Jedi were pretty good. But they weren't *that* good.

"Ever seen an akk herding nerfs?" Niner said. "Well, it's just like this."

The squad had separated Yelgo from the flock, akk-style. His chances of getting off the station were slim. For most beings it would have been zero, but this was a Jedi, and Darman took nothing for granted.

Niner aimed his Deece at Yelgo. "I don't suppose you're going to surrender."

"Would you?" Yelgo asked, reaching for his lightsaber.

He was a Knight, low enough on the league table to be a dead-or-alive job. Imperial Intel wanted Jedi they could *turn*, their word for an agent they could threaten, torture, brainwash, or—just sometimes—persuade by rational argument to come over to their side.

"Probably not," Darman said. "So, the easy way or the hard way, Jedi?"

It was too much to hope that Yelgo would fall on his lightsaber or accept a quick end with a round from a Deece. Yelgo looked at Rede for a moment as if he'd identified him as the squad's weak link. "You could walk away from this, you know."

"Not this time," Darman said, and opened fire.

Yelgo batted away the stream of bolts with his lightsaber and spun to deflect Niner's shot. Then he took a run at the side wall. As soon as his boot hit it, he flipped himself over in a back somersault, dodging Rede as he moved in for a point-blank shot, and landed ten meters away as only a Force-user could. Rede spun around, firing. And that was probably what Yelgo wanted: to make them empty their magazines. The commandos had twenty seconds continuous fire and then they had to reload, so if Yelgo timed it right, he could grab the seconds he needed to leap over them, Force-rip a door open, and vanish into the bowels of the station.

But Rede paused and just held his aim.

Darman thought it was a stoppage, that the Deece had frozen on him. But Rede didn't look troubled. He was definitely just aiming. Darman and Niner took up the slack, too stunned to yell at him for a moment.

He's too green. He's going to get killed. Idiot. Stupid kid.

"Rede!" Niner barked. *"Move!"*

Rede darted behind Yelgo. And just as Niner ran out of ammo, Rede opened fire. The kid wasn't so dumb after all. Yelgo was still forced to fend off two streams of fire. If he'd been an ordinary being, someone would have got a shot past him sooner or later and brought him down. But he was a Jedi. He could spin and bat away bolts with the accuracy of a slingball practice droid. This firefight was like finishing off a dying keller-buck, knowing that its horns could still rip you open if you got too close.

Maybe we should have brought a fourth man after all.

The *dapp-dapp-dapp* of rapid fire from three Deeces sent the civvies screaming for cover. The sealed-off corridor was all white-hot staccato light, noise, and the flashing green beam of the lightsaber leaving afterimages in a blurred wake behind it. Ricochets from the lightsaber spat everywhere, searing the walls and scorching black patches on the synthmarble floor.

He could leap over us, try to rip out a side door. No problem. But then he'll be deep in a crowd of civvies.

Is he going to bank on us not shooting?

The crowd at Darman's back, trapped by the other

emergency bulkhead at the far end of the shopping arcade, could only watch—and scream. *Shab,* they didn't stop. Darman hoped they stayed put and didn't run, because the only place they could go was back into the squad's arc of fire. Yelgo was edging away a step at a time toward the transparisteel wall of a snack bar. This had to be a trick. He was going to pull something out of the bag.

Darman reloaded, snapping a clip out and in again in seconds. He tried to anticipate what Yelgo would try next. He saw the Jedi's left arm go out to the side as if he was holding something back, then Rede reloaded, and Niner ran across to the far wall firing as he went.

Grenade round? Risky. Too confined.

Rede got his clip back in. Darman had one eye on the transparisteel wall, one huge transparent sheet decorated on the inside with a glittering green foil logo from floor to ceiling. Rede moved closer, taking out his sidearm and firing the Deece one-handed. Nobody could say those Spaarti instant-jobs didn't have guts.

Darman saw Yelgo close his eyes—still fending off shots with the lightsaber. The transparisteel wall started to shiver, then vibrate. Darman could guess what was coming next. He'd seen Jusik bring down whole buildings with the Force.

Oh, shab—transparisteel.

Seven meters by four meters, two and a half kilos per square meter per millimeter thickness—that's—

Nearly two tons of razor-sharp shards were about to hit Darman at explosive velocity, Force-smashed, Force-channeled into a tidal wave that would miss the crowd but slice through the squad.

And Yelgo. Yeah, he's dead, too, but he doesn't care now.

"Dar, Rede!" Niner yelled. *"Down!"*

Rede suddenly swung his aim a meter above Yelgo's head and emptied his clip into the bulging transparisteel. Maybe it was the enormous stresses the sheet was now straining under; maybe Rede was a genius at calculating weak points. Either way, the wall shattered and fell, raining glittering fragments like an avalanche of diamonds instead of blowing outward toward them. Yelgo lost concentration at the premature collapse of the wall. Rede was on him in a heartbeat. He rammed into him, inside the sweep of the lightsaber. His fist punched down and in. The moment seemed to drag on forever, but it was a blink, a second, and Yelgo was on his knees, staring at the dark blood welling from his tunic as Rede staggered back a pace and then fired twice into the Jedi's head.

And it was all over: done and dusted.

The silence was one communal gasp. Then it broke, and there was more screaming. No, firefights never ended like that in the holovids. Civvies were always shocked to discover that.

"Rede," Darman said. "Rede, *ner vod*, I'll never say a bad word about you instant troopers ever again. That was *ori'kandosii*."

The emergency bulkheads lifted, and station security guards appeared to usher the civilians away. Rede scuffed his boot on the ground, trying to get rid of broken transparisteel that had embedded itself in the tread.

"I take it that means I did good," he said.

"*Shabla* brilliant, kid." Darman felt suddenly old, as old as *Kal'buir* and just as responsible for a young commando. "You can stay."

The security chief, a tubby Sullustan, crunched across the carpet of fragments and surveyed the damage. "Could have been worse, I suppose. Nobody else hurt."

"Charge it to the Emperor's account," Darman said. He went over to Yelgo's body and picked the lightsaber out of the debris. Yeah, some things were worse than being dead. He couldn't imagine what Palps did to Jedi he caught and that scared him, because Darman had seen enough in the war to imagine more than was good for his peace of mind.

Right call, Yelgo.

Darman handed the lightsaber to Rede. "Don't cut yourself," he said. "If you were a *Mando'ad*, you'd wear that on your belt to show how *ori'beskaryc* you were."

"I can work that one out, too," Rede said, admiring the weapon. Darman thought it would be a nice touch if Melusar let the kid keep it and wear it. *Inspirational for everyone. He's doing okay for a one-year-old.* "Niner? I'm just sloping off for a while. Back in fifteen."

Niner knew what he planned to do. And out here, nobody was watching the chrono or wondering where the squad was.

"In your own time," Niner said, and walked off with Rede. "We'll be in the security office drinking their caf."

Darman strolled along watching the stores and booths reopening now that the emergency was over, looking for a quiet spot. Eventually he found a janitorial closet and bypassed the lock. In the sealed environment of his suit, it didn't actually matter where he made comm calls, but he felt self-conscious and needed to hide.

What do I say to him?

Kad was a baby. He just needed to hear his dad's voice. Was it the middle of the night at Kyrimorut? Too bad. If Darman woke everyone, they'd understand. He spent a few moments calming himself with deep breathing before finally selecting the Nulls' secure channel on his HUD with a couple of blinks.

Jaing—or that droid buddy of his—knows what he's doing. This comm can't be traced.

There was no flashing icon to indicate the status of the comlink, another hallmark of Jaing's caution. Anyone casually picking up the helmet wouldn't see anything different from the standard issue.

Darman waited.

Eventually, he heard a pop of static and a voice he recognized.

"Dar, that had better be you."

"Ordo? Did I wake you up?"

"Not exactly. Where are you?"

"Coth Fuuras station. Just caught a Jedi."

Ordo didn't answer for a moment. "Which one?"

"Borik Yelgo. Hey, can I talk to Kad? To Fi? Any of the *vode*?"

"How long have you got?"

"Fifteen minutes or so."

"Wait one."

Ordo sounded as if he moved away from a mike, all scuffing noises and the occasional distant thump. Darman found himself drumming his fingers on his thigh plate. Eventually, someone came back and picked up the comlink with a loud scraping noise.

"Dar? How are you, *vod'ika*? It's me—it's Fi."

Fi sounded different. The last time Darman had seen him, he was starting to come out of a deep coma. It didn't matter. This was his brother. *Shab*, he'd missed him. He felt his eyes sting with tears.

"Fi, it's good to hear you."

"It's going to be all right, Dar. When you come home, you'll see." Fi gulped in a breath. "I'm sorry about Etain. I don't know what else to say. I'm so sorry."

Another voice interrupted. "Dar! Stop slacking, you lazy *shabuir*, and come home. The roba need mucking out." It was Corr. "How are you doing?"

"I miss you guys. Come on, where's Atin?"

"He's getting Kad up to talk to you."

"What's he like? Is he growing fast? Is he—"

"Dar, this is Atin. Here's your son. He wants to say a few words." Darman heard Atin whispering. "*Kad'ika*, that's Dada. He's talking to you from a *long* way away. Say hi to *Buir*."

Darman shut his eyes to concentrate, trying to imagine what his son looked like now. When he heard his voice, it almost stopped him breathing.

"Boo. I want Boo." Kad was still getting to grips with *Buir*. "Where's Boo?"

"I'm here, son," Darman whispered. He wasn't sure how much a toddler could understand. He realized how little he knew about nonclone kids. "Dada loves you. I'll come home as soon as I can."

There was a long silence. Atin sounded as if he was encouraging Kad to go on, but getting nowhere.

"I think he's gone all shy," Atin said. "But he knows

it's you. He's grinning from ear to ear. When are you coming back, Dar? Don't wait too long."

"Things to do first."

"Uthan's working on the aging thing," Fi said. "You'll never believe it, but we've got a thousand-year-old aiwha-bait Jedi here, and the doc's working out how they engineered her. And guess who showed up the other day? Zey. That's right. Maze *didn't* cap him after all."

Darman felt his scalp prickle with an awful fear. He heard the word *Zey* and didn't care who was alive, or what Uthan was doing, because his brain stalled at the word *Jedi*.

Jedi. Jedi at Kyrimorut. No. No, no, no.

"This is a joke, right?" Darman said. *Jedi, living under the same roof as my kid?* "Tell me it's a joke."

Fi seemed to realize he'd said too much. "No, Dar, it's true. But it's okay. *Kal'buir*'s keeping an eye on everything. It's all going to be all right."

Darman couldn't concentrate on the conversation. All he could think was that Kyrimorut was full of Jedi, and it was the place where Kad was supposed to be safe from them. He could feel his pulse hammering in his throat. How could Skirata let them in? What was he thinking?

"Dar? Dar, are you still there?"

"I'm here," he said, numb and shocked. He wanted to tell them to get Jusik, but he couldn't stand to sit here a moment longer, helpless and scared, a galaxy away from his son. "I've got to go. Tell Jusik to keep Kad safe. Make him swear it. Tell him that if the Jedi take my boy, I'll come after him. *Tell him.*"

"Dar, it's okay, it's not like that—"

"*Tell him.*"

"Dar?"

"I'll call back later."

He shut the comm channel without waiting for a reply, and sat shaking, hands braced on his knees.

Jedi, in *his* haven, with *his* son. *Jedi.* He wasn't going to take that. He had to calm down, think things over, and come up with a new plan.

There was no point fighting the war against Force-users at Melusar's side if the Jedi Order had a foothold in his own home.

Kyrimorut, Mandalore

"Is he responding, *Ord'ika*?" Skirata asked. "Is that thing working?"

Ny thought Ordo was starting to look ragged from lack of sleep, but his patience with his father never failed. He handed over the comlink.

"It's working," he said. "I've just raised Niner. Dar's taken it badly. *Kal'buir*, there was never going to be a good way to tell him about the Jedi. Don't blame Fi."

"I'm not blaming Fi. I'm blaming *me*."

Skirata paced around the *karyai*, one hand in his pocket, the other to his mouth, head down and staring at the floor. Ny had never seen Skirata wilt under pressure. The more problems he had, the stronger he seemed. She wondered how he'd cope when things finally settled down and everyone lived a routine life here. He was going to miss his wars.

But that's never going to happen. Is it? It's always going to be this way.

"Ny, you don't have to stay up," he said. "Get some rest. It's nearly two in the morning."

"I can't sleep now. How do you think I feel? I was supposed to bring Dar home."

"*I* should have told him. *Again*. I never leveled with him about Etain being pregnant with Kad. I let him hold that kid without telling him he was the father. I can't keep doing that to him, or he's never going to trust me to tell him so much as the time of day."

"The Jedi weren't a secret," Ordo said wearily. "We just never got the chance to mention them. It's not like we chat to Dar and Niner all day. Look how long it took us to establish comm contact with them. And it's still risky."

Ny could hear the faint burble of hushed conversations elsewhere in the house. Besany wandered into the room, bathrobe pulled tight around her. Even in a scruffy robe, hair uncombed, and no makeup, she looked effortlessly glamorous.

"Is this a making lots of caf kind of crisis, or worse?" she asked.

Ordo moved up to make room for her on the padded bench. "Dar's gone off in a huff. He found out the Jedi were here."

"That's no surprise. He's hunting them while they're here watching his son grow up. That has to hurt, especially with Etain gone."

It was brutal and true. Besany was a clearheaded woman who got to the point. But even in this outspoken, unapologetic society, nobody had ever said the obvious. Nobody had railed at Ny for wanting to bring two Jedi here. And nobody had criticized Skirata for agreeing to it. Ny felt this was one more problem she'd landed them with.

I've put them all in danger. Even if Kina Ha is the key to solving the aging problem, is it worth this?

Skirata stopped dead and straightened up. He had that rabid look in his eyes that said he had a plan. "Okay, ideas. We can't go on collecting trouble."

"The immediate problem is reassuring Dar," Ordo said. "Niner seems okay about it. Shocked, maybe, but not like Dar—but then he's not got a half-Jedi child to worry about. The bigger problem isn't going to go away as easily."

"You think reassuring Dar is easy?"

"Anything that keeps Kad away from Jedi or any other Force-user will placate him."

"If he'd got his *shebs* back here like he was told to, he wouldn't *need* to be worrying now." Skirata shook his head, eyes screwed up in self-disgust for a second. "Okay, I shouldn't have said that. I'm sorry."

Ordo gave Ny his back-me-up look and steered the

conversation back again. "The Jedi are a time bomb. You know it."

"I should have quit when I was ahead with Uthan, and not got greedy for Kina Ha, too." Skirata put his hand on Ny's shoulder. It felt comradely rather than romantic. A'den's matchmaking efforts might have been corralling both of them into something that wasn't meant to be. "So I get my just desserts for taking advantage of your good nature, freight-jockey."

Ny tried to be objective. If these had been her sons, would she have done anything different? "I can't claim you weren't honest about it. Can I?"

"Well, it's bitten me in the *shebs*. It's going to cause strife in this clan, and it's my job to resolve it. The fact that I'm standing here debating about it instead of doing the obvious tells me that Vau's right. I don't have the *gett'se* to stick to a hard line on Jedi. It was all talk. When it comes down to it, I'm too much of a moral coward to shoot them."

"Actually," Ny said, "I think that's moral courage."

Skirata just looked at her as if she'd made a terrible gaffe that everyone else could see and she couldn't. He shook his head.

"You don't get it," he said.

Ordo cut off any explanation. "Once Uthan has whatever she needs from Kina Ha, then the choices are to find somewhere to off-load the Jedi, or to terminate them." He used the same word the Kaminoans had used for exterminating him and his brothers. Normally, he spoke like the soldier he was and said *neutralized* or *slotted*. Ny wondered if he was consciously treating Kaminoans as they'd treated him, or if he'd been so inured to the lives being snuffed out for being inconvenient or falling short of imagined standards that he used it as casually as his creators. "And if they remain alive, we need to be sure that they won't lead the Empire to us—willingly or otherwise."

Skirata ran his hand down his face, clearly struggling with his options. Ny suspected he wouldn't have been so torn if she hadn't been around. He'd have been hearing the same message from everyone. *Just get rid of them. You don't owe them a thing. They'll be our downfall.* Instead, he looked into her eyes and saw the dread, that she'd hate him for taking the brutal but certain option.

She wasn't even sure she'd hate him, though, and that scared her.

"Just asking them to keep their traps shut isn't enough," he said. "And you can't make folks forget things to order."

"Yes, you can," Besany said. "Jusik can."

"What, that mind-rub thing?"

"He told me how he wiped some Twi'lek's memory of being questioned by him and Scorch, when you were trying to grab Ko Sai before Delta got to her."

Skirata snorted, amused. "So he did. And that one sordid episode sums me up. I even deceived Vau's boys—all in a noble cause, of course. Just like Jedi. Ends justify means."

Ordo's jaw clenched. "Drop the guilt now and concentrate on solutions, *Buir*. We were all willing participants in that mission. We're not kids. We make decisions for ourselves."

He might have been trying to snap his father out of wallowing in guilt, or he might have meant it. Ny could only see complete devotion in Ordo when it came to Skirata. But he could be pretty cutting when he put his mind to it.

"Sorry, son."

"Let's ask Jusik whether he can erase memories in other Jedi. And how."

Besany nodded and put her arm through Ordo's. "I'm up for that. If I have a vote."

"Your life's on the line with ours, *Bes'ika*. Vote away."

"I say we aim to help our Jedi guests to forget Kyrimorut, and then get Altis to take them," Ordo said. "Because if we can't, I'm going to take the decision out of your hands and do it myself. I love you, *Buir*, and I'd willingly give my life for you, but I won't risk it for a Jedi.

Not even a kind one. It makes a mockery of everything we've been through." Ordo stood up to leave. "Now *Bes'ika* and I are going to get some sleep, and in the morning you'll talk to Dar and Niner and smooth them over. Okay? You're their father. They'll listen to you."

Skirata stood staring at the floor for a while after Ordo had gone, lost in thought. Ny didn't want to leave him to stew alone.

"He's doing it to spare me getting my hands dirty," he said at last.

"I think he's doing it because he really wants the Jedi out of his life, Kal."

"Am I being a bigot? About Jedi, I mean."

"Well, you *are* a bigot, but you gave Jusik a chance. And you haven't shot Kina Ha or Scout yet."

"You left out Zey."

"*And* Zey. You feel sorry for him."

Skirata didn't take the bait. He put his boots up on a chair and shut his eyes. "Maybe."

Ny boiled a pot of water and started making caf. Skirata played the knife-wielding thug to perfection, and it wasn't an act. His job was to kill people for payment. But there was still that intelligent, compassionate core that drew her to him. He was an extreme man living in an extreme world. She wasn't sure he'd had a chance to ever be anything else.

He saves lives. He also takes them without a second thought. I have to live with that.

"Do you seriously think that the garrison isn't going to hear about you anyway, Shortie?" she asked. "You went into the cantina. They had our images on the wall—on the bounty hunters' job sheet."

Skirata opened his eyes and reached for a cup of caf. "There's *hearing,* and then there's *finding.*"

Ny watched him for a while, wondering how a little boy from a regular working-class Kuati family grew up into a gangster. He didn't seem to mind being watched. She found they could sit together in silence and not feel uneasy about it.

A few pots of silent coffee later, Jusik wandered into the kitchen, followed by a worried-looking Zey. Skirata gave them both an appraising stare. Ny didn't pick up any signs of animosity. If anything, he seemed baffled by the Jedi.

"I heard about Dar," Jusik said. "Fi's mortified."

"It's not Fi's fault." Skirata gestured to the caf pot. "But we've got to clear this up." He raised his eyebrows at Zey. "You heard, too, I take it."

"Kal, I wish I knew why Darman thinks I'm a danger to his child."

"Well, apart from being on the Empire's most wanted list—not that we aren't *all* on it—he thinks you'll take Kad and turn him into a saber-jockey, and Etain didn't want that. And neither does Dar."

Zey looked at Jusik in a where-did-I-go-wrong way. Ny wondered how he coped with seeing his former underling go native without so much as a backward glance at his Jedi days.

"You really see us as baby-stealers?" Zey asked.

"You wouldn't like the answer," Skirata said.

"How about you and your clone sons? Didn't you take them before they were old enough to vote on it?"

"That's *different*. I did what was best for those lads when everyone else treated them as *disposable*."

Ny winced. Skirata had spectacular double-standards, and the extraordinary thing was that they convinced her. But when she stood back, all she could see was how many qualities—and terrible flaws—Mandalorians had in common with Jedi. One day, she'd have a sensible conversation with him about it. Now wasn't the best time. Even Zey, who didn't strike her as the retiring type, didn't pursue the case.

"I'm going to find you, Kina Ha, and Scout a safe haven," Skirata said. "It's a long way from here, and you're going to have to forget you ever saw this place."

Poor Zey. Here he was, a man who'd held serious power and responsibility, reduced to a refugee and being bounced around like an unwanted stray.

"You know I'd never do anything to compromise your family's safety, Kal," he said. "I know what I have to atone for, both as a Jedi and a man. And I'd never seek to recruit Kad. I swear it."

Skirata gave him a five-second stare, the sort that usually shook anyone down. "I believe you," he said. "But could you still keep your mouth shut after Palpatine's thugs had been working on you for a week or two?"

Zey didn't answer.

"Very few could," Skirata said. "And I can't bet the safety of this place on the chance that you're the exception. If *Bard'ika* can erase your memories of being here, I'm going to ask a Jedi sect to take you in. Altis."

Ny watched Zey's shoulders stiffen. "Altis?"

"Don't go all doctrinal on me, Zey," Skirata said. "You Jedi Order guys are all but extinct, so this isn't the time to tell me you wouldn't be seen dead in his temple."

"I wasn't. I just had no idea he'd survived, let alone that you knew him."

"I don't. But I will." Skirata turned to Jusik. "You know how to find him, *Bard'ika*. And you, Zey—all I'm asking is that you saber-jockeys *learn,* and stay out of politics. Because if you don't, and I'm still alive to hold a knife, I'll personally find you and cut your throat."

Skirata got up with slow care, wincing at stiff joints, and went outside. Ny heard the 'fresher doors close. Zey turned to her as if she was the umpire and he wanted her to tell him how the game was going.

"And he'd *let us go,* for all that?" Zey said. "He knows where Altis is, and he hasn't turned him in?"

Ny could only shrug. "And would that save us?"

There were no deals to strike with this Empire.

She was fiercely proud of Skirata at that moment. It wasn't about being kind to Jedi who'd almost become friends. She liked to think Skirata was ignoring his instincts and trying to do things differently, to break the cycle of revenge, even though history told him he was a fool to try.

He probably knew that. And Ny realized that nothing

would change, and that if she lived long enough, she'd see the same old wheel turn. But Skirata was the first to put the blaster aside. It didn't matter if he failed. He'd done it.

You're a good man, Shortie. I wasn't wrong about you.

Jango Fett wouldn't have agreed, but he was dead, and Skirata had a duty to the living.

Meserian, Outer Rim

Jusik didn't need to check any hard data when he landed the Aggressor starfighter. He was definitely in the right place. He didn't even have to concentrate or check his instruments.

The place hummed with the Force presence of a *lot* of Jedi.

It's like walking into the Temple again.

He'd forgotten that feeling. Being away from the company of Jedi for so long, the sensation hit his senses afresh, and he was briefly disorientated by the sheer wealth of information in it. He shut his eyes and let it wash over him. If the *feel* of the Temple had been serene, restrained, a plain *gray* kind of sensation, then this gathering felt like . . . a patchwork, a vivid quilt, no two parts of it matching but somehow harmonious.

Djinn Altis's community—or a large proportion of them—was very close. The sensation was oddly comforting.

Does this speak to me? Do I miss what I used to be?

Jusik was constantly alert now for signs of backsliding. It worried him. Despite the fear any Jedi must have felt at that moment, the Altis sect seemed *happy*. Not serene, not purged of passions; happy, *actively* happy, in the way of people with fully lived and sometimes turbulent lives.

"*Bard'ika,* have you nodded off?" Fi demanded.

Jusik opened his eyes. "Just feeling the Force. Who's who, where's where."

"And?"

"They're here."

"Well, you did comm them first."

"That poor woman. 'Look, lady, no comm number stays secret from *me* forever . . .' I hate myself for enjoying this sort of thing."

"You going to tell them their information was compromised?"

"I ought to, but I won't. *Kal'buir* can put the frighteners on them. He's good at that."

Fi put his helmet on, the red and gray one that had once belonged to Ghez Hokan. "Okay, let's do it."

"Fi, do *you* think this is a good idea?"

"Well, I like it better than killing old ladies. Even aiwha-bait old ladies. And little girls. Killing kids is plain wrong, even if she *is* older than me. Oh, unless they open fire on me first. Then they're fair game."

Jusik counted on his fingers. Yes, Scout had probably been born a year or two before Fi was hatched. He needed to remember that. It kept him focused on what Kyrimorut was all about. This off-loading of Jedi, this ducking and diving—that was a diversion, a sideshow. The main agenda was to give his brothers back their rightful *time*. He would grow old with them, not watch them fade fast and far too young.

He secured the Aggressor and stood surveying the area. It looked as rough as a bantha's backside. The low-rise buildings were huddled together like conspirators, stucco walls peeling, and wherever there was a wall or a gulley it was full of windblown garbage. He could smell raw sewage. Some of the walls had blaster damage, their skim coat of garishly painted plaster gouged out in places to reveal the ferrocrete blocks beneath. Most of the stores seemed to be cantinas. Speeders in various stages of decay or dismantlement dotted the streets.

"Not a place to take a lady," Fi said. "Unless she's *especially* rough."

"Nothing that a little urban regeneration grant wouldn't fix."

"Or a turbolaser. From orbit."

"Okay, I know where we are now. Follow me."

"I still think it's ever so clever."

"What?"

"Your homing instinct. It's like watching Mird track borrats."

"Yeah, well this borrat's going to be armed and he can use the Force a lot better than I can, so let's not alarm him."

"You think the *beskar'gam* is a good idea? Too intimidating? Too dressy?"

"Safer than the alternative, *ner vod*."

Jusik walked casually, surrendering to an instinct that made him want to turn his head in a specific direction as if trying to hear a faint sound. He tried to stay fully aware of every Force sense that he used, *un*-learning every lesson they'd tried to teach him at the Jedi Academy about feeling rather than thinking.

You have to challenge what you feel. You can't just feel things and act on them. If we'd thought a bit more and felt a bit less, the galaxy would never have ended up like this.

Fi started laughing. It jerked Jusik out of his inner debate, and for a foolish moment he thought Fi had picked up what he was thinking. It turned out that he was laughing at some kids who looking over the Aggressor at a cautious distance. Aggressors were popular bounty hunters' ships, and seeing two Mandalorians swagger out of this one had probably guaranteed Fi and Jusik an uneventful visit. Jusik still wore his lightsaber on his belt. Nobody needed to know that it was his and that he hadn't killed a Jedi to get it.

"Would you ever go back to being a Jedi?" Fi asked. "I mean, if Altis is what they say he is, and it's all anything goes and *egalitarian,* would you think about it?"

"No, I wouldn't. I'm Mandalorian now. Why does everyone keep asking?"

"They're not. And I'm just checking."

"Why?"

"Well, having your old boss around . . ."

"They say that you can run into an old flame who once broke your heart and not understand what you ever saw in her," Jusik said. "I think it's like that with me and the Order. Except I fell out of love with it over a couple of years—at least."

"So you met us on the rebound."

The sooner Zey and the others left, the better. It raised unnecessary specters for Jusik. "Okay, I'm an all-or-nothing type. Fodder for any cult. But you lot had the cool armor."

They did a little backtracking and diversion just in case they were under surveillance, even though Jusik *felt* they weren't. Eventually they ended up on the banks of a canal that seemed to contain more rusting speeder parts, rubble, and dumped garbage than water. It could have called itself a very wet road. A rainbow film of oil gave it an incongruously iridescent beauty.

A sudden feeling of Jedi—anxious, wary Jedi—hit Jusik like a punch in the chest. The old boatyard on the other side of the canal was Altis's choice for a neutral meeting place. That should have reassured him.

"Okay, I'll go first," Jusik said.

"You told him what we'd be wearing, right? Because the helmet tends to upset those of a nervous disposition. Not to mention the Verpine piece."

"He'll know who we are. He can sense me by now."

They picked their way across locked gates so overgrown with weeds that it would have taken a direct hit to open them. Jusik walked into the boat shed and looked around. It still seemed to be in use. There were two long, shallow wooden-hulled boats up on blocks with half their varnish removed.

"Master Altis, you can come out now."

Jusik waited, hands well away from his sides, trying to look as harmless as he could. Fi was trying, too, but Fi was a big guy even now, and he still moved like a soldier despite his disability.

"Left," Fi said. "Armed and unhappy-looking."

Jusik didn't take off his helmet. He and Fi had a good infrared image in the gloom of the shed, and there was no point being rash. The male human who walked slowly toward them was a Force-user all right, but there was something different in the impression he left in Jusik's mind. For a moment Jusik thought they'd been set up by a dark sider, but it wasn't that at all. And this man wasn't a Jedi. He was something else. He stood four meters in front of them, a square-built man in an ancient ankle-length coat with deep vents and leather shoulder panels that made him look like he'd stepped out of a costume drama. But the rifle he held on Jusik was absolutely real.

"Master Altis will see you now," he said stiffly. "Follow me."

Jusik didn't recognize the strong accent at all. He was starting to feel disoriented by not knowing things that he'd always taken for granted. Suddenly all the beings he'd sensed—a dozen males and females of various species—emerged from hiding places and stood watching.

He didn't need to be told which one was Djinn Altis. He felt him before the eccentric Master stepped forward and stared for a moment.

"Bardan Jusik," Altis said, breaking into a bemused grin. "I've heard *so* much about you. Except for how the blazes you managed to track us down. Let me shake your hand, boy."

"Master Altis." Jusik's fingers were trapped in a handshake like a vise. This man was a legend, albeit one they didn't talk about much in the Temple. "A pleasure to meet you."

"So you're the man of conscience who ran away to join the Mandos and scared all the little Padawans, eh? If you think I can help you, I'll do my best, but you've probably noticed we're in a sticky spot ourselves at the moment."

Jusik took off his helmet and nodded to Fi to do the same. He could be forgiven for a little theater. It would make the point so much better than an impassioned speech.

"This is my brother," he said. "Fi Skirata."

If anyone needed a poster boy for the clone army, Fi was the first choice. He was still charming, funny, and disarming. It was much easier to tug heartstrings with Fi for a prop than with Maze or Sull, who didn't look like they needed saving from anything and exuded resentment at the very thought of rescue.

"I bet everyone tells you that you've got a familiar face, young man," Altis said. "Now, I know they don't retire clone troopers, so let me guess—you're on the run as well."

"It was just a parking fine," Fi said. "But you know how these things escalate."

"Ah, you want to hide with us? You're very welcome. We're a mixed bunch. Jedi, other Force adepts, all sorts of Sector Rangers, a couple of Ffib Nonconformists, and plenty of non-Force-sensitives. We even have a renegade spy. No obligation beyond pulling your weight in the community."

"Actually," Jusik said, "we'd like you to take three Jedi off our hands."

"Ah . . . *that's* what you're running."

"No, we're running an escape and rehab network for *clones,* Master. But we have Jedi who would be safer elsewhere, and we also need them to forget they know where we're based. For everyone's safety. We've *really* upset the Emperor. I mean at Intel level. It's better that you don't know the detail."

Altis tilted his head. "Of course we'll take them. Are you going to try *memory-wiping* them, though? That's . . . risky."

"I know."

"Have you done it before?"

"Yes." Jusik knew what was bothering Altis. Mind-rubs were regarded as a dark side practice. But then allowing marriage and families was anathema to orthodox Jedi thinking, too, and Altis didn't seem to have any problem with that. It hadn't sent his sect rushing to the dark side. "I erased a courier's memory of meeting me and a squad of clone commandos. For safety reasons. *Ours*."

Altis just looked at him for a while. "Let me know how you get on."

"Put it this way, Master—the alternative is to leave no witnesses. Do you understand me? And my father doesn't want to take that route."

"Father?"

"It's a long story."

A brown-haired woman a little older than Jusik—rather pretty, he thought—sidled up to Altis as if to interrupt. She looked and felt eager, half smiling.

"These three Jedi," she said. "Is one a human female called Etain? I met her at Nerrif Station. She had a son. We talked about her joining us with her child and her partner. Did she mention me? I'm Callista Masana."

Jusik was taken aback. He hadn't known Etain had approached the Altis sect at all. "Did she say why she . . ."

He couldn't go on. Every Force-sensitive in that boat shed could feel his distress. Callista caught his arm.

"What is it?"

"Etain was killed," Jusik said. Realizing that she could have left and found a safer place—that if she'd gone with Altis, she'd probably be alive now—was almost too much to take. "She's dead."

Callista gulped in air the way people did when they were caught out by shocked tears. She composed herself quickly. "What about her son?"

"He's fine. We have him. His father . . . he's fine, too. Look, if I can deliver these Jedi to you without anything in their memories to connect them to our base, will you take them?"

"Absolutely," said Altis. "May I know their names?"

"Master Arligan Zey, a Padawan called Tallisibeth Enwandung-Esterhazy, and a Kaminoan Jedi Knight—Kina Ha. She's rather *senior*."

"A Kaminoan? Good grief, I thought that was a *myth*."

"She's about a thousand years old, we think."

Altis blinked a couple of times, then laughed to himself. "At last, someone I can grumble with about young whippersnappers and dreadful modern music. Are you *sure*? No, of course you are. How *extraordinary*."

Jusik felt a flood of relief. He'd almost expected Altis to be too wary of a trap to cooperate, but he'd forgotten that he was dealing with Jedi, and one thing he could be sure of was that they felt his true intentions. He looked around at the group. Yes, it was a very mixed bag indeed, six different species, male and female, young and old. And he felt that some weren't Force-sensitive.

The man with the ancient coat still perplexed him. So did a striking woman with flawless black skin that looked almost polished. She dissected Jusik with a glance—not unkind, simply thorough, as if she was used to making fast judgments—and went to speak to Fi.

"Do you know anyone in the Five-oh-first?" she asked.

"Yes ma'am."

"Really?"

"Yes."

"I knew some very fine troopers from the legion. I'm glad there's another life for them if they want it."

"We never close, ma'am. Open all hours."

"Remember that Imperial Intel is full of dark siders and would-be Sith," she said. "So watch your back, soldier. It was looking a bit too mystic even when I worked for them. I'm Hallena, by the way. I used to be a spook, but I'm all better now."

"I leave the intel stuff to my crazy brothers," Fi said. "I just shoot things. And feed the nuna."

"Very wise," Hallena said. "How are we going to do this handover, then? It's not without risks."

"Neutral planet," Jusik said. "We won't burden you with our location."

"Are you going to tell us how you found us?"

"Probably not." It was Skirata's job to do the bargaining when necessary. Jusik had the feeling the problem would be stopping Altis from being too helpful and ending up on everyone's comm list. At least they had a resident spook to keep their paranoia fit and healthy. "I'll stay in touch. When they're ready to leave, I'll comm you."

Altis shook his hand again, and Fi's. "You sound like *very* interesting folks. I'd like to meet your father." He turned Jusik around by his shoulders. "Now vanish. Because we will. You can't trust anyone here."

Jusik resisted the urge to look back. Fi glanced over his shoulder just once as he walked, then faced forward again and whistled tunelessly under his breath.

"Nice lady," he said. "Well, that's one problem solved. But Mij is going to miss Scout. So will Uthan."

"Yeah, I know. I might be out of my depth with a memory wipe."

"You repair brains. How hard can it be?"

"Might be easier with subjects who can consent and cooperate."

"It's that, or it's endex for them."

"No pressure, then."

"Nah. Can I drive?"

"Okay. Once we leave orbit."

Jusik scattered the small knot of local kids with a tilt of his head and climbed into the Aggressor's cockpit. They looked at him like he was the most *ori'beskaryc* gangster this side of Hutt space. If only they knew his self-doubt at that moment.

He was going to have to wipe his old Master's memory. It wasn't the same as healing injury. He wondered how much Zey wanted to forget besides the coordinates of Kyrimorut.

"Are you going to tell *Kal'buir* that Etain had an invite to join Altis?" Fi asked.

"Yeah," Jusik said. "Somehow."

Skirata had to be told. It was the kind of thing he'd want to know, even if it hurt.

15

*It had never crossed my mind that these men felt perse-
cuted by me, that they felt I was a threat and would
take Darman's child. I was horrified. I was raised to
believe I was a soldier for the light, defender of the op-
pressed, a righter of wrongs. But Skirata and Darman
saw me as just a baby stealer, a monster who would
drag Kad into a cult. And so did Etain, it seems. And
that breaks my heart.*
—Jedi Master Arligan Zey, confiding in Kina Ha

Special Operations barracks,
501st Legion headquarters, Imperial City

"**A**s far as I'm concerned," said Melusar, leafing
through the Coth Fuuras report, "that's a *result*. Tidy
job. Especially you, Rede. Good thinking. If Intel wants
to up their departmental midi-chlorian count, they can
do it some other way. One more Jedi off the list."

And Melusar really *did* have a list. He'd had it neatly
printed out on large flimsi poster that reminded Niner of
a bolo-ball league table, with colored lines showing
which Jedi was linked to another and how. He got up
from his chair, scanned the list of names—more of
which were crossed out with a red line each week—and
ran his marker stylus through YELGO, BORIK.

"There really aren't that many left," he said. "Look.
Scattered ones and twos. Occasional groups of five or
six. The only big tranche left seems to be Djinn Altis and

an assortment of other fringe Force-user groups linked to him. Makes sense. He was never part of the mainstream Jedi Order, so his people just weren't there when Order 66 was called. Never hung out with the Yoda faction. Never got into politics. Never worked for the government. Never led clone troops. Fought the Seps, yes, but only later in the war, and then on their own terms. So more of them survived. And they're nomadic—based on some ship."

Niner quite liked the sound of Altis. He guessed that Darman didn't. As soon as Holy Roly had told that briefing that Altis let his followers marry and have families, Niner could imagine what was going on in Dar's head. It must have made him as bitter as *haran*. It wasn't Altis's fault that the other Jedi banned attachment, but he could see why Darman might blame them all for their dumb rules.

Rede just studied the list on the wall, squinting slightly. Melusar stood in his way and got his attention. "Rede, can you get me something, please? I need the details of the *beskar* extraction deal with Mandalore, and the latest geological survey you can find for the sector."

"On it, sir."

Rede trotted off. Melusar carried on talking generally about Jedi numbers, and then switched topics as soon as the office doors closed.

"It's not that I don't trust Rede," Melusar said. "But he's all raw enthusiasm, and I need to know him better before I tell him everything that I tell you. Now—I want you to go after Altis."

Niner wanted to check. "Us, or multiple squads, sir?"

"You."

"I think we might be a bit outnumbered, then."

"Not a frontal assault. Surveillance, intelligence gathering, and eventually we bring the whole lot down in one operation. It won't be an overnight job. It'll take months."

"Is he that important?"

"Yes, I think he is. We've got more than enough commandos to deal with the other odds and ends. But Altis is the kind of leader that other Jedi might regroup around, not just his own dippy freethinkers. He's a potential threat now that almost all the other Masters have gone. And he might be a charming chap, but the ones who flock to him will be the usual kind of Jedi, and before long they'll be back, running the galaxy from behind the scenes."

It was a helmets-off meeting, because Holy Roly preferred to make eye contact, but Niner—like most clones—liked to keep his helmet on because it gave him precious privacy. No officer could tell what was going on under that frozen mask. A guy could be mouthing obscenities, but as long as he kept his head still his commander would be none the wiser. It was a safety valve.

And it was Niner's bugging device, too. He hoped it was picking up some of this briefing for Ordo.

He could see Darman's jaw muscle clenching and unclenching. Melusar probably could, too. *Shab,* as long as that was *all* Dar did; he was still seething because he'd found out the hard way that there were Jedi at Kyrimorut. Instead of calming down, he was getting angrier and more agitated.

Dar was always the laid-back one. Never lost it. So calm that we used to think he was asleep.

"We'll rely on our own intelligence," Melusar said. "I'll get cover in place so that they don't start taking an interest in what we're doing. Right now, all they seem concerned about is recruiting Force-users. Fine. At least I'll know where they all are, come the glorious day."

Darman still didn't say a word. Melusar wasn't a fool. He was a soldier's soldier, and he was good at reading his troops.

"Is this a problem I can help you solve, Darman?" he asked.

Darman had to respond now. Niner willed him not to blurt out something he'd regret.

"No problem, sir."

"You're a smart man," Melusar said. "That's what

whoever bankrolled the army paid for. Really top-notch soldiers. So I don't think you ever switched that brain off. You know you've been used. You're mad about it. Maybe it's even personal, *really* personal. And that's fine. But the deal is that I level with you, and you level with me. I'm taking a big risk here. That's why I'm keeping this very small-scale. Concealable. *Deniable.*"

"Can I ask why it's personal for you, then, sir?"

Melusar blinked a few times. "You were right about Dromund Kaas, Darman. My family did come from there. It's the cesspit of the Outer Rim. It never had a government, just a cabal of Sith monks. The Prophets of the Dark Side." He sat on the edge of his desk and folded his arms. "Guys in black robes with black beards. Absolute power. Everything they predicted always came true, and if it didn't, they'd help it along— death and destruction, usually. But there were never any Republic missions or Jedi armies to liberate us, because Dromund Kaas was erased from the star charts a long time ago. So we *rotted.* And somebody in the outside world must have *known* we were rotting to take us off the chart in the first place. It's what you do when a reactor blows, isn't it? Tough luck on the poor fools working there. Lock them in, and stop the contamination getting out." Melusar leaned forward a little and lowered his voice. Niner could see the pulse flickering in his throat. He definitely wasn't playing for effect. "My father tried to get people to change the world themselves rather than wait for help that was never going to come. I was six when I watched him get killed. The Prophets predicted he'd be a long time dying. They were right. They always were."

Melusar seemed to shake himself out of the memory, and stood up with his back to Darman and Niner for a moment before smoothing the front of his tunic and sitting down behind his desk again.

"I'm sorry, sir," Niner said. "This must be really hard for you." He had to ask. Ordo would want to know, but

Niner *needed* to. "Has this got anything to do with Imperial Intelligence?"

Melusar shuffled the files on his desk. "They're all the same," he said softly. "Whatever brand of cant they mumble, they're all about power. They're not on our side. And we have to do something about that."

Niner found that he'd actually held his breath without realizing it. Darman was frozen. Melusar had *issues,* vast ones. He also had good reasons.

"Understood, sir," Darman said.

Rede reappeared with three datapads, and the talk of Force-users stopped. "Got it, sir."

Rede handed them over, and Melusar tapped a few keys. "You should have the documents and plans in your HUD systems now," he said. "Familiarize yourself with them."

Every mention of Mandalore now knotted Niner's gut. It was all getting too close to home in every sense. But that was exactly why he'd stayed. "And the objective, sir?"

Melusar looked up without raising his chin. "Good stuff, *beskar.* Never tackle a Jedi without it. Now get some lunch."

Niner had no idea what he actually meant—whether he'd just sent Rede on an errand for any old thing, and *beskar* mining was still fresh in his mind, or whether he was introducing them to yet another angle in his personal war on Force-users. Niner needed to check what Ordo or Jaing had picked up via his helmet link, so he steered Darman toward the quartermaster's store.

"Rede, go grab us a quiet table, will you?" he said. "I'm going to the stores. Won't be long."

Rede never questioned why Dar and Niner seemed joined at the hip. He was the new guy. Niner longed to have a tight squad again, where everyone knew everything about their brothers and they didn't have to think before they spoke. He wanted to bring Rede into that circle of trust, but Melusar was right: he had some way to go yet.

Niner and Dar slipped into a corridor and put on their helmets. They could both hear what was going on when they were connected to the Kyrimorut link now. Niner felt better for that.

"Ordo? Jaing?" Niner said. "Did you get that?"

There was a long breath. It sounded like Jaing. "Wow." Yes, it was. "Holy Roly makes *Kal'buir* look like the Jedi appreciation society. And that whole Sith thing. No wonder he loves his job."

"But you got it all, right? I'm going to transmit the Mandalore mining data, too, in case there's something you don't have."

"Great. Just a word, though."

"What?"

"Best to find a way of stalling the boss on Altis."

"Sorry?"

"Avoid Altis. Leave him be until we tell you it's okay."

"Why?"

"Because," Jaing sighed, "we need him for the time being. We've done a deal with him. It'd be very awkward if you crashed in and found him now."

Niner was still struggling to understand that news when Darman lit up like a flare. "What, is this another Jedi you've chummed up with now? Which *shabla* side are you on, Jaing?"

"It's *business.* You want Zey and the others out of Kyrimorut, don't you?"

"Don't patronize me. I'm going to get back one day and find Kad gone and a thank-you note from the Jedi saying it was all for his own good. What the *shab* is wrong with you people? Why are you helping them after all that happened to us?"

Niner put a restraining hand on his arm. "Steady, Dar. *Udesii.*"

"No, you butt out of this, Niner." Dar shook him off. "I'm not going to take this. I'm fed up with Jedi always sticking their oar in. They're history. It's not our job to save their *shebse.* You're all way too cozy with them."

"Dar, shut it. I know you're upset, but—"

"Ah, forget it. *Forget it.*" Darman turned around and stalked away, pulling his helmet off.

He'd calm down. He always did. Niner was all for a deal with this Altis if it removed the risk to Kyrimorut. He thought it was weird that Skirata was in league with another Jedi, but Jusik had turned out okay, so maybe Altis would, too. Sometimes, you just had to be pragmatic. It wasn't like the guy was General Vos or any of the real *shabuire.*

"Niner, he's not going to go off and screw things up for us, is he?" Jaing asked quietly. "It's a few weeks, max. That's all. He needs to shut up about Altis."

"Don't worry, I'll keep him on a leash," Niner said. "It's all too soon after Etain."

"Sooner he comes home, the better."

"*Oya.* You're not wrong there."

"*K'oyacyi.*"

"Yeah, you look after yourself, too."

Niner went to the stores and signed for a couple of tubes of sealant for his boots just in case Rede was the checking kind. By the time he found Darman, his brother was already in the canteen, chatting to Rede as if everything was just fine and demolishing a plate of nerf steak.

He wasn't fine, though. Niner could see the tension in him. He probably felt helpless, so far from Kad and desperate to be there to protect him, even if he wasn't sure what the threat was. Funny; the Imperial garrison at Keldabe never even got a mention. Dar just wasn't worried about it. He seemed to have complete faith in *Kal'buir* and the others to keep that at arm's length.

But he didn't seem convinced that Skirata could take a tough line with Jedi. Knowing how *Kal'buir* felt about them, even Niner began to wonder what the *shab* was really going on.

It was just a few weeks' stalling. Then it was a couple of months setting up the Altis surveillance, when the Jedi were long gone from Mandalore.

By then, Niner thought, Dar would be missing Kad so

badly that he'd be ready to be persuaded to desert for good.

Laboratory, Kyrimorut, Mandalore

"Someone's got to test it," Uthan said. "And it might as well be me, because I started all this nonsense."

She ran a detector around the seal on the biohaz room doors, checking the flashing light that would turn continuous if there was the smallest leak—small enough to let a nanoscale virus escape. Ordo was convinced there had to be an easier and safer way to test the immunogen. It had taken him all night to convince himself that this wasn't some plot to release the FG36 virus after all so that Uthan could have the last laugh.

She'd lost her world. Ordo thought that if he'd been in her situation, he'd have happily spent his own life taking his revenge on those responsible. But Uthan wasn't him. She seemed sweet on Gilamar, and she'd even taken Scout under her wing, so maybe she had plenty to live for, and meant what she said. People did, sometimes, even those who dealt in death on an industrial scale.

"Okay," Ordo said. "But give me the vials first."

"Ordo, dear, I'm going to give *everyone* a shot before I do this. Even Kina Ha, and Kaminoans aren't affected by FG thirty-six at all. I've been working with pathogens all my adult life and I'm *still alive.*"

"Okay." He was going to make sure she did it. "But I still think you're rash."

"If I die, you won't get your aging therapy . . ."

"I wasn't thinking of that."

"You should." Uthan flexed her fingers like a keyboard virtuoso as she looked at the small transparisteel enclosure, more like two snack vendor's food display cabinets bolted side by side than a biohaz containment area. She wasn't as relaxed about it as she tried to make out. "Now, I should be fully cooked in an hour. Don't forget to baste me halfway through. Be a dear and get everyone assembled in the *karyai*—that's *everyone*, even Cov and his boys. And *nobody* moves in or out until I'm satisfied we're in the clear."

When Ordo and Kom'rk had herded the whole clan into the *karyai*, Ordo was suddenly struck by how unlikely it would have been for this odd group of individuals to cling together in anything but a desperate war and its aftermath. Enemies, strangers, blood relatives and adoptees, those without roots and those who clung fiercely to their ancient cultures—it wasn't a recipe for harmony.

Besany put her arms around his waist and kissed him on the cheek. "Kal can make *anyone* feel they belong," she said, answering the question in his head and scaring him. Wives always did that, *Kal'buir* warned him. "Jilka's talking to me at last. Normally, I mean. Not frosty-frosty. Corr's a good influence."

"Will you miss the Jedi when they leave?"

"Yes. Kina Ha is a treasure. While you're off sabotaging the Empire, she's the one I end up talking to most of the day."

My wife, my Bes'ika, friends with a kaminii. I should draw some great moral message from that, but Kina Ha isn't Ko Sai or Orun Wa. I'd still shoot Orun Wa on sight.

"Point made," Ordo said. "Who's making sure Arla gets her shot?"

"Bardan. Actually, the point I was making was that I spend less time with you now than I did when you were in the army."

"But we're married now."

Besany stared at him for a second, then laughed. "If romance isn't dead," she said, "it's certainly coughing up blood."

Sull and Spar had both shown up, doing a double act based on how very unimpressed they were by all this. They'd still been cautious enough to present for treatment, though.

"So there's some shot you can give me to make me immune from the Empire's bioweapon," Spar muttered. "*Another* one. Whoopee. You know how many times clones were immunized against the latest super-duper-mega-deadly viral agent some Sep quack dreamed up? My backside's like a pincushion. We're immune to *everything*. Even flattery."

Uthan took a vial from the box and inserted it into the hypospray. "I *am* that Sep quack," she said, "and I can assure you the pathogen this protects you from *is* lethal. Now drop your pants, or roll up your sleeve. I don't mind which."

Sull raised an eyebrow and presented his upper arm. "Have you had *your* shot?"

"Yes. Now you, Spar."

"So when do we get the fix for premature gray?" Spar asked. "Is that your recipe, too?"

"Soon, I hope," Uthan said. "You want to volunteer for trials?"

"Yeah. Yeah, I do."

"You're awfully trusting."

"And Sergeant Gilamar is an awfully good shot, ma'am. I can *afford* to trust you."

"I might just engineer you some unusual and embarrassing physical characteristics to teach you never to mess with a menopausal woman." Uthan finished administering the hyposprays and held up the empty box. "Friends—if you do get any symptoms, onset should be within an hour. Just sniffles and a slight fever. This does *not* entitle any males to take to their beds claiming they have acute pneumoscoria and *yes* Corr that does mean you and *no* you cannot have a candy for being a brave boy . . ."

Everyone laughed. Ordo rated her at 9 on a fear scale of 10. If she was wrong, and not half as good at her job as she thought she was, she had less than an hour to live. She walked out, Gilamar and Scout trailing behind her, and there was a noticeable drop in the volume of conversation, as if everyone had the same thought at once.

It took the best part of the next hour to run all the

safety checks on the biohaz chamber. Ordo simply watched, because he needed to know if she lived or died. Scout hung around outside the main door of the lab, hands in her pockets and looking downcast. Gilamar fidgeted, more anxious than Ordo had ever seen him. When Uthan stood in front of the chamber with her hand on the locking mechanism, taking deep breaths that she seemed to think nobody noticed, he couldn't hold back. As she slid the door aside, he simply wrapped his arms around her and gave her a desperate kiss. She responded.

It was a very touching moment. Ordo had to look away.

"I can't lose two good women in my lifetime." Gilamar sounded hoarse. "You better be right about this, Dr. Death."

Ordo decided he'd have to work on his lines to reach Gilamar's effortless line in affectionate abuse. The chamber closed behind Uthan, and the door seal hissed. Once she opened the finger-sized durasteel container and inhaled or touched the contents, she'd infect herself with a planet killer.

She paused, then pulled out a thin plastoid spatula. Ordo wondered if she thought of Gibad at that moment. It hadn't occurred to him before that she might be punishing herself in some act of atonement.

"*Shab . . . ,*" Gilamar said, shutting his eyes for a moment.

Ordo hadn't *seen* her use the hypo on herself.

And if she hadn't, it was too late now.

Scout came and clung to Gilamar, sometimes burying her face in his tunic because she couldn't bear to watch, sometimes steeling herself to look at Uthan. She really was just a kid, lonely and afraid in a galaxy that wanted to kill her just for what she was. He understood that fear.

Uthan kept taking her own pulse and checking her eyes with a small piece of mirrored metal. She pulled down both lower lids and gave Gilamar a thumbs-up sign.

"Hemorrhaging," she mouthed. "Just checking. Nothing."

It was a very, very slow hour. Toward the end of it, she took a blood sample from her arm and put it in a steribag. Gilamar shook his head. "Got to teach that woman to use a sharp *properly*. Eh, Scout? You, too."

Ordo checked the chrono. Uthan was well beyond the onset period now, and she still looked fine. After another half an hour, she stepped into the adjacent chamber and pressed the controls to flood the whole space with decontaminant as thick as white smoke. Ordo found that the worst part of it. When she opened the door, the smoke rolled out like fog and she was coughing.

"Where the stang did you get that thing, Mij?" she demanded. "It looks like an old GAR field biochem decontamination unit."

"It is," he said, hugging her. "They just left it unattended. I always thought I'd find a use for it."

Ordo wasn't sure how to take his leave of them, but they seemed happy enough. Scout didn't. She turned to Ordo.

"If Bardan wipes my memories of this place, am I going to forget Mij and Qail?" she asked, utterly miserable. "Is it *all* going to disappear?"

"I don't know," Ordo said. "I'm not sure anyone does."

"I don't want to leave," Scout said. "Not yet, anyway. Do I have to? I'd never tell anyone this place was here. I'm learning so much."

Gilamar put his arm around her shoulders like a father. "And you don't *have* to go, *ad'ika*. I'll talk to Kal. Don't you worry."

"He'll have you in armor in no time," Ordo said.

"Oh, thanks, but I'm a Jedi. I can still be a Jedi, can't I? It's all I ever wanted to be."

Ordo heard Gilamar pause for a fraction of a second before replying.

"Of course you can," he said. "Leave it to me."

Ordo decided that this was going to be . . . *interesting*.

Kyrimorut, next day

"Ah, it's good to hear your voice again, Kal," Shysa said. "Feel safe using a comm now?"

Skirata tried to phrase the offer sensibly. The more he tried to cover all the bases that had been troubling him, the more insane it sounded. Uthan stood within earshot to guide him on the technical stuff. But he couldn't imagine Shysa wanting to ask about antigens and T-cells.

"Safe enough," Skirata said. "I've got something to offer Mandalore."

"The services of that fine young Force-using *Mando'ad*?"

"Not that." Shysa never forgot *anything*. Skirata took a breath. "You know what happened to Gibad."

"I do. Filthy business. But then we know who we're doing business with."

"If the old *hutuun* plans to use the virus on *us*, we've beaten him to the punch. But we need to keep it quiet, or he'll just get a tame scientist to invent another one."

"So what trick have you got up your sleeve?"

"An immunogen. Or some word like that." He glanced at Uthan and she nodded emphatically. "A virus that makes folks immune to the thing. And they pass the immunity to their kids. I don't understand the science, but we can spread it to everyone on Mandalore so we don't have folks lining up for hypos and making the Imperials curious."

Shysa made a *hmmmm* noise. "Is it safe?"

"Well, *we're* not dead yet. You just get a mild fever and a runny nose. But I wanted your blessing to spread it. It's not like we can ask everyone for their consent."

"Ah . . . Kal, I never thought I'd see the day when you got a bad case of medical ethics, you old *shabuir.*"

"We've just got better scientists than Palps has."

"You won the Corellian lottery, then. Again."

"Yeah." Skirata felt a sudden chill down his spine as he realized he hadn't checked the clan accounts with Jilka for days. The numbers multiplied like bacteria. He could bankroll a small army for Shysa. "Natural born winner."

"I'll mention to the clans that there'll be a little bug doing the rounds but that we'll be all the stronger for it."

"Then we can all laugh at Palps when he tries to wipe us out."

"I'm glad you're on our side, Kal. You're a strange and dangerous wee fella. Will this make the Imperials here immune, too?"

"Yes, if they mix with us. Win some, lose some."

"Then it's back to shootin' 'em when they outstay their welcome. Drop by for a glass or two, Kal. Door's always open."

Skirata closed the comlink and looked to Uthan for approval. She gave him a baffled frown.

"You Mandos are thoroughly contradictory," she said. "One minute you'll kill the first person to try to impose rules on you. The next you think it's okay to infect your entire population without their knowledge or consent."

"Forgive me if I say that's rich coming from you."

"Face it. You're all split personalities." She looked at her chrono, lips moving as if she was calculating. "We'll stay infectious for a few more days, so better get on with it. Pity we're on the run. I would have *loved* to submit a paper on this."

It was a good excuse to take a few of the *ad'ike* into Keldabe. Everyone was getting a little restless, and Skirata wanted to check for himself exactly who was in town. He stuck his head around the kitchen door.

"Walon, are you still sulking, or are you coming with us?"

Vau wiped his nose. "Okay. Change of *beskar'gam,* though. No point asking for trouble."

Jusik, Gilamar, Vau, the Nulls, and Skirata swapped out armor plates from the stores and emerged in unrecognizable colors. It was enough to avoid the attention of any dumb Imperial who had a checklist of wanted Mandos wearing certain colors of *beskar'gam.* All the *vode* had to do now was take their helmets off in tapcafs when prying Imperial eyes weren't watching, cough in confined spaces, and touch as many surfaces as they could. Keldabe was a hub for the whole planet. Eventually the infection would spread like the wirt-cough epidemic had forty years before, across the planet and throughout the Mandalore system by travel, and—eventually— around the galaxy.

Slow. But covert.

"Can they charge us with bioterrorism?" Jusik asked.

Skirata thought of Jaller Obrim for a moment, and missed their long rambling discussions in the CSF staff club over an ale. "They can nick us for looking at them funny and being willfully Mandalorian with malice aforethought in a public place."

Vau opened the hatch of an old agricultural shuttle laid up in one of the barns and ushered the rest of them inside. A whiff of roba dung and straw rolled out. Mird trotted up expectantly, tail whipping, but Vau pointed back to the house. "Zey, *Mird'ika.* Guard the *jetii.*"

Mird ambled back through the kitchen doors, grumbling to itself. Skirata knew that it was going to shadow Zey even into the 'freshers until Vau got back and told it to stand-down. It was a pity most sentient species weren't that smart.

"When we finish spreading the plague, we need to get on with offloading our Jedi," Skirata said.

Gilamar coughed, and this time it wasn't the virus. "I was meaning to talk to you about that, Kal. Scout wants to stay, poor kid."

"Plenty of room for strays."

"She wants to stay as a Jedi."

Skirata strapped himself into his seat and choked back his reflex rejection. "Okay. It's not like she's the first."

"No, Kal, *she wants to stay a Jedi*. Not become a Mando. But it's okay. We've got Togorian Mandos. If *they* can fit in, Scout can, too. It's only temporary—she seems to need Uthan at the moment."

"Interesting choice of mother figure." Skirata could hardly blame Gilamar for wanting to be the archetypal Mando *buir* to any child in need. He decided to worry about Scout later. "So has anyone else got a surprise for me?"

"Yes," said Jusik. "Djinn Altis. Etain was invited to join them with Kad and Dar if she felt like it."

Jusik blurted it out as if he wanted to rid himself of the knowledge. Skirata felt his chest sink under the weight of loss.

Etain could have survived Order 66, then.

Skirata was learning to stop himself running through endless what-ifs, because a different fork in the road had been taken. He couldn't change history, and he couldn't live with the pain of being reminded that things could have been different. He had to walk away and accept that was how things had turned out.

It was a massive effort. He usually failed.

"Bard'ika," he said, "if I ever make you feel you have to pick the right time to tell me things, I'm sorry. You should never have to tread on eggs with me, son"

He didn't mean it as a rebuke. He really did worry that his temper scared his family from telling him things.

"I just don't like opening wounds," Jusik said. "Altis said he'd like to meet you sometime."

"I'd like to meet him, too. Especially as Dar and Niner are keeping tabs on him."

"Dar's spitting blood about it." Jaing didn't sound as chipper as usual. "He still thinks we're going soft on Jedi. Betraying our principles."

"I can see that, son. But I can't win with Dar at the moment whatever I do, because he's hurting too much." *No, I decided to behave all nice like an* aruetuii, *not a Mando, and he called me on it.* "Let's take one hurdle at a time."

The shuttle skimmed over familiar woods and fields and then followed the course of the Kelita River into Keldabe. Vau parked the shuttle near the animal market.

"Seeing as your girlfriend failed to secure a proper bone for Mird, I'm going to see the butcher," Vau said. "Never break a promise to a strill."

"She's not my girlfriend," Skirata said. "And Mird got the cookies."

Gilamar caught his arm by the biceps as they walked into the maze of alleys at the rear of the *Oyu'baat* cantina. "You're a long time dead, Kal," he said. "I know you put your needs a poor second to the lads', but you've been a widower way too long."

"Is this a trend? You and Uthan, Jilka and Corr . . ."

"Ruu and Cov."

"*What?*"

"Your own daughter, and you don't know where she spends her free time?"

Skirata was stunned for a moment. He really needed to catch up with Ruu. He felt worse every day about neglecting her. Now she had a sweetheart, and he hadn't even noticed.

"You sure?" he said. "Cov? He's just a kid."

"He's roughly twenty-seven. Ruu's thirty-six, thereabouts. In eight years or so, they'll be the same age. Then he'll start getting older than her."

Skirata never needed reminding that the clones were on borrowed time and that his personal priority was to put that right. But Gilamar's stark analysis in relation to his own daughter really smacked him around the head. When he got back to Kyrimorut, he'd do whatever it took to get that gene therapy out of Uthan.

The group split up, very casual, very random. Ordo went off with Gilamar. Now Skirata had to carry out his bizarre mission. He had to cough his guts out and give as many *Mando'ade* a mild dose of genetically modified rhinacyria as he could. Market day, held twice a week, meant the town was heaving with shoppers, drinkers, and scrappers, so Skirata slipped off his helmet one-handed to share his viral gift.

Any Imperial who happened to venture into Keldabe wouldn't even spot him. Skirata was out of practice, but he could still disappear simply by altering his body language and becoming a skinny old man nobody took any notice of until he wanted them to. It was an assassin's skill. It was also a thief's.

It had been years since Skirata had gone anywhere with nothing to do except mooch around, and he wasn't very good at doing nothing. He stopped at each tapcaf along the Chortav Meshurkaane and had a mug of hot shig, then ambled along the market stalls that lined the alley. One end was all leather items, from gloves and belts to kamas. The other was precious metals and gems, and somewhere in the middle the two trades met and mixed. Gilamar was right. He had to sort out where he stood with Ny. It affected the whole clan.

Skirata looked over the gems and wondered what was an appropriate betrothal token for a man whose bank accounts had more zeros than he could count. It wasn't his personal wealth. It was the clones' fund. But he still had access to more creds than he would ever have a use for.

Ah, shab. He didn't even know what Ny liked. He'd buy something for Ruu, too, because he hadn't bought his little girl a gift—a personal gift, not creds sent to her mother—for more than thirty years. He put his helmet back on, comforted by the instant access to comms and data, and took his virus further into town.

The end of Meshurkaane opened onto the ancient paved square in front of the *Oyu'baat,* a space filled today with food stalls. A couple of stormtroopers strolled up and down the aisles. Skirata wasn't sure if they were patrolling—why would they need to?—or if they were just exploring. Maybe the Imperial army had learned a lesson and worked out that men needed stand-easy time and a little breathing space.

Empire or no Empire, his subconscious reaction to white plastoid armor was that these were his boys. Under their helmets, they would *look* like his boys. But they were not. If they were doing their jobs right, they'd check this scruffy little *shabuir* against their ID images in their HUDs, see the personal death warrant from Palpatine, and they'd pull him in. Thirteen years of constant, sleepless devotion to the liberation of their slave army wouldn't count for *naas*.

Instead of turning and retracing his steps down the Meshurkaane, Skirata carried on without deviating and walked slowly past them. He even stopped to buy a packet of spiced leathermeat. He didn't see the stormies react. They were still facing dead ahead. But then he knew anything could have been happening under that helmet, and they could have been looking right at him.

He carried on. They'd be looking for sand-gold armor with red sigils anyway, not this dark sea green. When he got to the far side of the square, he leaned on the rail to watch the Kelita River crashing over the granite rocks below while he unwrapped the leathermeat.

Another great thing about his *buy'ce,* the distinctive Mandalorian helmet, was that the visor could not only give aging eyes a sharp view in infrared, low light, and UV, with a range of two kilometers, but also enlarge the infuriatingly small print on food packaging.

But there was nothing wrong with his distance vision. When he turned around, something in the crowd drew his eye as familiar things did. It was out of time frame and context, something that rang a bell but took him a couple of slow seconds to pin down to a specific memory.

It was a woman in yellow and gray armor, leather kama swinging as she walked, and a man in red and

black. He'd seen that in some place or other every day of
his life for the best part of eight years, and the place was
Tipoca City.

Ordo had warned him. It was Isabet Reau and Dred
Priest.

If Gilamar saw them, there'd be trouble. He loathed
them with a passion. If anyone thought Jango Fett's
handpicked team of special forces experts had been one
happy unit, then they really needed to understand what
it was like to be marooned indefinitely on Kamino with
folks you hated on sight and nowhere to escape them.

Priest had run a fight club in one of the shadowy
maintenance areas of the stilt city. He was a sick *shabuir*.
He enjoyed seeing men really damage each other in fist-
fights, and nobody needed that when they were training
lads for armed combat. His girlfriend, Reau, was even
worse, always harping on about restoring the glory of
the Mandalorian empire through the iron will of the
warrior.

Skirata was all for *Mando'ade* kicking the *osik* out of
anyone who got in their faces. That didn't mean that
aruetiise were inferior species; just enemies. But Reau
and Priest really believed they were in need of the firm
governing hand of a master state.

"Kal?" Vau's voice whispered over his helmet audio.
"I can see you. Can you see what's heading your way?"

"Yeah. Where's Mij?"

"Ordo's with him. It's okay. But have you *seen* them?"

"*Yes*. You going deaf as well, Walon? Right in front of
me, almost on a collision course."

"Well, look harder."

Skirata doubted they'd recognize him. It had been
more than three years since he'd last had to breathe the
same air as those two, and he no longer had his distinctive limp. His only worry was that he wouldn't be able
to resist the urge to finally slide his three-sided blade
into Priest where it would do the most damage. But he'd
had plenty of chances on Kamino, where the Kaminoans

were scared of the *Cuy'val Dar* and left them to run their affairs. It was lawless. And he still hadn't done it.

Gilamar had punched Priest senseless, though. He didn't like young commandos showing up blinded in one eye or collapsing with brain hemorrhages. The fight club stopped for good after Jango gave Priest a good hiding.

Skirata was five or six meters away from Priest and Reau now. If they'd been here during the war, he'd have known. It was a very small city in a world of only four million people. They'd come back with the Imperials.

We're mercenaries. Professionals. It's no big deal. But those two . . .

Skirata still couldn't work out what Vau was so insistent he ought to see. It was only when Reau turned a little to her left that he saw the full surface of her shoulder plate, and the dark blue emblem on it.

He thought it was a stylized *jai'galaar* at first, wings spread and half-folded back to swoop on its prey, talons outstretched, forming a vague W shape. But it wasn't. And he had no idea how this woman had made it through Keldabe without getting a punch in the face at the very least.

Shab, Priest had one of the emblems on his shoulder plate, too.

Didn't *anyone* else here know what that was?

Skirata was now level with them, forced by the crowd to stop by the roba pie stall for a few seconds. He looked at Reau's plate straight on.

It wasn't the same as the Death Watch emblem, but it was enough to almost trigger his reflex to swing a punch. It looked like a ragged, stylized silhouette of a shriek-hawk in dark blue paint. Dred and Reau moved past him and vanished into the crowds.

Skirata just carried on walking, shaken. Vau caught up with him and they headed in silence for the *Oyu'baat.* They didn't speak until they got inside, checked for Imperials, and took off their helmets.

The barkeep gave them a weary look and set up two mugs of *net'ra gal.*

"I told you—we asked the garrison to stay out of the place." The thin head of pale amber foam settled on the black liquid like a mat of pond-barley as he contemplated it. "I'd lose half my custom if nobody could take off their *buy'ce* without being arrested."

Skirata noted his mug shot was still on the bounty poster behind the bar, along with everyone else's. The sheet was splashed with some unidentifiable dark stain that might have been blood or even gravy. Some wag had inked in pointy *schutta* fangs on his image. Vau and Skirata grabbed their ales and found a quiet booth near a noisy hot-air unit, where they huddled over the mugs and tried to keep their voices down.

"Well?" Vau said. "I know what I think that is."

"So do I. But nobody else seemed to be taking any notice."

"When did anyone last see the Death Watch here? Nearly thirty years ago. Update the badge, change from dark red to dark blue, and there you are. Nobody remembers. Some fancy diner used a symbol exactly like the winged circle of the Guuko Pure Light party and nobody under fifty thought there was anything wrong with it. Folks forget, and kids don't get taught. And so these *hut'uune* get reinvented."

Skirata shut his eyes for a second to recall the symbol. It was a definite W shape. Older Mandos reacted to the Death Watch emblem just like the Guuko reacted to the Pure Light circle, which would always spell genocide to Guukosi who remembered the invasion.

"Maybe we're letting the personalities of the two *hut'uune* concerned shape our judgment," said Skirata, realizing he was clutching at straws.

"You know that's *osik.* This isn't the time of life to suddenly discover benefit of the doubt." Vau leaned closer, almost nose-to-nose across the table with Skirata. "I don't care if they're cozying up to the Empire or the Holy Children of Asrat. It's not the company they keep.

It's what they *are*. No true Mandalorian can live alongside the Death Watch."

Skirata wondered how many *Mando'ade* had given a mott's backside about the power struggle between Jaster Mereel and the Death Watch. It hadn't touched Mandalorians living off-world. It probably hadn't even touched most of those living in the Mandalore sector. It was between two factions, relatively *small* factions. But it swallowed up the core of the full-time army and the leading clans, and it had been a battle for the heart of *Manda'yaim*—the very culture, how Mandalore would conduct itself for generations to come. The Death Watch represented the worst excess of an ancient imperial Mandalore.

They're rotten to the core. They're dangerous.

Skirata knew that no compromise could be reached with them. He could rationalize about the folly of trying to rebuild old empires, but in the end it was something he felt in his guts like a reflex revulsion at finding a decomposing body. He couldn't help seeing the Death Watch as something disgusting.

"Like we don't have enough to keep us busy," Skirata said. "So who do we deal with first?"

Vau's lean face betrayed every twitching muscle. He wasn't just angry. He was possessed. Skirata knew it was stoked by his guilt at not being at Jango Fett's side at the Battle of Galidraan.

"We haven't fought a war of expansion for thousands of years," Vau said. "We're strictly home defense or mercenaries. Whatever the Death Watch have in mind, they'll always drag us into the kind of war we can't win."

The Death Watch had melted away after Fett finally defeated them. But they had enough Mandalorian spirit in them to guarantee one thing.

They knew the strategic value of *ba'slan shev'la*. And that meant they'd be back one day.

That day could be coming all too soon.

Keldabe, half a kilometer from the Oyu'baat

"I hope Mereel isn't getting *Bard'ika* into bad ways." Ordo checked his chrono, trying to work out where in the city they'd be by now. "Corr was the quiet stay-at-home type before *Mer'ika* got hold of him."

But Gilamar wasn't going to be distracted by small talk. He wasn't strolling, spreading his virus carefully, but walking with his head thrust forward like a hunting strill on a scent. Ordo knew what was on his mind; Dred Priest and Isabet Reau.

"*Kal'buir* shouldn't have commed you," Ordo said.

Gilamar shook his head. "I knew they were here. It was only a matter of time."

"I meant about the Death Watch angle."

"That," Gilamar said, "only makes me want to kill them *twice*."

Ordo found himself wondering how hard a stranglehold he'd have to put on Gilamar to break up a fight without hurting the man. Keldabe wasn't a big place. The public areas—marketplaces, alleys full of shops, the main cantinas—were all crammed into a small sector, and on a busy day like this the entire population seemed to be circulating around it just waiting to run into folks they knew. But Gilamar was a pro, a man used to keeping a low profile. He wasn't going to start a brawl and draw attention to himself.

"So where have the Death Watch been all these years, then?" Ordo said.

"Depends who you ask." Gilamar obviously kept tabs on them, which was worrying in itself. "Anywhere from half the planets on the Outer Rim to Endor. Also holding hands with Black Sun and any other crime syndicate that'll pay them."

Ordo tried to calm him down. "Let's distinguish between the lowlife sporting a badge to look tougher to their criminal buddies, and the real Death Watch. If someone wants to be a designer thug, that's not our problem."

"But anyone who wants to change Mandalore and its culture to achieve galactic domination—that's very much our problem. You remember Priest, Ordo. You know what he's like. And they're all like that, all of them. Ask Arla."

Gilamar's resolve to leave the galaxy's ideologues and firebrands to rebel against Palpatine seemed to have been swept aside by a knee-jerk urge to start an equally dangerous fight with other Mandalorians. Ordo scanned every unhelmeted face he passed, hoping that he'd spot a familiar one before Gilamar did.

"I still don't see what the Death Watch would get out of siding with Palpatine," Ordo said. "If they want to restore the Mando empire, he's not the power-sharing kind."

"Maybe he's franchising dictatorships. The Death Watch gets this concession to keep an eye on the place."

"That won't be enough for them."

"No, not if they're still spouting Vizsla's party line."

"What was Jango doing recruiting them? He had more reason to hate the Death Watch than anybody"

"Priest and Reau weren't exactly card-carrying members. Jango thought they were all talk. He only cared about results."

So even legends made bad choices. Ordo found that oddly comforting. Gilamar took off his helmet as he walked and slipped on a sun visor. Combined with a bandanna tied over the hair, the visor gave Gilamar some anonymity in this crowd, and even his broken nose wasn't as distinctive in Keldabe as it might have been on Coruscant. A lot of people had one—including females.

I feel like I'm roasting. This fever had better be over as fast as Uthan promised.

Ordo could still smell frying food whether his nose was running or not. He opened the filter on his helmet and savored the scent. Gilamar, a pace or two ahead of him, was forced to slow down by the press of bodies as they got closer to the market square.

"I'll be glad when this is done." Gilamar's voice

rasped. "I feel as rough as old boots. Qail can make me a nice pot of shig when I get home, maybe with a splash of *tihaar* in it."

"We're hard as nails," Ordo said. "Not."

He willed the day to be over without incident. Just a couple more turns around the block, and they could meet up with the others in the *Oyu'baat,* then head back to Kyrimorut, job done, population immunized. The next problem was waiting to be solved; erasing the memories of their Jedi guests before transferring them to Altis's care.

Ordo spotted a few items on the stalls that Besany might like—a decent butchering knife, a ruby glass vial of perfume—and paused to check them over. Gilamar scanned the crowd, managing to look casual. The stormtroopers had vanished. Ordo paid for the knife and the perfume, then commed Jusik for a routine check.

"How's it going, *Bard'ika?*" he asked.

"Mereel's just met a new woman. I'm sure she'll be sneezing and coughing very soon."

Ordo couldn't begrudge Mereel grabbing whatever chances he could to be young and carefree but he wanted to tell him to keep his mind on the job. "Can't ever call that boy *slow.*"

"What's the problem? I can feel a lot of angst around."

Ordo still tended to forget that Jusik sensed things. "Oh, Priest and his crazy woman are in town, and *Kal'buir* said they had Death Watch insignia or something."

"That explains what I can feel."

"See you later. Make sure Mereel doesn't wear himself out."

Ordo shut the comm and turned to share the joke with Gilamar. He'd only taken his eyes off him for a few seconds. For a moment, he lost him in the sea of shoppers; then he spotted his brown bandanna, and realized Gilamar had moved on a few meters. He stood on the

corner of an alley that became steep steps leading down
to the river.

Better stick with him. Can't be too careful.

Ordo edged through the crowd and reached out to tap
Gilamar's shoulder. Gilamar turned slowly, but it wasn't
toward Ordo. It was as if someone had called him and
he wasn't sure it was a good idea to respond.

"Fancy seeing you here," said a voice that Ordo
hadn't heard in years.

By the time Ordo got to Gilamar, he could see Dred
Priest almost face-to-face with him, and Ordo knew
he'd have to intervene.

Come on, Mij, udesii. *Stay cool. Don't make a scene.*

Ordo saw Gilamar literally hold himself back, straining to walk away and save his anger for later. But it was
too late; Priest had cornered him. There was nowhere to
run, too dense a crowd. Gilamar stood his ground.

"Small world," he muttered.

Priest took off his helmet. *Kal'buir* had described him
as having the sort of face he could punch all day; it was
that thin, lopsided mouth that did it. There was no sign
of Isabet Reau. She was no work of art, either.

"You never were the kind to worry about the wanted
list, were you?" Priest said. "Been a long time." He
glanced at Ordo. "Who's this?"

"My nephew," Gilamar said. Ordo took that as a hint
to keep quiet and not give Priest a clue who was under
the helmet. "I'd like to say I'd missed you, but you'd
know I was lying. So . . . working for the Empire?"

The emblem on Priest's shoulder plate really did look
like the old Death Watch badge. Even Ordo could see
that, and he hadn't lived with it as a specter of dread like
Gilamar and the others had. He kept his arms at his
sides, but flexed his right fist discreetly to make sure the
vibroblade in his gauntlet was primed to eject. Gilamar
still had his thumbs hooked on his belt, deceptively casual.

"You know how I prefer winners," said Priest.

Gilamar stared pointedly at Priest's emblems. "Interesting paint job."

"Is that a question?"

"Was that an answer?"

"No hard feelings about the pounding you gave me."

"Oh good."

"And if you're worried I'm going to turn you in to the garrison, I've got more pressing business." Priest looked around. Maybe he was checking for Reau. "Times change. Are you looking for work?"

Gilamar froze. Ordo thought he was bracing to throw a punch. "Not with the Death Watch, *hut'uun*."

"Things have changed since Vizsla." Priest took that ultimate insult calmly. "The galaxy's a different place. Mandalorians need to look after themselves better. Not just scramble for crumbs like the deadbeats here."

Ordo couldn't just walk away now that Priest had identified Gilamar. Plenty of folks here knew that Skirata and his clan were back somewhere on Mandalore, and even if they did some work for the garrison, that didn't make them Imperial sympathizers. But Priest was different, almost an enemy to start with. There was no telling what he'd do.

"So—new Death Watch?" Gilamar said quietly. His voice was steady, as if he'd suddenly forgotten the past and every blow he'd ever landed on Priest. "New policies?" Then he looked around as if he was checking for eavesdroppers. "You better tell me about it."

Gilamar turned and jerked his head at Priest to follow him. Ordo took the cue instantly, closing up behind them. Gilamar led the way down the alley. It grew steeper and became cobbled steps that dipped down to the level of the river, deserted and damp with spray. It was just a dead end that had once led to a sluice gate or something, but the gate had long gone, and now the archway cut from the solid granite foundations of Keldabe was sealed off by a metal safety rail. Foaming, hammering white water rushed beneath them, echoing under the arch and drenching the walls with a permanent mist.

Deep green frond-grass thrived in the cracks. It was the kind of hidden spot where you could lean on the rail and lose yourself in contemplation of the raging river, or meet a lover, or just hide.

It was a great place to discuss the Death Watch without being overheard. But Ordo had no idea what Gilamar was up to.

He's going to shake Priest down. Double agent stuff. I hope he knows what he's doing.

Gilamar put one hand out to lean on the wall, which would have looked relaxed to anyone who didn't know him. Ordo stood back, ready to do whatever needed doing. Priest kept glancing at him. He'd obviously pegged him as the hired muscle who'd give him a clip around the ear if he got out of line.

"I never did like you much, Dred," Gilamar said. "Or your *chakaar* of a girlfriend. What could I possibly do for you?"

"Same as always. You're either with us, or you're against us."

"And *us* is . . ."

"Lorka Gedyc has big plans for us. Forget your petty personal squabbles with the *aruetyc* Empire and start thinking about our rightful heritage. We weren't always the *aruetiise*'s latrine-cleaners. We've got the *beskar*—and we can use it."

"Say it."

"Say what?"

"Are you still calling yourself the Death Watch, or have you hired an image consultant to give you a racy new name?"

Gilamar looked Priest straight in the eye with just enough hostility to be convincing. Ordo had guessed right. He just hoped *Mij'ika* knew how far to go with this stunt.

"We're not ashamed. Death Watch it is."

"So how are you going to build your new Mando empire?" he asked. "There can't be more than a few thousand of you vermin, tops. And you won't be fighting little girls this time."

"I can't reveal troop strengths to you." Priest shook his head. Gilamar didn't voice his usual objection to the Death Watch using the word *troops* instead of *thugs.* "Still as sanctimonious as ever, Mij."

Gilamar paused and pushed himself away from the wall one-handed to stand upright. Ordo braced for trouble, keeping an eye on Priest's holstered blaster. His hand wandered just a fraction too close to it for comfort.

"Yeah," Gilamar said. "I have trouble forgetting all the lads on Kamino I had to patch up from your fight club. And the ones who didn't make it."

"The strong survive, the weak die. That's the way the galaxy works. The day we forgot that, we became everyone's lackey."

Gilamar looked down for a moment. The river was so noisy that they had to stand as close as friends to hear each other. Then Gilamar's shoulders sagged as if he was sighing.

"It's not vengeance," he said. "It just has to be done."

Ordo was fast. But he wasn't fast enough. Gilamar dropped to a crouch and drew the blade on his belt, bringing it up into Priest's belly in the time it took Ordo to inhale. Priest staggered back, eyes wide with shock, and fell against the slippery wall. For a heartbeat Ordo couldn't work out how Gilamar had put the knife through Priest's armor; but then he saw the blood, spurting blood, *arterial* blood, and knew that Gilamar had aimed with a surgeon's precision for the gap between the plates at the top of the thigh. He'd sliced through the femoral artery.

Priest had minutes to live. He'd bleed out in minutes.

"Oh . . . oh . . . you *scum* . . ." Priest's voice had suddenly taken on a high-pitched shakiness, all surprise. He slumped at the foot of the wall, trying to stem the blood with his hands, but he was already too weak to apply much pressure. "You . . . you . . . why?"

"It'll take too long to list." Gilamar just watched him. Ordo had never seen that side of the doctor before. "But I can't let you live, for so many, many reasons."

"Isabet? Issy? Help me . . . *help me . . .*"

Reau wasn't going to hear him. Nobody would, with the racket the water was making. They were going to have a dead body on their hands very soon. Ordo had to think what to do next.

"*Shab*, Mij, did you have to?" he said.

"Yes." Gilamar squatted down and looked Priest in the eye. "I can't let your kind come back to Mandalore. You know that, don't you? And it's the least I owe Jango. And all those boys who got broken for your entertainment."

Priest was panting now, semiconscious, and all he managed was an animal noise that faded into nothing. There was an awful lot of blood pooling on the cobbles. Ordo looked down from the archway to see if there was any runoff staining the water, but the churning foam was as white as ever.

How can I tell Besany that my first thought was how to cover this up?

It was a war. It didn't matter which war. And Besany had seen him do far worse.

Ordo watched Gilamar check the pulse in Priest's neck as if he was doing a house call. "*Kal'buir*'s going to be furious."

"You got a better idea, son? This *chakaar* would turn us in if it suited him, too."

"We'd better dump the body in the river."

"Yeah." Gilamar took something from his belt and held it under Priest's nose. It looked like polished dura-steel. The man's eyes were half open. Gilamar nodded. "He's gone. Kinder exit than he deserved. Help me tip him over the side. Mind you don't get blood all over your plates."

Gilamar searched Priest and took his datapad, com-link, and ID chip, then unclipped one of the shoulder plates with the hated Death Watch emblem and slipped it into his belt pouch. The opening in the granite wall wasn't overlooked. Unlike Imperial City, there were no snoop cams to monitor the place, either. Ordo took a grip of Priest's belt and backplate, Gilamar grabbed the other side, and together they heaved the body into the torrent. They didn't even hear a splash.

"He'll wash up somewhere downstream," Gilamar said. "The buffeting and the rocks will mash the body a bit, but we don't have Jaller Obrim or the CSF Forensics Service here to worry about. Come on. I'll make my peace with Kal."

"Who's going to make the most noise when they realize Priest's missing?" Ordo asked. He checked himself for blood before climbing the steps again. "Other than Reau?"

"Does it matter?" Gilamar cleaned his knife in the spray from the river and shook off the water. "We're all borked anyway. Might as well hang for a bantha as a jackrab."

It was time to bang out of Keldabe. They'd infected enough people by now anyway. And Reau—Ordo knew they'd have to deal with her sooner or later.

It would take her a long time to work out who'd killed Priest.

Your prowess with a lightsaber is childish vanity. Your physical Force powers are no more than a conjuror's trick, sleight of hand to dazzle the ordinary beings you should be serving. You profane these powers by using them as weapons in war. And you fail to grasp the single, simple, uncompromising duty of the true Jedi. The Jedi is the rock-lion at the gate who says, "I will defend these beings with my life, and that is the sum of me." Etain Tur-Mukan died to save one life, a man she did not even know, but felt compelled to save, and that is what made her stronger in the Force and a truer Jedi than any of you acrobats, tricksters, and specious, empty philosophers.

—Kina Ha, Jedi Knight; unsure of her exact age, but at least a thousand years old

Kyrimorut, Mandalore

"**A**rla? It's me. Can I come in?"

Jusik rapped on her door and waited for a response. It was locked from the outside, but he had to give her some control over the only sanctuary she had. Laseema listened, head tilted in concentration.

"She's been awful while you were down in Keldabe." Laseema adjusted the balance of dishes on the tray. "Hallucinations, muscle spasms, vomiting, the lot. I had to get Fi to give her medical aid while Scout kept her calm. He's really good."

"He trained as a squad battlefield medic," Jusik said. "I always think of him as just the sniper. I tend to forget the medic side."

"This is the first time she's been too far out of it to wash and dress herself. That's why I'm worried."

"What were the hallucinations about?"

"The only thing I could understand was that she thought she was burning. There were flames coming toward her."

Jusik didn't know enough to even guess if that was a clue to an underlying problem. And he'd never seen anyone suffer withdrawal symptoms before. It was distressing. When he opened the door, Arla was thrashing around on the bed, clearly in pain, panting for breath. Her eyes were half open.

"Let me die," she mumbled, apparently lucid. "If you understood, you'd end this for me."

Jusik turned to Laseema. "Better get *Mij'ika*." This was medically beyond him. "Arla, this is going to pass. I know it doesn't feel like it, but it *will* be over soon."

He put his hand under her head, feeling the matted, sweaty hair, and wondered how medics ever coped daily with the smell of illness. She struggled to focus on him.

"It *won't* pass," she whispered. "It's not the drugs. It's *me*."

"When that stuff is out of your system, then we can fix you. We can."

"No. It's still there. It always will be."

Gilamar arrived with an assortment of hyposprays. For a man who'd just killed a former comrade, he looked oddly calm. "What's wrong, Arla? Stomach cramps? Throwing up? Head hurt?" He placed a blood pressure sensor in the crook of her elbow. "That's a bit low. Let's fix that first."

"Twitching muscles . . . stang, my legs . . ."

"Two for two, so far." Gilamar gave her two shots and stood back. "Should be kicking in anytime, Arla. Hang in there. Now, where are you, and what can you see?"

"Bedroom . . . window . . . you . . . Bardan . . . and Laseema was here."

"You're not hallucinating, then. You're going to feel like a speeder wreck for a couple of days yet. What's your biggest problem right now?"

Arla rolled over on one side and flung off one of the blankets. "I want to stop thinking. I want it all to stop."

Gilamar bent down to whisper in Jusik's ear. "She's lucid and feeling ropey. Apart from monitoring her blood pressure that's all I can do until something else mechanical or chemical goes wrong."

Jusik sat with Arla for half an hour, trying to feel her mental state, and all he could get was a sensation in his mind of her constantly trying not to look at something hanging in front of her eyes. He tended to see solid images superimposed at a point that felt somewhere behind his eyes and level with the roof of his mouth. Then he felt Zey and Kina Ha approaching. Kina Ha was distinctive in the Force, such a weight of time and experience stored in her being that the Force felt as if it curved around her. Zey was an odd mix now: the old Master, impatient and frustrated like an escaping sigh, but almost completely engulfed in a terrible regret that peaked and fell on a cycle like a heartbeat.

"If we can help," Zey said. "Just say."

Kina Ha settled down with majestic slowness and dipped her long neck to gaze into Arla's face.

"I'm *old*," she said. "And there's nothing you have done that can shock me. I've seen *so many*. Whatever it is, you're not the most terrible being who ever lived. It won't let you go, so you can't run from it, but you can grab it and hold it where you can see it for what it is."

Jusik had no idea what the Kaminoan was going on about, although she seemed to sense that thing that Arla was trying not to see. It was obvious: a terrible memory. It would be agony to relive what the Death Watch did to her family and then to her, but it seemed to be the only option left.

Zey just watched. Jusik moved back a little. Kina Ha took Arla's arm and examined the cuts and deep wounds.

"What are you trying to cut out of yourself?" she asked.

Jusik tried not to jump too far ahead, but he could guess guilt, taste guilt, *calculate* guilt. Arla didn't know her brother Jango had survived. But there wasn't a happy ending to that, either, so Jusik decided to save it until she was a lot stronger.

"What I am," Arla said at last.

"And what are you?"

"One of them."

"Who?"

Jusik looked at Zey, who seemed just as lost as he was. Kina Ha's thousand years of life—what had she seen and experienced? More than any human, ten times over, even more than any Hutt, even if she spent it all in secluded contemplation. She'd had time to listen to whole *worlds*.

"Look," Arla said. "I can't say it."

She scrambled into a sitting position, and struggled to lift the back of her shirt. Jusik didn't know what to expect; he just knew that she'd been hurt, physically and emotionally. Jango had told Vau just the barest detail about the Death Watch punishing his father for harboring Jaster Mereel, and his mother shooting one of them dead so Jango—eight, maybe—could get away. That was the last he saw of all of them, his mother shielding fourteen-year-old Arla, his father on his knees yelling at him to run.

Jango thought they'd all died. Arla seemed to think she was the lone survivor, too. Between those two views lay a mystery.

Arla still fumbled with her shirt. Jusik didn't dare touch her to help her. He left it to Kina Ha.

"Look," Arla said. Kina Ha lifted the fabric higher. "I can't reach it. If I could, I'd cut it out. But *I'd* still be in here. It's me who needs to go."

Jusik steeled himself to look. He was expecting worse. He wasn't sure if the dark brown mark was a tattoo, or a scar, or a branding mark, but he knew exactly what it was because he'd seen one only hours ago, or a version of it: the Death Watch emblem, the ragged winged W shape. It didn't surprise him. She'd been spoils of war as far as they were concerned, an animal to be used, and marked as their property.

"A surgeon can remove that," Kina Ha said. "Would that help?"

Arla pulled down her shirt again. "You don't get it. You can't guess because it's so bad."

"Whatever it was, you were a child of fourteen, Walon tells me. When we're adult, we look back and judge our childhood actions by unfairly adult rules."

Arla didn't turn around. "It's not a wound or a humiliation. It's a badge."

"Explain."

"After I was kidnapped, after it stopped being a nightmare, I stayed with them. I became one of them. I *stayed*. I could have run away. But I *stayed*." She looked over her shoulder at Jusik. "Could you stand being me?"

"Oh, *shab*," Jusik said.

"Stop me remembering it all," she begged. "Let me die, or kill me, but I can't live in this head anymore. I kept trying to die. But the doctors wouldn't let me."

Arla was frighteningly lucid now. Jusik wasn't sure if Kina Ha had induced some state of clarity, but whatever it was, he'd rescued a woman who didn't want to stay rescued. There was no point telling her that kidnap victims, hostages, and abused, helpless kids often found themselves depending on the very people hurting them, and even growing to like them, because their own lives were held in those hands. Humans generally weren't the magnificent heroes of holovids who fought back, but simply normal beings doing instinctive things just to stay alive.

"You know you're not evil or unusual for doing that," he said. "Don't you?"

"Maybe." Arla started scratching her forearm, as if the muscle relaxant was wearing off. "But that doesn't change how hard it is to make it through the next second from the moment I wake up to the moment I fall asleep."

"When did you get away from them?"

Arla went quiet for a moment. "When I got arrested for the last shooting. Five, six years? Something like that."

"Try ten," said Jusik.

Arla shut her eyes for a second. "That long?"

Zey didn't even seem to be breathing. Kina Ha looked as if she was resting now, having unlocked that mental door. Now Jusik had to sweep up the Arla that was falling out of it. He wasn't going to start asking her about the killings, not now.

"Your brother Jango survived," he said. "He went on to be a legendary soldier and—well, most of my brothers here were cloned from him. He founded the finest army in galactic history."

"I sort of knew he was doing okay as a bounty hunter," Arla said. "The Watch was aware of stuff. But you talk as if he's dead now."

That was a shock; Jusik had no idea she even knew he'd survived. But that was before he knew she'd been living with the Death Watch for most of her life. She'd shifted from tragic lost youth to something he didn't understand yet, a sister who never let her brother know she was still alive, but still observed him from afar.

I need to stop filling gaps in history with pieces from the obvious.

"He was killed at the outbreak of the Clone War. I'm sorry." It didn't feel like a good idea right then to tell her that a Jedi killed him, and how much Jango had grown to loathe them.

"We were all good shots," Arla said. "That was why I did so many assassinations for the Death Watch." She looked over her shoulder again. "*Now* are you going to give me a quick way out? What do you think Jango would have done to me if he'd known I was with them."

Jusik felt Jango would have forgiven her. "Would the Death Watch be looking for you now, if they were still around?"

That made her flinch. "Are they?"

"If they are, they won't get near you."

Arla looked at Jusik for a long time. "You know," she said at last, "that this lull will wear off, and I'll crash again, don't you?"

"You don't want the medication, obviously."

"Try it sometime. It doesn't stop you remembering. Just stops you doing something about it."

Jusik knew what he might be able to do. He was about to do it to Kina Ha, Scout, and Zey, after all: he could blank out parts of her memory. He didn't know whether to offer.

Shab, he had to. She was his personal responsibility.

"I used to be a Jedi," he said. "I can erase memories. But beyond just removing recollection of the last five minutes or so, I don't know how safe it is, or what else I'll remove in the process."

Arla reached down for the discarded blanket and pulled it around her.

"I was going to die first chance I got anyway," she said. "If you can make this go away—no, I don't think I deserve to feel better."

Jusik moved automatically into that game of guessing the motivator. She was still trying to atone for letting her parents' murderers become her family. "Well, if I practice on you," Jusik said, "I'll be much safer when I come to wipe my Jedi friends' memories, and you can still give me useful intel on the Death Watch. A few years out of date beats zero any day."

Zey gave him a look that said his little earnest Jedi Knight had grown up rather fast since leaving the Order.

"Do it," Arla said. "And if you turn me into a vegetable, you shoot me. Deal?"

Jusik nodded. "Deal," he said.

Kyrimorut

Skirata couldn't find it in himself to be annoyed with Gilamar, let alone angry. Priest got what was coming to him. And leaving him alive to tell the tale—no, that hadn't been an option. Gilamar had done what Skirata should have done years ago, just by way of cleansing the Mando gene pool. Vau agreed.

But things were still getting a little too close to home. Clan Skirata didn't have the monopoly on Mandalorian resourcefulness. Sooner or later, someone was going to track them down. Skirata flipped Priest's shoulder plate between his fingers like meditation beads, staring at the emblem and wondering just what was out there waiting to return from *ba'slan shev'la*.

Does it matter who kills you in the end? Yes, I think it does.

"So what if Reau works out it was one of us?" Ordo leaned on the roba pen wall, watching one of the sows with her new litter. Fi was going to get his smoked roba slices one day soon. "Is that going to make us any more wanted by the Empire than we already are? There's no trail back to this place either way."

"Bardan's planning a relocation for Kyrimorut in case the worst happens. *Ret'lini.*" It was the Mando watch-word for prudence; *just in case*. Everyone had a plan B. Jaing, in his business-minded way, had taken to calling it *offsite hot standby*. "I'm thinking that we should have a bolt-hole on Cheravh."

"Why stay in the Mandalore sector?"

"Yeah, we could just walk away from Mandalore and the Empire," Skirata said. "Find a remote planet. Build a small town. Move in. Let the Death Watch make a big mistake with Palps and get eaten alive, or let Shysa fight his guerilla war. Churn out cutting-edge pharmaceutical products. Drink *ne'tra gal* on the porch, indulge a vast army of spoiled grandchildren, get old, and let everyone else do the fighting."

Ordo gave him a little frown. "Logistics, *Kal'buir*. We'd have to ship in everything on a dump like Cheravh, and freight gets noticed."

That was Ordo, all common sense. Skirata reminded himself that this whole thing was about Ordo and the rest of the boys.

The sow got to her feet and trotted off, pursued by her litter. Skirata liked Kyrimorut. The stay so far had been short, but it was already full of bittersweet memories.

The unfinished memorial for the fallen clone army, the crops breaking the surface of the soil, and the idyllic spots around the lake where he could fish were all things he didn't want to leave. And wherever he looked, he could see Etain, from the moment she let him first hold newborn Kad to the moment he stood by her funeral pyre. This was his *shabla* clan home, and everyone living here had put their blood and sweat into it. So had Rav Bralor. She'd restored the place brick by stone by plank for him. Part of Skirata refused to be driven from it. It was a very un-Mandalorian thought.

We're nomadic. Isn't that what Mando'ade *were all about? Isn't that what we still are at heart? It's danger-ous to get too attached to one place.*

He thought of Master Altis, smart enough to base his Jedi academy on a ship. He was actually looking forward to meeting the man. He had to. He wasn't sure why. He was certain that a Jedi Master would know how to take care of his own kind. In a few hours, he'd rendezvous with him in neutral space and look the man in the eye.

"They're very appealing when they're little," Ordo said absently.

"What are?"

"Roba. They're cute."

The babies were play-fighting, ramming one another with their snouts and squealing as if they were having fun. They still had coats of striped ginger hair that cam-ouflaged them in undergrowth until they were big enough to cope without their mother. Roba sows were fearsomely protective. Skirata gave them a wide berth.

"Doesn't pay to get too attached to them," he said. "That's going to be our breakfast." He felt bad about that for a moment. "Like Mij getting too fond of Scout. She's going to want to go back to her Jedi buddies one day soon."

Ordo was still staring at the baby roba. "Where do you draw the line?"

"What, between house pet and food?"

"Protectiveness. Saving folks. Maze saved Zey, just like

you saved us. Mij and Uthan seem to want to save Scout. When does it become crazy to keep rescuing things?"

Rescue was an instinct, a moment's unconscious reflex. Skirata hadn't even had to think about stepping between Orun Wa and the young Nulls to save them. It was simply something that demanded doing. He didn't regret a second of it; it never occurred to him that it might risk his own life, or cause endless ripples of trouble down the years, and even if he had he wouldn't have cared. It just didn't matter. Maze obviously felt the same about Zey. Soldiers would die for their buddies. It was the way of the galaxy, the best part of it, that beings cared so much for others that they did dangerous things so that someone else could live.

"Is this another hypocrisy lecture?" Skirata asked.

"Never, *Buir.*"

"It's okay. Even I can see that I've got double standards. Ny keeps me fully aware of that."

Skirata realized he'd started referring to her as casually as if she were his longtime wife. He edged into the open pen and stood still, one eye on the huge sow. The animal would break his legs if she charged him, and he didn't want to think what her sharp tusks would do to soft tissue. Two of the litter broke away from the others and trotted up to him.

Breakfast or pets? You're right, Ordo, there's no logic in it.

The babies just wanted to see if he had food for them. They were already learning to root in the mud and find their own dinner. He felt a tug at his heart, but it wasn't quite an overwhelming drive to pick them up and keep them in the house, although he knew many folks would do exactly that.

"In the end," he said, "we know which lives we have to save, and those come first. Even if we take insane risks to do it."

Ordo just nodded. The sow turned toward Skirata and let out a long warning grunt that sounded as if she was gearing up to ram him. As soon as her head dipped for her attack run, Skirata found agility he thought he'd lost twenty years ago and almost vaulted over the wall. She raced up to the half-open gate and stood rumbling a warning, even though she could have carried on and chased Skirata around the yard. This was her turf. She wanted the filthy human interloper to leave her kids alone, that was all.

"She knows she'll be on Fi's plate one day," Ordo said. "What has she got to lose?"

Skirata decided to leave a couple of weeks before he let anyone venture into Keldabe again to check if there was any aftermath from Priest's death. They might not have found his body yet. But Reau would know something bad had happened to him.

"Come on," Skirata said. "Let's clean our boots and then go rendezvous with Altis."

Altis was due to comm them anytime now to say he was inbound. All Skirata could think of was how different things might have turned out if this Altis had run the Jedi Council, and not Yoda and his cronies. That was the trouble with the people who *should* have been in charge. They never really wanted the power that they were better equipped than others to wield.

Jusik let Ordo take the Aggressor for the journey. It made sense to pack some firepower and speed, even if Altis and his gang were as peaceful as beings could get. Skirata took no chances these days. The fighter dropped out of hyperspace and waited at the coordinates, giving Skirata time to simply gaze out of the viewport at the sheer emptiness of speckled space, something he rarely had a chance or inclination to do. It really was beautiful, clean, so utterly miraculous and perfect compared to the sordid events on most planets that he wondered if Uthan's virus ever looked up at an apparently majestic ruby sky and didn't realize it was inside some shabby humanoid that cheated and killed.

This was why he didn't spend time contemplating starscapes. He remembered now.

Ordo cocked his head, listening on his comlink.

"Here we go, *Kal'buir*. It's a cargo ship, *Wookiee Gunner*. They're preparing to let us dock alongside."

"I admire a man who doesn't overcompensate with a Star Destroyer," Skirata said. "I'm going to treat him with caution."

Trust was a funny thing. They were now going to dock with a ship, not inside its bay but alongside, with a fragile corridor of flexible plastoid and durasteel as their only shield against hard vacuum. Somehow, both sides thought this was less risky than landing on a planet. Skirata felt suddenly foolish. Ordo maneuvered the Aggressor into position and the docking ring sealed with a grinding sound that reverberated through the fighter's airframe.

"Pressuring up," Ordo said, and hit the control. "You can board when the light shows green, Master Altis."

It was a demonstration of goodwill, Skirata knew. The Jedi was prepared to step aboard a Mandalorian starfighter alone, taking all the risk. Maybe the docking hadn't been such a rash move after all.

Skirata eased out of his seat and stood watching the inner hatch. The plate retracted, and he found himself staring at an ordinary-looking human male—gray hair, late sixties, maybe even seventies.

So this was Master Djinn Altis.

He walked like a workman or a scruffy college professor, with no brown robes, tunic, or monastic look. And he just felt *different*.

"I'm Kal," Skirata said. "This is my son, Ordo."

Altis held out his hand. "We're in the same line of work," he said. "Salvage."

"People-salvage."

"We could form a union, then."

"My boy *Bard'ika* likes you." Skirata winked. "And that's a powerful recommendation. You still up for helping us out?"

"When do you want us to take your guests?"

"One of them asked to stay for a while. Kina Ha and Arligan Zey—I want their memories of my base wiped first."

"You can always reach us, anytime you're ready."

"But we already knew you were willing to take the Jedi off our hands, so we're here to talk more broadly, aren't we?"

"We are." Altis unsettled Skirata. He managed somehow to be both very ordinary and also radiate an ancient authority. "We're all on the run."

"I had this idea," Skirata said. He heard Ordo inhale, rightly so, because he hadn't fully discussed any of this. "*We* want to rescue clones and keep our planet free of scumbags. We hear stuff from extraordinary places and there's nothing we can't buy, build, invent, steal, or slice. *You* have all kinds of extra talents most of my clan don't have, and a different intelligence network, so I think we could occasionally help each other out."

Altis chewed his thumbnail. "There's a but. I hear it."

"*But* I'll only help you if you don't play a part in putting the Jedi Order back in power. Because we hate those *shabuire* for more reasons than I've got time to list."

Altis roared with laughter. He seemed to find it genuinely funny, as if Skirata was sweetly naïve about Jedi politics.

"We've never been close, us and the mainstream Jedi Order. We're the crazy relative in the attic that nobody talks about." Altis coughed to clear his throat. "About half of our community these days isn't Force-sensitive, so you can imagine how hard this is for a more ascetic school of Jedi thought to handle."

"Well, here's something for free, to show goodwill. You might think you're the harmless eccentrics, but the Empire's singled you out as a potential rallying point to rebuild the Jedi Order, and it thinks that lots of the surviving Jedi will try to regroup around you."

Altis wasn't inscrutable or serene, and he didn't look as if he was trying to be. He frowned. "Oh, that's worrying."

"Plett's Well." It was just a trick, throwing in one scrap of half-understood information to see what else fell out. Jaller Obrim would have been proud of him. "You're still moving kids there?"

That was a *real* flier, based solely on a snatched line of

radio comms mentioned by Darman. Skirata watched Altis's pupils flicker.

"Ah, Kal, you *are* well-informed. I ought to be scared of you."

"Not at all. Only if you hurt my boys. All I'm saying is that if you help us out occasionally, we'll help you out. You might want to start by faking your death. We're good at making that look convincing. And we'll help you find somewhere to hide that's not on the database that your more careless colleagues managed to lose."

Skirata paused for breath as much as effect. Yes, he'd definitely got Altis's attention.

"One day, I know I'm going to get the bill for this," Altis said.

"It'll be a favor. Probably for one of the boys. Maybe for their families. Like you, we just want to be left alone to get on with our lives."

"So where do we go from here?"

"I'll comm you when we get our Jedi situation sorted out."

"We'll be there. Stay safe, Kal Skirata."

"*K'oyacyi*, Master Altis."

Altis winked. "*Djinn*, please."

Skirata stood and watched in silence while Altis crossed back through the narrow sleeve of plastoid and the air lock at the far end snapped shut behind him. Ordo sealed the Aggressor's hatches, waited for the red indicator to turn green, and disengaged from the docking ring.

"Worth the journey?" he asked, moving the fighter away from *Wookiee Gunner*'s hull.

"I think so." Altis was different. Skirata didn't want that. It blurred the line. Before long, he'd be what Darman accused him of being; soft on Jedi. He couldn't afford to forget the bigger picture just because Djinn Altis wasn't the kind of Jedi he was used to. "If only because he can give us tips on how to handle housing a whole community on a wandering ship."

"If you can't get rid of Force-users," Ordo said, "then you might as well buy a bunch of your own."

"Not that I think Altis is buyable, but he knows a mutual interest when he sees it." Skirata decided he probably had been a bit generous in his offer, and the dumbest way to open negotiations was with a concession. But nothing had been traded yet. Two old guys who had to find a way to work together in a galaxy that wanted them dead had sized up one another and decided they could get on. That was all that had happened, nothing more. "Jaing was right. We'll find a use for them, and they'll find a use for us."

"So here we are, drawing a line between one kind of Jedi and another."

"Isn't that what we did with Bardan and Etain?"

"Yes," Ordo said. "I suppose it is."

Ordo was an outspoken lad. If he had any real misgivings about Altis, he would say so plainly and undiplomatically. Instead, he programmed a course for Mandalore on the nav computer and took the *Aggressor* up to jump velocity. The transition to hyperspace always left Skirata feeling off-balance for a moment or two. When he focused on the viewport again, the serene starscape that made the galaxy look like a really nice place to live was gone.

I gave Altis another bonus, didn't I? Maybe I'll save that card for later.

Skirata had shaken the man's hand. And he was still infectious, still carrying a virus that would protect against the FG36 bioweapon. Now Altis would spread that to all his followers, and another population would be immunized.

"I should have billed you," he muttered to himself. "Never mind."

**Gym locker room, Special Operations barracks,
501st Legion headquarters, Imperial Center**

Darman had his best ideas in the 'freshers.

He always did. It was something about the soothing effect of hot water hitting the crown of his head, and the continuous rainfall sound of the shower. He hovered in a relaxed state closer to dozing off than being awake.

He knew now that he'd made a serious mistake by not grabbing the chance to desert to Mandalore when Ordo came for them. There was no point trying to do the best for Kad from so far away when he was always going to be relying on others to take the information he'd gathered and do something productive with it.

"Dar? You asleep in there or something?"

Darman let the voice drift over him. It was Niner. He could wait.

No, he was going about this all the wrong way. He could be stuck here for the rest of his life, and that wasn't going to be as long as a regular human's. He didn't have time for another mistake. There was one solution. Examples of it had been staring him in the face for a year or more.

"Dar! You're going to be as wrinkled as a strill's *shebs* if you stay in there much longer."

Darman couldn't break off from his train of thought to answer. When Fi needed help, when Skirata needed to get him out of that medcenter before they pulled the plug and let him die, Besany and Obrim went in and *got* him. When Skirata needed to save the young Nulls from the Kaminoans, he went and *did it himself.* Even the evacuation on the night of Order 66—even though it ended so terribly for him and Etain, and for Niner— Skirata and the team went in and pulled people out.

You have to do things for yourself.

Kal'buir showed you everything you needed to know to be a good father.

What would he be doing now?

Darman was certain that he wouldn't be standing here in a shower stall when his son needed him. *Kal'buir* was a wonderful father, a kind and patient man, and the best example of how much you could change the galaxy when you didn't accept the hand you were dealt.

But he had a lot of other clone sons all relying on him, and he let too many Jedi spin him sob stories and take advantage of his guilt about Etain. Darman was feeling worse by the hour about all those Jedi being under the same roof as Kad.

Etain wouldn't have wanted it. That reason alone was enough for Darman to do something *now*.

He was going to Mandalore—which he always thought of now as *back* to Mandalore, even though he'd never been there—and he was going to be a proper father to his son. Darman wanted to stay at Kyrimorut, but it was obvious that it was going to be a more dangerous world now that the Empire had dug in there. It was no place to raise a kid who was half Jedi.

Darman now knew firsthand what would happen to Kad if the Empire's dark side spooks got a whiff of him. Roly Melusar was a great guy who knew exactly what needed doing, but Darman couldn't wait that long for the revolution.

Got to do it yourself.

He was going back to Mandalore to take his son, and then get away somewhere that nobody could find them. He was a commando; he was great at extractions, and if he wanted not to be found, he was pretty good at that, too.

Sorry, Kal'buir, *but you've got too much on your plate at the moment. I missed the first eighteen months of Kad's life because nobody even told me he was mine.*

Darman had it all planned now. He didn't even have to sneak out of the barracks. He'd been tasked to find Altis, and Melusar had no idea how easy that was going to be for him.

"Dar, are you okay?"

"Yeah. Keep your hair on."

He turned off the spray and toweled himself dry. Niner gave him a worried look and dropped his voice to a whisper.

"Dar, you need to stop worrying about the Jedi. Kal's on the case. He'd gut anyone who so much as looked at Kad the wrong way."

"I know."

"You sure you're okay?"

"Yeah. Let's go see Holy Roly. I've had an idea."

"What?"

"Bet you I can persuade him to let us carry out an op on Mandalore."

Niner just stared as if he was checking Darman's eyes for signs of madness. Darman found it hard to be anything less than totally honest with his brother, but Niner was a worry-guts, and what he didn't know couldn't hurt him. If Darman leveled with him completely about what he had in mind, then he knew what would happen; Niner would try to stop him. He'd do it out of love, but he'd get it all wrong. He just didn't understand how much having a kid changed everything.

It was okay to keep a few cards up your sleeve if it saved your brother from harm. Niner had kept things from him for exactly the same reason.

"That's your desertion plan?" Niner said at last. He whispered so quietly that Darman could just about see his lips move. Maybe they should have switched to *Mando'a*—but too many of the Kamino commandos would understand that, too. "Just stroll out with an Imperial vessel and a full fuel tank?"

"That's about it."

"What about Rede? Or have you got a plan for convincing the CO it just needs us?"

Darman was pretty sure he could do that, too. He pulled on his fatigues. "Let's go see."

"If we end up taking him," Niner said, "then we better be clear what's going to happen to him when he works out we're doing a runner. He won't want to desert."

"He's a blank sheet. He'll respond to a sensible argument."

"No, he's not a *blank sheet*. He might be a Spaarti job, but he's a man like us. You've seen how fast he learns. What if he really objects? What if he turns us in?"

"Then I'll do what I *have* to do."

Niner's face fell. He never did like that kind of dilemma. He tied himself up in ethical knots about duty, and he found the really dirty work—turning on his own kind—one step too far. Darman didn't want to harm a brother, but he'd shot two covert ops troopers because it was a matter of them or him, and Darman was trained to survive at any cost.

I've got a son to worry about now. I'd shoot the whole Imperial Army if I had to.

"There'll be a better way," Niner said.

"Well, you think about that, and I'll work on Roly."

It never occurred to Darman that Melusar might have gone home at this time of night. And he hadn't. He was still sitting in his office, poring over intelligence reports. The man had a mission, a quest, and at its heart it was about family—a family that had been taken from him. Darman understood that perfectly.

Is he married? Has he got kids? Or can't he face that until he avenges his father?

Darman didn't ask. He rapped on the door frame, Niner fidgeting behind him, and waited.

"Yes?"

"Got five minutes, sir?"

"Certainly."

Darman waited for the doors to close behind them and stood in front of Melusar's desk. Whatever he said next, he would be dragging Niner behind him. He had to be sure it was worth that risk.

How can I lie to Melusar, after all he's been through?

"I think I can find you Altis and his people, sir," Darman said. "In fact, I'm sure I can. Niner and I just need to find some old intel contacts."

He didn't look at Niner. He didn't need to. He knew his brother's pulse rate had just gone through the roof.

Melusar nodded. "Go on."

"We need to go to Mandalore."

Melusar looked slightly puzzled. "Very well. Is there anything special you need from me?"

Darman had been expecting to argue his case for being let off the leash. The new army wasn't like the old

GAR. He was taken aback. *This* was how much faith the commander put in them.

I can't betray this guy. It's not right. But I have to get my son to somewhere safe.

"Just your permission, sir," Darman said.

"You have it. Tell me what you need and I'll make sure it gets supplied without any awkward questions." Melusar pulled out a datapad and tapped it. "Are you planning to take Rede? Might be easier than leaving him here to speculate."

It sounded like an order. Darman wasn't going to push his luck and make an excuse for refusing. And Melusar had a point. Rede would ask questions, and the last thing anyone wanted was for other commandos to realize that Squad 40 was off the roster for unexplained reasons.

"It'll be good for him, sir," Niner said. "I'll make sure he doesn't get into any scrapes."

Niner turned to leave, but Melusar beckoned Darman back.

"Whatever the Jedi did to you, Darman, remember what they say about a dish best served cold." He gave Darman that look—head slightly tilted, eyebrows raised, chin down—that said he'd thrown his lot in with his troops, 100 percent. "Vengeance makes you take crazy risks. I *know*. Remember—*cold*."

Darman felt the guilt starting to eat him alive. "Got it, sir."

He didn't say a word to Niner until they got back to their quarters. He checked that Rede was snoring like a vibrosaw before he even risked a whispered conversation at the far end of the room.

"I know it's no different from what we planned to do before," Niner said. "But I feel rotten lying to Holy Roly. And Rede."

"I'm not lying," Darman said. "I'm going to give Melusar all the Jedi he wants."

Yes, Darman would. And if that didn't fit with Jaing's plans for finding some Jedi an escape route—it was too bad.

His son came first.

Read on for an excerpt from
Star Wars: Darth Bane: Dynasty of Evil
by Drew Karpyshyn

Published by Del Rey

" . . . **a**dhering to the rules established through the procedures outlined in the preceding, as well as all subsequent, articles. Our sixth demand stipulates that a body of . . ."

Medd Tandar rubbed a long-fingered hand across the pronounced frontal ridge of his tall, conical cranium, hoping to massage away the looming headache that had been building over the last twenty minutes.

Gelba, the being he had come to the planet of Doan to negotiate with, paused in the reading of her petition to ask, "Something wrong, Master Jedi?"

"I am not a Master," the Cerean reminded the self-appointed leader of the rebels. "I am only a Jedi Knight." With a sigh he dropped his hand. After a moment's pause he forced himself to add, "I'm fine. Please continue."

With a curt nod, Gelba resumed with her seemingly endless list of ultimatums. "Our sixth demand stipulates that a body of elected representatives from the mining caste be given absolute jurisdiction over the following eleven matters: One, the determination of wages in accordance with galactic standards. Two, the establishment of a weekly standard of hours any given employee can be ordered to work. Three, an approved list of safety apparel to be provided by . . ."

The short, muscular human woman droned on, her voice echoing strangely off the irregular walls of the underground cave. The other miners in attendance—three human men and two women crowding close to Gelba—were seemingly transfixed by her words. Medd couldn't help but think that, should their tools ever fail, the miners could simply use their leader's voice to cut through the stone.

Officially, Medd was here to try to end the violence between the rebels and the royal family. Like all Cereans, he possessed a binary brain structure, allowing him to simultaneously process both sides of a conflict. Theoretically, this made him an ideal candidate to mediate and resolve complex political situations such as the one that had developed on this small mining world. In practice, however, he was discovering that playing the part of a diplomat was far more trying than he had first imagined.

Located on the Outer Rim, Doan was an ugly, brown ball of rock. More than 80 percent of the planetary landmass had been converted into massive strip-mining operations. Even from space, the disfigurement of the world was immediately apparent. Furrows five kilometers wide and hundreds of kilometers long crisscrossed the torn landscape like indelible scars. Great quarries hewn from the bedrock descended hundreds of meters deep, irreparable pockmarks on the face of the planet.

From within the smog-filled atmosphere, the ceaseless activity of the gigantic machines was visible. Excavation equipment scurried back and forth like oversized insects, digging and churning up the dirt. Towering drilling rigs stood on mechanical legs, tunneling to previously unplumbed depths. Gigantic hovering freighters cast shadows that blotted out the pale sun as they waited patiently for their cavernous cargo holds to be filled with dirt, dust, and pulverized stone.

Scattered across the planet were a handful of five-kilometer-tall columns of irregular, dark brown stone several hundred meters in diameter. They jutted up from the ravaged landscape like fingers reaching for the sky. The flat plateaus atop these natural pillars were covered by assemblages of mansions, castles, and palaces overlooking the environmental wreckage below.

The rare mineral deposits and rampant mining on Doan had turned the small planet into a very wealthy world. That wealth, however, was concentrated almost exclusively in the hands of the nobility, who dwelled in the exclusive estates that towered above the rest of the planet. Most of the populace was made up of Doan society's lower castes, beings condemned to spend their lives engaged in constant physical labor or employed in menial service positions with no chance of advancement.

These were the beings Gelba represented. Unlike the elite, they made their homes down on the planet's surface in tiny makeshift huts surrounded by the open pits and furrows, or in small caverns tunneled down into the rocky ground. Medd had been given a small taste of their life the instant he stepped from the climate-controlled confines of his shuttle. A wall of oppressive heat thrown up from the barren, sun-scorched ground had enveloped him. He'd quickly wrapped a swatch of cloth around his head, covering his nose and mouth to guard against the swirling clouds of dust that threatened to choke the air from his lungs.

The man Gelba had sent to greet him also had his face covered, making communication all the more difficult amid the rumbling of the mining machines. Fortunately, there was no need to speak as his guide led him across the facility: the Jedi had simply gawked at the sheer scope of the environmental damage.

They had continued in silence until reaching a small, rough-hewn tunnel. Medd had to crouch to avoid scraping his head on the jagged ceiling. The tunnel went for several hundred meters, sloping gently downward until it emerged in a large natural chamber lit by glow lamps.

Tool marks scored the walls and floor. The cavern had been stripped of any valuable mineral deposits long before; all that remained were dozens of irregular rock formations rising up from the uneven floor, some less than a meter high, others stretching up to the ceiling a full ten meters above. They might have been beautiful had they not all been the exact same shade of dull brown that dominated Doan's surface.

The makeshift rebel headquarters was unfurnished, but the high ceiling allowed the Cerean to finally stand up straight. More important, the underground chamber offered some small refuge from the heat, dust, and noise of the surface, enabling them all to remove the muffling cloth covering their faces. Given the shrillness of Gelba's voice, Medd was debating if this was entirely a good thing.

"Our next demand is the immediate abolition of the royal family, and the surrender of all its estates to the elected representatives specified in item three of section five, subsection C. Furthermore, fines and penalties shall be levied against—"

"Please stop," Medd said, holding up a hand. Mercifully, Gelba honored his request. "As I explained to you before, the Jedi Council can do nothing to grant your demands. I am not here to eliminate the royal family. I am only here to offer my services as a mediator in the negotiations between your group and the Doan nobility."

"They refuse to negotiate with us!" one of the miners shouted.

"Can you blame them?" Medd countered. "You killed the crown prince."

"That was a mistake," Gelba said. "We didn't mean to destroy his airspeeder. We only wanted to force it into an emergency landing. We were trying to capture him alive."

"Your intentions are irrelevant now," Medd told her, keeping his voice calm and even. "By killing the heir to the throne, you brought the wrath of the royal family down on you."

"Are you defending their actions?" Gelba demanded. "They hunt my people like animals! They imprison us without trial! They torture us for information, and execute us if we resist! Now even the Jedi turn a blind eye to our suffering. You're no better than the Galactic Senate!"

Medd understood the miners' frustration. Doan had been a member of the Republic for centuries, but there had been no serious efforts by the Republic Senate or any governing body to address the injustices of their societal structure. Comprising millions of member worlds, each with its own unique traditions and systems of government, the Republic had adopted a policy of noninterference except in the most extreme cases.

Officially, idealists condemned the lack of a democratic government on Doan. But historically, the population had always been granted the basic necessities of life: food, shelter, freedom from slavery, and even legal recourse in cases where a noble abused the privileges of rank. While the rich on Doan undoubtedly exploited the poor, there were many other worlds where the situation was much, much worse.

However, the reluctance of the Senate to become involved had not stopped the efforts of those who sought to change the status quo. Over the last decade, a movement demanding political and social equality had sprung up among the lower castes. Naturally, there was resistance from the nobility, and recently the tension had escalated into violence, culminating in the assassination of the Doan crown prince nearly three standard months earlier.

In response, the king had declared a state of martial law. Since then, there had been a steady stream of troubling reports supporting Gelba's accusations. Yet galactic sympathy for the rebels was slow to build. Many in the Senate saw them as terrorists, and as much as Medd sympathized with their plight, he was unable to act without Senate authority.

The Jedi were legally bound by galactic law to remain neutral in all civil wars and internal power struggles, unless the violence threatened to spread to other Republic worlds. All the experts agreed that there was little chance of that happening.

"What is being done to your people is wrong," Medd agreed, choosing his words carefully. "I will do what I can to convince the king to stop his persecution of your people. But I cannot promise anything."

"Then why are you here?" Gelba demanded.

Medd hesitated. In the end, he decided that straightforward truth was the only recourse. "A few weeks ago one of your teams dug up a small tomb."

"Doan is covered with old tombs," Gelba replied. "Centuries ago we used to bury our dead . . . back before the nobility decided they would dig up the whole planet."

"There was a small cache of artifacts inside the tomb," Medd continued. "An amulet. A ring. Some old parchment scrolls."

"Anything we dig up belongs to us!" one of the miners shouted angrily.

"It's one of our oldest laws," Gelba confirmed. "Even the royal family knows better than to try and violate it."

"My Master believes those artifacts may be touched by the dark side," Medd said. "I must bring them back to our Temple on Coruscant for safekeeping."

Gelba glared at him with narrowed eyes, but didn't speak.

"We will pay you, of course," Medd added.

"You Jedi portray yourselves as guardians," Gelba said. "Champions of the weak and downtrodden. But you care more about a handful of gold trinkets than you do about the lives of men and women who are suffering."

"I will try to help you," Medd promised. "I will speak to the king on your behalf. But first I must have those—"

He stopped abruptly, the echo of his words still hanging in the cavern. *Something's wrong.* There was a sudden sickness in the pit of his stomach, a sense of impending danger.

"What?" Gelba demanded. "What is it?"

A disturbance in the Force, Medd thought, his hand

dropping to the lightsaber on his belt. "Somebody's coming."

"Impossible. The sentries at the tunnel outside would have—ungh!"

Gelba's words were cut off by the unmistakable sound of a blaster's retort. She staggered back and fell to the ground, a smoking hole in her chest. With cries of alarm the other miners scattered, scrambling for cover behind the rock formations that filled the cavern. Two of them didn't make it, felled by deadly accurate shots that took them right between the shoulder blades.

Medd held his ground, igniting his lightsaber and peering into the shadows that lined the walls of the cave. Unable to pierce the darkness with his eyes, he opened himself to the Force—and staggered back as if he had been punched in the stomach.

Normally, the Force washed over him like a warm bath of white light, strengthening him, centering him. This time, however, it struck him like a frozen fist in the gut.

Another blaster bolt whistled by his ear. Dropping to his knees, Medd crawled to cover behind the nearest rock formation, bewildered and confused. As a Jedi, he had trained his entire life to transform himself into a servant of the Force. He had learned to let the light side flow through him, empowering him, enhancing his physical senses, guiding his thoughts and actions. Now the very source of his power had seemingly betrayed him.

He could hear blaster bolts ricocheting throughout

the chamber as the miners returned fire against their unseen opponent, but he shut out the sounds of battle. He didn't understand what had happened to him; he only knew he had to find some way to fight it.

Panting, the Jedi silently recited the first lines of the Jedi Code, struggling to regain his composure. *There is no emotion; there is peace.* The mantra of his Order allowed him to bring his breathing under control. A few seconds later he felt composed enough to reach out carefully to try to touch the Force once more.

Instead of peace and serenity, he felt only anger and hatred. Instinctively, his mind recoiled, and Medd realized what had happened. Somehow the power he was drawing on had been tainted by the dark side, corrupted and poisoned.

He still couldn't explain it, but now he at least knew how to try to resist the effects. Blocking out his fear, the Jedi allowed the Force to flow through him once more in the faintest, guarded trickle. As he did so, he focused his mind on cleansing it of the impurities that had overwhelmed his senses. Slowly, he felt the power of the light side washing over him . . . though it was far less than what he was used to.

Stepping out from behind the rocks, he called out in a loud voice, "Show yourself!"

A blaster bolt ripped from the darkness toward him. At the last second he deflected it with his lightsaber, sending it off harmlessly into the corner— a technique he had mastered years ago while still a Padawan.

Too close, he thought to himself. *You're slow, hesitant. Trust in the Force.*

The power of the Force enveloped him, but something about it still felt wrong. Its strength flickered and ebbed, like a static-filled transmission. Something—or someone—was disrupting his ability to focus. A dark veil had fallen across his consciousness, interfering with his ability to draw upon the Force. For a Jedi there was nothing more terrifying, but Medd had no intention of retreating.

"Leave the miners alone," he called out, his voice betraying none of the uncertainty he felt. "Show yourself and face me!"

From the far corner of the room a young Iktotchi woman stepped forth, holding a blaster pistol in each hand. She was clad in a simple black cloak, but she had thrown her hood back to reveal the downward-curving horns that protruded from the sides of her head and tapered to a sharp point just above her shoulders. Her reddish skin was accentuated by black tattoos on her chin—four sharp, thin lines extending like fangs from her lower lip.

"The miners are dead," she told him. There was something cruel in her voice, as if she was taunting him with the knowledge.

Gingerly using the Force to extend his awareness, Medd realized it was true. As if peering through an obscuring haze, he could just manage to see the bodies of the miners strewn about the chamber, each branded by a lethal shot to the head or chest. In the few seconds it had taken him to collect himself, she had slain them all.

"You're an assassin," he surmised. "Sent by the royal family to kill the rebel leaders."

She tilted her head in acknowledgment, and opened her mouth as if she was about to speak. Then, without warning, she fired another round of blaster bolts at him.

The ruse nearly worked. With the Force flowing through him he should have sensed her deception long before she acted, but whatever power was obscuring his ability to touch the light side had left him vulnerable.

Instead of trying to deflect the bolts a second time, Medd threw himself to the side, landing hard on the ground.

You're as clumsy as a youngling, he chided himself as he scrambled back to his feet.

Unwilling to expose himself to another barrage, he thrust out his free hand, palm facing out. Using the Force, he yanked the weapons from his enemy's grasp. The effort sent a searing bolt of pain through the entire length of his head, causing him to wince and take a half step back. But the blasters sailed through the air and landed harmlessly on the ground beside him.

To his surprise, the assassin seemed unconcerned. Could she sense his fear and uncertainty? The Iktochi were known to have limited precognitive abilities; it was said they could use the Force to see glimpses of the future. Some even claimed they were telepathic. Was it possible that she was somehow using her abilities to disrupt his connection to the Force?

"If you surrender, I will promise you a fair trial," Medd told her, trying to project an image of absolute confidence and self-assurance.

She smiled at him, revealing sharp, pointed teeth. "There will be no trial."

The Iktochi threw herself into a back handspring, her robe fluttering as she flipped out of view behind the cover of a thick stone outcropping. At the same instant, one of the blasters at Medd's feet beeped sharply.

The Jedi had thought he had disarmed his foe, but instead he had fallen into her well-laid trap. He had just enough time to register that the power cell had been set to overload before it detonated. With his last thought he tried to call upon the Force to shield him from the blast, but he was unable to pierce the debilitating fog that clouded his mind. He felt nothing but fear, anger, and hatred.

As the explosion ended his life, Medd finally understood the true horror of the dark side.